F
AF

*Glam**ͫ͞͞us Sydney...***

Sophisticated millionaires...

The world's most eligible men!

Dreaming of a foreign affair? Then, look no further!
We've brought together the best and sexiest men the
world has to offer, the most exciting, exotic locations
and the most powerful, passionate stories.

This month, in *Australian Attraction*, we bring back
two hot and spicy stories by best-selling Modern
Romance™ authors Miranda Lee and Helen Bianchin.
To get to know the sexiest playboys from Down
Under, read on!

Enjoy!

MIRANDA LEE

Miranda Lee is Australian, living near Sydney. Born and raised in the bush, she was boarding-school-educated and briefly pursued a career in classical music, before moving to Sydney and embracing the world of computers. Happily married, with three daughters, she began writing when family commitments kept her at home. She likes to create stories that are believable, modern, fast-paced and sexy. Her interests include reading meaty sagas, doing word puzzles, gambling and going to the movies.

Look out for more new novels from
Miranda Lee in Modern Romance™!

HELEN BIANCHIN

Helen Bianchin was born in New Zealand and travelled to Australia before marrying her Italian-born husband. After three years they moved, returned to New Zealand with their daughter, had two sons, then resettled in Australia. Encouraged by friends to recount anecdotes of her years as a tobacco sharefarmer's wife living in an Italian community, Helen began setting words on paper and her first novel was published in 1975. An animal lover, she says her terrier and Persian cat regard her study as as much theirs as hers.

A Passionate Surrender is Helen's new Modern Romance™
– on the shelves now!

australian
attraction

MIRANDA LEE & HELEN BIANCHIN

SYDNEY'S MOST ELIGIBLE PLAYBOYS

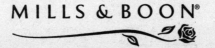

MILLS & BOON®

*MILLS & BOON and MILLS & BOON with the Rose Device
are registered trademarks of the publisher.
Harlequin Mills & Boon Limited,
Eton House, 18-24 Paradise Road, Richmond, Surrey, TW9 1SR*

Australian Attraction © Harlequin Enterprises II B.V., 2002

The Bride in Blue and *The Marriage Campaign*
were first published in Great Britain by
Harlequin Mills & Boon Limited in separate, single volumes.

The Bride in Blue © Miranda Lee 1995
The Marriage Campaign © Helen Bianchin 1998

ISBN 0 263 83191 4

126-0902

*Printed and bound in Spain
by Litografia Rosés S.A., Barcelona*

australian attraction

THE BRIDE IN BLUE

THE MARRIAGE CAMPAIGN

THE BRIDE IN BLUE

MIRANDA LEE

CHAPTER ONE

'IT'S time, Sophia.'

A shudder rippled down Sophia's spine at the sound of the quietly spoken words. Taking a deep steadying breath, she turned from where she'd been standing at the bedroom window, staring blindly out at the lengthening shadows.

She tried not to look as wretched as she felt. After all, a bride was supposed to be happy on her wedding-day. But it was impossible to smile, or feel anything other than depressed.

The man who was about to become her husband filled the open doorway, looking impressive in a beautifully tailored grey three-piece suit. Sophia had always thought him a strikingly handsome man, with his strongly sculptured face, jet-black hair and compelling blue eyes. But it was a cold, forbidding kind of beauty, and she had never warmed to it. She shivered when his dark brows drew together, narrowed eyes sweeping over her.

'You're not wearing white,' he said brusquely.

Gulping, she glanced down at the pale blue suit she herself had chosen, mostly because the softly pleated skirt and thigh-length jacket disguised her rapidly changing figure. It had a matching hat—a small soft thing with a blue flower on one side and a wispy veil that came down over her forehead.

When Wilma had tried to steer her towards something white, she'd been firm in her refusal. White would have been hypocritical. Not because she thought herself impure, but because her wedding was not a romantic wedding. It was simply the fulfilling of a deathbed promise.

'No,' she said. 'I'm not.'

Her succinct answer was not inspired by defiance but by fear. Jonathon Parnell frightened the life out of her.

Sophia had never met a man as intimidating as Godfrey's younger brother. Not even Joe, her bullying stepfather, had produced the sorts of reactions in her *this* man could produce. She fairly quailed in Jonathon's presence, becoming tongue-tied or simply stupid. Sometimes she even stammered, which was why she tried to answer him in monosyllables.

'You were entitled to wear white,' he growled. 'Any wrongdoing lay entirely with my brother.'

Her dark brown eyes flung wide at this unjust misreading of what Godfrey had supposedly done. Perhaps he should have told her he was married, but there had been no heartless seduction, no taking advantage of her tender age, or forcing her against her will. She'd gone to his bed willingly and would have done it more than that one time, if she'd had the chance.

But of course, she hadn't had the chance. Godfrey had collapsed the following day and within a few short weeks, he was gone. She would never see him again. He would never see his baby...

Tears filled her eyes.

'Come now, don't cry,' Jonathon ordered curtly, drawing a snow-white handkerchief out of his jacket pocket as he strode across the room. 'What's done is done. Don't go messing up those lovely eyes of yours.'

This most uncharacteristic compliment flustered Sophia, as did the feel of Jonathon's large hands pressing the handkerchief into her tremulous fingers.

That was another of the things about him that she found intimidating. His size. He was a very big man. Not only tall, but powerfully built with broad shoulders, a massive chest and long muscular legs.

Godfrey had been much shorter and of a slight build, with elegant, almost feminine hands. He hadn't towered over Sophia's five-foot-two frame as his brother did; hadn't made her feel like a child by comparison. Jonathon could pick her up and snap her in two, if he wanted to.

'Th-thanks,' she said, her voice and hands both shaking as she dabbed at her eyes.

'Why do you always act as though you're scared to death of me?' Jonathon growled.

There was something other than exasperation in his voice that made her glance up at him through her soggy lashes. But the hard blue eyes that looked back at her were as remote and unreadable as ever.

'I...I d-don't mean to,' she whispered, but her husky stammering belied her words.

A guilty remorse curled her stomach. The man deserved better than her irrational and no doubt irritating nervousness whenever he came within three feet of her. His treatment of her since Godfrey's death had been impeccable. He'd brought her to live in his own home, provided her with every material thing she could possibly want, even had his own secretary befriend her so that she wouldn't be lonely for female companionship.

And now…now he was about to give her what no other person could. The name of Parnell for her baby. Her beloved Godfrey's name.

The least she could do was show gratitude, not fear. After all, he wasn't expecting anything from her in return. The marriage would be in name only, to be quietly terminated at some future date.

'Smile, then,' he commanded.

The smile she dragged up proved acting was not her forte. When Jonathon sighed, Sophia's smile faded, her wretchedness returning. Only by a supreme effort of will did she keep the tears at bay.

His hand on her arm was as firm as his voice. 'Come along. People are waiting.'

Instant alarm had her resisting his pull. 'People? But I thought…I mean…'

Jonathon's face carried frustration. 'For pity's sake, don't get me wrong. *People* does not mean a crowd. There's only Mother, Harvey, Wilma, Maud and the celebrant. OK?' he asked with exaggerated patience.

Her eyes told him that things were far from OK, but she nodded her compliance.

'Shall we go, then?'

'I suppose so,' she replied resignedly, the first smoothly delivered answer she had ever given him. Odd that it seemed to irk him as much as her usual gibberish.

Sophia realised at that moment that Godfrey's brother found *everything* about her a trial of the first order, not just her lack of confidence and sophistication. He'd done his best to hide his frustration with her and the unenviable position his vow to his brother had put him in, but she could see now that the coolly aloof manner he adopted with her hid a very real annoyance.

The thought upset her, so much so that as Jonathon was leading her down the wide sweeping staircase, she felt impelled to say something.

'Jonathon,' she began, doing her very best not to stammer or bumble her way over his name.

Unfortunately, he stopped walking and looked over at her, the last thing she wanted. That cold blue gaze was as unnerving as the rest of him. 'What?'

Sophia licked dry lips before launching forth. 'I just wanted you to know how much I appreciate what you're doing today. I…I also wanted to reassure you that I'll set you free of me as soon as possible.'

There! She'd managed to say it all with only the one little slip-up. She even managed a small smile.

Not, however, with any good effect. That wintry gaze grew frostier, if anything.

Dismay washed through her as her earlier conclusion about Jonathon's feelings was confirmed. Nothing she could say or do would ever really please him. *As soon as possible* was not soon enough.

'I think, Sophia,' he returned coolly, 'that Godfrey had a more permanent arrangement in mind when he made me promise to marry you. He wanted his child not only to carry the name of Parnell, but to be brought up a Parnell with all the advantages that would give him or her. Of course, I appreciate that you might wish to be free to find another man like Godfrey to share your life with, which is why I originally suggested a divorce after your baby is born. But please do not feel any pressure to set *me* free of this marriage.'

'But I can't *stay* married to you,' she protested. 'Not…not forever!'

His shoulders lifted and fell in a nonchalant shrug. 'I am not suggesting you do. I am, however, telling you that there's no hurry on my part to get another divorce. You've lived here for several weeks without disturbing my equilibrium. In fact, you seem to have fitted into the household exceptionally well. Both Mother and Maud have grown quite fond of you. Since I have no intention of ever marrying again, feel free to embrace the sanctuary of being married to me for as long as you like.'

His mouth pulled back into a sardonic smile. 'If you are concerned for my sex life, then don't give it a second thought. I have never had any trouble finding women to keep me well satisfied in that regard and see no reason why I shall in future. Naturally, I will be discreet. And I expect you to be the same,' he finished on a sharper note.

She stared at him, her eyes rounding. Did he mean what she thought he meant? Did he honestly think that at four months pregnant she would go looking for…for…?

A fierce blush invaded her cheeks. 'I don't think you'll have to worry about me on that score,' she flung at him, outrage making her words flow. 'I loved Godfrey, and I will love him to my dying day. There will be no other man for me. Not ever!'

The corner of his mouth lifted in a cynical fashion. 'A nobly romantic sentiment, I'm sure, but not a very realistic one. You're only nineteen, Sophia. A young woman not yet in her sexual prime. Some day, there'll be another man for you.'

'Maybe so,' she said heatedly, 'but certainly not in

the next five months. I don't know how you could suggest such a disgusting thing. I'm carrying Godfrey's child!'

Their eyes clashed and for a split-second Sophia could have sworn she glimpsed something dark and dangerous swirl within those icy blue depths.

'Is there anything wrong, Jonathon?' came a shaky query from below.

Both of their heads snapped around and down.

Ivy Parnell stood at the bottom of the staircase, a frail, white-haired figure dressed in a grey chiffon dress that had a draining effect on her equally grey face. She was looking up at them with a worried expression in her faded blue eyes.

'Not at all, Mother,' Jonathon returned smoothly. 'Sorry to keep you waiting.'

'You sounded as if you were arguing,' came her plaintive remark when they joined her on the Persian rug that covered the black and white tiled foyer.

'Sophia was under the misconception that I might want a divorce as soon as her baby is born,' Jonathon explained. 'I was reassuring her that wasn't the case.'

Ivy turned alarmed eyes towards Sophia. 'Dear child, you shouldn't be worrying about such things at this moment. Why, even when you and Jonathon do eventually get divorced, you're going to stay here with us and we're going to look after you and your baby just as poor Godfrey wanted. We all love you already, don't we, Jonathon? You're the daughter I never had, the sister Jonathon never had. Tell her she must stay.'

Though touched by Ivy's warmth and kindness, Sophia only needed a quick glance Jonathon's way to see he didn't concur with his mother's sentiments.

There was no affection for her in his staunchly held
face, not even a brotherly one. She was a burden he
had to endure, a cross he had to bear. All she could
hope was that time would soften his hard heart
towards her. Maybe when his niece or nephew was
born, his attitude might change. Babies had a way of
winding themselves around even the hardest of hearts.

And she did want Jonathon to warm to her. He was
the brother of the man she'd loved so very deeply.
She wanted her baby's uncle to like her at least. It
hurt her that he didn't seem to, especially when she
didn't know why exactly.

To be honest, she didn't like him much either. He
made her so uncomfortable. Maybe she made him just
as uncomfortable. One didn't always need a reason to
dislike someone. It could be an instinctive reaction.

Come to think of it, Jonathon had been cold to her
from the very first moment they'd met, in Godfrey's
hospital room. At the time she'd thought he was embarrassed, because he'd walked in on them embracing, but, looking back, she believed there had been
an instant antagonism on his part.

'I've already told Sophia she was welcome to stay,'
Jonathon informed his mother somewhat impatiently.
'And that there's no hurry for a divorce. What there
is some hurry for, however, is the marriage itself. The
celebrant told me he has another appointment at six,
so let's go in.'

The celebrant looked relieved as the three of them
entered the formal sitting-room where the ceremony
was to take place. So did the others.

Wilma shot Jonathon a reproachful glare, which
brought a tiny smile to Sophia's lips. Wilma did not
fit the stereotyped image of a tycoon's private secre-

tary. She wasn't at all beautiful or glamorous or gush-ingly attentive of her boss. She was pushing forty—skinny, plain, opinionated and downright prickly.

She had been Mr Parnell Senior's secretary before he died, Jonathon inheriting her, along with the family business. In Wilma's words, their relationship had been rocky for a while, but in the end, she and Jonathon had forged an understanding.

Sophia was astounded at the way Wilma spoke to her boss at times, but there again, Jonathon gave as good as he got. Worse, most of the time. Sophia sus-pected that if *she'd* been his secretary she'd have quit within a week. In a weird way she gained a degree of secret satisfaction at Wilma's liberated stance.

Wilma's scowl vanished when she shifted her re-gard to Sophia. Now she smiled, mouthing, 'You look beautiful.' Sophia smiled back, feeling a warm grat-itude swell her heart. Wilma had become a good friend over the past few weeks. If it hadn't been for her sound common sense and pragmatic advice, Sophia suspected she might have cracked up entirely.

The lady standing next to Wilma had been similarly supportive. Maud had been the housekeeper in the Parnell household since the year dot. No one knew how old she was, but sixty-five would not have been far astray, though she was very sprightly for her age. And a hard worker.

She'd been cool to Sophia at first, till Sophia had made it clear that she had no intention of lounging around Parnell Hall like some parasite. From day one, she'd insisted on doing her own room and en-suite, as well as helping in any way she could.

Sophia had had plenty of practice with housework during her growing-up years and saw no reason to sit around like a useless lump, simply because she was pregnant. Maud had become her champion in this regard a week or two after her arrival when Jonathon expressed the opinion—quite dogmatically—that she shouldn't be doing the cleaning in her 'condition'.

'The girl's pregnant, not sick!' Maud had argued with a forthrightness reminiscent of Wilma. 'When I had my Jerry, I worked right up till they carted me off to the hospital. Provided the girl is healthy, then no harm can come to her. What do you expect her to do, sit around painting her nails all day?'

Sophia had been astounded when this last remark seemed to strike Jonathon dumb, though his eyes spoke volumes. He'd given Maud a savage look and marched off, clearly furious. Maud's grin of secret triumph had sparked a curiosity within Sophia that she hadn't as yet satisfied. Though she did suspect that the lady who had filled in her time painting her nails must have been Jonathon's ex-wife. Who else could have inspired such a reaction?

Sophia found herself thinking of Jonathon's exwife again as they stood, side by side, in front of the marriage celebrant. All she knew about Jonathon's first marriage was that the divorce had become final only recently. Had his wife been beautiful? Had he loved her as much as she had loved Godfrey? If so, who had divorced whom, and why?

Wilma had implied once or twice that Jonathon had been deeply hurt by his divorce, suggesting that his wife had been at fault. Maybe she'd had an affair...

Sophia found it hard to imagine any woman being unfaithful to Jonathon. Who would *dare*?

She slid a surreptitious glance over at him, standing ramrod-straight, his shoulders as squared as his chiselled jaw-line. There wasn't a weak line in either his face or his body. Sophia realised some women might be attracted to Jonathon's strong silent type, but she knew she could only ever be drawn to a man who showed a degree of sensitivity and compassion.

Godfrey had been *all* sensitivity and compassion.

Sophia could still remember the day they'd first met, when she'd stumbled, weeping, into the old orchard behind the deserted farmhouse next door. She'd thrown herself down into the cool sweet grass under the spreading branches of an ancient apple tree and cried and cried till there were no tears left.

It was then that Godfrey's gentle voice reached her ears.

'What has happened, lass, to upset you this much? Sit up and tell your Uncle Godfrey all about it.'

Frightened at first, she had shot to her feet, about to run, but the sight of Godfrey sitting at his easel, looking so unlike an accoster of young ladies, eased her fears. His eyes were a gentle grey, his soft brown hair already receding, and he had a way of looking at one that warmed and gladdened the soul.

Jonathon accused his older brother of being a dreamer and a fool, but to her he'd been a saint and a saviour. She hadn't fallen in love that first day when she'd poured out her heart to him. But by the time he'd given her sanctuary two years later he'd meant the world to her.

Her whole chest contracted, her eyes shutting momentarily as she struggled to gather herself. She shouldn't have started thinking about Godfrey. Biting her bottom lip till the pain propelled her out of her reverie, Sophia still found that her fingers had begun twisting feverishly together.

Jonathon clamped both of his large hands over hers, holding them in a rock-like grip as the celebrant started speaking.

'We've come together on this lovely September afternoon to celebrate the marriage of Jonathon and Sophia…'

He droned on, Sophia hating the sentimental words, hating the way Jonathon was holding her still, hating *Jonathon*. It should have been Godfrey standing beside her, not this cold, heartless individual. Godfrey, with his love of everything fine and gentle and romantic. He'd taught her so much, about music and poetry and literature and art, shown her a world she hadn't known existed, a world he'd always loved but had been denied him most of his life.

Not that Sophia had known about Godfrey's background prior to his falling ill. She hadn't gleaned much about his past life even then, from either Godfrey or Jonathon or Mrs Parnell, who was so upset by her son's advanced cancer that she was incoherent most of the time.

Wilma had finally filled in the missing pieces for her: how Henry Parnell's first-born son had not taken after his father at all, inheriting instead his mother's softer nature, as well as her appreciation of culture and gentility. As an adolescent, Godfrey had yearned to become first a dancer, then a painter, only to have both his ambitions scorned as effeminate by his domineering father.

Godfrey, as the elder son, was supposed to follow in his father's footsteps in the family property development business, but he'd hated the ruthless cut and thrust of the real estate world from the start. Not that he hadn't tried to conform to his autocratic father's wishes. He had, even to marrying the daughter of another wealthy property tycoon, though his failure to sire an heir had only added to his general sense of inadequacy.

When he'd deserted the family company and his unhappy marriage shortly after his father's death of a heart attack, no one had been seriously surprised. Neither had anyone been surprised when Jonathon had slipped into his father's shoes to make Parnell Property Developments more successful than ever. He was the spitting image of his father in looks, business acumen and ambition.

While the family business had benefited by Godfrey's defection, his mother hadn't. Ivy had become ill with worry over wondering where Godfrey was and what he was doing. His only communication had been a letter with a Sydney postmark which he'd sent shortly after he left, saying he was all right but that he had to live his own life and not to worry about him.

Jonathon had tried to trace his whereabouts but could never find him, not knowing that Godfrey had changed his surname to Jones and was living in a run-down farmhouse just outside the old mining town of Lithgow, over a hundred miles from Sydney.

Any happiness and relief Ivy had felt when Godfrey had finally contacted his family had been superseded by her devastation at his illness and subsequent death. Sophia took some comfort from the fact that in five months' time she would be able to put Godfrey's child in Ivy's arms. Maybe then the woman would come really alive again.

An elbow jabbing into her ribs jolted Sophia back to reality.

'Say "I will,"' Jonathon hissed into her ear.

'I…I w-will,' Sophia stammered, to her mortification.

'God,' came the low mutter from beside her.

Jonathon bit out his 'I will' as if he were giving a guilty verdict for murder. When the celebrant pronounced them 'as one' in a flowery way, followed by a sickening smirk and a 'you may kiss your bride', Sophia darted Jonathon an anxious look.

She didn't want him to kiss her but she couldn't really see how they could avoid it. Everyone else knew their marriage was a sham, but the celebrant didn't. Jonathon looked just as reluctant to oblige, but, seeing perhaps that he had no alternative, he took Sophia firmly by the shoulders, turned her his way and bent his head.

Sophia steeled herself for the cold imprint of his mouth on hers, so she was somewhat startled to find that the firm lips pressing down on hers were quite warm. Her eyelashes fluttered nervously, her mouth quivering tremulously beneath his. His mouth lifted, and for a second he stared down into her surprised face. Something glittered in that cold blue gaze.

Then he did something that really shocked her.

He kissed her again.

CHAPTER TWO

SOPHIA'S first response was a bitter resentment. Who did he think he was, forcing another kiss on her when he knew she hadn't wanted him to kiss her at all?

But as those determined lips moved over hers a second time, Sophia's resentment was shattered by an astonishing discovery. Jonathon's mouth on hers was not an entirely unpleasant experience.

Of course, I'm not really *enjoying* it, she kept telling herself for several totally bewildering seconds.

When Jonathon made no move to end the kiss, the pressure of his mouth increasing, if anything, Sophia began to panic. What must the others be thinking? The grip on her shoulders increased as well, his fingers digging into her flesh. When Sophia felt his tongue demanding entry between her lips, she gasped and reefed her head backwards.

Her eyes, which had closed at some stage, flew open, flashing outrage. But Jonathon was already turning away to shake the celebrant's hand.

'I never tire of seeing couples genuinely in love,' the man said, pumping Jonathon's hand. 'But if you don't mind, Mr Parnell, could we sign the appropriate documents straight away? I really must dash.'

Jonathon turned back to Sophia then, his eyes and demeanour as unflappable as ever, while *her* face was burning up, her heart still beating madly in her chest. How dared he presume to kiss her like that?

Not that she didn't know what lay behind it.

Frustration. He was frustrated with the situation his deathbed promise to Godfrey had put him in. A kiss, Sophia imagined, could be an expression of anger as well as love—both emotions capable of evoking a fiery passion.

It just showed what kind of man Jonathon was. Nothing like Godfrey at all! Godfrey would never have kissed her out of anger or frustration. Why, Godfrey hadn't even kissed her at all till that fateful night. Even then, *she'd* been the one to initiate the first kiss. Not that he hadn't kissed her back quickly enough, cupping her cheeks and covering her face with beautiful, gentle kisses.

Her eyes misted with the memory of the sweet pleasure they had evoked, of how they had fulfilled all those wonderfully romantic dreams she'd been harbouring about Godfrey for such a long time.

'Sophia.'

The impatient calling of her name snapped her out of her daydreaming, as did those harsh blue eyes glowering at her blurred vision.

'W-what?'

'Good God,' Jonathon muttered darkly.

'You have to sign the marriage certificate, Mrs Parnell,' said a gentler male voice beside her. 'It's all set up in Jonathon's study.'

She glanced over her shoulder up at Harvey Taylor's smoothly urbane face. In his mid-thirties, Harvey was as fair as Jonathon was dark. Apparently, he had inherited control of Taylor and Sons—Solicitors, around the same time Jonathon took charge of Parnell Properties. He and Jonathon had gone to school together, both of them excelling in their studies. But he possessed none of Jonathon's hard-edged strength, either in his face or his nature. He was a charming man, but a little weak, Sophia suspected.

Still, it was good to feel a kind hand on her arm for a change, and she liked the way he was looking at her. With admiration and respect. Not like her pretend husband. *His* eyes carried nothing but an ill-concealed exasperation.

'Best *you* bring her along, Harvey,' Jonathon said with a sardonic twist to his mouth. 'You seem to have the right touch. Mother, you can help Maud with the refreshments while we get the paperwork out of the way. Wilma! You have to come with us, being one of the witnesses. This way, Mr Weston. The study is just across the hall...' And he was striding away from them without a backwards glance.

'Yes, *commandant*,' Wilma saluted to Jonathon's rapidly disappearing back, and marched off after him.

Sophia couldn't stop a giggle from escaping her lips.

'You should take a leaf out of Wilma's book,' Harvey whispered as he ushered Sophia in the secretary's wake. 'Jonathon can't hurt you if you don't let him, Sophia.'

She lifted startled eyes. 'Why should you think he can hurt me at all? You better than anyone know this isn't a real marriage. Jonathon and I will be divorced as soon as the baby is born.'

'That is your intention now, I'm sure, but Jonathon is a very attractive man. What if you fall in love with him? What if he decides having a wife who looks like you is just what the doctor ordered?'

She ground to a halt in the doorway of the study and stared at Harvey, his last remark not even registering after his first ridiculous suggestion. 'I will never fall in love with Jonathon. Never!'

When Harvey suddenly frowned, his eyes darting to a spot behind her left shoulder, she spun round to find a stony-faced Jonathon standing there. 'Do you think we might get on with signing these papers?' he rapped out.

'Sure thing,' Harvey agreed smoothly, and waved Sophia into the room.

She hesitated, her emotions seesawing between embarrassment and guilt. Yet why should she feel guilty at Jonathon's overhearing her assertion? He already knew her feelings about falling in love again, and while she could concede she might love another man at some point in the far distant future, that man would never be someone like him. She could only love a man who made her feel good about herself, who made her feel special, not gauche and stupid.

'Sophia,' Harvey murmured, and urged her into the room.

But as she made her way across the polished parquet flooring on to the richly patterned rug that lay in front of the huge oak desk, flashes of the first time she'd stood in front of this desk jumped into her mind.

It had been the day after Godfrey's funeral, a cold, wet, windy August morning on which she hadn't been able to drag herself out of bed. She'd been lying there, watching the rain slap against the window, when Maud had come in with the message that Jonathon wanted to see her in his study when she finally did get up.

A guilty embarrassment had propelled her out of bed immediately, hating for Godfrey's brother to think she was going to be a lazy house guest. Showering hurriedly, she'd thrown on a pair of jeans and a pale peach sweater, put a few vigorous brush-strokes through her long dark hair, subdued its thick waves into a single plait then practically run down-stairs, only ten minutes having passed since Maud had come into her room.

Her knock on Jonathon's study door had been timid. Not so the barked, 'Come,' from within. Taking several hopefully steadying breaths, she'd gone inside, shutting the door carefully behind her. Her sidewards glances had been nervous, however, as she'd hesitantly approached the desk, the room being as intimidating as its owner. Wood-panelled walls, masses of bookshelves filled with heavy-looking tomes, dark curtains at the windows blocking most of the natural light from entering. Not a welcoming room at all.

'You…you wanted to see me?' she asked, feeling like a recalcitrant student who'd been hauled in front of the headmaster for misconduct.

When Jonathon looked up from his paperwork, he leant back in his chair, removing himself from the circle of light from his desk lamp. His face fell into shadow, making him appear more menacing than usual.

'Pull up a chair, Sophia,' he ordered. 'We have things to discuss.'

'D-d-discuss?'

He sighed. 'Perhaps it would be better if you just sat down and listened.'

Sophia agreed wholeheartedly, despising herself for stammering all the time. She couldn't understand why he had such an effect on her. She'd never stammered before in her life. There again, she'd never had anything to do with anyone quite like Jonathon Parnell before.

She settled into a large brown leather chair, happy to fall silent.

'I'm sorry to intrude on your grief,' he started, without much apology in his brusque voice. He wasn't even looking at her, some papers on his desk holding his attention. 'But there are legal matters I must make you aware of. Godfrey's will—made a few years back unfortunately—leaves everything to his wife. The one who didn't even bother to come to his funeral yesterday,' he muttered before glancing up and giving Sophia a long, hard look. 'Though perhaps it was as well she chose not to show up…'

He sighed a weary sounding sigh. 'Whatever, Godfrey left her his entire estate, which includes the home at Roseville he once lived in with Alicia, and which she has been occupying since he disappeared, plus its contents, as well as a third share in Parnell Properties, all up valued at approximately fifteen million dollars.'

Sophia simply gaped. Godfrey had been a millionaire? And yet he'd lived so poorly during the years she'd known him, never buying any new clothes, growing his own vegetables, cutting firewood from dead trees. It had been a hand-to-mouth existence, his only extravagance being his art supplies. She'd often teased him about what he could do with the money when he became a famous painter. Now she understood why he'd brushed aside her fantasies, telling her instead that money didn't bring happiness and never to believe it could.

'My solicitor informs me, Sophia,' Jonathon went

on, 'that you could contest the will on the grounds that you lived with Godfrey as his common-law wife for at least six months preceding his death, and are expecting his child.'

Sophia opened her mouth to protest that first assumption, then closed it again. She *had* lived with Godfrey, she supposed. What difference did it make that they hadn't consummated their relationship till that last night? Still…contesting Godfrey's will didn't feel right. He'd had enough time and opportunity to change his will, if that was what he'd wanted to do.

Godfrey's words came back to her about money not bringing happiness and she knew then that she didn't want any of the money he'd left behind, the money that had obviously made him miserable. But before she could open her mouth again, Jonathon preempted her.

'Knowing you,' he drawled, 'I'm sure you don't want to do that any more than I want you to. Besides, Alicia is not the sort of woman to go quietly in matters of money. Any contesting of Godfrey's will could get very nasty and very expensive. There's no guarantee of your winning, either. So I would not advise that course of action. Godfrey entrusted you to me, knowing I would never see you destitute, so I have set up a trust fund for yourself and the child, in exchange for which you will sign a legal waiving of your rights to Godfrey's estate and any more Parnell money. How does that sound to you?'

She hesitated. How could she refuse financial security for her child and herself? That would be crazy. And it wasn't the same as fighting for that obscene amount of money. Jonathon obviously wasn't talking about millions, just enough for her to live on.

The only problem was that it was Jonathon's money. Sophia hated feeling obliged to him for more than he'd already given her. Dear heavens, he'd spent a fortune on her already, having Wilma select her a new wardrobe and a host of other things. Still, she supposed he must be very rich too and wouldn't really miss it, so she swallowed and nodded her assent.

'Good,' he muttered. 'For a second there, I thought you were going to be stubborn and foolish. *Again*.'

Sophia blushed, knowing he was referring to her distress over the price-tags on some of the clothes Wilma insisted she buy. Sophia had telephoned Jonathon at his office in a panic, only to have her protest swept aside with total exasperation. Instead of his admiring her for not wanting to spend his money, he'd seemed angry at her worrying.

She'd since learnt not to complain when he ordered her to buy something he thought she needed. Her dressing-table was covered in jars of cosmetics and bottles of perfume she'd never opened, her drawers full of expensive and very delicate lingerie she felt it a sin to wear on an everyday basis. As if she'd been interested in material things, anyway, when her Godfrey was dying.

Jonathon came forward on his chair and cleared his throat. 'Now along to the matter of our getting married...'

Sophia sat up straight. She'd been wondering when he'd get round to that. Of course, he wouldn't want to go through with it. No one could condemn him for that. People said anything to make a person's last days happy.

'If you'll just sign where indicated,' he said, picking up a sheet of paper, turning it round and facing it towards her, 'we should be able to get married next month.'

'You mean you…you still want to m-marry me?'

His coming forward in the chair to pass over the document had brought him into full light, so that she saw the hard glitter in his blue eyes. 'The word "want" does not come into it, Sophia. I have no other option. I could not live with myself if I did not fulfil my promise to my brother, for it was the first and only thing he has ever asked me to do for him. I realise I am not the sort of man you would choose for a husband, but we only have to go through the motions. It will not be a real marriage. Later on, we can secure a discreet divorce.'

Sophia gulped when he directed a pen her way.

Her hand had trembled as she took it, her signature wobbly. Now, five weeks later, she was signing her marriage certificate on the same desk, and her hand was shaking just as much.

When she'd signed for the last wobbly time, Sophia heaved a sigh of relief and gave the pen to Wilma who stepped forward with her usual brisk confidence. Dressed in a severely tailored brown woollen suit with black patent accessories, her straight brown hair cropped mannishly short, she still exuded a strength of personality that was oddly attractive. In seconds, she'd whisked her distinctive signature in the allotted spaces, followed by an equally dashing Harvey.

Sophia watched them both with a degree of envy. One day, she would be like that, she vowed. Undaunted by any situation, and totally in command of herself.

Her sigh carried a certain amount of disappointment in herself that all Godfrey had achieved with her had turned out to be an illusion. She'd mistakenly believed he'd turned her from a shy, ignorant girl into a culturally informed young woman who would not have been at a loss in any company.

But she'd been wrong, realising within days of her arrival in the cosmopolitan city of Sydney and the elegant grandeur of Parnell Hall that she was still a country bumpkin, with few real social graces and no style at all. Wilma had done her best in the dress department—she'd certainly been given enough money to squander—but a presentable face and good figure could not disguise Sophia's innate lack of sophistication. Her recognition of her failings had obliterated her self-confidence, everything only made worse by her unfortunate reaction to Jonathon's bossy, almost bullying nature.

Perhaps if he'd been a bit more like Godfrey…

She sighed again, thinking to herself that she'd never known two brothers less alike.

All the formalities over, Jonathon saw the hearty Mr Weston to the door while the rest of them returned to the sitting-room where Maud was still laying out the buffet supper she'd been preparing all afternoon. Ivy was standing around, looking lost. Wilma immediately pressed a sherry into her hands, Sophia declining. Harvey moved off to pour himself a drink from the selection of crystal decanters lined up next to the food.

'I wanted to tell you how beautiful you look today, my dear,' Ivy complimented Sophia.

'Blue's not her colour, though,' Wilma joined in tactlessly before Sophia could say a word. 'She'd have looked much better in cream with her dark colouring, but Sophia thought it too close to white.'

'I can understand her not wanting to wear white,' Ivy murmured. 'If only poor Godfrey could have been here…'

The words hung in the air, the group falling silent as the wretched reality of the occasion sank in.

'Then there wouldn't have been a wedding at all, Mother dear,' Jonathon inserted drily into the emotion-charged atmosphere.

All heads turned to stare at him, Wilma recovering first.

'Hardly a fair thing to say,' was her tart comment, 'especially when Godfrey isn't here to defend himself.'

'Oh I have no doubt that Godfrey *meant* to marry Sophia,' Jonathon elaborated, that sardonic edge still in his voice, 'but he was, at the time of his death, still married to Alicia. It takes twelve months after the initial application to gain a no-fault divorce in this country and Godfrey had instigated nothing in the three years he'd been away.'

'Do we have to talk about that today, Jonathon?' Ivy looked quite distressed and Sophia's heart went out to her. 'We all know Godfrey meant to divorce that woman.'

Jonathon, however, was not about to be swayed.

'He didn't divorce her, though, did he?' he drawled. 'But that was just like Godfrey, wasn't it? Always meaning to do something but never getting round to it.'

'Jonathon, don't,' his mother cried brokenly, a hand coming up to flutter at her throat.

'I'm sorry, Mother, but I'm the one who's always had to pick up the pieces whenever Godfrey decided to run away from real life and embrace one of his fancies.'

Sophia sucked in a sharp breath, but Jonathon swept on, seemingly intent on assassinating his brother's character.

'The man never grew up, never developed a sense of responsibility. I'm prepared to forget his business fiascos, but when it comes to his personal life I find it hard to be as tolerant. Alicia might be a spoiled, mercenary bitch, but she didn't deserve being walked out on without a word. She's been in limbo for three years, for God's sake. The least Godfrey could have done was give her a divorce. Then what does he do? He takes up with a girl almost young enough to be his daughter and makes her pregnant when he knew, he *knew* dammit, that he was dying. What kind of selfish stupidity was that, I ask you?'

A hushed silence descended on the room once Jonathon ran out of steam, and it was while the air vibrated with everyone's tension that Sophia stepped forward and slapped him hard around the face. The sound of her hand cracking across his cheek echoed with the gasps of shock her action produced. But she heard nothing, saw nothing except a haze of red-hot fury before her eyes.

'Don't you *ever*,' she launched forth, her voice and body shaking with emotion, 'call my Godfrey selfish or stupid again, do you hear me? He might not have been perfect. He probably made mistakes. But Godfrey would never deliberately hurt another human being. He did whatever he did because he *had* to! As for his callously making me pregnant, nothing could be further than the truth! During the time I knew Godfrey, not once did he make improper advances to me, even after he took me in when I had nowhere else to go.

'If you must blame someone for my pregnancy, then blame me. I went to my Godfrey's bed when he was obviously distraught and I comforted him the only way I could think of. Neither of us thought of the child we might have as a consequence, but do you know what? I'm proud I'm having Godfrey's baby. Extremely proud. He was a fine man and would have made a fine father. But I am not proud of being your wife, Jonathon Parnell. The day cannot come quickly enough that I have done with you!'

So saying, she burst into tears and ran from the room, dashing up the stairs and along the hall into her bedroom where she threw herself on to the bed, weeping copiously into the green silk quilt.

Downstairs, Jonathon was still staring after her, his face ashen, except for the bright red mark on his cheek.

'Well, Jonathon?' Wilma mocked. 'I see the much vaunted Parnell charm is still intact.'

'Go after her, man,' Harvey advised. 'Apologise profusely. Beg her forgiveness.'

'Please, Jonathon,' Ivy pleaded. 'She's going to have Godfrey's child…'

His eyes turned slowly towards his mother, their expression haunted. 'Must I spend the rest of my life paying for the dubious privilege of being born in the image of my father?' he muttered.

When no one commented further after this cryptic statement, he whirled and strode from the room, mounting the stairs two at a time till he disappeared from the others' view. Maud returned from the kitchen at that precise moment to find three silent, drooping faces.

'What is it?' she demanded to know. 'What's happened?'

'Jonathon said something that upset Sophia,' Wilma volunteered.

'Oh, no, not again! What's wrong with that man? Can't he see what a prize that girl is? Why, if he had any brains he'd snap her up for himself good and proper.'

'Life isn't that neat, Maud,' was Harvey's wry remark.

'I don't see why not,' the old lady muttered crossly. 'She's a beautiful girl. He's a handsome man. They're married now. Why can't nature take its natural course?'

'She's having his brother's baby, for pity's sake,' Wilma argued. 'Give the man a break. This hasn't been easy for Jonathon. Besides, Sophia is still very much in love with Godfrey.'

'You're right,' Maud sighed. 'I'm just a silly old fool, thinking things can be all tied up with pink bows. So what are we going to do?'

'I know what I'm going to do,' Harvey said, lifting his whisky and draining every drop. 'I'm going to have another drink.'

'Good idea,' Wilma agreed. 'I'll join you.'

CHAPTER THREE

THE first awareness Sophia had that someone had followed her came when the bed dipped low on one side, but she never dreamt it was Jonathon sitting there. She presumed it was Wilma, or maybe Maud. Not Ivy. Godfrey's mother was not one to confront or even actively comfort. She was a gentle, but very passive creature.

So it wasn't till Jonathon actually spoke that she realised who it was in the room with her.

'I'm sorry, Sophia,' he began with a ragged sigh. 'I have no excuse for my appallingly thoughtless behaviour other than I've been finding it difficult to deal with certain aspects of Godfrey's life prior to his illness. I'm glad you've cleared up my misconception that he had somehow taken advantage of your youth and innocence. Please also believe me when I say I make no judgement of *your* actions, either with Godfrey or with me downstairs. I have nothing but admiration for the way you defended my brother just now. A man would kill to have a woman love him as you obviously loved Godfrey.'

Sophia lay there for a moment, unsure if his seemingly heartfelt words had soothed, or flustered her further. She did not associate Jonathon with apologies.

Rolling slowly over, she encountered a face so bleak her heart filled with instant remorse. She couldn't see into his eyes for he was looking down at the floor, but the uncharacteristic droop of his head and shoulders pulled at her heartstrings.

'I...I'm sorry too,' she whispered. 'I shouldn't have hit you.'

When his head lifted and he twisted round to face her, Sophia gasped at the still stark imprint of her hand on his cheek. She had no idea she'd hit him that hard. Appalled, she reached up blindly with shocked fingers, a guilty groan escaping her lips as her shaking hand made contact with the red mark.

'Don't!' he snapped, iron fingers enclosing her wrist and ramming her hand down on to the quilt, the action jerking her up into a semi-sitting position.

With the abrupt movement, her hat, which had been partially dislodged when she'd first flung herself on the bed, fell off, the large comb holding her hair up also coming adrift, sending her dark glossy waves tumbling down around her face and shoulders.

'Oh!' she cried.

When she tried to disengage her hand from his to push back her hair, his grip remained fast, his eyes boring into hers with such intensity that she was completely bamboozled by the whole situation. Did he think she'd been going to hit him again? Sophia couldn't see why he should. She'd already said she was sorry for that.

So why didn't he say something? Why did he just sit there, staring at her like that? And why, oh, why couldn't she seem to find her own voice?

The room, which was very large and luxuriously furnished, seemed to have shrunk, Jonathon looming large over her. His face was only inches from hers, so close now that she could no longer see the blue of his eyes. They were deep dark pools into which she seemed to be drowning…drowning…

In desperation she sucked in a breath of air, but this only seemed to remind her of the way her heart was suddenly hammering in her chest. The large hand cuffing her wrist tightened, and for a brief mad moment she thought he was going to kiss her again. Instead, she found her hand being ground further down into the mattress as Jonathon pushed himself to his feet.

'Don't let your tender heart lead you into any more trouble, Sophia,' he grated out, his face as harsh and humourless as ever as he glared down at her from his considerable height. 'I deserved hitting downstairs, and I almost deserved hitting again just now. When you touch a man like that in future,' he warned darkly, 'make sure you're not on a bed with him. Not all males are as saintlike as Godfrey.'

Sophia's eyes widened, colour coming to her cheeks. So he *had* been tempted to kiss her.

But surely he did not think she had been deliberately provocative, or that even subconsciously she might have been inviting him to…to…

Her cheeks burnt even more fiercely at such a mortifying thought.

Jonathon spun away from the bed with a scoffing sound. 'I was right the first time,' he growled as he stalked across the deep gold carpet. 'Godfrey should have been hung, drawn and quartered for taking you under his roof the way he did. I refuse to forgive his appalling lack of judgement. If he couldn't foresee the consequences of such an action, then the man was more of a naïve, idealistic, airy-fairy fool than I always thought him to be!'

Grabbing the knob of the bedroom door, Jonathon whirled to face her one last time. 'Hate me all you like for saying as much, Sophia, but that's the way I see it. I loved my brother, believe it or not, but he was a dreamer who left a trail of destruction behind him. He's left you literally holding the baby, and me in a situation no man would relish.'

Sophia scrambled off the bed, straightening her clothes and pushing back her hair with agitated hands. 'You didn't have to marry me!' she cried. 'I didn't expect you to, but you insisted!'

'More fool me,' he snarled. 'But I'm not so blind that I can't see my own mistakes. You will have your wish, Sophia. A divorce as soon as the baby is born. I also think a house of your own is called for. Somewhere nearby, of course, where Mother can easily visit you and the child.'

But not you, she thought agitatedly. I don't want you visiting me, you hateful man!

'Now I suggest you go wash your face and fix your hair,' the hateful man ordered. 'It's rather a mess. I will expect you to make an appearance downstairs shortly.'

'But I don't want—'

'We all have to do things we don't want to do occasionally,' he cut in sharply. 'If you don't come down, everyone will look at me with accusing eyes, and I will be forced to return to bring you down myself. If you can't do this for me, then do it for Godfrey. I'm sure he would have expected the mother of his child to conduct herself with ladylike decorum in his home, which means keeping childish tantrums to a minimum.'

With that, Jonathon politely but firmly shut the door, leaving Sophia to stare after him.

Childish tantrums?

Childish tantrums!

She would show him childish tantrums.

Her eyes darted savagely around the room, looking for something she could throw. *Anything*!

Her hat was the only item within arm's reach. She scooped it up from where it lay on the pillow and launched it in the direction of the door like a frisbee. But, being a rather light hat, it fell a good deal short of its target with a highly unsatisfying plop. Marching over to where it had landed, Sophia glared momentarily down at the pathetic little wisp of nothing before she gave into another irrational burst of temper and began stomping it to death.

After a few feverish seconds, she stopped, eyes rounding with horror as she bent to pick up the poor mangled thing, the veil now ripped, the flower totally destroyed. Sophia blinked her shock as she stared at what was left of the once pretty blue hat, a sob catching in her throat.

I've gone mad, she thought. Quite mad.

No, you haven't, the voice of brutal honesty inserted. You're simply behaving very badly. Jonathon was right. Godfrey would not be proud of you today. Not at all.

Tears threatened as her thoughts filled with Godfrey…her kind, gentle, warm, wonderful Godfrey. Oh, God, how she missed him!

But not in bed, as others in this house might imagine, she thought bitterly. In hindsight, her one intimate experience with Godfrey had been an utter failure in the physical sense. How could it have been otherwise, with her a virgin and Godfrey upset and unwell?

What she missed was Godfrey's companionship. Their long talks into the night. Their listening to music together. His just being there, his calm and collected presence always having a soothing influence on her occasional burst of restlessness.

Their relationship had been a meeting of souls long before it had finally become a meeting of bodies. Sophia had no doubt that in other circumstances the physical side would have eventually become just as satisfying. She had not allowed herself to be too disappointed at the time, brushing aside any dismay over the brief and rather painful experience actual intercourse had turned out to be. She'd told herself there would be other nights. Next time, it would not hurt so much. Next time, things would be different.

But there had been no other nights, no next time…

When Sophia snapped back to the present, she was startled to find that she was standing there in the middle of the room, twisting the already mangled hat round and round in her hands. It took considerable effort for her to stop. What on earth was wrong with her? She had never felt quite like this before, so uptight and angry and knotted inside, as though she was a volcano waiting to erupt.

She still couldn't get over hitting Jonathon as she had downstairs. And now she had obliterated a perfectly innocent hat. Yet still it wasn't enough. The urge to scream out loud echoed in her head and she bit down hard on her bottom lip.

Tasting her own blood brought her up with a jolt.

Shock was swiftly followed by shame. What would Godfrey think of her, carrying on like this? It had to stop. Right now. This very second. She was a married woman, a mother-to-be, a grown-up, not a wild, uncontrollable child.

Jonathon's parting words about her putting on a childish tantrum popped back into her mind, infuriating her with its potential accuracy. She would show him, she vowed fiercely. From this moment on she would be the epitome of female composure and maturity. There would be no more losses of temper, no more juvenile blushings. And no more silly stammering!

It was a subdued but steely Sophia who walked down the stairs a few minutes later, her face freshly made-up, her thick dark waves held back behind her ears with some combs. With each step she focused her mind on staying cool, calm and collected, but, from the moment her foot moved on to the Persian rug at the base of the stairs and she was faced with actually presenting herself at the drawing-room door, her composure began to crumble.

What would everyone be thinking about the dreadful exhibition she had made of herself earlier? No doubt they were wondering what Godfrey ever saw in such a hysterical ninny. They were also probably feeling very sorry for Jonathon, having been lumbered with a wife he didn't want and a child that wasn't his.

Sophia groaned her inner distress. Oh, why couldn't Jonathon have just let her stay upstairs? He could have said she had a headache. Maud could have brought her a tray. God, if only she were more like Wilma. Wilma could handle any situation. She didn't care what others thought, especially her boss.

Sophia had to literally force her legs to carry her across the foyer towards the drawing-room. When she moved gingerly into the thankfully open doorway, no one noticed her at first. Wilma was seated on the silk brocade couch, sipping sherry and chatting to a wan-looking Ivy. Jonathon was standing with Harvey next to the fireplace, both of them with large scotches in their hands. Maud was fiddling with the food on the sideboard.

When Sophia gave a nervous clearance of her throat, everyone stopped doing what they were doing to turn and look at her. She froze under their curious gazes, unable to take another step into the room. An awkward silence fell and she was contemplating bolting back upstairs when Jonathon extracted himself from Harvey's side and strode forward, his blue eyes locking with hers and forcing her to remain exactly where she was.

'Feeling better now?' he enquired in his usual cool manner. The mark on his cheek had faded, she was glad to see.

'I'm fine, thank you,' came her somewhat stiff reply, but without a stammer in sight, thank God. A sigh of relief puffed from her lungs. Maybe she would survive the next few minutes after all.

'Good. Come and I'll get you a drink, then,' he said, and taking her hand in his, began to draw her across the room.

His grip was oddly gentle, such a contrast from the last time he'd held her hand upstairs, a few minutes ago. But it had no less of an effect on her, bringing a disturbing rise in her pulse-rate which she determinedly put down to nerves. Sophia refused to admit it could still be fear. Why should she fear Jonathon?

The idea was ridiculous. Fear should be reserved for one's enemies, and Jonathon was not her enemy. Nor did she really hate him. That had been the silly child within her thinking that a while ago.

She didn't want anyone else thinking she hated him, either. Sophia came to a sudden decision, grinding to a halt and extracting her hand from Jonathon's as she turned to face everyone else in the room.

'I...I have something to say,' she began, clasping her hands nervously together in front of her. 'I...I'm very sorry for causing a scene earlier. And I'm very, very sorry for having hit Jonathon. No, please, Jonathon,' she insisted when he went to interrupt, a grimace on his face. 'I have to say this.'

She scooped in another steadying breath before continuing in a reasonably composed fashion. 'It was very wrong of me to do what I did when you've been so kind. I can see the way Godfrey acted might have looked a little irresponsible to your eyes and I can understand why you feel angry with him. I can't think of many brothers who would do what you have done here today.' Tears pricked at her eyes but she held them back. 'I'm sure Godfrey would have wanted me to co-operate with you, not...not make your life difficult. I...I feel as if I've let him down somehow.'

By this time, she was also finding it extremely hard not to cry. Wilma, probably seeing her distress, leapt to her feet.

'What rubbish! You have done Godfrey proud today,' she insisted firmly, coming forward to take both Sophia's hands in hers. 'Hasn't she, everyone?'

There were murmurs of assent all round. But not, Sophia realised unhappily, from Jonathon. He stood beside her in stoical silence.

'And I'm sure Jonathon holds no grudge against you for giving him a little slap,' Wilma raved on. 'I would imagine it's not the first time a lady has given his cheek the taste of her hand,' she added mockingly.

'I can think of one woman who might benefit from the back of some man's hand,' he muttered under his breath so only Sophia and Wilma could hear.

The interchange quite startled Sophia out of her threatening misery. Her eyes darted to Wilma, who seemed delighted to have evoked such a reaction in her boss. When a drily amused smile pulled at Jonathon's mouth, Sophia's confusion was complete. Truly, she did not understand their relationship at all. Were they friend or foe?

'Let's sample some of this mouthwatering food Maud's been bringing in,' Wilma continued. 'I'm starving.'

The evening went reasonably well for a while after that. Maud had prepared mainly finger-food which was easy to eat either standing up or by sitting with a small plate in one's lap. Conversation revolved mostly around Maud's delicious food and the recent spate of rainy weather, which were both very safe topics.

Not that Sophia was really enjoying herself. The strain of the day was taking its toll, the beginnings of a tension headache pressing in over her eyes. When Harvey poured her a glass of red wine she took it readily, settling down on the couch Ivy and Wilma had recently vacated. A small smile came to her lips as she sipped the drink and recalled the many evenings she had sat with Godfrey either before the fire or out on the back porch, drinking cheap claret and discussing the latest book she was reading.

She was completely off in another world, not noticing when Harvey sat down beside her, so that when he said, 'Penny for your thoughts,' she jumped in surprise. But her reply consisted of nothing but a sad little smile, knowing that a man like Harvey would never understand what she and Godfrey had shared; what she had felt for him. In his eyes—as in Jonathon's—Godfrey had been a loser, a plain, balding thirty-seven-year-old loser who had no right to the love of a pretty young girl.

She'd seen everyone's shocked looks when she'd been brought here to Parnell Hall and introduced as Godfrey's *de facto* wife. Even his own mother had been surprised, despite Godfrey's having been her favourite son. The news that Sophia was expecting his baby had initially been met with a stunned silence. Sophia was hurt for Godfrey, once she realised they hadn't even believed he was man enough to father a child.

Well, they were wrong, weren't they? she thought defiantly as she sat there, her fingers linking over her gently swelling stomach. He had fathered a baby, and next week, after she'd had her ultrasound, she would know if it was a boy or a girl. She hoped it was a boy. And she hoped he was just like Godfrey!

'I can see you're not in the mood for chit-chat,' Harvey said quietly from her side. 'I just wanted to say I think you're great and I hope everything turns out well for you. But if it doesn't and you ever need a shoulder to cry on, give me a call.'

Sophia was touched by the offer and turned a grateful smile his way. 'That's very kind of you, Harvey. I'll remember that. Thank you.'

Harvey patted her wrist and stood up, almost brushing shoulders with Jonathon as he did so.

'Leaving, are you, Harvey?' Jonathon said in clipped tones.

Harvey seemed taken aback for a second before glancing at his watch. 'Not yet,' he returned. 'I was just going to get myself another glass of wine.'

'No more for Sophia,' Jonathon ordered brusquely, glaring down at her near empty glass.

'That's up to her, isn't it?'

Sophia was thinking the very same thing.

'Jonathon,' his mother interrupted, materialising by his side and thereby saving the awkward moment. 'Why don't you put some music on? Something nice and relaxing. Mozart, I think. You like Mozart, don't you Sophia? You were playing him the other day.'

'I adore Mozart,' she agreed. 'He was Godfrey's favourite composer.'

Ivy's sigh was wistful. 'Of course… You know, I played him Mozart from the day he was born. It always put him to sleep.'

'Mozart would put anyone to sleep,' Jonathon muttered, his irritation obvious as he stalked over to the stereo and started flipping through the CDs.

'Don't take any notice of Jonathon,' Ivy whispered as she sat down next to Sophia. 'For some reason he's always been a little jealous of Godfrey. Lord knows why. Poor Godfrey wasn't born with any of his brother's natural advantages. He was a sickly child, whereas Jonathon never even got colds. I couldn't count the number of nights I had to spend sitting up with Godfrey, especially when he had asthma.'

Sophia began thinking that maybe Jonathon was jealous, not of Godfrey himself, but all the love and attention his mother obviously lavished on her older son. She'd never had any brothers and sisters herself, but she could well imagine it must be very hard growing up knowing a brother or sister was favoured over you. Still, it seemed Godfrey's father had favoured his second son so maybe the love and attention bit was balanced out in the end.

Mozart's Flute and Harp Concerto in C major brought a brief end to any conversation as its pristine notes cut through the drawing-room. Jonathon's choice sent Sophia's heart squeezing tight, plus a host of vivid memories to the forefront of her mind. She almost expected to look over at the empty armchair opposite and see Godfrey materialise, his head tipping back and his eyes closing as they did whenever he listened to this particular piece.

'Aah,' Ivy sighed next to her. 'What magic…what bliss…'

Sophia gritted her teeth against the unexpected pain the music was evoking, knowing she could hardly ask for it to be turned off. But she couldn't help grimacing a little as she glanced over towards the stereo. Jonathon turned around at that moment and their eyes met, Sophia shivering at the austere hardness in his face as he walked back towards her.

And sympathy for him disappeared. The man was pure granite, not the sort to ever feel deprived of a mother's love. Or any other person's love for that matter. She doubted he'd ever felt anything even approaching love in his whole life. It was no wonder his first marriage broke up. No normal woman could endure living with a block of stone.

'You're looking tired, Sophia,' he announced

brusquely on returning. 'I think it's time you went up to bed.'

'Yes, you do look tired, dear,' Ivy agreed.

She was about to argue when common sense intervened. She *was* tired, and her headache was getting worse. On top of that, the prospect of staying here and listening to Mozart was more than she could bear.

'Yes, you're right. I *am* tired.'

When Jonathon held out his hand, she hesitated, then resignedly placed her hand in his. It closed, large and strong, around her fingers, drawing her to her feet. Once again she was reminded of how big he was. And how tall. Even with high heels on, she had to crick her neck back to look up into his face.

'I'll walk you upstairs,' he offered.

Sophia's panic was instant, as was her return to stammering. 'N-no, I…I…' When she tried to pull her hand out of his, his fingers tightened.

'Don't be ridiculous,' he hissed. 'I'm not going to eat you. I'm just taking Sophia up to bed,' he announced out loud. 'She's exhausted. Say goodnight, everyone.'

Everyone said goodnight, Wilma coming forward to give her a kiss on the cheek, after which she frowned down at where Jonathon was still holding Sophia's hand. Sophia was appalled to feel a flustered heat sweep up her neck and into her cheeks. Wilma's eyes rounded a little, which only served to make Sophia even more mortified. She recalled how Wilma had told her one day that a lot of women were drawn to Jonathon's darkly brooding personality, finding him challenging and extremely sexy.

But I'm not one of them! she wanted to scream at her friend, her eyes flashing her distress.

She didn't manage to get her message across, however, Wilma's face turning drily knowing when Jonathon began to lead a seemingly meek and compliant Sophia from the room. My God, she thinks I'm attracted to the man. She thinks I want him to hold my hand. Maybe she even thinks I want him in my bed!

Sophia yanked her hand out of his grasp once they reached the top of the stairs. Jonathon immediately ground to a halt to glare at her, clearly at the end of his tether. 'What the hell's wrong with you?' he snapped. 'Am I some kind of monster in your eyes that my holding your hand frightens the life out of you? Or is it that you think Godfrey is looking down at you from his place in heaven and disapproving of your allowing any other male to touch you in any way at all?'

'No!' she denied, stunned that he would think such a thing. Godfrey had never been a jealous or a possessive man. That kind of thing wasn't in him.

'Then why are you so frightened of me?' Jonathon asked, his tone totally exasperated.

'I'm not!'

'Yes, you are,' he bit out. 'You very definitely are. I only have to come within three feet of you and you get the jitters, stammering when you never stammer with anyone else. The only time you speak normally with me is when you're so infuriated, you forget your fear. Wilma tells me all the time that I'm a natural bully so I suppose that might explain some of your reactions. But I have to tell you, Sophia, I can't abide it. I can't abide it at all!'

'I—I'm s-sorry.'

'See what I mean?'

She hung her head, unhappy and humiliated.

'Don't do that!' he ordered. 'Look up at me!'

She did so, her eyes blurring with tears.

His groan sounded tortured. 'I've done it again. Hell, I don't mean to. I really don't. God, don't cry. I can't stand it.'

Before Sophia could resist, he had drawn her into his arms, holding her tight and stroking her hair. 'I mean you no harm,' he rasped. 'Honestly... If I have been brusque, then I apologise. But you've no idea...how difficult...I have found all this. God, if only you weren't so...so...'

His arms tightened around her for a few astonishing seconds before he abruptly put her away from him, his breathing ragged, but his face as grim as ever. Grimmer, maybe. 'I'm sorry,' he ground out. 'I've made a mess of things with you, as usual. Go to bed. I'll try to do better in future.'

Whirling, he disappeared down the stairs, Sophia staring after him. Her own breathing was as ragged as his had been, her head spinning.

Good heavens, she thought breathlessly, and stared down at the palms of her hands which were still tingling from where they'd rested against the hard expanse of his chest. Why hadn't she used them to push him away? Why had she simply spread her fingers wide, placed her cheek between them and sagged into him?

She supposed there was some excuse for her wallowing in the warmth and comfort of his embrace. It had felt so good to be held and stroked, his strong arms like a haven from all her recent pain and distress.

She hadn't thought there would be any harm in it. Or danger.

She just hadn't thought.

It was still hard to believe that what had happened had happened.

Jonathon…aroused. Jonathon…desiring her. Jonathon…not a cold, unfeeling machine after all.

There had been *nothing* cold or unfeeling about what had risen between them, pressing its hard, throbbing life into her stomach.

Her shock was still with her an hour later as she lay in bed, staring blankly up at the ceiling. For the first time since coming to live in this house her nighttime thoughts were not of Godfrey, or of her coming child. Her mind was occupied trying to recapture the very moment she'd become aware of Jonathon's arousal, when she'd realised what it was she could feel.

There was no doubt in her mind that he hadn't pushed her away immediately. He'd given in to his frustration for a few seconds before his conscience had got the better of him.

Of course, none of it meant anything. Not really. Everyone knew men were much more easily aroused than women. Jonathon might as easily have been turned on by hugging any number of women. It didn't mean he particularly fancied *her*. He couldn't! Why, he didn't even *like* her. She irritated the death out of him.

But Sophia was still disturbed. She wished it hadn't happened. How was she going to face him in the morning? It was awkward, and embarrassing, and… and…

She rolled over and punched her pillow. Several

times. It didn't make her feel any better. In fact, it made her feel much worse, reminding her forcibly of her earlier irrational behaviour with the blue hat.

Self-disgust had her forcibly lying still, with her hands jammed down at her sides.

'I am going to go to sleep,' she told herself out loud. 'I am not going to get up. I am not going to go downstairs. I am not going to risk running into Jonathon again tonight.'

Sophia repeated this litany of advice over and over and, eventually, she did fall asleep.

CHAPTER FOUR

SOPHIA woke feeling wrung out the next morning. Yet the bedside clock showed after eight, which meant she'd had plenty of sleep. The state of the bed-clothes, however, indicated a restless night.

Her groan echoed this fact. She hadn't felt this rotten since the day after Godfrey's funeral, which probably meant it was more an emotional condition rather than a physical one.

Yes, she gradually realised. It was. She felt terribly down. And awfully alone.

No. Not alone. Lonely.

Not even thinking about her baby made her feel better. He or she was not going to be born for nearly five months and, while Sophia was absolutely certain she was going to enjoy being a mother, there was no baby for her to love and hold at that very moment.

At that very moment, she was just a grieving girl who had recently lost the man she loved, who had yesterday married his brother for the most well-intentioned reasons, but who was now wishing whole-heartedly that she hadn't.

She should have refused, despite Jonathon's death-bed promise to Godfrey. She should have gone her own way, been her own boss, lived her own life. Instead, she had weakly allowed Godfrey's domineering brother to take her under his wing, to draw her into the bosom of his family and to make all her decisions for her.

Sophia knew that she was not as submissive a creature as Jonathon thought her to be. Though not normally given to the wild outbursts of temper she'd suffered from yesterday, she could still be very stubborn and wilful, as her stepfather had found out in the end. That was why she was so astonished at how she always reacted to Jonathon. It was testimony to his formidable personality that she went to mush in his presence, giving in to his demands most of the time without a quibble.

Sophia took some consolation from the fact that he'd now decided to divorce her once the baby was born. Also that he was going to get her a place of her own. She was sure she'd be a much more content and confident person away from Jonathon. He did not have a good effect on her all round. She'd also be lying if she denied that what had happened last night at the top of the stairs wasn't an added concern.

Jonathon was nothing like Godfrey and, while she didn't really see him as a potential rapist, the incident had blown apart her misconception that Jonathon was cold and passionless. There had been nothing cold or passionless about the man who had held her and stroked her. Heck, no! Just thinking about the incident made her stomach flutter nervously. It was going to be difficult to face him today without making a fool of herself.

With a shudder, Sophia threw back the bedclothes and climbed out of bed. At least she didn't have to worry about any awkward encounters till this evening. At this hour on a Monday morning, Jonathon would already be in his big fancy office in North Sydney, wheeling and dealing, planning how to make his next million and giving Wilma a hard time.

The man was a workaholic, Sophia decided rue-fully as she dragged herself into the bathroom for a wake-up shower. The hours he kept would kill a brown dog. Eight till six at the office six days a week. Home by seven, dinner at seven-thirty then into his study for more work. The light was always still on under the study door when Sophia went to bed, which was sometimes quite late, if she'd watched a movie on television or the video. She didn't know how he kept it up. Sunday was his only day off, spent mainly on the golf-course.

By the time she was ready to go downstairs half an hour later, Sophia felt a hundred per cent better. Things could be worse, she supposed. She could be throwing up every morning, as some women did dur-ing the early months of their pregnancies.

To be honest, sometimes she forgot she *was* preg-nant, especially when dressed in something like the loosely fitting maroon tracksuit she'd chosen to wear that day. Maybe when the baby started moving it would be different. But up till now, all she had to show for her pregnancy was a disappearing waistline, slightly swollen breasts and a gently rounded tummy.

The house seemed very quiet as she made her way down the stairs. There again, Parnell Hall was often quiet, the double brick walls and heavy doors muf-fling any noise from within the individual rooms. The street was quiet too, with little traffic passing down the no-through road.

When Sophia had first been brought here, she'd been very impressed by the grandeur of the house and its surrounds. Since then she'd come to realise that all the neighbours' homes were similar in style and size, some being even larger and more opulent.

Turramurra was apparently one of Sydney's well-to-do but older suburbs on the upper North Shore, with most of the residences having been built before the war.

When she'd asked Maud about Parnell Hall's history, the housekeeper had revealed that the house had originally been built in the thirties by Jonathon's great-uncle William, with Jonathon's father Henry inheriting it during the war when the old man died, childless. It was two-storeyed and Victorian in style, and Henry had allowed Ivy to renovate and refurbish the house considerably during their marriage, which accounted, Sophia thought, for its air of quiet elegance.

The house was still Ivy's to do with as she pleased till she died, a fact Ivy had reminded Jonathon of last week when she'd removed some of the original artworks from the walls and replaced them with the paintings of Godfrey's which Sophia had brought with her and given to his mother.

Sophia had found the incident—and Jonathon's angry objections—quite distressing. The last thing she'd wanted was to cause dissension in the family. At the time she'd thought Jonathon insensitive and lacking in compassion. Now, in light of other incidents and comments, she felt some sympathy for him. After all, they weren't even *good* paintings!

Sophia ground to a halt at the bottom of the stairs, shocked by this new insight into Godfrey's artistic talent. Or lack of it.

For a few seconds, she felt terribly disloyal to his memory. How many times had she lavished praise on him for his paintings? How many times had she told him that one day he would be a famous artist, that his work would hang in galleries and on the walls of millionaires' mansions?

Had she always known she'd been lying?

No, she accepted with a sigh of relief. She hadn't. It had only been when she'd come here to Parnell Hall and seen the truly magnificent paintings on the walls that she'd recognised Godfrey's work fell far short of genuine talent. His paintings were, at best, very mediocre, their amateurishness only obvious after she'd been able to compare them with the works of truly fine artists.

Sophia frowned. Had Godfrey known? When he'd shaken his head at her compliments, smiling that soft sad smile of his, had he been acknowledging the hidden truth? That he wasn't a good painter, that he wasn't really good at anything...except perhaps making her love him and need him.

Tears pricked at her eyes.

Oh, Godfrey...

For a few moments Sophia allowed herself to wallow in a type of remorse before growing impatient with herself. Enough of that, she decided staunchly, and began to blink madly.

Once she was totally under control, she turned and marched along the downstairs hallway, past the various closed doors on either side and down to the door that would bring her into the room which was the hub of the household.

At the back of the ground floor, and approachable from several angles, the kitchen-cum-family-room was where dinner parties for twenty were prepared, informal meals were eaten, television was watched and company was sought. It was large and sunny and warm, and Sophia loved it.

Sophia opened the door, relieved to find the room empty except for Maud. For a second there she'd worried Jonathon might have stayed home for some reason. But it seemed their marriage yesterday was not going to change his daily routine in any way, for which she was grateful. Even in the few short weeks she had lived at Parnell Hall, she knew his presence brought a different atmosphere into the home. Tension vibrated in the air. Conversation was stultified. Ivy withdrew into herself even more than usual, and Maud, who was the sweetest of old ladies, became a little short, her delightfully dry sense of humour turning slightly caustic, especially with Jonathon.

The lady herself spun round at Sophia's entrance, an instant smile further creasing her wrinkled face.

'Well if it isn't Mrs Rip Van Winkle herself,' she teased.

Sophia smiled back. 'I did sleep in, didn't I? Ivy up yet?'

'She's in the morning-room with a pot of tea and the morning papers.'

'Then I'll leave her to it.' Ivy could spend the whole morning on the papers, reading them from cover to cover, then doing all the crosswords, even the *Herald* cryptic. Mostly she finished it, but occasionally the answer to one or two clues eluded her. Only rarely could Sophia or Maud ever help her with these, because they were always the most difficult and obscure.

Sometimes—but not often—Ivy would ask Jonathon's help when he came home in the evening, and he would invariably have the answer for her within seconds. Once, he had filled in the blank

squares himself when he saw the unfinished crossword lying on the kitchen table, only to have Ivy
complain that he'd spoiled the page with his big ugly
printing and that he was just like his father, with a
heavy hand and no natural neatness.

Remembering that incident again now sent a frown
to Sophia's face. Why did she keep thinking of things
that made Jonathon appear the wronged person in this
family? Surely Godfrey had been the son who had
drawn the short straw? Jonathon had it all. Looks.
Drive. Intelligence. He'd shone as a student and an
athlete, according to Wilma. He'd had girls running
after him by the score. His father had apparently lavished praise and approval on him by the bucketful.

So what if his mother hadn't loved him? So what
if his wife had left him? So what if he'd had to marry
a girl in name only, just so that his brother's child
could achieve legitimacy?

Something moved within Sophia that felt awfully
like pity, yet not quite. It was stronger, more emotional, more…*what*?

'How was Jonathon this morning?' she demanded
of Maud, so abruptly the housekeeper shot her a startled look.

'Why do you ask that?'

Sophia shrugged, the action an echo of her own
inner confusion. 'I just wondered,' she said.

'He was like a bear with a sore head. Frankly, I
think he had a hangover.'

'A hangover?'

Maud nodded wryly. 'He's been hitting the bottle
lately. Has been ever since Godfrey died. He did the
same when that bitch of a wife of his left him for that
movie producer.'

'What movie producer?' Sophia pounced, eager to know about the break-up of Jonathon's marriage.

Maud scowled. 'Some rich American who was out here on a talent-scouting trip. She went back to the States with him. Dear Charmaine always had acting aspirations, though for my money she couldn't act her way out of a paper bag. Had a good figure, though, I'll give her that. Her face was passable as well, I suppose, though her hair was obviously fake blonde. Maybe her boobs as well. Who knows these days?'

'How long was Jonathon married to her?'

'Just on two years. Frankly, I think he wasn't think-ing straight when he got mixed up with that floozy. His father had just died, Godfrey had done a bunk, and he'd been working twenty-hour days to salvage Parnell Property Developments when *she* walked into his life. The poor devil never stood a chance.'

Sophia was startled by Maud's unexpected sym-pathy for Jonathon. She'd always thought Maud didn't like her employer very much. 'Did he love her?' she asked.

'He was *crazy* about her, the deluded fool.'

'Oh...'

'She used to spend hours and hours on her appear-ance, bathing in perfumed oil every afternoon then whisking Jonathon off up into the bedroom the second he got home. It was disgusting, the way she kept him bewitched through sex. She made him think he was her life, then up and dumped him, just like that!' Maud snapped her fingers.

Sophia grimaced.

'Yes, that's exactly the way his mother and I felt,' Maud agreed. 'But there was nothing we could do or say against her. Love is blind. Or lust is. Jonathon is just like his father in that regard. Henry was a very physical man too. Maybe I shouldn't be saying this but Jonathon's father was not the most faithful of husbands. Ivy pretended she didn't know, but I'm sure she did. She...'

The telephone ringing interrupted Maud's gossiping, Sophia feeling rather relieved about that. She really didn't want to hear the personal and private details of Ivy's marriage, though the bit about Jonathon's first wife had been informative. What a bitch!

'Parnell Hall,' she heard Maud say in the background. 'Oh, yes, Wilma... He *is*...? Where...? For how long...? I see... Yes, it'll be ready... Bye, dear. See you soon.'

Maud hung up with a sigh. 'Speak of the devil,' she muttered.

'What was that all about?' Sophia asked.

'I have to pack an overnight case for the Lord and Master,' Maud said drily. 'Wilma's on her way to pick it up. He's going away for a couple of days.'

'G-going away?'

'Yes, flying up to the Gold Coast this afternoon. On business. Or so he says,' she muttered.

Sophia fell silent, knowing in her heart that what Maud had just implied was probably true. He was not going away on business. He was going away to rid himself of the sexual frustrations that had caused what had happened last night. Logic told her he was doing the right thing, the 'discreet' thing. There was no reason for her to feel upset in any way by his very sensible decision.

So why was she?

Sophia finally decided she wasn't. It was

Jonathon's going away without having the common decency to say goodbye to her personally that was irritating her. She might only be his wife in name only, but he could still have asked to speak to her. He could have said goodbye to her, not to mention his mother as well. The man was downright rude!

A slow-burning resentment simmered within Sophia the rest of the day, especially after Wilma dashed in and out like a whirlwind, on instructions from her boss not to stay and chat but to get back to the office, pronto. Sophia revised her opinion about Jonathon's not being an unfeeling machine. He most definitely was. She decided his betraying his sexual needs the previous evening had nothing to do with real feelings. *Real* feelings came from the head and the heart, whereas what Jonathon was suffering from came from strictly below the waist.

It particularly annoyed Sophia to think of how exactly he was going to go about satisfying those needs. Did he have a little black book with names and addresses of accommodating ladies in it from all over Australia? Was he taking some secret mistress with him? Or was he contemplating picking up some woman from a bar somewhere?

Surely, oh, surely he didn't plan on paying for a professional's services! Her eyes blinked wide, the very idea turning her stomach.

Revulsion plus common sense quickly discarded this last thought. Jonathon would not have to resort to paying for sex. Neither was he the sort of man to take stupid risks with his health. The women he consorted with would all be intelligent, sophisticated females who would be as concerned with their own well-being as their partners'. Safe sex would be the name of the game; mutual satisfaction their only aim.

She still shuddered at the thought.

By lunchtime Sophia found herself so nervy and unnerved that she decided some physical work was the only antidote for her agitation.

'Why don't we start spring cleaning the house this week?' she suggested to Maud over a cheese and to-mato sandwich. 'You told me a few days ago that you always gave it a good going over every September. Since it's a nice sunny day today, I could start on the windows.'

Maud dragged her eyes away from the Midday Show to give her an exasperated look. 'For pity's sake, Sophia. I defended your right to do a few chores around the place but you're hardly in a fit state to start climbing up on ladders, cleaning windows and such. Frankly, I'm too old for such nonsense as well; have been for years. We always get a cleaning service in to do the hard stuff like the blinds and the win-dows.'

'Fair enough,' Sophia agreed. 'But I could at least wash and iron the curtains. Or what about the floors? I could polish the floors.'

'Definitely not! Jonathon would skin me alive if I let you do such heavy work. No, I'll be sending the curtains out to be dry-cleaned as usual. As for the floors—there are far too many for you to do. It would exhaust you. If you must do something, there's a lot of silver to be cleaned. That's a nice safe sitting-down job.'

'What's a nice safe sitting-down job?' Ivy asked as she wandered in, a folded newspaper in her hands.

'Sophia's going to clean the silver.'

Ivy smiled her approval. 'What a good girl you are. Here, have a look at this last clue for me, Sophia? I can't get it and Jonathon isn't here to ask...'

By bedtime that night, Sophia hoped never to see another piece of silver—or a cryptic crossword— again. Her poor brain had gone round and round for hours, only to have Ivy walk back in and do the damned thing herself in a sudden inspiration. Trying to untangle cryptic clues, Sophia decided, was almost as tiring and tedious as cleaning endless pieces of cutlery. Frankly, she'd rather milk cows, and she'd never particularly liked that job, either.

The only reward for her day's labour was that she was blessedly tired and fell asleep without any of the restlessness that had plagued her the night before. The following morning, the cleaning service Maud had called arrived first thing, the blinds and curtains and rugs being carted away for cleaning elsewhere while a team of overalled workers stayed behind. Two men set to washing the many windows inside and out, a very fit-looking girl waxing and polishing the wooden floors downstairs while a third male person steam-cleaned the carpets upstairs.

By the middle of the Wednesday afternoon, all the blinds and curtains were back in place and the place looked and smelt fresh and clean. Sophia was wandering through the house admiring everything when she spied a job that had been overlooked. The ceiling fans needed dusting.

Without saying a word to the others—Maud was fortunately busy preparing dinner and Ivy was resting upstairs—Sophia quietly collected a small set of steps and a feather duster from the cupboard under the stairs and set about doing the fan in the study first, making sure she was extra careful when climbing the ladder and reaching up to stroke the duster along the first blade.

When a shower of dust landed on top of her head, Sophia stopped, sighed, then climbed back down again and went to get a scarf to tie over her hair. She had remembered seeing an old tartan one on a peg under the stairs a few minutes before.

Back up the steps again with the scarf securely in place, she resumed carefully dusting each of the four blades and was on to the last one when two large male arms suddenly wrapped around her waist and lifted her off the ladder into mid-air.

Sophia dropped the duster, her gasp of shock forming into a scream just as Jonathon's angry voice filled her ears.

'And what the hell do you think you're doing, you silly little fool?'

CHAPTER FIVE

BY THE time Jonathon lowered her to the floor, turning her in his arms to face him, Sophia's shock had long turned to outrage. What in hell did he think *he* was doing was more like it, scaring the life out of her like that? And what was he doing home anyway? He wasn't expected for another couple of hours.

But she said nothing, glaring up into angry blue eyes with angry eyes herself, her lips pressed firmly together in mutinous silence for fear that this time her temper might make her run off at the mouth with decidedly unwise words.

Jonathon wasn't similarly reticent. 'I thought having Godfrey's baby meant the world to you,' he flung at her. 'Whatever possessed you to get up on that ladder? You might have fallen.'

Hurt that he would imply she would recklessly risk Godfrey's child drove her to protest. 'I was perfectly safe,' she flung back, 'till you grabbed me and dragged me off into thin air. That nearly gave me a heart attack!'

Which was no exaggeration, Sophia realised. Why, her heart was going so fast that a heart attack was still on the cards!

Suddenly aware that his hands were still around her waist, she brushed them off in a type of panic and hurriedly spun away from him, almost tripping over the steps in the process, knocking her shin against one of the legs. The sharp pain, plus her uncharacteristic clumsiness, made her mad as a hatter and she rounded on him.

'Now look what you've done?' she snapped.

His sigh had a martyred sound to it. 'I haven't done anything, Sophia, except try to look after you. Godfrey put your welfare in my hands. I wouldn't be able to sleep at night if I let him down where you were concerned.'

Sophia's dismay was instant. She was the one letting Godfrey down. Here she was again, acting like a shrew and generally being a right pain. Underneath, she knew she'd been a bit silly getting up on that ladder. Maud had warned her not to do anything of the kind but she'd thought she knew better. Remorse mingled with guilt and an undermining awareness of her own stupidity.

'I'm sorry,' she said in a voice raw with emotion, her eyes dropping to the floor. 'I won't do it again.'

'I hope not,' he grumped. 'But I'm still going to give my mother and Maud firm instructions the next time I go away. You obviously can't be trusted to use common sense when it comes to this passion you have for cleaning.'

Her eyes jerked up to his, alarmed at the thought she might have caused trouble for Maud and Ivy. 'Oh, please don't say anything to them,' she begged. 'It wasn't their fault. Truly. They didn't even know what I was doing. Maud was busy in the kitchen and your mother was lying down.'

His expression was disbelieving. 'You mean you sneak around this house, cleaning things while no one is looking? What is it with you? Is cleaning some sort of secret addiction of yours? Are you one of those maniacally house-proud females who can't walk past a surface without running their finger along to check for dust?'

'No, of course not! But I do like to see a job done properly. Maud had the whole house professionally spring-cleaned while you were away, and I was thinking how great everything looked. When I noticed all the dust on the ceiling fans, I just had to do them.'

'She just *had* to do them,' he repeated drily.

Sophia's chin lifted in defiance of his sarcasm. 'Yes,' she shot back waspishly. 'My passion for cleaning got the better of me!'

'Well well,' he drawled, one eyebrow lifting in surprise at her counter-attack. 'Not such a frightened little kitten after all, are you? I've noticed you've also finally got over that infernal stammer, thank God. Can I hope it's permanent?'

Sophia glared at him, thinking again that he was as far removed from Godfrey as night was from day.

'I certainly hope so,' she bit out.

He folded his arms and leant back against the desk behind him, a drily amused smile tugging at his lips. 'So, have you decided I'm not such a monster after all?'

Sophia couldn't help staring at him. Not once, in all the time she'd known Jonathon had he smiled at her in any way, shape or form. It quite transformed his face, bringing some warmth to his coldly handsome features, his cruel mouth softening to a sensual curve, his icy blue eyes actually glittering with a surprising degree of humanity and humour.

It threw her to be suddenly confronted with the Jonathon Godfrey had once described to her, but which she had never seen for herself, the Jonathon who wouldn't have to work too hard to have women throwing themselves at his head. Or was it his feet?

For a few disarming seconds, she felt the pull of his physical appeal before a bitter resentment surfaced, totally obliterating any vulnerability to such a superficial and strictly God-given charm. Godfrey had been worth ten of this man!

'I've never thought of you as an actual monster, Jonathon,' Sophia said stiffly.

'You could have fooled me,' he said, his smile widening.

Sophia's heart fluttered anew under its impact, her stomach immediately clenching down hard in dismay. Surely she couldn't be attracted to Godfrey's brother. She just couldn't!

But it seemed she was...

'Some people bring out the best in a person,' she snapped in self-disgust. 'Others the worst.'

The smile faded. And so did the charm. It was like a light being switched off, and Sophia was flooded with relief. It had been a momentary aberration, that was all. How could she possibly feel anything for Jonathon like that?

He straightened abruptly, his arms falling to his sides, his large chest rising and falling with a ragged sigh. Suddenly he looked and sounded very tired, his bleakness dredging up some of Sophia's earlier sympathetic feelings for him.

'Yes,' he admitted grudgingly. 'Godfrey had that talent. I'll give him that. He made people love him, despite his obvious failings. I have no idea how he managed it,' he added, shaking his head.

The word 'failings' evoked a fierce, maternal-style protectiveness in Sophia. 'You're always implying

Godfrey was a failure and a loser,' she accused. 'But he wasn't. If success is measured by how much a person is truly valued by others, then he was the greatest success of all time.'

Jonathon stared straight at her, yet right through her, his eyes oddly dead. 'You could be right, Sophia. You could be right.' He turned and walked around behind the desk, flopping down into the large leather chair and briefly leaning back with his eyes closed before opening them again and glancing over at her.

'Go and tell Maud I'm home, will you?' he asked rather wearily. 'Dinner at seven, if possible. I have a lot of paperwork to catch up on tonight.'

'Would…would you like me to bring you a cup of coffee?' she offered hesitantly as a type of apology. The last thing she wanted was to be at odds with Jonathon all the time.

'Right now, you mean?'

'Yes.'

'No, thanks. I need something a little stronger than that. I'll get myself a proper drink in a minute. Oh, for God's sake, don't go picking up that damned ladder!' he suddenly roared, snapping forward on his chair. 'And for pity's sake take off that ghastly scarf. You look like Sadie the cleaning lady.'

Sophia coloured as she realised she had forgotten all about the scarf. She whipped a hand up to drag off the offending scrap of tartan, feeling mortified at having looked silly in front of Jonathon, who was always the picture of sartorial splendour, his expensive business suits never creased, his shirt as dazzlingly white as his teeth, his black wavy hair never out of place.

'There's no need to yell,' she said unhappily. 'And there's no need to make me feel awful.'

His sigh carried self-irritation. 'I wasn't trying to make you feel awful. If anyone feels awful around here, it's me.'

'I don't know why,' she muttered. 'You're the one who's been away, living it up on the Gold Coast.'

'Hardly living it up, Sophia. I was there on business.'

'Oh, yeah, sure.'

They stared at each other, Sophia with obvious cynicism in her eyes and Jonathon with shock.

But he wasn't shocked for long, his face growing hard and resentful as cold blue eyes raked over her. Sophia gulped, already regretting her foolhardiness at revealing she knew the purpose of his little trip away.

'I don't understand your attitude,' he bit out. 'All I ever promised you was that I would be discreet. I was. *Very*. And I will continue to be till we're divorced. Meanwhile, don't you ever sit in judgement of me. I won't stand for it!' He thumped the desk with his balled fist and glowered at her. 'I certainly won't be made to feel guilty when I have done nothing to feel bloody guilty over! So I spent a couple of nights with a woman? Big deal. What did you expect me to do in these conditions? Satisfy myself like some schoolboy? God, girl, grow up! This is real life here and in real life, real men go to bed with real women. *Comprends*?'

She shivered under the force of his quite terrifying fury. 'Y-yes,' she said in a small, quavering voice. 'I...I...understand.'

His face twisted into a grimace at the sound of her

stammering again. 'Go,' he ordered with a groan, waving an impatient hand as he slumped back in the chair, his eyes closing. 'Just go…'

She went.

CHAPTER SIX

DINNER that evening was a strain. Sophia sat down at the table in fear that Jonathon would say something to Ivy or Maud about finding her up a ladder, dusting.

But he didn't.

Frankly, he hardly said a word all through the meal, eating his food in a darkly brooding silence, his mind obviously a million miles away. Whenever his mother or Maud spoke to him, he seemed to have to drag his thoughts back to the present with a real effort. His answers to their innocent questions about his trip away were curt and largely uninformative.

Sophia knew why. There hadn't been any business conducted. Jonathon had gone to the Gold Coast for one reason and one reason only.

Her appetite for the food in front of her dwindled as she contemplated that reason, wondering how long it would be before he took himself off again. Once, she glanced sideways down the table at him, and their eyes met. He looked right through her, then back down at his dessert.

Sophia was glad when Jonathon took his coffee into the study.

'Couldn't have been a very successful trip,' Maud muttered as she and Sophia cleared the plates away. Ivy had already scuttled off to her bedroom to read.

Sophia didn't know what to say to that, knowing it was the altercation with her that had put him in such a bad mood. His trip to the Gold Coast had undoubtedly been *very* successful. 'Maybe he's just tired,' she muttered, hating the disturbingly explicit images that kept popping into her mind.

'Then he should stop burning the candle at both ends,' Maud said sharply. 'The man doesn't get enough sleep. And he drinks too much. I checked the liquor stocks in his study while he was away, and there was hardly a drop of whisky left, not to mention brandy, vodka and cognac. I hope he's not going the way of his father. Henry drank too much in the years preceding his death. Put on too much weight too. Sixty was far too young to die in my opinion.'

'My father was only thirty-nine when *he* died of a heart attack,' Sophia said, gulping down the lump that formed in her throat whenever she thought of her father.

'Yes, I remember you telling me that,' Maud mused. 'That was young, Sophia. And your mother was how old when she died?'

'Thirty-eight.'

'How sad for you.'

Sophia scooped in a deep breath and let it out slowly. 'Yes, it was,' she agreed, then busied herself, stacking up the rest of the dishes.

That night, once again, Sophia had trouble falling asleep. There was a dull throbbing behind her eyes and she had a slight tummy upset. On top of that, she was also still perturbed over the run-in she'd had with Jonathon.

He was right, of course, she'd begun to appreciate. She had no right to judge him over the private and personal side of his life. What in heaven's name *did* she expect him to do? He was a man in his prime.

Only thirty-four, for pity's sake. Healthy. Handsome. Full of energy and drive and hormones.

A man of Godfrey's nature might have been able to embrace celibacy without it disturbing his equilibrium too much—clearly he had!—but his younger brother was a different kettle of fish entirely. Jonathon had obviously always been a big winner where the opposite sex was concerned, with a strong libido to match. He wouldn't be used to doing without in the bedroom.

When Sophia finally began to drift off to sleep, she was wondering exactly what kind of woman Jonathon was attracted to. Did she have to be tall, blonde, shapely, sophisticated?

He was sure to like tall women, she decided with a yawn.

Sophia's last fuzzy thought was a resolve to ask Maud in the morning exactly what Charmaine had looked like, even though an image was already forming in her mind, that of a tall, sexy creature with come-hither blue eyes, a mane of exquisitely styled blonde hair, a model-perfect figure and long, long legs that went on forever, nothing like a five-foot-two half-Italian brunette with big brown doe-eyes, long wavy unstyled hair, and a figure far too lush and curvy for her height.

Sophia woke with the pain.

For a few seconds she was disoriented, not sure what was wrong till another cramp twisted at her insides. Her groan echoed her horror, and disbelief. No, no, it couldn't be. It just couldn't.

She lay there in denial for another minute or two, till more cramps forced her to crawl out of bed and into the bathroom where her worst nightmare was revealed. Her underwear was spotted with blood.

'Dear God, no,' she cried, her hands shaking as she stuffed a few tissues into her pants then made her way slowly back into the bedroom, hunching over with the pain. The bedside clock showed two-fifteen. Everyone would be in bed, sound asleep, at this late hour.

Sophia began to panic. What was she to do? She would have to wake someone. She needed help.

It would have to be Maud. Ivy took sleeping tablets every night and was impossible to rouse once they'd taken effect. Jonathon she refused to consider. She could not bear to see the accusing look in his eyes when she told him what was happening. He would think it was her fault somehow. She just knew he would.

No, it would have to be Maud.

The trouble was that Maud slept in her own granny flat behind the garages, quite some distance away.

Another pain ripped through Sophia, stronger, sharper. It propelled her across the room and out into the upstairs hallways. Arms crossed and hugging her stomach, she made her way slowly to the top of the stairs, her discomfort increasing. She had occasionally had painful periods, but this was sheer torture, the physical discomfort made worse by her emotional distress.

She was going to lose Godfrey's baby.

As she started to creep down the stairs—each step an agony—total despair was kept at bay with some straw-grasping thoughts. Maybe there was still some hope. Maybe she wouldn't really miscarry. Maybe a doctor could give her an injection or something to stop what was happening.

When Sophia reached the bottom of the stairs, she was surprised to see that the light was on under the study door. Jonathon was still up. Suddenly, another cramping pain struck. It felt like a hot dagger being plunged into her belly and she couldn't stop crying out loud.

The study door was wrenched open and a bedraggled, bleary-eyed Jonathon stood there, staring at her. If she'd been capable of noticing the appalling physical state *he* was in, she might have stared at him in return. But pain was dulling her mind and tears blurring her eyes. It was taking all of Sophia's strength to remain standing upright. The urge to simply sink down on to the floor was intense.

Jonathon's eyes widened on her pale, pain-filled face and he took a hesitant step out into the hallway. 'What is it, Sophia?' he demanded hoarsely. 'What's wrong? Are you ill?'

'I'm bleeding,' she said, her words coming out in a shaky whisper.

'Bleeding?' he repeated rather blankly.

'Yes,' she said, and a moan of pain punched from her throat. The tears which had been threatening suddenly spilled over and started running down her cheeks. 'Oh, Jonathon,' she cried, her voice raw with emotion. 'I think I'm losing Godfrey's baby!'

For a second he seemed struck dumb, but then Sophia began to double up with the pain and he raced forward, scooping her up high into his arms, then enfolding her hard against him.

'No you're not,' he ground out. 'Not if I can help it.' And he began carrying her back up the stairs.

With a sob she wrapped her arms tightly around him and pressed her wet cheeks against the warm expanse of his chest. 'Don't be angry with me,' she choked out as he angled her through the doorway of her bedroom. 'I didn't do anything silly. Truly I didn't.'

'No, of course you didn't,' he agreed thickly, throwing her an anguished look as he laid her gently on the bed and pulled the quilt over her. 'Is the bleeding very bad?'

'Not too bad,' she said, trying not to thresh about. But the pain was getting worse, if that was possible.

'I'm going to ring your doctor,' Jonathon told her. 'I don't suppose you know his number.'

She shook her head. 'Not off by heart,' she bit out, clenching her teeth hard. 'But I...I wrote it down in the telephone book on the hall table...under H for Henderson.'

'I'll go and call.'

Sophia didn't want him to leave her, but she knew he had to. The next five minutes were interminable. Her eyes were glued to the opened doorway, her pain-racked body relaxing a little when Jonathon returned. He came to her across the carpet with brisk, efficient strides, sitting down and taking her hands soothingly in his. How strong he was, she realised somewhat dazedly. And how kind. She'd been so wrong about him. So very wrong.

'Please don't be alarmed,' he began gently, 'but Dr Henderson wants you in hospital. He's sending an ambulance straight away and will meet you there. They'll be here shortly. I've woken Maud. She's getting dressed. She's going to go with you.'

'Can't you come with me?' she asked tremulously.

He seemed taken aback by her request. 'You want *me* to come with you?'

Her eyes swam. 'Yes. I think I'd be braver with you. Please promise me you'll come. Promise me you won't leave me. *Promise.*'

His hands tightened around hers. 'I promise.'

Sophia closed her eyes with a shuddering sigh. 'Thank you,' she whispered.

She lost the baby. And Jonathon did have to leave her eventually, when she was taken away into Theatre for a precautionary curette.

But he was sitting there in her hospital room when she was brought back in from Recovery a couple of hours later, rising to his feet as she was wheeled in, watching in grim silence as she was lifted into her bed and made comfortable before the wardsman and the sister left the room.

'You should have gone home, Jonathon,' were her first quavering words once they were alone. 'You must be awfully tired.'

'Tired I can live with, Sophia,' he said. 'But a promise is a promise.' He dragged a chair up to the side of the bed and sat down. 'I wouldn't have been able to sleep if I'd gone home, anyway. How are you feeling?'

Her shoulders lifted in a resigned shrug. 'All right, I guess.'

'Don't keep on trying to be brave, sweetheart. If you want to cry, cry. I won't mind. I feel like crying myself.'

Surprised eyes slid over to his. 'You, Jonathon?'

He did, indeed, look very bleak. Not only bleak but dishevelled, she realised. Her gaze travelled slowly over him, from his creased clothes to his stubbly chin to his bloodshot eyes.

'I know,' he said wearily, and ran a hand back through his messy hair. 'I look terrible.'

'You look exhausted. You really should go home.'

'No,' he said firmly. 'I'm staying.'

A short silence fell between them and Sophia closed her eyes, swamped by depression. The overwhelming feeling that she had somehow let Godfrey down would not leave her. Perhaps she should have warned the doctor about her mother's medical history. Maybe if she had, this could have been prevented. The fear that she might have inherited her mother's inability to carry a child full-term brought a low whimper of distress.

'I hope you're not blaming yourself for this.'

Sophia's eyes fluttered open at Jonathon's stern words. She shrugged again, unable to deny or confirm what she was feeling. Was it guilt? Or despair?

'I spoke to the doctor earlier,' Jonathon went on, 'and he said this is nature's way when there's something wrong with the development of the foetus. He said he'd had a niggling concern during your last visit that something was wrong, which is why he ordered an ultrasound. But he didn't say anything for fear of worrying you.'

'My mother was a habitual aborter,' she said unhappily. 'Maybe I'm the same.'

'I doubt that, Sophia.'

'But I *might* be.' The thought terrified her, for she'd always wanted lots of children.

'Don't jump to conclusions. Ask the doctor when you see him.'

'All right,' she sighed, and fell wretchedly silent again.

'Tell me about your mother, Sophia,' Jonathon

asked after a while. 'All I know is that she died shortly before you came to live with Godfrey. He also said something about how your stepfather had tried to force you to marry him. Is that right?'

She nodded. 'He was Italian too, my stepfather. My real father wasn't. He was Australian. Mum met him when she was at school. He was her English teacher.'

'I'll bet her parents didn't like that.'

'Her parents were dead, killed in an earthquake back in Italy. She'd been sent out here to Australia to live with an aunt and an uncle. Apparently she was a bit of a rebel, and they were never able to control her much.

'Anyway, she married Dad the year after she left school and I was born nine months after the wedding. It seems something went wrong with Mum's uterus when I was born. When she had two miscarriages after me, the doctors told her not to try any more, that it was dangerous.'

'But she did?'

'Not with my real Dad. But after he died unexpectedly early of a coronary, she married Joe. He was a second cousin of hers. That's when we moved to the farm outside of Lithgow. Joe wanted a son. He was a very good-looking man, but very traditionally Italian in his ways. Poor Mum tried to have a baby every year, and every year she lost it. I used to argue with my stepfather about how it was killing her, trying to give him his precious son.

'One day, when I was sixteen and Mum had just had her fifth miscarriage, he and I had a really big argument. He said women were for having *bambinos* and that if my mother couldn't give him one then he would find a younger woman who could. Out of the blue he…he tried to…to…you know. I fought him off and grabbed a knife and told him if he ever came near me again, I'd kill him.'

'I'd like to kill the bastard myself,' Jonathon growled. 'Did he ever try again?'

'Not till Mum died. And even then, he didn't try to force me to go to bed with him. His idea by then was that I marry him first. When I said I'd rather die he locked me in my bedroom, boarded up the window and told me I wasn't going to get any food and water till I came to my senses.'

'What did you do?'

'It took me all night but I managed to work a couple of boards off the windows, climbed out and went racing to Godfrey. He lived next door, you know.'

'Yes, I know. What did Godfrey do?'

'He told me I could move in with him till I knew what I wanted to do with my life, so I did.'

'What did your stepfather do then? Surely he must have done something!'

'He came storming over, ranting and raving, but my Godfrey was magnificent.' Sophia smiled widely at the memory. 'He had this old rifle which didn't even work but Joe didn't know that. He pointed it straight at Joe's head and told him if he ever came near me again, he'd splatter his brains from there to Lithgow.'

'Good lord! *Godfrey* did that?'

'He sure did.'

'The power of love,' Jonathon muttered. 'So what happened next?'

'Joe sold up the farm and moved to Melbourne. I haven't heard from him since.'

'I dare say you haven't missed him.'

'Hardly.'

Jonathon began shaking his head. 'I still can't believe it. Godfrey…my meek and mild brother, actually physically threatening someone.'

Sophia's smile was rueful. 'Maybe I should tell you what happened after Joe left…'

'Maybe you should.'

'Godfrey fainted dead away. I had to carry him inside and put him to bed.'

Jonathon's nod was as dry as his voice. 'Now that's more like the Godfrey I knew and loved.'

Sophia's heart turned over and she looked at Jonathon, her eyes blurring suddenly. 'You did love him, didn't you?'

'Very much.'

'He loved you too, Jonathon.'

'I hope so, Sophia. I really hope so.'

'He was a very special man.'

'Very special.'

'And he's gone,' she cried softly. 'And his baby's gone. There's nothing left for people to remember him by. It's not fair. It's just not fair…'

'Life was never fair to Godfrey,' Jonathon agreed with a weary sigh.

'I loved him so much.'

'Yes…I know.'

'I'll never forget him.'

'Yes…I know.'

The utter desolation in Jonathon's voice pricked at her conscience. He was suffering too. She should try not to be so maudlin. Godfrey would not have liked her to be maudlin. He hated dreariness in any way shape or form. And hatred. Godfrey always said it was a pity human beings could not all love one another, no matter what.

She reached over and picked up the nearest of Jonathon's hands, the unexpected action sending his eyes jerking up to hers. 'Don't be sad, Jonathon,' she soothed. 'If there's one thing that has come out of all this, it's that we've become friends. Look, I haven't even stammered once tonight and I'm not at all angry with you.'

He simply stared at her, so hard and long that she began to feel self-conscious. And then it hit her. She was no longer having Godfrey's baby. There was no longer any reason for her to be welcome in the Parnell home. Their friendship had come a little late.

She extracted her hand from his, a sharp pang of dismay jabbing at her heart.

'What is it?' Jonathon snapped. 'What's wrong?'

'Nothing…'

'Don't give me that, Sophia. Your face is an open book. What's suddenly worrying you?'

'I…I was wondering what I was going to do now?' she admitted unhappily. 'Where I was going to live?'

'Why, you'll go on living at Parnell Hall, of course!'

'There's no *of course* about it, Jonathon. All my reasons for coming to live with you are gone now. All your reasons for marrying me are similarly gone.'

'What nonsense you speak.' He stood up and began pacing around the room, clearly agitated. At last he ground to a halt, glaring over at her. Yesterday, she might have quailed under such a dark scowl. But now she knew Jonathon was nothing like she'd originally imagined. Underneath the wolf lived a lamb. Underneath the hard shell lay a tender heart.

'Mother would have my hide if you didn't come back to live with us. So would Maud. You light up the house, Sophia. You're like a spring day after the gloom of winter. You will not leave us. I command it!'

Sophia blinked her astonishment at Jonathon's passionate and almost poetic outburst.

'We will find you a job when you're fully recovered,' he swept on. 'Or, if you'd prefer, you might like to go to university and study something. Have you passed your HSC?'

Sophia nodded, though her pass was nothing to write home about. She might have done much better if Joe hadn't kept her away from school so much to help on the farm. She'd had more days off than anyone else in her class.

'That's settled then. I don't want to hear any more of this leaving nonsense. You must think me a heartless bastard if you would imagine I would turf you out at such a time. Good lord, Sophia, have some compassion for me before ever suggesting such a thing again. Think of what Wilma would do if she found out? My life wouldn't be worth living!'

Sophia gave him a watery smile which ended in a yawn, followed by a shuddering sigh of exhaustion.

Jonathon groaned. 'I'm being selfish, raving on when you must be dying to go to sleep. I was just trying to take your mind off things. You should have told me to shut up and get lost.'

She managed another weak smile. 'Shut up and get lost.'

He smiled, then came forward and bent over her,

giving her a kiss on the cheek. 'Go to sleep now,' he murmured. 'And don't worry. I'll look after you. I promised Godfrey...'

CHAPTER SEVEN

'WHAT a madhouse!' Wilma exclaimed. 'Anyone would think it was Christmas tomorrow, instead of a full week away. Every man and his dog must be in Chatswood buying presents. I think we would have been better off going to a smaller shopping centre, Sophia. Oh, look, there's a coffee-lounge with some spare tables. Let's go and sit down for a while. I'm bushed.'

'Me too,' Sophia agreed. 'I didn't realise buying Jonathon a camera would be so difficult, or that they'd be so expensive.'

Sophia and Wilma angled their way over to a table against the wall and sat, happy to put their parcels down and rest their weary feet. A harried-looking waitress bustled over and was relieved when they only ordered iced coffee.

'You shouldn't have to worry about money, Sophia,' Wilma commented once the waitress moved off. 'Didn't Jonathon set you up with a special bank account for your everyday expenses?'

'Yes. Yes, he did. I have the book safely put away in a drawer in my bedroom.'

Wilma frowned. 'It sounds as if you haven't used it yet.'

'Well, no, I haven't. I haven't had any need. Jonathon's already bought me everything I could possibly want in the way of clothes and cosmetics. Maud keeps my bathroom cupboard stocked full of toiletries. Ivy insists on paying my way in whenever we go to the movies, and you always insist on paying for whatever we eat and drink every Saturday.'

It had become something of a ritual, her spending Saturday with Wilma. Sometimes they just went to Wilma's unit at Hornsby for lunch and a few hours' female chit-chat, but more often than not Sophia accompanied Wilma out shopping somewhere. Wilma, she decided, was a shopaholic.

'Frankly, Wilma, I'm not comfortable with the amount of money Jonathon's given me all round. It's far more than I expected even when I was having Godfrey's baby. I've been thinking about asking Jonathon if he wants some of it back again.'

'Good God, don't do that!' Wilma exclaimed. 'He'd be most annoyed. He *likes* thinking he's looked after you properly. He'd want you to spend some of the money, too.'

'But not to buy him his own Christmas present,' Sophia insisted. 'That wouldn't have felt right.'

'Then where on earth did you get the four hundred dollars you just spent on that camera?'

'I earnt it.'

'Earnt it? How?'

'Ironing.'

'*Ironing*?'

'Yes, I talked Maud into paying me to do what she usually sends out. Then I put pamphlets in the letter-boxes down our street, undercutting the other local ironing services. I've got four regular clients already. I've been earning an average of a hundred and fifty dollars a week for the past month or so.'

Wilma was looking at her with appalled eyes. 'Does Jonathon know about this?'

'Of course not. And he's not going to. He'd probably have a pink fit.'

'Pink is not the colour I would choose to describe the sort of fit he would have,' Wilma said drily. 'You know, Sophia, I doubt you've ever seen Jonathon in one of his full-blown black rages, have you?'

'I've certainly seen him less than happy.'

'Not the same, I assure you.'

'I can't imagine the Jonathon of the last few months getting up the energy for a full-blown rage, be it black, pink or otherwise. What's wrong with him, Wilma? Is he still grieving the loss of Godfrey and Godfrey's child? I know Ivy is. She's like a wet blanket all the time. It's very depressing, really. Maud's the only one around the house who's ever cheerful. Sometimes, I feel quite cross with Jonathon and his mother. Don't they think I'm sad too, that I'm feeling the loss maybe more than they do? Ivy's moods I can perhaps tolerate. She's an old lady. But Jonathon should be big enough to snap out of it, yet he never smiles, never laughs. He only comes home to eat, work and sleep. When he has to talk, he's quite curt. And he's drinking like a fish. Maud's quite worried.'

'And you, Sophia?' Wilma said quietly. 'Are you worried? Do you really care what happens to Jonathon?'

'Of course I do! I care about Jonathon a lot. I just wish he really cared about me in return. I thought we'd come to an understanding the night I lost Godfrey's baby. He was incredibly sweet to me that night, Wilma, and amazingly supportive. I thought...' She shook her head in a type of confusion. 'Oh I don't know what I thought except that I was so pleased—

and relieved—that we'd finally become friends. Godfrey would have wanted that. But now...now I can see I'll never be Jonathon's friend. I'm his *responsibility*, that's all. And that's all I'll ever be.'

'Oh, I wouldn't say that...'

Wilma's drily knowing tone startled Sophia and she was about to say something when their iced coffee arrived. It rather broke the moment, though it gave Sophia a few seconds to think about what Wilma might be implying. The answer to such a speculation had Sophia's breath catching in her throat. Wide eyes found Wilma's cool grey ones across the table. Wilma's smile was just as cool.

'I see you've finally opened your eyes in more ways than one. I've been wondering how long it would take.'

'But...but that's crazy, Wilma! Jonathon's not attracted to me at all, and I...I...I'm still in love with Godfrey,' she finished in a panicky rush.

'I'm so glad you didn't lie and say you weren't attracted to Jonathon,' Wilma returned drily. 'A girl would have to be deaf, dumb and blind not to be attracted to him. The man is exceptionally good-looking and as sexy as all get-out.'

Sophia stared at Jonathon's secretary. Had she been wrong all this time? Was Wilma secretly in love with her boss?

'No,' Wilma drawled. 'I'm not in love with Jonathon. He's far too young for me. And far too physical. Frankly, I like much older men, ones who prefer a woman's brain to her body.' She smiled at Sophia's ongoing shock. 'But you, Sophia, are another matter. You're a beautiful girl. And very physical too. I refuse to believe that your youthful hormones haven't been responding to Jonathon on a purely sexual level. As for Jonathon…if you think he's not attracted to that lush, nubile young body of yours then think again, my dear. I would imagine his moods of late are nothing to do with grief and everything to do with frustration.'

Sophia bent her head abruptly and sucked up some iced coffee into her straw. She desperately needed some cooling down, not to mention some time to think. Perhaps there was some truth in what Wilma was saying. She'd always admired Jonathon's looks, and there had been a couple of moments when she'd felt drawn to him, especially when she'd been emotionally vulnerable.

But on a purely sexual level? No, she couldn't honestly say her feelings for him had been that. As for Jonathon's being attracted to her… She'd already accepted that that was a possibility in a superficial sense, but she doubted she was the cause of his losing sleep at nights. He'd been taking his little trips away on a regular basis over the past three months. There was no reason whatsoever for him to be suffering from frustration.

His suffering, she believed, was something entirely different, something deeper, something very private and personal.

Her mind turned to Jonathon's ex-wife for the first time in months. She'd never asked Maud about the woman as she'd once meant to, the loss of Godfrey's baby having consumed her thoughts and feelings for a long, long time. Now her curiosity was piqued again.

'Tell me about Charmaine, Wilma. What was she like?'

'The most strikingly beautiful woman I've ever seen on first viewing. But the closer you looked, the less perfect she seemed. She was all flash and flesh, if you know what I mean. Masses of golden-blonde hair, a Miss America smile, big boobs, long legs. Real Penthouse Pet material. Not dumb, though. Behind the blonde bimbo image was a mind as smart as a whip. She played Jonathon like a fish and landed him good and proper. He was besotted right up to the day he found out the truth.'

'Which was?'

Wilma frowned. 'Maybe I shouldn't tell you this, though Jonathon can't possibly think I don't know. If you're going to air dirty linen in your office with your secretary seated right outside, then you should keep your voice down.'

'Wilma, don't drag this out. Just tell me what she did.'

'She was taking the Pill. That's what she did.'

Sophia must have looked as blank as she felt.

Wilma sighed. 'Apparently, Jonathon and Charmaine had been trying for a baby since the day they were married. When Charmaine hadn't conceived after a year or so, she'd pretended to be concerned, pretended to have herself checked out and cleared. She even had Jonathon go for tests. The day his tests came back showing he was potent as a stud ram, he rang Charmaine's doctor to see what else he could do to help her conceive.'

'And the doctor told him she was on the Pill?'

'Well no, not straight out. He wouldn't be able to do that. But his initial confusion over Jonathon's questions must have bothered Jonathon and when Charmaine dropped by later to take him to lunch—

that was the sort of thing she did—he tackled her about his suspicions. Under intense and very loud questioning, she finally admitted to having taken the Pill all along. At that point, Jonathon totally lost it. He called her all sorts of names, at which she screamed at him that she had never had any intention of ever spoiling her figure by having any brats and that he was a fool to want her to.'

Sophia grimaced.

'She capped it all off by saying that having a baby would have spoilt their sex-life, then made the fatal mistake of also claiming she loved him too much to do that. Jonathon told her in no uncertain terms that she had no concept of what real love was all about, after which he warned her that when he came home to Parnell Hall that night, she'd better not be there. She came storming out of his office threatening to take him to the cleaners. Jonathon threw after her that he'd be only too happy to give her whatever she wanted just to get rid of her so that he could start feeling clean again.'

Sophia was shaking her head. 'Poor Jonathon. He must have felt very bitter at being deceived like that. He obviously loved her very much to react so strongly.'

'Yes, Charmaine certainly left her mark on him.'

'I dare say she's why he vowed never to marry again,' Sophia murmured.

'But he did marry again,' Wilma pointed out. 'He married you.'

'Oh, but that's different.'

'Yes, it was. But it needn't be, Sophia. You could make it a real marriage if you wanted to. You could offer to give Jonathon the family he's always wanted. He wouldn't turn you down. I'm certain of it.'

Sophia was stunned, not only by the suggestion itself, but her own inner response to it, especially to the possibility of having children in the near future. She'd thought, after her miscarriage, that she wouldn't be able to face having another baby for ages, but such wasn't the case at all! The idea of having a baby filled her with nothing but the most amazing feelings, not the least of which was a deep maternal longing. She wanted a baby to love and care for; wanted it with all her heart.

But *Jonathon's* baby?

As much as Wilma's revelation about Jonathon's first marriage had touched her, she wasn't sure her sympathy extended to offering herself as mother to his children.

'It's not such a shocking idea once you get used to it,' Wilma said matter-of-factly. 'Don't dismiss it out of hand. Think it over for a while. You're not worried about what Godfrey would think, are you?'

Godfrey, Sophia knew, would be delighted. As she'd once said to Jonathon, it wasn't in Godfrey's nature to be jealous or possessive, or to begrudge anyone any happiness. If she could find some sort of life with his younger brother, there would be no one more pleased than Godfrey.

Any problems did not lie with her loyalty to Godfrey's memory, more in her ability to think of Jonathon as her lover. For her, making love had always been associated with being in love. The romantic in her automatically cringed away from anything else. She could not deny, however, that this was a special case. For some weird and wonderful reason, it also felt right.

'I don't mean to be cruel,' Wilma continued in her usual pragmatic fashion, 'but Godfrey's gone. You can't make a life out of memories. Neither can you make a baby. You need a flesh and blood man. Frankly, you couldn't get a better arranged flesh and blood man than Jonathon.'

A shudder rippled through Sophia and Wilma frowned.

'Surely you can't be repelled by the idea of going to bed with a man like Jonathon.'

'Not repelled exactly,' she admitted shakily. 'I'm just not sure how I would handle it. I...I only went to bed with Godfrey the once and it wasn't such a big success, despite our being madly in love. There again, I *was* a virgin.'

'Goodness! I had no idea. Looking at you, I would have thought you'd have had other lovers before Godfrey.'

'I was only eighteen when I moved in with Godfrey,' Sophia protested in shocked tones. She'd been brought up very strictly in a moral sense, her mother brainwashing her that a good girl never gave herself till she was very much in love, and preferably engaged. 'I'm only twenty now,' she added.

'You look older,' Wilma commented, her gaze travelling from Sophia's face down to her chest.

Sophia blushed, the woman's explicit scrutiny embarrassing her. 'It's my Italian heritage,' she muttered. 'Italian girls mature young.'

Wilma's laugh was dry. 'Don't be shy about it. Lord, I'd give my eye teeth to have *half* your bust.'

'I'd give *my* eye teeth to have only half of it,' Sophia countered just as drily.

'Don't be silly, most men love breasts. And yours aren't too big. They're nicely rounded and still beautifully high. Don't knock them. And don't take too much notice of your first experience with Godfrey. First sexual experiences are rarely memorable for a female. Besides, I don't think that...' Wilma broke off, mumbling something under her breath which Sophia couldn't catch. When she looked up, her thin lips pulled back into a encouraging smile. 'So what do you think you might do?'

'I don't know, Wilma. I'll have to think about it, as you said.'

'There's no hurry. I don't think Jonathon's going anywhere.'

Sophia began wishing he *would* go somewhere that very same night. After her conversation with Wilma, she suddenly became awfully conscious of him in a physical sense. Several times over dinner she found herself staring at him. At his hands particularly...and his lips. They weren't as thin as she'd thought. They were, in fact, very nicely shaped, the bottom one fuller than the top.

Once, he looked up while forking cheesecake into his mouth and caught her staring. His brows drew together in a puzzled frown. For a long, awfully tense moment their eyes remained locked, Jonathon's frown increasing. Sophia felt frozen, unable to look away, appalled with herself, yet fascinated with the way her heart was hammering away behind her ribs.

'Have I grown horns?' Jonathon drawled when the staring had long passed the point of politeness.

Both Maud and Ivy looked over at Sophia who coloured guiltily. 'No of course not. I was just wondering…'

'Wondering what?' he persisted.

Her mind searched desperately for something to say. 'I was wondering how to go about asking you to buy a Christmas tree.'

'We already have a Christmas tree,' he returned in a droll tone. 'Haven't you seen the silver one Maud put up in the drawing-room?'

'Yes, but that's not the same as a real one,' she went on, trapped by her white lie. 'Godfrey always said that Christmas wasn't Christmas without a real tree.'

The mentioning of Godfrey brought a hushed silence for a moment. Till Jonathon spoke. 'Then a real tree we will have by all means. I'll go get one first thing in the morning.'

Sophia thought she detected a rueful note behind his crisp voice, but even so, his agreeing to the suggestion seemed to spark some life into his mother, who said she would go up to the attic that very night and bring down some more decorations.

'There's things up there which we haven't used since you and Godfrey were boys, Jonathon,' she said quite excitedly. 'Remember how Godfrey always insisted on putting the angel on the top of the tree?'

'Yes, Mother,' Jonathon said. 'I remember.'

'And we had to sing carols while doing it,' she went on, her eyes shining with the memory. 'He was such a dear, sensitive boy,' she finished with a wistful sigh.

Sophia's heart squeezed tight when she saw the wry twist on Jonathon's mouth. Yes, of course

Godfrey must have been a dear sensitive boy, for he had been a dear sensitive man. But he didn't have a monopoly on sensitivity. Couldn't Ivy see Jonathon was hurt by her ongoing *insensitive* favouring of Godfrey? No doubt this was just a continuance of the way she'd always acted. My God, maybe Jonathon might have liked to put the angel on top of the tree sometimes. Or hadn't that ever occurred to her?

Sophia vowed silently that this time he would do exactly that. She would make a special point of asking him to, knowing neither Maud not Ivy would climb up on a ladder to do such a precarious task. Truly, Ivy needed telling some day that Jonathon had feelings too!

When Sophia looked across the table she noted a similar irritation written on Maud's face. She was frowning, first at Ivy, then at Jonathon. Perhaps for the first time, Maud saw the unfairness of her old friend's attitude to her younger son. Hopefully, she might say something to her. Sophia knew *she* wasn't in a position to; it would look very bad coming from her.

Jonathon stood up abruptly at that point. 'Bring my coffee into the study, will you, Maud? I have some calls to make.'

'Certainly, Jonathon,' she said with a ready smile. 'And I'll bring you a slice of my special Christmas cake. I made it early this year. You know the one.' She gave a sheepish laugh. 'It has more rum in it than eggs.'

Jonathon was taken aback but obviously pleased by the housekeeper's uncharacteristic warmth. His surprised smile moved Sophia unbearably. The man was starved of love, she realised. Positively starved.

Wilma's suggestion slipped back into her mind. Jonathon would never love her as he had loved Charmaine. She would never love him as she'd loved Godfrey. But they could learn to love each other in a fashion, especially if they had a child together.

The doctor had assured Sophia that there was nothing physically wrong with her, that her miscarriage was a one-off thing. He'd investigated her mother's problem, getting her medical records from the Lithgow doctor who had treated her, dismissing Sophia's worry as groundless. Her mother's weakness had not been congenital, but the result of damage caused by a difficult childbirth.

There was no medical reason why Sophia shouldn't conceive easily again and carry the baby full-term. Dr Henderson had been most reassuring, thinking no doubt that the baby she lost had been Jonathon's, and that they would want to try again soon for another child.

Sophia swallowed when she thought of going to bed with Jonathon. She'd told Wilma the truth when she'd expressed extreme nervousness over such a prospect. Right from the start she'd found Jonathon an intimidating man in a physical sense, both with his size and his overpowering aura of authority and decisiveness.

That had not changed, despite her having got over her excessive fear. She was also terribly nervous over the idea of actually approaching him and suggesting that they make their marriage a real one, that they try to have a child together.

For she wasn't sure what his reaction would be. Wilma might feel confident that he found her desirable enough to agree. But she wasn't so sure. Other than the one awkward moment on the stairs when he'd hugged her and been unexpectedly aroused, Jonathon had never shown, by look, word or deed, that he fancied her any more than any other young attractive woman he might meet.

Still, a lot of men were not too fussy when it came to sex, it seemed. They could go to bed with any number of women without being in love, without any great depth of feeling at all. Clearly Jonathon had been sleeping with a variety of females, his trips over the past few months rarely being to the same place. Sophia doubted he'd been taking the same woman with him every time. Wilma would know if he had since she made all the bookings for him, and it was clear from their conversation that day that Jonathon was not in the clutches of some secret mistress.

No…Sophia had to admit that Wilma was probably quite right. Jonathon would have no trouble actually taking her to bed if he wanted to. But would he want her to have his baby?

There was only one way to find out, she supposed. She would have to ask him, if and when she could find the courage.

CHAPTER EIGHT

SOPHIA should have guessed that Jonathon would avoid the decorating of the tree like poison. Yet when he brought home such a magnificent specimen, taking time to cement it firmly in a large bucket of sand in one corner of the main living-room, she'd hoped he was going to help with the rest of the proceedings. But he left the house as soon as the first coloured ball was drawn from the various boxes Ivy had brought down, saying he had an appointment.

Sophia's disappointment was sharp. What appointment could he possibly have before lunch on a Sunday? In the end, she put the darned angel on top of the tree herself, climbing back down the step-ladder with a heavy heart. But when Ivy turned on the coloured lights that they'd threaded through the branches, it was hard to remain down. There was something about a real live Christmas tree all lit up that was impossible to resist. Godfrey had been right. Christmas wasn't Christmas without it.

Immediately Sophia started to think about the presents she'd bought everyone. She hoped they'd like them.

The rest of the week dragged, but at last Christmas morning dawned, Jonathon surprising everyone by accompanying them to church. He looked very handsome, Sophia thought, in a dark blue suit and tie. And much more cheerful than usual. He even opened some champagne after breakfast, so that by the time the four of them assembled around the tree to give out the presents around eleven, the general mood was quite bright. Even Ivy was chirpy.

Maud suggested she receive her presents first, saying she had to get back to the kitchen and the turkey dinner. She seemed very pleased with the Italian cookbook Sophia gave her, having often expressed curiosity and interest in the Italian dishes Sophia had been cooking the family lately. Ivy's present to Maud of a summer nightie and matching robe was also much appreciated, but when Jonathon gave her an envelope with a cash bonus in it Maud's eyes almost popped out of her head.

'But that's way too much, Jonathon,' she protested.

He waved a dismissive hand. 'Send some of it to that son of yours, if you like. He needs a helping hand from what you've told me.' Maud's only child, Jerry, who was a logger in Tasmania, had been retrenched a few months back. With his five children, he had to be finding life pretty tough.

Tears pricked at the old lady's eyes. 'I'll do that. Thank you, Jonathon. What a good man you are.'

Amen to that, Sophia thought, and slid an admiring glance his way. It caught his eye and he looked back at her, his own gaze travelling down over her body. Sophia tried not to blush, well aware that she looked pretty that day, the softly flowered sundress flattering her voluptuous figure by skimming rather than hugging her curves, the flaring skirt reaching down to just above her ankles, giving her the illusion of more height. Her long dark hair was caught back behind her ears, small but expensive gold hoops decorated her lobes and a deeper red lipstick than she usually wore outlined her mouth.

His eyes lifted to rest on that mouth and she swallowed. Today would be a good day, whispered a little voice. I look nice and Jonathon seems very relaxed. Maybe I will ask to speak to him after dinner…

Sophia's pulse-rate immediately went haywire. Dear God, how would she ever find the nerve?

Maud blessedly interrupted her panicky train of thought by handing out her presents. It seemed she always gave stationery, Ivy expressing the opinion that she'd outdone herself this year with some simply beautiful sets. Which they were, Sophia's delicate and flowery; Ivy's gold-embossed and classical, Jonathon's very business-like, with an accompanying pen-set.

'Just what I always wanted,' he drawled, but smiling. He even gave Maud a kiss on the cheek, which flustered her for a moment, she was so surprised and pleased. Ivy looked startled as well, as though seeing a different Jonathon from the one she'd always known.

After Maud departed to attend to the dinner, mother and son exchanged gifts, Ivy delighted with her crystal ornament in the shape of a castle, Jonathon making all the right noises over his pewter desk set.

When Ivy coyly presented Sophia with two gifts, not one, Sophia was taken aback, as they had earlier agreed only to buy each other the one gift. The larger of the two turned out to be a small portable CD player, the other a selection of Mozart CDs.

'The player's small enough to put on your bedside table,' Ivy explained. 'You could play it when you go to bed at night, especially when you find it hard to go to sleep.'

Sophia darted a quick look Jonathon's way, but his

face had taken on that rather remote unreadable expression he wore sometimes.

'You shouldn't have spent so much money on me,' she told Ivy.

'Don't be silly. We wanted to. Besides, it was Jonathon's idea. This is from him as well.'

'It's a lovely present,' Sophia said, amazed at Jonathon's selecting that particular gift. She knew exactly what he thought of Mozart. It showed he was a lot more mature than his mother. 'Thank you both. I hope you'll like what I bought you.'

Ivy seemed genuinely thrilled with her early edition leather-bound copy of *A Tale of Two Cities*, which Sophia had found in a nearby second-hand book shop. No doubt Jonathon thought he was getting a book too, for when he ripped the paper off his present and saw the latest zoom compact camera lying in his lap, surprised blue eyes snapped up to Sophia. Maud chose that moment to come back into the room, carrying a serving dish full of cherries, nuts and lollies.

'I see you've opened Sophia's present,' she said. 'I hope you appreciate it. She worked darned hard to earn the money to buy you that camera.'

Everything inside Sophia tightened as she stared at Maud. She hadn't said anything specific to the woman but she'd been sure Maud understood Jonathon wasn't to know about her having taken in that ironing. Ivy had certainly understood, for she too was staring wide-eyed at Maud.

Jonathon wasn't staring. He was frowning.

'What are you talking about, Maud? What work?'

'About a hundred hours' ironing,' Maud revealed airily, not looking at Sophia as she sailed from the room again.

Jonathon's straight black brows met. 'You took in ironing to buy me this?'

Sophia held her breath and bit her lip. 'Yes,' she choked out.

'For God's sake, why? You have plenty of money. I *gave* it to you.'

Sophia scooped in a deep steadying breath and lifted her chin. 'I wasn't about to buy you a present with your own money,' she told him with remarkable composure, though aware her stomach was tight with tension.

'And how did you come by this ironing?'

'Maud paid me to do what she usually sent out, and I...I did some of the neighbours'.'

'The neighbours',' he repeated, shaking his head. 'Good God.'

An awkward silence fell, during which Ivy cleared her throat and Sophia got steadily angrier. If Jonathon spoiled everyone's day, she was going to let him have a piece of her mind.

When he looked up again, however, his attitude was quite calm. 'Mother, could I perhaps have a few moments alone with Sophia?'

Worry was written all over Ivy's face. 'You... you're not going to have an argument, are you? Not on Christmas Day.'

'Not at all,' was his smooth reply. 'I just wish to speak briefly to Sophia in private. Perhaps Maud could do with some help in the kitchen?'

Ivy's departure was clearly reluctant, her parting glance quite anxious.

'Now,' Jonathon began with a weary sigh. 'Would you like to tell me how the neighbours found out that a guest in my home wanted to take in ironing?'

Sophia's simmering irritation with Jonathon made her fiercely unrepentant, and extremely defiant. 'I put pamphlets in their letterboxes,' she admitted boldly.

'You put...' He rose to his feet, eyes and nostrils flaring. 'Good God, whatever possessed you? Haven't you any pride? Or any concern for mine? You're my wife, dammit!'

'No I'm not,' she countered, her surface coolness in stark contrast to his out-of-control fury. 'Not really. No one in this street even knows we went through that sham of a ceremony and I certainly haven't told them. They probably think I'm some poor relative or other.'

'Which is just as bad,' he ranted. 'What do you think they're saying amongst themselves? That bastard Parnell is so mean his poor cousin, or niece or whatever they think you are, has to take in ironing to make ends meet.'

Sophia flushed. 'I...I never thought of that.'

'No, you certainly didn't. I can't imagine why Maud and Mother let you do such a thing.'

'They didn't *let* me, Jonathon. I just did it. Besides, I think they thought it took guts.'

'No one's ever denied you've got guts, Sophia. But there's a limit to what I can allow. Hell, whatever am I going to do with you?'

'You could do one of two things,' she said, her voice steeling as she decided to take the plunge and put Wilma's suggestion into action. 'You could give me a divorce and let me make my own way in life. Or...or...'

'Or what?' he snapped impatiently.

Sophia gulped. In for a penny in for a pound, she

supposed. 'Or you could make me your real wife,' she blurted out.

The next few seconds were excruciatingly nerve-racking. Shock held Jonathon's handsome face frozen for a moment till he gave an odd little shudder, as though having to physically shake himself out of his stunned state. Even then, he didn't speak for a few moments, bewildered blue eyes raking over her.

'Might I ask what is behind that amazing offer? And please don't say anything stupid about how you've fallen in love with me, as you and I both know that's not true.'

'I wouldn't insult your intelligence by saying as much,' Sophia said stiffly, while underneath her courage was quickly crumbling. 'I...I can't see myself falling in love with anyone really. Not as I loved Godfrey. But I...I would like to marry and have a family some day and...well...you seemed almost as upset as I was when I lost Godfrey's baby, and I thought maybe you might have wanted a child around the house too. Since we're already married, and we've put that silly antagonism behind us—well, I wondered if...if...'

Sophia's voice trailed away as Jonathon's face filled with a knowing cynicism. 'Wilma's been talking to you, hasn't she?' he said on a sardonic note.

If only she could have hidden her guilt.

'I thought as much,' Jonathon said curtly. 'God, I can see it now! I suppose she waxed lyrical about how my bitch of a first wife embittered me by refusing to give me children, at which point your sweet and far too generous heart was immediately filled with pity for poor childless Jonathon, spawning this amazingly sacrificial offer. Never mind that that same heart still belongs to my very own poor departed brother! Do you honestly think I would use you to give me what should rightly have been his? What kind of a man do you think I am?'

Jonathon's astonishing outburst struck Sophia speechless for a few moments, till the confusion his high emotion evoked cleared away and she felt impelled to answer his accusation.

'What kind of a man do I think you are?' she launched forth, her heart thudding painfully. 'Why, I think you're a very disillusioned man if you think Godfrey would mind my having your baby. Didn't you know your brother at all? There was nothing petty about him. Nothing small-minded or envious. I'll bet he made you promise to marry me because he hoped we might end up together. That's the sort of brother you had, Jonathon. As for my pitying you…I doubt you would ever be the object of a woman's pity,' she snapped heatedly. 'You inspire far different feelings in females from pity!'

Jonathon's eyes narrowed on the rapid rise and fall of her chest. 'Are you saying you *want* to go to bed with me?' he asked, his voice disbelieving.

Sophia kept her eyes steady on him, even whilst her cheeks were burning. 'I can't say I do, but I can't say I don't. I haven't had much experience in such matters. But you must know you're a very attractive man, Jonathon, and I'm sure, a very experienced one. What do *you* think?' she rashly flung at him. 'Could you make me want to go to bed with you?'

Those blazing but oddly cold blue eyes seemed to seer through her dress, their fire heating her skin, their ice freezing her nipples into hard little pebbles. With breathtaking and incredibly sensual slowness, his gaze travelled upwards, leaving behind a parched throat and parted panting lips. At last he reached her eyes, her large, liquid brown eyes which grew larger as they glimpsed the power within that ruthlessly sexual gaze.

Oh, yes, she realised breathlessly, he could make her want to go to bed with him. But it would be nothing like what she had experienced with Godfrey. His kisses would not be sweet or soft or romantic. There would be no meeting of souls, only a meeting of bodies. Hard, panting bodies, reaching for each other in a strictly primitive passion.

The starkly explicit images bombarding her mind brought a gasp of shock, and shame. For this was not the sort of lovemaking she had always dreamt about. This was nothing but sex. Raw, naked sex.

When he took a step towards her, she staggered backwards, pale and shaken. His mouth twisted in a cynical smile, his hand reaching out to lie with odd tenderness against her cheek.

'We will forget this conversation ever took place, Sophia,' he said in a low, thickened voice. 'But do not make such an offer to me again. Or such a challenge.' His hand dropped from her cheek, his shoulders squaring as his face resumed its usual harsh remoteness. 'Now go out to the kitchen and smile for Maud and Mother,' he ordered. 'We don't want to upset them on Christmas Day, do we?'

CHAPTER NINE

THERE was an annual tradition in the Parnell household. On New Year's Eve, they threw a lavish party for the employees of Parnell Property Developments. This year, however, there was a problem.

Sophia.

How was she going to be introduced? No one at Parnell's, other than Wilma, knew of their marriage of convenience. Though it seemed it was more a marriage of inconvenience nowadays, Sophia thought bitterly as she viewed Jonathon's frustrated face.

'I'll just stay in my room,' she offered, which brought a howl of protest from Wilma who'd come over to help with the preparations.

Jonathon gave his secretary a quelling look, but Wilma was unquellable. 'Your mother will not allow that and you know it,' came her curt reminder.

Jonathon sighed, and gave in. 'We'll say you're an old friend of the family,' he told Sophia. 'Harvey's the only person attending the party who knows any different. I'll call him right now and tell him not to let the cat out of the bag.'

'Don't worry, I'll do that,' Wilma offered swiftly. 'You have to go out and pick up the drinks I ordered for tonight. I told the man in the liquor shop you'd pick up everything by two.'

Jonathon glanced at his watch. 'It's already after two. Why didn't you tell me before this?'

'I did. You weren't listening. You were probably

thinking of...other things,' she finished drily, then turned to smile at Sophia. 'Come along, Sophia, let's go pick out the right sort of dress for an "old friend of the family" to wear.'

Sophia trundled up the stairs after Wilma, resigned to being told what dress to wear, what shoes and accessories, how to do her hair, plus her make-up. Wilma was an incorrigible organiser. Still, she had impeccable taste and Sophia was quite happy to put herself in her hands.

She wasn't quite so happy at five to eight that night when she stood in front of her dressing-table mirror, surveying the result of all her friend's suggestions. The black dress Wilma had drawn out of the wardrobe had seemed a simple and elegant ankle-length style with its high round neckline, cut-in shoulders and a skirt that flared slightly from the hips, falling in soft folds around her legs. What Sophia hadn't realised was that her bra would show in three places. On her shoulders, inside the deeply cut armholes, and at the back where the back seam was split to the waist, the neckline being cinched at the back of her neck with a large crystal button.

Sophia had discarded her bra with reluctance, knowing her full breasts had a tendency to jiggle alarmingly when unrestrained. Thankfully, the black colour had a slimming, minimising effect and the lined material meant that there was no obvious nipple outline. But still...

I'll be fine, she told her reflection ruefully, as long as I don't move!

A knock on her bedroom door had her whirling round, giving her a splendid example of exactly what she was fearing. Her breasts slid right and left against the cool taffeta lining, bringing her into hot awareness of their naked state.

Flustered, she walked towards the door in the outrageously high black shoes Wilma had chosen, the short walk reinforcing even further her sudden determination to find a dark corner for herself at this infernal party and not move an inch all night. She was nervous enough as it was, her upbringing on a dairy farm hardly equipping her for such socialising. She wished wholeheartedly that Jonathon had not given in to Wilma, that he had agreed to her hiding away in her room all night.

Sophia opened the door, expecting Wilma, whom she'd made promise to come get her at eight and accompany her down to the party. Wilma at her side would give her dutch courage.

'Oh!' she exclaimed on finding Jonathon standing there, looking devastatingly handsome in a white dinner jacket and bow-tie. 'I…I was expecting Wilma.'

'She's busy bullying the caterers. She sent me up to bring you down. Now I can see why,' he finished drily.

'What…what do you m-mean?' Sophia was appalled to see that she was back to stammering with him. And blushing. But she wished Jonathon would stop looking at her like that. Yet it wasn't admiration in his eyes. Or desire. It was irritation. A coldly mirthless irritation.

'That woman doesn't know when to give up,' he muttered.

The heat in Sophia's cheeks changed from fluster to embarrassment, for she knew what Jonathon meant. Wilma was still intent on matchmaking her with her boss. Why, she had no idea. What did it matter to her?

'I dare say that hairdo is Wilma's handiwork as well,' he went on testily.

Sophia gnawed uncomfortably at her bottom lip. She'd been putting her hair up herself an hour earlier when Wilma had come in, tut-tutting and shaking her head.

'None of those schoolgirl plaits or maiden-aunt buns for you tonight!' she'd insisted. '*I'll* do your hair for you.'

Which she had, piling the long, glossy dark waves on top of her head in a haphazard yet highly attractive fashion, anchoring it quite firmly with myriad hidden pins, then pulling down lots of wispy bits to curl softly around her face and neck. The sexy, tousled image was completed when she slipped long dangling earrings made of black crystal beads into Sophia's lobes.

'A little Christmas present from me,' Wilma had whispered, and given her a sisterly kiss on the cheek.

Sophia had guessed what Wilma was up to, but she hadn't known how to stop her.

'Do not do this, Sophia,' Jonathon warned darkly.

'I'm not doing anything,' she said, feeling wretched.

'You're letting Wilma manipulate you, but you don't know what you're playing at. Let me assure you it's a dangerous game and way out of your league. You should stick with safe, gentle men like Godfrey. I'm not for you.'

His coldly condescending tone finally got to her, bringing a resurgence of spirit. Her dark eyes flashed, her nose and chin lifting to glare up into his arrogantly handsome face. 'I fully agree with you, Jonathon. I made a mistake the other day, offering myself to you. I don't know what possessed me. You're not half the man Godfrey was. Believe me when I say I won't be making the same mistake again.'

There! Take that!

For a few seconds, Sophia was filled with a type of triumph, her pride having been restored with her dignified outburst. Till she glimpsed the hurt deep in those suddenly bleak blue eyes. Immediately, remorse welled up within her, like a huge wave, engulfing her totally. Her hand lifted to hover over his shirt buttons, her eyes pleading with his. 'Jonathon, I'm sorry. I...I...'

'Don't apologise, for God's sake,' he snapped, his right hand jerking up to grab her wrist. 'Anger is good. Truth is good. It will protect you. Sympathy is bad. Pity is bad. Don't succumb to it.'

For a few excruciating seconds he scowled down at her, his fingers tightening on her wrist. But then he did the most peculiar thing. He groaned, lifted her hand to his mouth, closed his eyes and kissed it.

It was a gentle, tender kiss, yet it shook her.

For a few seconds, a hushed silence seemed to encapsulate them. Her whole being strained towards him, to his mouth breathing warm air into the palm of her hand, to the lips sipping softly at her prickling skin.

But then he opened his eyes and lifted his mouth, smiling a wickedly sardonic smile down into her still enraptured face.

'See?' he taunted softly. 'Even *I* can masquerade as gentle.'

Stung that he would mock her—and his brother—she wrenched her hand away. 'You bastard,' she rasped.

'I can be,' he muttered. 'But not tonight, beautiful Sophia. Tonight I'm going to escort you down to that party and be a proper gentleman all evening. But afterwards…afterwards, I suggest to scuttle on back to this very room and lock your door. You look far too sexy tonight for a bastard like me not to try to take advantage of you. Especially since I virtually have your permission.'

'No!' she gasped. 'I…I took that back.'

'No, you didn't. I turned you down. Careful I don't change my mind.'

'I wouldn't let you!' she protested breathlessly.

The devilish gleam in his eyes told her she wouldn't stand a chance of stopping him.

'I'm going to leave this house come tomorrow,' she threw at him in a panic. 'Wilma would let me move in with her. I know she would.'

'What a splendid idea,' he drawled. 'I wish you'd thought of it several months ago. Now, are you sure you don't want a few minutes to compose yourself before you come down and join everyone? You're looking a little—er—rattled.'

She stared at him, at this stranger who *had* been perpetrating a masquerade—as a good kind decent man. He was nothing but a predator, a…a…blackguard, a *villain*!

She gritted her teeth and fought to control her pounding heart. 'I'm fine,' she bit out, and slid a brave trembling arm through his. 'Let's go.'

He laughed. Drily. 'As I said once before, you've

got guts, Sophia. But you're so naïve, so impossibly, incredibly naïve.'

If it hadn't been for Harvey, Sophia would not have stayed downstairs at that party. From the first moment she walked into the room with Jonathon on her arm and a hundred curious eyes turned her way she was a quivering quavering mess.

But no sooner had that last vestige of her courage begun to fail her than Harvey had come forward out of the laughing, chatting, dancing throng of people and rescued her. How kind he was, taking her away from Jonathon, getting her a drink then finding them a quiet, dimly lit corner out on the terrace where they could sit and talk away from prying eyes.

'I was very sorry to hear about the baby, Sophia,' he said once they were alone. 'But maybe it was for the best…'

'Perhaps,' she sighed.

'So what are you going to do now?'

'I'm not sure.' She took a sip of the dry white wine he'd brought her, thinking she much preferred red. 'I'm thinking of moving out of Parnell Hall into a flat of my own. I was hoping Wilma might take me in.'

Harvey looked startled. 'Does Wilma know about this?'

'Er…no, not yet.'

'I didn't think so.'

'Why do you say it like that?'

'What? Oh…um…no reason, really. But I got the impression she thinks you're happy here.'

'I have been,' she said stiffly.

He frowned at her. 'Has Jonathon done or said something?'

'He's a difficult man to get along with,' she hedged.

'True. But I'm not.' He smiled at her, displaying an easy, relaxed charm which she found soothingly unthreatening. Yet after ten minutes of Harvey's bland conversation her eyes started flicking around the terrace, unconsciously searching for Jonathon. There were a few couples dancing around the edge of the pool, music coming from a stereo set up on the barbecue, but he wasn't one of them.

Sophia twisted slightly in her deckchair so that she could look back through the open french doors and into the living-room, filled at that moment with an assorted group of well-dressed and predominantly young people. Parnell Property Developments, it seemed, had a youthful staff.

Eventually, she found Jonathon over near the bar in earnest conversation with a blonde woman, a very pretty blonde woman no older than she was. Her feelings as she watched him dance attention on the girl, smiling and laughing as he never had with her, made Sophia sharply uncomfortable. Surely she couldn't be jealous!

'Care to dance?' Harvey asked.

She turned back to face him with an apologetic smile. 'I can't dance,' she admitted. When she'd been old enough to go to local dances, she hadn't been allowed, her Italian stepfather very traditional in his ideas about the proper upbringing of females. She hadn't been allowed to go to parties either, or even some of the school excursions. Her mother, who'd long had her rebellious spirit tamed by a man given to using his fists when crossed, had backed her husband, much to Sophia's dismay and disappointment.

'Nothing to it,' Harvey said. 'Here. Put down your wine... Now give me your hand...' He drew her to her feet and into his arms. 'Put your arms up around my neck and just move your feet in time to the music. Two slides to the right, then one to the left. Yes, that's right. Very good. You have a natural sense of rhythm.'

'But no natural common sense,' Jonathon drawled at her shoulder, 'if she lets a rake like you dance with her in a dark corner.'

When Sophia went to pull away, her head whipping round to encounter Jonathon's glowering face, Harvey's hold tightened, flattening her breasts against his chest. One of his hands slipped into the slit in the small of her back, his fingers spreading across bars of skin.

Sophia was too stunned to do a thing.

'That's the pot calling the kettle black, friend,' Harvey returned silkily as he continued to move Sophia slowly around their private corner. 'Besides, Sophia's a free agent, isn't she? I would imagine you two will be getting a discreet annulment shortly. She's already talking about moving out of your house, so you can drop the ''disapproving guardian'' act. Once Sophia's out on her own she can do what she likes and see whomever she likes. I hope she'll like to see me.'

He smiled a devilish smile down into her startled face while his hand started roving under her dress, making Sophia's eyes widen and her skin break out into goose-bumps of alarm and sudden revulsion. Yet she felt totally powerless to do anything about it.

'Not if I can help it,' Jonathon snarled, grabbing her arm and wrenching her out of Harvey's embrace.

She sighed with relief at being free of that disgusting hand, almost happy to find herself in Jonathon's comparatively safe arms, even if his grip was bruisingly hard.

'Get lost, Harvey,' he ground out.

Harvey laughed. 'You never did know how to share, Jonathon.'

'This isn't a matter of sharing. It's a matter of protecting. Leave…Sophia…alone.' Each word came out with a razor's edge and she shivered.

'Why should I?' Harvey tossed back. 'Godfrey wasn't *my* brother. I made no deathbed promise. Besides, Sophia's not a child. She's a fully grown woman. Or hadn't you noticed?'

'Yes,' Jonathon bit out. 'I've noticed. But in experience she's still little more than a child.'

Sophia opened her mouth to protest, then closed it again. Jonathon was right…in a way. She hadn't much experience with life, and men. If she had, she'd have known what to do a moment ago, when Harvey had started mauling her.

'Experience has to start somewhere, friend,' Harvey went on wryly. 'Besides, you're talking as though Sophia's a shy, retiring, wide-eyed virgin. She's hardly that. Don't be such a spoilsport, man. If you don't want the girl, there are a lot of other men who will. But I don't want to argue with you about this tonight. It's New Year's Eve. I have another couple of parties I promised to drop in on, so this might be an appropriate moment for me to take my leave. As for you, lovely Sophia…I'll be in contact. Soon.'

He was gone before Jonathon could say another word, which was perhaps why he rounded on Sophia, angrily pulling her back in the shadows against the wall.

'I suppose I shouldn't blame you,' he said frustratedly. 'But damn it all, can't you recognise an inveterate womaniser when you see one? Harvey's thirty-five years old. He's never been married and he never will be. He's loved and left more women than I can count. He is not the sort of man for you!'

Sophia remained silent, confused by Jonathon's tirade.

Was he jealous? Or merely annoyed?

'I want you to stay by my side for the rest of the night,' he ordered brusquely. 'You obviously can't be let loose in this company, certainly not with all these randy young men pouring beer and spirits down their throats as if there's no tomorrow. And certainly not while you're wearing that dress!'

'What's wrong with this dress?' she stupidly asked.

'Nothing…if it was on Wilma.'

Sophia blushed.

'My God, you're a real babe-in-the woods, aren't you? A man like Harvey could eat you up and spit you out for breakfast.'

'No, he couldn't!'

'Oh, yes, he could. I saw what he was doing, groping you under your dress. And I saw you weren't exactly liking it. But you didn't say a word. You let him go on groping. If you go out with him, he might try to do a damned sight more than grope. What would you do then, Sophia? Would you just lie there, speechless with fright, when his hand finds a damned sight more intimate target than your back, when he pulls down your pants and…?'

'Stop it,' she gasped, her face burning. 'Stop it!

You…you've got your message across. I'm a fool,' she cried. 'A silly little fool.'

His face softened at her distress, his eyes almost apologetic. 'No, not a silly little fool. A sweet, trusting soul who needs a crash course in life if she's to survive in this world. You lived a fantasy life with Godfrey, Sophia. It wasn't real. My brother always ran away from life, and, for a while, so did you. Maybe I'm to blame for trying to protect you further. Maybe it's time you joined the real world…saw what *real* men are like!'

'What…what do you mean?' she croaked out, her throat drying as his hard blue eyes came to rest on her tremulous mouth.

'You know damned well what I mean.'

Sophia's eyes rounded with a burst of fear, but he wasn't looking at her eyes. He kept looking at her mouth as he slowly drew her against him, one hand sliding up the back of her neck into her hair, the other assuming the same position that Harvey's had, settling into the small of her back and holding her firmly captive.

Jonathon's hand, however, did not inspire revulsion. A soft moan escaped her lips as it moved caressingly against her bare skin, her immediate goosebumps carrying a far different meaning this time.

'I shouldn't be doing this,' he muttered against her lips, groaning a type of despair, she thought, as the last millimetre between them was crossed.

And then she didn't think anything. There was nothing but his mouth, hard on hers, his hands tightening on her flesh.

When his mouth lifted momentarily on a raw moan, she gasped for air, only to instantly have his lips back covering hers and his tongue, hot and wet, surging deep inside. Wild swirls filled her head, the blood pounding in her temples. She pressed her hips against his, whimpering a need she had never felt before.

His mouth was wrenched from hers so abruptly, that for a few confusing seconds, she stared up at him, her lips still apart, red and swollen. He groaned, then gathered her back against him, this time burying his face in her hair.

'Tell me you want me,' he said hoarsely.

'I want you,' she whispered, her voice shaking, her thoughts a blur, but her body very very sure.

'You won't change your mind if I let you go?'

'No.'

'I want you to go to your room and wait for me. Don't come down again.'

'All right,' she agreed dazedly.

'I'll come to you as soon as everyone's gone.'

She nodded dumb acquiescence to his will. At that moment she would have done anything, anything he wanted.

'Kiss me, before you go,' he urged hoarsely.

She did so, blindly, hungrily, inviting his tongue to drown in her mouth again, demonstrating without words that desire had her securely in its tenacious grip.

'It's not midnight yet,' said a dry voice, blasting through Sophia's mindless passion.

Jonathon grudgingly eased his mouth from hers and turned round, holding her firmly against his side with a possessive arm around her waist.

Wilma stood a short distance away, where the shadows in their corner were dispelled by the lights from the house. She was surveying them both with a knowing satisfaction on her sharp, plain features.

'I had to get in early,' Jonathon drawled, showing a shocked Sophia how experienced he was at reducing women to mush whilst retaining superb control himself. His cool voice belied the thickened tones he'd just whispered in her ear. She almost wondered if she'd imagined them.

'Sophia's come down with a headache,' he went on blithely, 'and she's decided to go off to bed.' He bent to give her a chaste kiss on the cheek. 'Goodnight, love. I'll pop in and see how you are later.'

Sophia found herself saying an amazingly calm goodnight to an astonished Wilma and drifting off back into the house, as though hypnotised. When she reached her bedroom, she turned and locked the door, not to keep Jonathon out, but to keep everyone else out, everyone who might ask her awkward questions and who might see what was in her face.

Jonathon had warned her that he was way out of her league. He was. But it was too late now. Too late. He'd set her on a path she'd never travelled along before, a dangerous but insidiously attractive path, far more powerful than conscience, or loyalty, or even love; a primitive path, promising pleasures that needed nothing of the soul but everything of the senses. She'd recognised once before that going to bed with Jonathon wouldn't be anything like she'd experienced with Godfrey. It would not be making love. It would be having sex, nothing more, nothing less.

She'd always believed that type of thing was not for her, that it would hold no appeal.

She'd been wrong.

Once her door was securely locked she took off everything, including the earrings, and showered very slowly, aware of the water beating against her skin as she'd never been before, aware of her body as she'd never been before. She closed her eyes and lifted her face into the spray, opening her mouth and letting the water fill it, remembering how it had felt to have Jonathon's tongue filling it. She shuddered, but stayed with that thought and reached for the soap, moving it in ever widening circles over her stomach and ribs.

She moaned softly when the soap found her breasts, her insides tightening whenever the slippery surface grazed over the nipples. When she could bear the sensations no longer she dropped the soap and arched her body into the hot wet spray.

After the shower she stood naked in front of the vanity and took all the pins out of her hair, brushing it down with long, languorous strokes, wincing whenever the sharp bristles came into contact with her breasts. She toyed briefly with the idea of staying naked for him, but in the end slipped on one of the nighties which had lain unworn till this moment in her bottom drawer.

It was cream, with a low-cut stretch-lace bodice which moulded her full breasts into a deep tantalising cleavage; the rest was satin, falling in slippery folds from its princess line to the floor. It felt cool against her heated skin, cool and decadent. She should have been disgusted with the image she was presenting. Instead, she felt so excited she could hardly stand it.

When there was nothing more to be done—her make-up had been touched up and perfume applied everywhere—she lay down on top of the bed and waited till the last guest had gone and the house was quiet. At that point, she rose, shivering, the cool satin folds slapping against her naked thighs as she moved across the plush-piled carpet to unlock the door.

It was at that point that she began to tremble quite violently. Knowing she could lie in supposed patience on that bed no longer, she walked over to stare, wide-eyed, through the window down at the now deserted terrace. She wondered how long it would be before he would come, how much longer he would make her wait. She hoped not too long.

CHAPTER TEN

THE sound of splashing snapped Sophia out of her blank staring. Her eyes, already wide and glittering, focused on a male figure cleaving his way through the moonlit pool.

It was Jonathon, of course. There was no other male in the Parnell House.

Sophia watched him swim up and down at a punishing pace, his head rarely leaving the water. Then, when she'd begun to fear he might stay doing laps till he drowned, he swam over to the side and abruptly hauled himself out of the water, standing there, heaving, while the water dripped from his glistening body to form a pool around his feet.

Sophia stared at him.

This was the closest she had come to seeing Jonathon naked since entering Parnell Hall, only a brief pair of black swimming trunks between him and total nudity. The sight took her breath away. She'd always been in awe of his physical size and strength, even when dressed in one of his sleekly expensive business suits, but he seemed larger without his clothes on.

She hadn't realised, either, how much body hair he had. Godfrey had had very little. There again, Godfrey had had very little hair even where he should have had some. He'd told her once he'd been going bald since he was twenty-three.

Jonathon's head, however, was covered with luxuriant black waves, at that moment plastered thickly wet around his well-shaped skull. There was also a matting of damp black curls over most of his chest arrowing down to where it disappeared from sight underneath the black swimming trunks.

Standing there as he was in the moonlight, with his shoulders squared and his fists curled, his chest still rising and falling with the physical effort of that savage swim, he presented an image rather similar, Sophia fancied, to that of a primitive man who'd just forded a flooded river. Soon, he would stride on home to his cave where his woman would be waiting with food cooking over an open fire.

But this caveman wouldn't want to eat straight away. He'd been away, after all, for days, seeking out new hunting fields. What he suffered from was hunger of a different kind.

Sophia could see him now, eyeing his scantily clad mate with hot eyes, then coming forward to grab a clump of her hair at the back of her head, bending her body back till he could suckle on one of her bare breasts like a starving infant before dragging her back on to their rough bed of furs at the back of their cave and vanquishing his hunger, not once, but several times.

She was still enthralled in this fantasy when Jonathon's head suddenly snapped up to see her staring glazedly down at him through the window. Their eyes met and locked, Sophia unable to breathe while that intense gaze remained riveted to hers. And then he moved, striding purposefully towards the house, his eyes only leaving her when they had to. She spun round, her breath coming in swift shallow pants as she stared at the bedroom door.

It was soon flung open, and he stood there, a huge dark silhouette against the light which was always left on in the hall. She licked dry lips, glad there was no other light on in the room. When he moved abruptly inside, shutting and locking the door behind him, she braced herself against the windowsill, her stomach churning wildly, her heart thudding almost painfully in her chest.

He crossed the carpet with huge strides, looking larger and larger with each step till he towered over her. She lifted rounded eyes to his narrowed ones, her tongue suddenly thick in her mouth. A flood of nerves consumed her, bringing with it a trembling deep inside.

But even as her apprehension built, so did her desire, her eyes clinging to his, her body unconsciously straining towards him.

He ripped the nightie from her body, rent it in two from top to toe and threw it aside before sweeping her shaking body up into his arms and carrying her to the bed. He held her briefly against his damp body, hot eyes raking over her naked flesh before spreading her out on the quilt then swiftly stripping himself. Sophia was stunned by the speed with which he loomed over her, a dark silent force that breathed but did not speak.

She gasped when he pushed her legs apart and settled on his haunches between them, gasping again when, as though he had mind-read her earlier fantasy, he bent to scoop an arm around her waist and pull her into a sitting position, his free hand winding into her hair and pulling downwards, arching her back till one breast came into position for his searching mouth.

He nuzzled it hungrily, rubbed his five o'clock

shadow over it, licked it, nibbled at it, and then, when she thought she could bear no more, drew the entire aureole into his mouth. Shuddering with pleasure, Sophia closed her eyes and gave herself up totally to the experience.

She didn't try to stop herself from moaning. There would be no stopping, she accepted blindly. There was no tomorrow. There was only here and now, with Jonathon's mouth on her breast. She didn't know what lay in store for her this night. She only knew that she wanted whatever he wanted. She was his, totally, utterly, to do with as he willed.

He tormented her other breast before he lowered her back to the bed, before his mouth began a frantic, feverish journey down her body. He shocked her when he left nothing unkissed or unexplored. But the shock wasn't nearly as overwhelming as the sensations his lips and tongue evoked. She'd never dreamt her body housed such hidden delights.

Not hidden to Jonathon, however. He showed his experience with women by knowing exactly what would bring her intolerably close to ecstasy, what would make her gasp and moan and writhe beneath him, what would make her beg him not to stop.

'No, don't stop,' she cried a second time when he abandoned what he was doing.

He didn't stop. He merely started replacing his mouth and hands with his body, making her gasp when she realised he was as large there as he was everywhere else. A sob caught in her throat, her eyes squeezing tightly shut against the pressure of his titanic desire seeking entry into her almost virginal body.

When he suddenly achieved the unachievable, slipping deeply inside, Sophia's eyes flung wide. All discomfort had ceased, the only sensation one of being thoroughly and very satisfyingly filled. What Jonathon was feeling, she couldn't tell. He didn't look at her from where he was still kneeling between her legs, his hands under her buttocks, his concentration seemingly on that area where their flesh became one. His face was in shadow, but his stillness suggested a silent savouring of their union.

His hands moved to grip her hips and lift them from the bed, pulling her forward across his thighs as he settled back on to his haunches. When his head tipped back on a low groan, a ray of moonlight slanted across his face, revealing tortured, twisted features. He looked as if he was in pain as he began to pump slowly into her, pulling her hard against him whenever he urged his own flesh fully into hers, then easing her away as he withdrew a few inches.

Sophia wasn't in pain. She was deep in pleasure. It was like riding a storm-tossed sea, she imagined, being lifted up on to a crest of a wave, then plummeted down into a trough, only to be scooped up again, even higher than before. Higher she went, and higher, her soft moans of delight slowly turning to almost tormented groans. Her hips writhed under his increasingly ruthless grasp, her mouth gasping wide, her eyes screwing tightly shut as pleasure did indeed become a type of pain.

Was this what he'd been feeling all along? Oh, surely not. He wouldn't have been able to stand it this long.

'No, no,' she moaned before suddenly being gripped in sensations so sharp, so electric, so exciting that she cried out aloud. Her hands gripped clumps of the quilt at her sides, her flesh pulsating with seemingly endless waves of pleasure.

Sophia dazedly understood that this was a climax, that it was the desired result in making love, the ultimate. She suspected now that she would never have experienced this with Godfrey. The one time she had gone to bed with him, she'd felt nothing at all like what she'd felt here tonight, Godfrey's kisses and touches not evoking even the first inkling of real arousal or desire.

Jonathon, however, had driven her mind and body into a crazed frenzy from the first moment he'd kissed her tonight. Yet they weren't in love with each other. It hadn't been making love, what he'd done to her on this bed, what he was still doing to her...

His name was torn from her lips, a lost, bewildered cry which called for him to explain how she could feel like this when there was no love involved, to comfort her in her confusion, to hold her till this cataclysmic experience released her from its tenacious grip.

He didn't do any of those things. He stayed right where he was till his own body finished shuddering into her, till her own spasms had long stopped and she lay there, limp and exhausted. Then he withdrew with a groan and collapsed beside her on the bed, leaving her feeling emotionally empty yet so physically sated she could hardly find the energy to breathe.

One last shuddering sigh puffed from her lungs and her head lolled sidewards to look at him. His eyes were shut, his chest still rising and falling quite raggedly, as though he'd just run a long, long race.

The room was bathed in enough moonlight for her

to see his body quite clearly, her eyes travelling down from his massive chest to his much trimmer hips, and what lay between them. He was still partially erect, she realised, his desire not totally spent.

Her surprise was quickly replaced by speculation. Did that mean he might want to do it a second time?

Her stomach turned over at the prospect. She gulped then stared blankly up at the ceiling. Could she bear to be taken to the razor's edge again so soon? To be teased and tormented, then practically torn apart?

Sophia gasped when one large hand suddenly found the flat of her stomach, her eyes flying to his when it began sliding slowly up her body. He had rolled on to his side, his eyes heavy-lidded as he continued to move his hand up over her right breast, kneading it gently then rubbing his thumb over and over the nipple till it became a hard little ball. Her breathing picked up again from where it had become deep and languorous, her lips falling softly apart.

'If only I'd realised,' he said cryptically, 'I would have done this sooner.'

'Realised what?' she said blankly in a voice like treacle.

'That Godfrey wasn't your first lover…' His mouth descended to lick at the highly sensitised bud, so that he didn't see her startled expression. And then she was too involved with what he was doing to speak, her head whirling wildly. Once again she was on the treadmill, only this time it was worse. This time she knew what was ahead of her, fearing it yet wanting it even more than before.

When he rolled her away from him and spooned his giant body around hers, clamping a firm arm around her waist she moaned an anguished protest. But there was no further protest once he'd lifted her top leg back over his hip and fitted himself into her, when he cupped her chin and twisted her face round so that he could kiss her panting mouth.

She was his once more, whimpering beneath his driving tongue, writhing beneath his driving flesh.

Her second climax was no less tumultuous than her first, leaving her totally drained afterwards. This time, however, he cradled her back against him. Possessively, she thought, one hand enclosing a breast, the other on her stomach.

'Beautiful,' he murmured, kissing her ear, her hair, her neck. 'Beautiful…'

Sophia sighed, aware that in an odd way she felt more Jonathon's woman than she'd ever felt Godfrey's. Maybe it was only sexual, but sex was obviously a powerful force—highly possessive, over-whelmingly pleasurable and addictively satisfying. And while her brain told her that it was only lust that had impelled Jonathon to her bed tonight, that any number of women would have served his purposes as well, she could not help smiling to herself in the dark-ness, her feminine intuition telling her that she had pleased him more than any woman had for a long long time.

Sophia was lying there in his arms, their bodies still joined, when she suddenly remembered the odd com-ment he'd made about Godfrey not being her first lover. She frowned and stiffened.

'What is it?' he said. 'What's wrong? Tell me…'

'I…I was wondering why you thought I'd been with other men before Godfrey.'

The hand around her breast tightened, the caressing

palm stilling on her stomach. She felt his instant tension along a thousand different nerve-endings.

'Are you saying Godfrey *was* your first lover?' he asked tautly.

She nodded.

His silence was excruciating.

'Did you enjoy going to bed with him?' he asked at last, his voice strained. 'Did he satisfy you?'

The tone of his question suggested that he already knew Godfrey had not been the best lover in the world. Had they shared brotherly confidences? Or had Godfrey's first wife complained openly over her husband's lack of skill in the bedroom?

Sophia gritted her teeth as a bitter resentment surfaced in Godfrey's defence. Jonathon had pretended he hadn't wanted to take what should have been his brother's. But he had in the end. Quite ruthlessly. And now he wanted her to compare notes about their individual performances in the bedroom. Be damned if she would belittle her beloved Godfrey. Be damned if she would let Jonathon think he had won in everything. He might have secured her passion but he would never have her love, or her loyalty.

'Of course I enjoyed it,' she said with fierce resolve. 'I *loved* Godfrey. There is more to making love than technique, Jonathon. Sometimes, it is more a meeting of souls, rather than bodies.'

'Is that so?' he drawled, his hand moving lazily on her breast again, playing with it till she had to bite her bottom lip to stop herself from making a sound. 'I suppose you would rather I read you poetry than do this,' he taunted softly. 'Or maybe you'd prefer a spot of Mozart playing in the background.'

'Don't be cruel, Jonathon,' she choked out, tears filling her eyes.

He abandoned her, so abruptly she cried out.

'But I can be cruel,' he bit out, rolling her over onto her back and glaring down into her distressed face. 'I'm an opportunist, my darling wife. Now don't look so shocked. Didn't you realise this little tumble legally consummated our marriage? Your offer has been well and truly taken up, Sophia. I decided tonight I'd be a fool not to. You're young and beautiful and sexy, and you'll make a marvellous mother.'

He laughed into her stunned face. 'Don't tell me you'd forgotten the other possible consequence to what we've just been doing? My, you do get rather carried away once you're turned on, don't you? No need to blush, my sweet. I like my women a little wild. And you are my woman now. Make no mistake about that. Godfrey can keep your soul, and your love. I'll just take those bits he has no use for any more.'

Bending, he kissed her open mouth, showing her with a few short savage strokes of his tongue that she was indeed his in a sexual sense. But she'd known that since he'd first sent her up to this room, long before he'd joined her.

'I think you're wicked,' she said shakily when his head lifted.

'And I think you're gorgeous,' he returned, totally flustering her.

'I'm going back to my own bed now,' he went on with surprising nonchalance. 'I suggest you dispose of that ripped nightie and get some sleep. Tomorrow we're going away together.'

She blinked her shock. 'Away where?'

'I have no idea…yet. Somewhere with room service, a large bed and a spa.'

Sophia groaned silently at how her heart leapt at his words. My God, in her mind she was already there in that room, in that spa and in that bed, with him. 'But…but what will we tell your mother?' she asked, a shameful heat flushing her entire face. 'And Maud?'

'The truth, of course. We've decided to make our marriage a real one, and we're off on a belated honeymoon.'

CHAPTER ELEVEN

'WHY, that's wonderful!' Maud exclaimed when Jonathon relayed his news over breakfast. 'Isn't it wonderful, Ivy?'

'I...I suppose so,' Ivy agreed weakly, startled grey eyes moving from her son to a rapidly colouring Sophia who was busy hoping neither Ivy nor Maud had concluded the honeymoon had already started.

Sophia closed her eyes briefly against the memory. Dear God, she could hardly believe any of it herself. When she'd woken this morning, alone in her big bed, it all seemed unreal, till Jonathon had knocked then barged straight in, striding over to snatch up the totally destroyed nightie from where it still lay on the floor under the window. She had meant to pick it up but had fallen asleep.

When she clutched a sheet over her nakedness he'd laughed before ordering her to get dressed and present herself for breakfast as soon as possible, which she had. Somehow, when Jonathon said jump, you jumped.

'Where are you going?' Maud asked excitedly.

'Now, Maud,' Jonathon reproached with a rueful smile. 'No one tells where their honeymoon is. I will leave a number with Wilma with strict instructions that it is only to be used for emergencies. Sophia and I want peace and privacy.'

'Of course you do,' Maud said with a wide smile.

'We wouldn't dream of spoiling your honeymoon, would we, Ivy?'

Ivy looked as if it was only just dawning on her that Sophia had abandoned Godfrey's memory in favour of his better-looking, more successful and younger sibling. She was looking at Jonathon with a bitter resentment in her eyes, then at Sophia with a weary disappointment.

A type of resentment of her own surged through Sophia. If Godfrey wouldn't have minded, why should his mother? Besides, she just wasn't able to help herself. Jonathon had cast a spell over her, a sensual, sexual spell that was so powerful, no woman could have resisted. Even sitting across from him at this breakfast table was agony. She had to forcibly stop her eyes from feasting on him, had to block her mind from the images that kept demanding entry. Jonathon…his mouth on her breast…his hands cupping her buttocks…his body blending perfectly with hers…

She gave a little shudder of defeat and looked over at him. He looked back, his face cool and shuttered, nothing at all like that face she'd glimpsed in the moonlight, that tortured passion-filled face. God, but she would do anything to see that face again.

'Eat up, Sophia,' he suggested smoothly. 'You have some packing to do.'

Ivy came into her bedroom while Sophia was packing, her hesitant steps betraying that possibly for the first time in her life she was actually going to confront a problem rather than simply complain, criticise or put her head in the sand.

'Sophia dear,' she began gingerly.

Sophia bit down her irritation and looked up, smiling. 'Yes?'

'You…you do realise what you're doing, don't you? I mean…Jonathon is nothing like Godfrey. Godfrey was a gentle romantic soul, whereas Jonathon's just like his father. A very physical man, if you know what I mean…'

Sophia knew exactly what she meant.

Ivy put a hand on her arm. 'You're not doing this for Godfrey, are you?'

'For Godfrey?' Sophia repeated blankly.

Ivy flushed. 'Well, he did make you and Jonathon promise to marry, and…and maybe you think this is a way of keeping close to Godfrey, by being with his brother. But they are not the same, Sophia,' she warned in a panicky voice. 'It won't be at all the same! Jonathon is nothing like Godfrey. He takes after his father.'

It came to Sophia then that Jonathon's father must have been as sexual a man as Jonathon was, and that Ivy had not been able to cope. Maybe she hadn't liked sex at all. Maybe her husband's virility had frightened the life out of her. It would explain why he looked to other women to satisfy his physical needs.

Sophia looked into the woman's pale frightened face with understanding and pity. Poor thing…

But she wasn't about to let the woman think she was making some mammoth sacrifice, or that she wasn't well aware of the sort of man Jonathon was. She took Ivy's hand in both of hers and patted it back.

'Don't concern yourself so, Ivy. I realise, more than anyone, that Jonathon is nothing like Godfrey, but that doesn't mean he's not a fine man, a man I'd be proud to have as my husband. We've thought this move over very carefully. I want children and so does Jonathon. Did you know that his first wife refused to give him children, that she pretended to be trying to conceive yet all the while she was on the Pill? That's why Jonathon divorced her.'

Ivy was clearly shocked. 'I...I didn't know that. Oh, poor Jonathon...'

'Yes, poor Jonathon. Your younger son does have feelings, Ivy. He's flesh and blood the same way Godfrey was flesh and blood. Sometimes I get the feeling you forget that...'

Sophia let her words hang, giving Ivy a few moments for them to sink in.

'A boy might do without a father's approval,' she added softly, 'but there's nothing like a mother's love. At least Godfrey always had that.'

Ivy gave her a horrified look. 'But I love Jonathon too!' she insisted. 'I always have.'

'I don't doubt it, but you rarely ever show it.'

'I...I...' Ivy sank down on the edge of the bed, clearly distressed. 'Jonathon never seemed to need my love as Godfrey did...'

Sophia didn't say any more on the subject and when Ivy left the room a few minutes later she hoped she had done some good. It was ironic, in a way, that she should care about Jonathon's relationship with his mother, or that she had defended him so staunchly when underneath she wasn't so sure he was such a fine man. It was all very confusing.

'What on earth have you been saying to my mother?' the man himself said as he strode through the still-open doorway. 'I met her on the stairs just now and do you know what she did? Gave me a big hug and a kiss, told me she loved me and wished us all the happiness in the world.'

Sophia turned a blankly innocent face to Jonathon's cynically knowing one. 'Maybe she regretted her bad manners over breakfast.'

'And maybe I'm Jack the Ripper,' came his dry reply. 'You've been doing your Tammy tricks again, haven't you?'

'Tammy tricks? What are they?'

'Never mind. I'd much rather see your other tricks, the ones which begin after your clothes come off.' He pulled her into his arms and kissed her, not letting her go till she was flustered and breathless.

'The door's open,' she protested when he started to undo the buttons that ran down the front of her dress. 'Someone might come in.'

He did the buttons back up again with an angry flick of his fingers. 'What I wouldn't give for a house of my own, where I wouldn't have to care about open doors or people walking in on us. No, don't bother objecting. I have no intention of really moving out. I'm not *that* cruel. But it's why I'm taking you away today. I want you all to myself for a while,' he growled, his hand reaching out to pick up the single plait that hung down her back, encircling it round her neck then pulling her slowly towards him. 'I have a mind to see this beautiful hair spread out on a pillow.' He smiled down into her wide eyes. 'I have a mind to do a lot of things to you…'

His head bent to sip with unexpected tenderness at her lips. When they fell apart on a soft moan, inviting the invasion of his tongue, he abruptly abandoned her mouth, dropped the plait, whirled and left the room.

Her heart was pounding as she watched him go,

her thoughts in turmoil. It was all getting out of hand, this sexual power he exercised over her. Where would it all lead?

To a hotel in a seaside suburb, it seemed. A beautiful hotel which overlooked the beach and the Pacific Ocean, with a honeymoon suite so corruptively luxurious and opulent that she could do nothing but stare at it in stunned silence, thinking this must have been specifically designed to tantalise and tempt the senses.

The decorating colours were visually rich—cream, red and gold. The furniture and furnishings were equally rich, with close attention paid to how they would feel to the touch—or underneath bare skin.

The large rectangular sitting-room boasted a plush red carpet, with two cream leather sofas and a low glass coffee-table down one end, and a table setting for two at the other, right in front of the floor-to-ceiling glass doors that opened out onto a balcony with a panoramic view of the Pacific Ocean. When a button near the light switch was pressed, billowing cream curtains slid silently across the view, their semi-transparent material giving an immediate sense of subtle intimacy and sensuality.

The bedroom was not so subtle. There, the carpet was cream and twice as thick, the room dominated by a huge circular bed covered by a red velvet quilt which was eclipsed for decadence only by the cream satin sheets underneath. Not that Sophia could see the sheets at first glance, but she could see the six satin-covered pillows propped up against the red quilted headboard.

Satin sheets and *six* pillows? Sophia was shaking her head as she moved on into the bathroom, only to have her eyes almost pop out of her head as she took in its crystal chandelier, carved gold taps and huge spa which stretched from one wall to the other underneath a plate-glass window.

Jonathon, who'd closely watched her silent tour, came up behind her, curving his hands over her shoulders and pulling her back against him. She tensed immediately, thoroughly intimidated by the thought of making love in broad daylight. Or of having a bath underneath a window, even though no one could possibly see in unless they went hang-gliding past the front of the hotel.

'What do you think of the view?' he asked softly, his lips moving over one of her ears, making her shiver uncontrollably.

'It…it's very nice.'

'It looks even better at night,' Jonathon murmured in her ear. 'More romantic.'

The penny dropped and she turned to face him, her face and heart tight with instant jealousy. 'You've been here before, haven't you? With one of your women.'

'No, I haven't,' he denied. 'But Harvey has. He told me about it when I called him this morning to let him know exactly what the situation was between us.'

'What…what did Harvey say? About us, I mean.'

Jonathon laughed. 'He wasn't at all surprised. Truth is, Sophia, we were both on the end of Wilma's plottings last night. She asked Harvey to come on to you. Not that he wasn't willing, mind. And he was quite ready to follow through if I didn't react as Wilma hoped.'

Sophia was taken aback. She'd known herself that Wilma had been trying to matchmake her with

Jonathon, but to inveigle Harvey into making a play for her seemed to be going a bit far, and she said so.

'Wilma has ulterior motives in wanting us together like this,' he explained drily. 'The woman's ruthlessly ambitious. She's been wanting to be more than a secretary in Parnell Property for years. Her first step up the ladder is to get more responsibility, to have the boss have interests other than work. Marriage to someone like you would qualify as having other interests...'

He started undoing the buttons on her dress again, and this time she didn't stop him. What would have been the point? Underneath her surface coolness she wanted him to undress her, so badly that she was shaking inside. She stood there, little tremors running through her, while he took off all her clothes, thankful that he made no attempt to kiss her or caress her as he despatched each garment.

By the time she was naked before him, her eyes were dilated, her skin flushed with heat, her heart racing madly.

But with him still totally clothed she also suddenly felt shy. The temptation to cover herself was great but she resisted, standing there proudly before him, though her hands had unconsciously clenched by her sides.

'You're so lovely,' he muttered, his eyes narrowed upon her. When he ran the back of his fingers across the tips of her breasts, she gasped aloud. He groaned, and dropped his head.

'God, Sophia, do you have any idea how much I want you?'

She simply stared at him, unable to say a word.

'I need to have you right now,' he went on, sweeping her up into his arms. 'No foreplay. Nothing for you but the knowledge that I've never been like this with any woman before. I haven't a hope of controlling myself as I did last night. Believe me, I guaranteed that performance by swimming in a cold pool till I was almost exhausted. It took the edge off my need. Not so this time,' he told her as he strode back into the bedroom. 'This time I will be appallingly quick. I don't want to hurt you. I don't want to frighten you, or disappoint you. But I must do this. Don't say no.'

He didn't wait for her to say anything, she realised in retrospect. He laid her face-down across that decadent red bed, making her feel just as decadent as he eased her legs apart and briefly, but only briefly, caressed her. She grew tenser by the moment as she listened to the sounds of clothes being discarded. But mingled with the tension was excitement, the thought of his looking at her lying there, naked and spread-eagled against the red velvet, sending the blood roaring through her head.

She gasped when he finally penetrated her, her fingernails digging into the velvet at the feel of his hardness driving deep. There was no denying that her body instinctively responded, eagerly awaiting each surging thrust. For a few moments, she was soaring upwards, but then it was abruptly over, leaving her heart pounding afterwards, her flesh suspended on some plateau which was in itself surprisingly pleasurable.

She lay there, almost savouring her lack of release, glad that it was not over for her. She heard the water running in the bathroom, and then he was turning her over, lifting her into his arms and carrying her to the spa. The hot gushing water was delicious against her still aroused body. He settled her comfortably into his lap but when she finally looked up into his face, she was surprised to find he was looking down at her with worry in his eyes.

Her smile totally threw him, she could see.

'You didn't mind?' he asked, still frowning.

'It was a lovely entrée.' She snuggled into him. 'When's the main course?'

His laughter carried surprise and relief. 'You are the most delightful, beautiful, sexy, generous-hearted girl. God, but I will never get enough of you!'

'I'm glad to hear that, Jonathon,' she said, startled at her own sauciness but revelling in it. This was a side to herself she had never known existed, this wickedly erotic side. Had Jonathon corrupted her? Or was it this place?

'You take this end,' he told her abruptly, and deposited her where he'd been sitting while he slid down to put his back to the window. Any initial disappointment that he had chosen to put space between them was soon obliterated when he picked up a sponge and began washing her feet, then her calves, her knees, working his way slowly upwards, sliding between her legs as he went, his own moving under her back.

Sophia's heart began to race as she realised where he was heading and what he was going to do. It had been one thing in a darkened bedroom, but here, in a bath, in broad daylight, in front of a window?

She swallowed several times while he washed her very intimately, but when he discarded the sponge and lifted her to his mouth, she squeezed her eyes tightly shut. Her back arched as her head tilted back, her hair fanning out on the surface of the water.

I shouldn't be allowing this, she told herself agitatedly. It was the ultimate in surrender, the ultimate in wanton behaviour.

But he's your husband, another voice said. And you're his wife. There's no such thing as a wanton wife...

Too late again, anyway. Her breath was catching, her blood firing, her body already on the edge of release. Sophia's eyes shut even tighter as she gave herself up to the sensations, her mouth gasping open. No use in fighting them. No use in fighting him. Oh, God...

The following two days would live forever in Sophia's memory as the most amazing forty-eight hours. Within no time, she ceased to question her actions, particularly her sexual responses to Jonathon and whatever he did or suggested. Soon, everything seemed incredibly normal and natural.

Perhaps this was because Jonathon was so loving, even when their encounters became a little torrid. Afterwards, he would always hold her with such tenderness, saying the most incredibly complimentary things. Praise was a powerful aphrodisiac, she found. Whatever he asked of her, she gave willingly, eager to please him, thrilling to the sounds of *his* pleasure much more than her own.

Her education was also greatly expanded. She found out that pillows had more uses than for resting heads on, that leather was as sensuous under naked flesh as satin sheets, that a woman could have many more climaxes in one lovemaking session than a man, but most of all, that Jonathon had to be the most wonderful, considerate, imaginative lover in the whole world.

They ate dinner in the nude both nights, room service setting up a table, complete with candles and champagne. Each time, Sophia became more than a little tipsy, so much so that after dinner, when she lay naked and replete in Jonathon's arms, she became rather talkative, telling him everything about her life so far.

He was a most sympathetic listener, especially when she told him about her father dying when she was only a little girl, her much loved schoolteacher father who had doted on her, read her stories and been such an important part of her young life. By the second night, she'd moved on to her years at the farm after her mother had married Joe, Jonathon saying all the right words to soothe these fresher and more turbulent memories. But when she tried to move on to her time with Godfrey, he stopped her dead straight away.

'No, Sophia,' he told her curtly. 'I do not wish to hear about what you shared with Godfrey. I realise you think he would understand all this…' His hand swept in a savage wave over their naked bodies. 'You could be right but I still have my doubts. I justify myself with the excuse that, in a perverse way, I am doing what my brother asked—protecting you.'

He laughed at her shocked expression.

'Oh, yes, Sophia, New Year's Eve showed me all too clearly that you had recovered from your grief at losing Godfrey and his baby, and that you were in danger of becoming a ready victim for some clever, conscienceless man. You're an extremely lovely and very desirable girl, full of life and love and passion. You needed a man in your bed that night as much as I needed a woman in mine. I chose to solve both our problems this way rather than let you loose in a world which is hard on naïvité and innocence.'

Again she looked startled and again he laughed.

'Don't think that anything we have done together in this hotel suite makes you any less innocent, or less naïve. So you know a few more sexual positions. So you know some more sophisticated ways to please a man. Neither makes you a woman of the world, Sophia. All it does is make you more vulnerable to the dark side of men, and more able to be exploited. Now I think you should get some sleep. First thing in the morning I'll be taking you home. The honeymoon, I think, is over.'

He rolled away from her and Sophia lay there beside him for ages, wondering if *he* was the conscienceless man he spoke of. Even if he wasn't, wasn't he happily exploiting this new-found sexuality of hers, hadn't he still made her a victim, vulnerable to his desires and his dark side?

She was lying there some time later when he rolled over and pulled her roughly to him. 'I hate women who don't go to sleep when I tell them to,' he muttered, his mouth covering hers. Sophia struggled with the urge to push him away, to tell him to go to hell. But it seemed she was some way off being able to deny herself, along with him.

Still, she would not let him have it all his own way. She did push him, but only on to his back, where she straddled him, her hair falling round her face in a dark curtain. He'd shown her how to make love to him this way, shown her exactly what drove him crazy. She needed to drive him crazy now, needed to see a shift in power in their relationship, even if it was only temporary.

'No, don't,' he groaned when she'd taken him to the edge a second time, only to retreat, forcibly bringing him back with her.

'But I thought this was how you liked it, darling,' she taunted breathlessly.

'I'll darling you, you little bitch.'

How he managed to reverse their positions so quickly, she had no idea, but suddenly she was flat on her back, her arms held wide in a brutal grip, her body impaled beneath his.

'And now we'll see who's boss around here,' he growled.

'Yes, we will, won't we?' she countered wickedly, using her internal muscles with ruthless resolve to propel him swiftly and savagely with her into the abyss.

CHAPTER TWELVE

SOPHIA and Jonathon were sitting at the table eating breakfast, Sophia in her bathrobe, Jonathon wearing white boxer shorts, when the telephone rang. The sound was so foreign to the last two days that they exchanged surprised looks for a moment.

'Probably Reception,' Jonathon said on the second ring. 'I called them while you were in the shower and asked them to make up the bill. Perhaps there's some query about the amount of champagne we've consumed.'

Jonathon rose and walked across the red carpet towards the telephone table. Sophia watched him admiringly, thinking how she no longer found his body or his size in any way intimidating. She loved both. Neither did she find his autocratic manner as intimidating any longer.

She had a feeling that in future, whenever he barked an order or scowled at her in disapproval, she would not quiver with fear but smile wryly to herself. For he was all bark and no bite, her husband. Passionate, yes. And as physical as his mother had warned her. But beneath his aggressive and sometimes difficult personality lay a depth of caring and consideration which he could not always hide. Sophia didn't think she would be afraid of him ever again.

Her musing was interrupted by his sudden snarling into the receiver.

'For pity's sake, Wilma, couldn't you have handled

that yourself? I would hardly classify a revised tender deadline as an emergency.'

When Sophia shot him a startled and perhaps slightly reproachful look, he astonished her by winking, while at the same time continuing with his dressing-down of the hapless Wilma.

'I suppose I'll just have to cut my honeymoon short and come into the office,' he said after an impatient click of his tongue. 'If this is an example of your decision-making skills, madam, then I think I'll have to reconsider my idea of offering you a promotion. No, no, it's too late now. I've lost faith in your judgement. I'll be there by one. Make sure you're in the office and not out buying one of those ghastly cottage cheese sandwiches you live on.'

He hung up, then grinned a malevolent grin.

Sophia was appalled at him. He'd been planning to go into the office anyway, after dropping her home later in the morning. 'Oh, Jonathon, that was cruel,' she chided as he came back to sit down at the table, still smiling with evil satisfaction.

'Cruel, my foot!' he scoffed, waving a dismissive hand. 'That interfering, manipulating witch needs taking down a peg or two. I haven't forgiven her yet for tarting you up on New Year's Eve, then sending hot-handed Harvey in to rile me up further. The woman's insidious.'

'You *like* her,' Sophia pointed out indignantly. 'And I was *not* tarted up! I looked very nice.'

'You were naked under that dress.'

'I was not naked! I…I simply didn't wear a bra.'

'With you, that's enough to make any red-blooded man's hair stand on end. Not to mention other unfortunate parts of his anatomy.'

'Don't be so crude,' she countered, flustered when she felt an embarrassed heat gathering in her cheeks. There she was, just a minute ago, thinking she was cured of Jonathon being able to rattle her. But it seemed she'd been wrong. 'I thought you liked my body,' she said, sounding rather sulky and childish in her irritation.

'You know I do. Why do you think I've kept you naked these past two days? Which reminds me, why are you all smothered up in that infernal robe? Take the damned thing off.'

'I will not,' came her indignant refusal, determined not to keep acting like a good little sexual slave, even if she had enjoyed it. 'Since you decided the honeymoon is over then my days of sitting naked at a table with you are also over!'

His eyes narrowed dangerously, and she did indeed quiver inside. But she was determined not to show it on the outside. 'I…I enjoy making love with you, Jonathon,' she said with a somewhat shaky attempt at firmness. 'But there is a time and place for everything. Godfrey wouldn't have minded your making me your real wife, but he would not have wanted you to corrupt me.'

'*Corrupt* you? You think being naked with your husband is *corrupting* you?'

'There's naked and there's naked,' she threw back, even as she realised she was becoming aroused underneath the voluminous bathrobe. This highly unwanted development heated her temper along with her blood. 'There's also husbands and husbands! I'm well aware you don't love me, Jonathon, but I would still like to feel that when we are intimate, it's like making love, not having sex. I want to feel like your wife, not a...a whore!'

Good God, whatever had possessed her to say such a stupid thing? Not once over the past few days had she ever felt like a whore, whatever it was a whore felt like! She had felt slightly wicked, and deliciously sexy, that was all. She had been with Jonathon every step of the way.

He was sitting very still, his face ashen under her accusation. 'You think I've treated you like a whore?' he asked, his tone grim.

Sophia couldn't bring herself to take back her lie, but neither could she go on with it. Suddenly—and she had no idea why—she burst into tears. Now Jonathon was looking totally appalled. He went to get up, possibly to come round and comfort her. But then he seemed to think better of it and sat back down again.

'I...I'm sorry,' he said bleakly. 'I had no idea. I thought...I hoped...' His obvious unhappiness propelled her to her feet. She raced round and knelt beside his chair, clasping his nearest knee and resting her wet cheek against his thigh.

'I don't think that,' she sobbed. 'I don't know why I said it. I don't know why I'm crying.' She looked up through streaming lashes, pleading with him for the answers.

His hand trembled as it stroked her hair back from where it had fallen around her face and his thigh. 'I think,' he said slowly, 'that you might be feeling a little guilty. About Godfrey,' he added when she blinked her bewilderment.

'But why would I feel guilty?' she asked in all innocence.

'Because he's not here and I am. Because you've been sharing with me the sort of passion you might prefer to be sharing with him.'

'But I never shared this sort of passion with Godfrey,' she blurted out. 'I…I loved him but I…I never felt the things with him that I feel when I'm with you!'

Oddly enough, her declaration didn't make him look any happier. 'I know,' he confessed in an extremely cynical tone. 'It's called sex, Sophia. Or desire. Or lust. I have a good record at inspiring such feelings in women. Don't set too much store by it. Don't confuse it for anything else, and for pity's sake don't start thinking you've fallen in love with me. I don't want your love. That belongs to Godfrey. What I do want from you is your body in my bed every night, and a baby some time in the future. Since you don't seem to mind either of those prospects, then there's no need for any of these tears, is there?'

'N-no, I suppose not,' she said with all the uncertainty in her heart, sighing as she settled her still damp cheek back down on his thigh.

But what if the words Harvey had spoken to her on their wedding-day had come true? What if she *had* fallen in love with Godfrey's very handsome and very sexy younger brother?

Such questions brought instant dismay. How could she have? She still loved Godfrey with all her heart and soul. She had not forgotten him in her mind and memory, not for a moment.

Her body, however, had other ideas. It loved Jonathon.

No, no, she agonised. This couldn't be love, this awful churning in her stomach, this wish to place her

lips to the flesh beneath her cheek, this yearning to
hold Jonathon so close to her heart that she could feel
his own heart beating under hers. It was what he just
said it was. Sex. Desire. Lust. I've fallen into lust, she
accepted bleakly, not love.

An instinctive aversion to this thought had her
scrambling to her feet, away from temptation, away
from Jonathon. 'I…I'll go and pack,' she said agitatedly, unable to meet his eyes.

She heard him give a weary sigh as she hurried
away into the bedroom, heard him mutter something
which sounded like, 'The honeymoon is, indeed,
over.'

'You're very quiet these days,' Wilma commented to
Sophia on their way to their weekly shopping excur-
sion. 'Aren't you happy with Jonathon?'

Six weeks had passed since Jonathon had dropped
his bride home at Parnell Hall and decamped to the
office for the rest of the day. Six weeks during which
the two things he'd said he wanted of her had come
to pass. Sophia had spent every night in his bed and
she was pregnant; had been, according to the doctor's
estimation last week, since New Year's Eve.

Jonathon's reaction to the news had been unexpectedly subdued. She'd gone to tell him in the study
after dinner—he still retired there to work every evening, sometimes not joining her in bed till well after
midnight. On those nights, he made no attempt to
touch her when he first slipped between the sheets,
but invariably, at some time during the night, their
bodies would touch and ignite with a type of spon-
taneous combustion. Jonathon's lovemaking had none
of the wild imagination he'd employed on their hon-

eymoon, but it seemed to have become more urgent, more impassioned, if that was possible.

His first reaction to the news of the baby was dead silence and a rather remote stare. Then he cleared his throat and shifted some of the papers around the desk before looking up at her again, this time with a still disappointingly bland look on his face. 'And are you pleased?' he asked.

'Very,' she said truthfully. 'I've always wanted children.'

He nodded, his mouth curving into an oddly wry smile.

'I thought you wanted children too,' she blurted out. 'I thought you'd be happy about it!'

'I'm very happy about it,' he said.

'You don't seem to be.'

'I'm just a little shocked that you got pregnant so quickly, that's all. Still, I suppose, in the circum- stances, it was a likely occurrence...' He frowned down at the floor for a few seconds before slowly lifting his eyes back to hers. 'Do you want to move back into your own bedroom?'

She was startled, both by the question and the hard- ness that had come to his face, and those beautiful blue eyes of his. 'Why...why would I want to do that?'

'I thought the doctor might advise it, in the light of your previous miscarriage.'

'No, he insists I don't do anything different to what I normally would. He...he specifically said there's no reason to abstain from normal lovemaking.'

'What's normal lovemaking?' Jonathon asked drily.

Sophia was flustered by the question. 'I...I didn't

ask. Normal, I suppose. I...I don't know.' She was blushing, yet didn't know why.

'I'll give him a ring and see what he means. Meanwhile, I think you'd better sleep in your old room.'

'But I don't want to!' she protested.

'It's only a temporary measure.'

'What will Maud and your mother think?'

'They won't think a thing after you tell them about the baby, except that I'm being a very considerate and sensitive husband. Don't make a fuss, Sophia. It is my job to look after you and your baby's welfare. Don't make it difficult for me.'

She stared at him, thinking it was going to be difficult for her as well. The hours spent together in bed at night were the only time they were alone, the only time she had respite from the feelings that welled up within her every night over dinner. She would sit across the table and eat him up with her eyes, having missed him terribly all day, but he would hardly even look at her, hardly speak to her. It was no wonder their time in bed meant so much. Now he was going to deny her the only part of the day she enjoyed, the part she looked forward to with every fibre of her being.

Yet she could hardly argue with him in the face of his common-sense consideration, even if it did seem unnecessary. She was only six and a half weeks pregnant at the most. How could making love at this stage be a danger to the baby growing inside her?

'Sophia, why won't you answer me?' Wilma went on impatiently. 'Is Jonathon being mean to you?'

Sophia snapped out of it to turn a shocked face her

friend's way. 'No, of course he isn't. He's been kindness itself since I told him about the baby last week.'

'Well I'm glad to hear that, because he's been like a bear with a sore head at the office. Lord knows what it would take to please that man consistently. He has a beautiful young wife who's going to have his baby, yet he's been acting as if he's got a permanent toothache.'

Wilma's words sent a huge wave of satisfaction flooding through Sophia. So he was missing their nights together as much as she was! She hugged the knowledge to herself, however. Wilma had done enough manipulating of their lives already. If she found out her protégées weren't sleeping together she would come up with some devilishly wicked plan to put things right.

Sophia knew how Jonathon hated that kind of thing. Now that she knew he was suffering as much as she was, she could almost bear the situation. But she wanted to kill that stupid damned doctor for telling Jonathon that, if his wife was unduly worried, they could abstain from sex till after she passed the three-month mark.

'I'll be glad to see the back of him for a while,' Wilma pronounced crossly.

Sophia's head snapped round. 'What do you mean? Is Jonathon going away?'

'You mean you don't know? God, isn't that just like him! Yes, he's flying up to the Gold Coast again tomorrow. Lord knows why. We haven't a prayer of getting that casino job no matter what he does.'

'What casino job?'

Wilma flashed her a pitying look. 'He really does keep you in the dark, doesn't he? If you don't watch it, you'll end up like one of those poor Mafia wives, seeing no evil, hearing no evil, speaking no evil. Now don't look so down-in-the-mouth, darling; if you want to know something just ask dear old Wilma. I'm a mine of information.'

'In that case, tell me about this casino job.'

'Well, we were one of the companies who put in a tender to the Queensland government for a new casino they want built on Gold Coast. I suggested to Jonathon that we should lower our bid, but no, the arrogant fool thinks being cheap is not the way to success. I tried telling him times had changed since his father built the company's reputation of quality alone. He's probably hoping that if he wines and dines the right people, he might be able to sway them at the nth moment.'

'But you don't think so.'

'No, I would have written that deal right off and moved on. To be honest, I'm surprised he's dug his heels in on this and insists on one last try. In my book, its dead money and dead time.'

Sophia sat there, in the passenger seat of Wilma's car, feeling sick. There was no doubt in her mind that Jonathon's trip away had nothing to do with that casino job. Any wining and dining he would do would be opposite some absolutely stunning-looking and highly sophisticated woman, the sort who only needed superficial romancing to end up in bed with a man like Jonathon. How many days would he need, she wondered bitterly, to rid himself of his growing frustrations? Two? Three?

She guessed three. That might hold him till after she had passed the three-month deadline.

'Have you booked his return flight?' she asked in a taut voice.

'Yes. He's tentatively coming back on Tuesday night, but he did say he might change that till Wednesday if he needs the extra day.'

Three days. Maybe four. He must really be in a bad way, she thought savagely.

Sophia wanted to scratch his handsome face to death, wanted to mar his beauty so that no woman would ever look at him again. Her jealousy was so painful, her envy so overwhelming, that she had to bite her tongue to stop herself from screaming.

'I suppose he hasn't mentioned his plan to take you out to dinner tomorrow night yet either, has he?'

Sophia's mouth fell open. Not once since their marriage had Jonathon taken her anywhere. They'd had Harvey and his latest girlfriend over to dinner one night. But, other than that, they had not socialised as a married couple in any way.

Not that Sophia had minded. She'd long come to terms with her being a home body. She wasn't one of those girls who wanted a career, or the bright lights. She enjoyed far simpler pursuits. Reading, going to the movies, watching television, gardening, cooking.

A real Tammy character, she'd come to appreciate after seeing one of the old Tammy movies on television and finally understanding what Jonathon had meant that day. Tammy was a country girl whose simple homespun ways endeared her to the hearts of the wealthy society family she comes to live with. Of course, fiction gave way to fact in her own case. Whereas Tammy won the love of the son in the family, all Jonathon felt for her was a lust that was easily transferred on to any other desirable female.

'I made the booking at the restaurant for him myself,' Wilma prattled on, 'so that's how I know. I think he's feeling guilty about going away, especially after working such long hours over the past few weeks. Of course, things aren't going too well in the real estate business at the moment. I think he's worried, which might go some way to explaining his bad moods.'

Sophia frowned at this. 'Jonathon's having money worries?'

Wilma laughed. 'Hardly. His family owns huge holdings in other much safer pies than real estate. Parnell Property Developments could fold tomorrow and Jonathon would survive. Handsomely!'

Sophia shook her head. It was the handsome part that bothered her the most. Would she feel this way about Jonathon if he were as ordinary-looking as Godfrey had been? Was his success with women all bound up in that superbly structured face and those compelling blue eyes? She didn't know. Neither did she know what she felt for Jonathon any more. If it was just lust, then it was growing stronger, not weaker. Wasn't lust supposed to wear off after a while?

'What kind of restaurant is it?' she asked wearily, her confusion seeming to drain all the anger and fight out of her.

'Now don't be like that. Jonathon wouldn't go away if he didn't feel he had to. The man's besotted with you!'

Sophia couldn't help the dry look she darted over at Wilma.

'He *is*!' the secretary insisted. 'And I should know. I saw him through his obsession with Charmaine. But this is different. Do you know he has a photograph of you on his desk? It's one he took of you on Christmas Day with the camera you gave him. I see him looking at it sometimes when he thinks no one is watching and the expression on his face almost moves me to tears. As for you, Miss Muffet, you don't fool me for a minute. You try to be cool when you talk about Jonathon but it's plain as the nose on *my* face that you adore him.

'Of course I realised that ages before the devil took you to bed, which was why I had to make sure he did! It's only natural that you adore him even more now. Dear old Charmaine would be spitting chips if she saw you two together. I'll bet she thinks she left behind one broken-hearted man. Instead, he has a beautiful wife whom he loves to death and who's having his baby. What more could a man want to be happy?'

Sophia was speechless. What more indeed, if it was true? Could it be so? Was it possible? Did they love one another?

'Have I embarrassed you?' Wilma asked when Sophia remained thoughtfully silent.

She thought of confiding in Wilma then dismissed it. 'No, no, of course not. What kind of restaurant is it you've booked?'

'Oh, very swank. It's not far from Parnell Hall, actually. It's attached to a five-star motel and extremely popular, which is why I booked early.'

'How should I dress?'

'That black number you wore to the party wouldn't go astray.'

'I think not, Wilma. I'll splurge and buy something new, something more…subtle.'

'Ooh, I like that. Subtle. What on earth are you up to, Mrs Parnell?'

Sophia merely smiled.

CHAPTER THIRTEEN

'YOU look very lovely tonight,' Jonathon said as he handed her into the passenger seat of his black Jaguar. 'Very…sophisticated.'

He could not have used a more pleasing word. It was the look she'd been striving for when she'd bought the elegantly tailored cream silk suit. Sophistication. The jacket was especially slimming, the long line minimising her breasts and hips, while still giving her a very feminine shape. Her hair was compressed tightly into a French roll, a curl hanging in front of each ear to soften the severe hairstyle, as did the gold and pearl drop earrings. Her cream shoes exactly matched the cream of the suit, and she carried a small gold evening purse.

The whole outfit, plus underwear, had hardly put a dent in her generous expense account, but it still seemed an enormous amount to her to spend on clothes. Still, she staunchly blocked any guilt over the extravagance. She would do anything, spend anything, if it brought Jonathon to her bed tonight. But she wasn't confident of success. Not at all.

'New perfume?' Jonathon asked after sliding in behind the wheel and sniffing the air in the enclosed cabin.

'In a way,' came her seemingly smooth reply. 'You had Wilma buy it for me months ago but I opened it for the first time tonight. I kept it for a special occasion.'

'How sweet,' he said.

Sophia swallowed and turned her face away from him to stare through the passenger window as he reversed out of the garages. Her nerves were becoming steadily worse. Jonathon was looking absolutely gorgeous tonight in a dark blue suit, pale blue shirt and burgundy silk tie. He was also being very charming, but in the most underminingly remote fashion, acting more like a hired escort than a supposedly besotted husband taking his wife out for a romantic dinner the last night before he was going away.

Wilma was wrong. Sophia could see that now. Jonathon was not in love with her. She could not explain the photograph business except that, somehow, Jonathon's secretary had got that wrong too. She must have misinterpreted his expression when he'd looked at it.

Dismay settled on her heart like a cold damp sponge. Wilma had at least been right about one thing. She did adore Jonathon Parnell. Maybe it was still a bad case of lust, but Sophia doubted it. It was not desire that was impelling her to try to seduce her husband tonight, but desperation. She needed to stop him from going to another woman's arms. She couldn't bear to think of it. She just couldn't bear it.

The restaurant was probably very, very nice, but Sophia hardly noticed its décor. The menu, too, was no doubt splendid, but she found herself duplicating Jonathon's order because she was too agitated to study it properly.

It was as well she liked seafood, since their meal started with oysters, then moved on to a lobster dish with an unusual sauce. The wine was white, chilled and dry. She drank it in gulps rather than sips, bringing frowning looks from Jonathon before he actually said something.

'I thought Godfrey had taught you about wine,' was his blunt comment. 'It's not meant to be downed like root beer. Keep that up and you'll be under the table before we get to dessert.'

Quite frankly, that was where Sophia would have liked to be at that moment. Under the table.

But her discomfort was nothing to how she felt a minute or two later when she noticed her husband's attention riveted on a blonde woman seated by herself against a front window. The light from some neon signs outside was shining on her strikingly beautiful and sultry face, highlighting the honey-golden colour of her glorious hair, as well as the well tanned cleavage on display above the deeply cut bodice of a skintight white dress.

As though sensing Jonathon's eyes on her, the blonde's head turned. Her eyes locked on to his and simply refused to let go. Her smile, when it came, was soft, sensuous and insidiously seductive, her lips falling sexily apart before the mouth lifted into a delicious curve. Sophia could not tell the colour of her eyes from that distance but she was sure they would be blue, just as she was sure that the woman's name would be Charmaine.

'Why don't you go over and talk to her?' she snapped. 'Since you're so wrapped.'

Jonathon's eyes carried surprise as they turned back to her rapidly reddening face. 'It *is* your ex-wife, isn't it?'

'Yes,' he admitted. 'It's Charmaine.'

Perhaps it was the wine which had loosened her tongue, but, once having started, Sophia found she couldn't stop. All the jealousy in her heart seemed to pour out in an acid tirade.

'Did you love her very much, Jonathon? I'd like to know. Was she good in bed? I wonder if you would have been able to stop making love to her if she had conceived your child. But above all, I wonder if you were as unfaithful to her as you're going to be to me this coming week?'

His stare vibrated with shock, and then anger. 'What the hell are you talking about it? I have no intention of being unfaithful to you, either this week or any other week.'

'Oh? Are you denying now that during all those trips away before Christmas you didn't sleep with other women?'

'That was different,' he hissed under his breath. 'And you damned well know it.'

Their argument might have continued if Sophia hadn't seen Charmaine move out of the corner of her eye. My God, the woman was actually going to come over. The hide of her! The gall!

Sophia lanced her with visual daggers as she sashayed over, undulating every inch of that tall unforgettable figure for Jonathon's benefit, as well as every other male's in the restaurant.

'I hope I'm not interrupting anything,' Charmaine said with saccharine sweetness, stroking a long blonde lock back over her shoulder from where it had fallen into the valley between her breasts, a valley which deepened as she leant artfully on the table in Jonathon's direction.

Sophia watched the obvious gesture with cynical disdain. Were men really taken in by creatures like this? If she was what Jonathon preferred, then he wasn't the man she thought he was.

'I just couldn't let you leave without coming over and saying hello,' she purred, totally ignoring Sophia's presence. 'As you can see, I'm back here in Australia, all on my lonesome ownsome. Naturally, my marriage to Chuck didn't work out. How could it, when I was still in love with you, darling?'

Sophia sucked in a stunned breath and was about to tell the woman where she could take her outrageously rude and brazen self when Jonathon got in first.

'Which just goes to show that you're still as big a liar as you always were, Charmaine,' he said in a voice dipped in ice. 'Now, if you don't mind, I'm having a quiet romantic dinner with my wife and we'd appreciate some privacy.'

Charmaine turned a colour between grey and green before turning viciously cold eyes upon Sophia. 'This sweet young thing is your wife?' Her low laughter was vile. 'That was quick, Jonathon. Still, it was only to be expected, I suppose. But a *brunette*? You told me once you weren't at all attracted to brunettes. You also told me that...' She broke off, giggling coquettishly. 'Well perhaps I'd better not relate any more of the things you told me, otherwise there might be another divorce on the horizon. Ah, I see my coffee's arrived. Ta-ta, darling. She *is* sweet, though. Enjoy.'

Sophia watched the woman undulate back across the room with turmoil in her heart.

'Don't let that bitch upset you,' Jonathon snarled.

'I...I...' Sophia rose onto unsteady legs. 'I have to go to the ladies',' she finished in a rush, almost knocking over her chair as she scuttled away in what she supposed was a very unsophisticated haste. But she didn't care. She couldn't sit there a moment longer. She certainly couldn't engage in a seemingly normal conversation with Jonathon at that moment. Maybe, by the time she returned, that hateful creature would have left, and maybe she might have regained control over her silly self. To find herself stammering again was mortifying in the extreme.

The ladies' room was blessedly empty, Sophia expelling a shuddering sigh as she leant against the twin vanity-units, her shoulders and head drooping. The door opening and shutting behind her sent her eyes jerking up in the mirror, only to find Charmaine's blazing blue eyes lying in wait for her. There was no smile on her face this time, and she didn't look half so lovely without it. In fact, she looked ugly, her mouth twisting with hate as she stood there with her back against the door, pretending to inspect Sophia.

'God, you're not even tall!' she sneered. 'Jonathon likes his women tall, didn't you know that? Tall and blonde…like me. With a decent bust…like me. I'll tell you why he married you, little miss nobody. Because he wanted someone young and compliant whom he could install in that ghastly old barn of a house as his private brood mare.'

Sophia stood there, frozen, when the woman came forward, grabbed her arm and spun her round. 'But don't think he won't be having other women on the side,' she raved on, her face contorted with fury. 'Women like me. Maybe even me! Don't go thinking that act out there means a damned thing. He hasn't forgotten me. He'll *never* forget me. I gave him better sex—and more of it—than any man has ever had.

Wait till you become pregnant and your body is gross.
He won't come near you with a bargepole.'

Something snapped inside Sophia, something quite
frightening. She wrenched her arm out of
Charmaine's hold and slapped her so hard the other
woman screamed and reeled backwards against one
of the cubicle doors, clasping her cheek and gaping
at Sophia. 'How dare you hit me?' she yelled. 'I...I'll
sue you for assault!'

'And I'll sue you for slander!' Sophia yelled right
back. 'My Jonathon wouldn't dream of being unfaithful to me. You know nothing, you stupid malicious
slut. You're everything he despises in a woman. He
would rather have *one* night with me than a million
nights with you, because he loves me.'

Charmaine laughed. 'Jonathon Parnell doesn't love
any woman.'

'Maybe he didn't once but he does now,' Sophia
argued. 'He loves me. And I love him,' she added,
her heart contracting as the truth of this last bit hit
home very hard. She'd suspected as much for some
time, but this incident underlined just how deeply she
did love him. If she lost him, she would die. Of
course, she didn't have the same faith in Jonathon's
love for her. Charmaine was probably right. It seemed
likely that the man who had been husband to both of
them was not capable of the kind of love Sophia
craved.

'What's going on in here?'

Both women turned to face Jonathon standing in
the doorway.

'Your bitch of a wife hit me,' Charmaine whined,
rubbing her cheek.

One of Jonathon's eyebrows shot up as he glanced

over at a flushed but unrepentant Sophia. 'I dare say you deserved it,' he drawled. 'When Sophia hits someone, they usually do. I suggest you keep out of her way, Charmaine. She's not nearly as meek and mild as she looks. Come, darling...' He extended a hand towards Sophia. 'I've fixed up the bill. I think we'll have our coffee back at home. Goodnight, Charmaine. If I ever see you again, it will be too soon.'

Sophia's fingers were trembling as Jonathon's large hand enclosed them. Somehow, she managed to ignore all the curious eyes that turned their way as Jonathon escorted her from the ladies' room and then the restaurant. How much had they heard, she wondered? How much had *Jonathon* heard?

'Did you believe her?' he asked during the drive home.

'Believe what?' Sophia hedged.

'Whatever lies she told you about me.'

Sophia smothered a relieved sigh. So he hadn't really heard anything. Their argument had probably been muffled by the heavy wooden door. No doubt it was Charmaine's scream that had brought Jonathon to investigate.

'I wouldn't believe anything that slut said,' Sophia said firmly. 'She has no integrity.'

Jonathon chuckled. 'That is a very Godfreyish expression.'

'Is it?' Sophia was startled.

'Yes. According to Godfrey, very few people have integrity.'

'He may have been right,' she muttered.

'Are you referring to me?'

Sophia said nothing.

Jonathon sighed. 'Do you honestly think I would have anything to do with that woman ever again?'

'I...I'm not sure,' she admitted at last.

'But you *are* sure I would have extra-marital affairs. You certainly implied as much earlier on.'

Again Sophia said nothing.

'Goddamn it, answer me!'

Tears pricked at her eyes. 'Yes,' she said in a small, broken voice. 'Yes...I am.'

He swore as she had never heard him swear before. He yanked the Jaguar into their driveway with a face like thunder, still muttering away under his breath.

There was no mention of coffee as he steered her inside, up the stairs and into her bedroom, Sophia having subsided into a fearful silence at Jonathon's black mood.

'Now,' he ground out once the door was safely shut and he'd plonked her down on the end of the bed. 'I want you to simply sit and listen. I do not want you to say a single word. Not a single word!'

Sophia nodded, happy not to have to talk.

He began pacing back and forth across the room, muttering darkly to himself. Finally, he stopped in front of the window, his hands gripping the sill as he drew in then expelled a shuddering breath. Finally, he turned to face her again, folding his arms and making a big effort to relax his tensely held shoulders.

'I want to tell you a story,' he said, his voice surprisingly low and controlled. 'About a man who married a woman he loved to distraction, but the woman was incapable of loving him back as he wanted to be loved...'

Sophia's eyes rounded. Was he talking about *their* marriage? Could he be confessing that he...?

'The man was my father,' he went on abruptly, totally obliterating her suddenly soaring hopes. 'The woman, my mother…'

Sophia's interest was captured, despite her disappointment. She straightened, her eyes fixed on Jonathon who was not looking at her but at some vague point on the far wall.

'My mother, you see, did not like the physical side of marriage. She found it…distasteful. She found my father's desires…disgusting. He confessed as much to me when I tackled him later in life on his many and increasingly less discreet affairs. But it was only when he told me the full story that I finally understood the puzzle that was my mother…'

Sophia couldn't say she was surprised by what she was hearing. She'd already suspected that Ivy had found her husband's obviously high sex drive an intimidating factor in their relationship.

'Apparently, my mother tolerated what she considered Dad's excessive demands till after she became pregnant with Godfrey. It was then that she started refusing him. Dad told me he was devastated, but since he loved my mother he tried not to stray, thinking that maybe after the baby was born things would get back to normal. Instead, she found every excuse she could think of not to resume marital relations. A year went by, then two. The strain of enforced celibacy began to take its toll and one night, in a fit of frustrated rage, he forced himself on her…quite violently…'

Sophia was shocked, yet moved. The poor man…the poor woman…what a horrible mismatch of natures!

'The result was me,' Jonathon said bleakly, 'plus

the end of all physical intimacy between them. To add insult to injury, I came out the spitting image of Dad. Can you wonder that she found it hard to love me, or that she has always favoured Godfrey?'

Sophia wanted to cry. Oh, poor, poor Jonathon...

'But your mother does love you, Jonathon,' she insisted. 'She really does.'

He nodded slowly. 'Yes, I actually think she does...now. I've gone up in her estimation considerably since I married you. But during my growing-up years she obviously found it hard to look at me and not...remember. I dare say I didn't help matters by following in Dad's footsteps in every way. I even committed the ultimate sin of liking sex as much as he did. That was the final straw around this house!

'It wasn't till I was a man and my father explained everything that I finally no longer blamed my mother for her attitude towards me. But I did blame her for making her husband turn elsewhere for what he should have received at home, quite willingly. I admit he was no saint. He had faults, not the least of which was his handling of Godfrey. Being a male of the old school, he didn't understand Godfrey's sensitive and slightly feminine nature, bossing and bullying him unmercifully, thinking he was making a man out of him.'

Jonathon began shaking his head. 'I have to admit Godfrey frustrated me too. I couldn't count the number of times I had to go to bat for him in the schoolyard. My father could never understand why Godfrey didn't fight back himself, why it was always me with the black eyes and not my older brother. When Godfrey wanted ballet lessons, my father enrolled him in boxing classes. When he wanted to do art, he had business studies rammed down his throat.'

Jonathon's laugh was rueful. 'But he did suffer for his transgressions, believe me. Guilt over his extra-marital affairs made him eventually turn to drink, and it was the drink that killed him. I loved that old bastard, Sophia. And I understood his pain. I vowed over his grave to never marry any woman who wouldn't give me everything I wanted in life. My idea of a married Utopia was plenty of sex interspersed with a large family. I wanted nothing of gentility or timidity. I wanted passion and no inhibitions at all...

'And so...I married Charmaine.'

When his face took on a faraway look, Sophia felt impelled to speak, driven by a jealousy that was as fierce as it was tormented.

'She...she said she gave you better sex—and more of it—than any man has ever had...'

His eyes turned to focus on her. Hard glittering eyes.

'I would give up every night I spent with her for one moment with you.'

She gasped as he walked swiftly over to her and pulled her up into his arms. 'I have not been unfaithful to you,' he whispered harshly into her hair. 'I have no intention of being unfaithful to you; I am going away tomorrow on business, nothing more.'

'But...but you did sleep with other women when you went away before,' she insisted shakily, afraid to naïvely believe all that he was saying. For all his ardour, there were still no words of love.

He drew back, peering down at her with anguish and regret in his gaze. 'Sometimes,' he groaned. 'Yes,

sometimes. But that was because I was terrified of
what I might do to you.'

'To me?'

'Damnation, Sophia, you're not that innocent! You
must have realised how much I wanted you that night
on the stairs. Why the hell do you think I took myself
off the very next day? I had to do something, anything
to stop myself from trying to take what I had no right
to.'

'I...I see...'

'No, you probably don't see,' he muttered, his
shoulders sagging as he turned away from her. 'How
could you possibly?'

'But...but you have a right now, Jonathon,' she
whispered, reaching up to place her small hands on
his wide shoulders, to rest her face against his back.
'We're man and wife now, and I want you as much
as you want me. Stay with me tonight. Make love to
me. I...I need you, Jonathon.'

He spun round on a tortured groan, sweeping her
hard against him and kissing her till they were both
shaking with desire. 'Are you sure it's all right?' he
rasped.

'Yes, of course it is. It always was.'

'I was worried I might be too rough with you, that
I might do something...dangerous...'

'Then let me make love to you,' she suggested, her
heart and stomach fluttering with excitement. 'I'll be
careful, and very, very slow.'

He groaned his pleasure at the thought.

'God, how I've missed you,' he said thickly, pulling the pins out of her hair and stroking it down her
back. 'You've no idea.'

'No more than I've missed you,' she murmured.
'Let me show you how much...'

CHAPTER FOURTEEN

WHEN the cramping pains woke Sophia in the early hours of the morning, her first reaction was disbelief. This couldn't be happening to her again. It just couldn't!

But it seemed it was. The pains were very familiar.

'Oh, no,' she moaned aloud, tears filling her eyes. 'No…' She covered her face with her hands in grief and dismay.

Jonathon was immediately awake beside her, rolling over to take her shaking hands down from her face. 'What is it?' he asked anxiously. 'Are you ill?'

'The baby,' she sobbed. 'It's the baby. Oh, God…'

'Are you bleeding?'

'I…I don't know,' she choked out, having been too frightened to look.

Jonathon snapped on the bedside lamp and threw back the quilt. 'No, you're not,' he muttered, then threw the quilt back over her. 'Try to relax. I'm going to get dressed then take you straight to the hospital. It might only be a false alarm.'

He dragged on some warm clothes double-quick, bundled her into one of his large warm dressing-gowns and carried her straight down to the car. By this time she was moaning continually with the pain, which was simply dreadful, much worse than the last time.

'Hang on, Sophia,' he told her. 'Just hang on.' But he looked horribly worried and pale.

Despair consumed Sophia. It's all my fault, she began thinking. I should never have insisted we make love. Never. Now I'm going to lose the only real part of Jonathon I will ever have to love with all my heart. His baby…

It wasn't her own doctor who examined her when they reached the hospital, but he was a gynaecologist, there to deliver a baby. Sophia was in so much pain at this stage that she was oblivious to the probing hands, the glaring lights and the muttering voices. She was shivering and shaking, her skin was clammy, and nausea was beginning to swim in her stomach. Suddenly, she was violently ill all over the side of the bed, her stomach heaving all its contents onto the floor as the casualty nurse flew to get first a basin, then a mop and bucket.

Eventually, Sophia flopped back on the pillow, exhausted yet amazingly feeling a lot better. Her eyes closed on a weary sigh, her head shaking with confusion and a sprinkling of hope. Maybe this wasn't a miscarriage at all. Maybe she was simply ill.

The doctor immediately echoed her thoughts. 'I think perhaps some of your fears can be put to rest, Mr Parnell,' she heard him say. 'Your wife's obviously eaten something that didn't agree with her. You wouldn't by any chance have had some seafood during the last twelve hours or so, would you?'

'Yes, we had oysters at dinner last night, then lobster.'

'Since you aren't ill yourself, then it was probably a bad oyster. It only takes one.'

'Then my wife *isn't* going to lose the baby?'

'I didn't say that…' These words had Sophia's eyes flying open again in renewed panic. 'I'd like to keep her in overnight for observation. I'd also like to sedate her. Her system's received quite a shock. It needs a little calming down.' He turned and ordered the nurse to get something in what sounded like medical gobbledegook to Sophia. Her still-worried eyes turned to Jonathon.

He came forward and took her nearest hand in both of his. 'It's just a precaution, darling,' he said softly. 'Don't worry. You'll be fine. You don't think I'm going to let anything happen to my baby, do you?'

The prick of the needle in her arm was hardly noticed as all her attention remained on her husband's word. *His* baby. Was Charmaine right? Was that all she was to him, a baby-carrier?

No, no, that didn't seem right. Last night, when she'd made love to him, she could have sworn he'd looked up at her with love in his eyes. For the first time as she'd moved over him, their bodies blended, she'd felt a powerful emotional bond surge between them, something that transcended the sex. At last, it had been a meeting of souls as well as bodies. She'd fallen asleep afterwards, hugging that wonderful thought to her heart.

She drifted off to sleep now, clinging to that memory, hoping against hope.

When she finally resurfaced to a woozy consciousness, the hospital room was filled with daylight. It was also empty, a private room with only the one bed. The door was open, however, and as her wits gradually returned she could hear Jonathon's voice in the corridor just outside.

'She's going to be all right? You're absolutely sure, Doctor? You're not just saying that?'

'Positive, Mr Parnell. We've checked her every

hour all day. Her vital signs are very good and she's resting comfortably. Please stop worrying. The baby's fine as well.'

'I wasn't so worried about the baby. There can always be another baby. There can never be another Sophia. God...I don't know what I would do if anything ever happened to her.'

Sophia was stunned at the way Jonathon's voice shook and broke during these last amazing words. It sounded as if he was almost in tears. Her heart flooded with emotion and flowed over. He *did* love her. She had been right last night. He did...

Tears filled her own eyes just as he walked in. On seeing that she was awake yet seemingly distressed, he raced over, anxiety on his ravaged face. He hadn't shaved and there were lines of worry etched around his mouth and eyes. 'What is it? Are you still in pain? Do you want me to call the doctor? He's just walked off down the corridor. I could...'

She shook her head vigorously from side to side, unable to trust her voice for a few seconds. He continued to look down at her with real concern and caring, and she wondered how she could have missed seeing that he loved her.

'Then what is it?' he persisted. 'Why are you crying?'

'You...you *love* me,' she said, and did her best to stop crying, gulping down the lump in her throat and blinking away the tears.

She saw his shock through her clearing gaze.

'No, I...'

'You *do*,' she insisted huskily. 'Don't lie.'

His hands lifted to rake his rumpled hair back from his forehead, his eyes anguished. Turning abruptly, he strode over to stare through the window for a few moments before turning back to face her across the room.

'All right,' he admitted almost despairingly. 'All right, I love you. I've loved you all along, from the first moment I damned well set eyes on you. I took one look at you in my brother's arms—so sweet and warm and caring, yet at the same time so lovely and sensual and earthy—and I knew that everything I had felt for Charmaine had been a sham, a shallow, disgusting sham.'

His laughter was full of self-mockery. 'She knew it, of course. I was the only fool to be deceived, thinking lust was love. My only excuse was that she was a damned good actress, promising all sorts of things that made me think my relationship with her was the real thing. I suspected as much when I first found out she'd deceived me, but once I met you and saw what real love was, I finally appreciated the ugly reality of women like Charmaine. It revolted me to think I had ever touched her.'

'I...I really thought you'd loved her,' Sophia said incredulously. 'When you said you would never marry again, I thought that was because your heart was broken.'

'The only reason I told you I'd never marry again was because I'd fallen in love with *you*. God, do you know what it was like, promising Godfrey to marry you? It was my deepest dream, and my darkest nightmare. I tried telling myself it would seem a noble sacrifice, that others would pat me on the back for my brotherly love, when all the while, down in the hell reserved for ruthless bastards like myself I was plotting to steal, if not your heart, then your body.'

'But you didn't,' Sophia protested. 'And you're not a ruthless bastard! You're a kind, good man, a fine man. You did everything you could not to do the wrong thing. In the end, I offered myself to you, remember? In the circumstances, I made it impossible for you to resist the temptation.'

His smile was wry and rueful at the same time. 'You did at that, my sweet. And I do thank you for your generous words. Yes, I could no more walk away that night when I saw Harvey pawing at you than I could have cut out my own tongue. And it was good, wasn't it? You've enjoyed being in my bed, haven't you? And now, we're having a baby together. Does it matter that I'm in love with you? Is that so disastrous now? God…'

He shook his head in an agony of emotional distress. 'How long do I have to carry this burden of guilt around with me? You told me often enough that Godfrey wouldn't mind us being together, wouldn't mind if you had my baby, and I did my best to believe you, even when underneath I found it almost impossible.'

He dragged in then expelled another ragged sigh. Sophia was struck dumb by what she was hearing. 'The only way I could justify what I eventually stole from him was to reason that I had only won that part of you which he obviously hadn't—your sexuality. I thought that if I kept our relationship to a strictly physical one, if I left your heart to his memory, if all we ever seemed to have were meetings of bodies and not souls, then I could live with the guilt.

'But I see now I was deluding myself,' he went on with a cynical laugh. 'My supposed sacrifice in leaving your love for Godfrey was all a lie. While telling myself I didn't want you falling in love with me, underneath I craved it far more than I craved your body. I know now that you'll never love me as you loved Godfrey, Sophia. But does it really matter if *I* love *you*? Does it, dammit?'

'You're right, Jonathon,' she managed to say in a strangled tone. 'I will never love you as I loved Godfrey...'

A huge lump gathered in her chest as Jonathon stiffened, squared his shoulders against the hurt her words might seemingly have delivered.

'Because the love I held for your brother,' she went on shakily, 'is nothing like the love I hold for you...'

Jonathon's eyes snapped wide, fixing on her face with an expression full of the most heart-rending hope.

'Godfrey was the father I had lost, the friend I'd never had, a fantasy-like figure who fulfilled some of my schoolgirl needs; but you were right...he was as far removed from the real world as the characters in the books he loved. Although we grew to love each other and lean on each other, he was not, and would never have become, my love and my lover in the real sense of the word. I can see that now. Godfrey was an undersexed man, far more comfortable thinking about love than making love. The one time we were together was a disaster, physically. Godfrey knew it, but I...I was naïve enough to think things would improve with time.'

She shook her head, smiling with sadness at the memory. 'Godfrey was far wiser, though, than either of us gave him credit for. I think he pushed us together because he sensed the chemistry that had vibrated between us from the start. Oh, yes, I can see that too now. Why else did I become such a ninny whenever you came within breathing distance of me? Do you think I normally go round blushing and stammering like some simpering eighteenth-century ingénue? I can assure you I don't! But with you...with you, Jonathon, I was a constant mess.'

'Are you saying you've loved me all along?' he asked, utterly taken aback.

'No, I don't think so any more than I think you loved me all along. It was desire we both felt in the beginning. But, somewhere along the line, our desire for each other did deepen to love. We grew to know each other and we liked what we saw.'

'So wise,' he murmured, 'for one so young.' He came slowly forward to stand beside her bed and take her hand. 'I'm not sure why you liked what you saw, but I know damned well why I liked what I saw. I don't think I deserve your love, my darling, but I'm going to take it and guard it as jealously as the most precious masterpiece. For your love is a priceless treasure. Priceless...'

He bent and lifted the palm of her hand to his mouth, closing his eyes and kissing it tenderly for some long wonderfully intimate moments. At last, he opened his eyes and put her hand down.

'Mother and Maud are down the corridor, waiting to see you,' he said. 'Can I call them in?'

'Of course.'

'And Wilma hasn't been off the phone. I should call her back now that I'm sure you're OK.'

'Of course.'

'Do you promise to love me forever and ever, till death us do part?'

She smiled. 'Of course...'

CHAPTER FIFTEEN

'You're sure you can cope?'

'I've had children of my own, Sophia,' Ivy said with a new firmness. 'One five-month-old baby boy won't give me any trouble, will you, Godfrey?' She clucked the baby under the chin.

Godfrey slept on regardless.

'He's such a good baby,' Ivy assured her. 'Stop worrying.'

Sophia glanced down at her son and marvelled anew. Although he was the image of his father, with masses of dark hair and long strong limbs, he certainly took after his namesake with his placid nature.

She'd been so thrilled when Jonathon had suggested Godfrey as his name, the gesture proving so much more than a million verbal reassurances. Since their baby had been born Jonathon had been a much more relaxed man all round. He adored little Godfrey.

Sophia herself was besotted with the child, though she tried to hide it a little. Being a wife and mother was a matter of juggling one's affections, she realised, which was why she'd agreed to Jonathon's suggestion that they go away for a while so that they could spend some time alone together.

Sophia was more than eager to have her handsome husband all to herself, but it was hard to let go of her maternal responsibilities.

'I left a copy of his routine on the kitchen notice-board,' she said for the umpteenth time.

'Yes, dear.' Ivy was patience itself. 'If I'm in any doubt, I can ask Maud. If I get desperate, I could even call on little Godfrey's godparents.'

Sophia felt a resurgence of panic. 'But Wilma's never had a baby! And Harvey's hopeless with children. He said so.'

'Stop fussing, Sophia,' Jonathon said affectionately as he came down the stairs, suitcases in hand.

Sophia sighed. 'I'm beginning to become a worry-wart, I think.'

'Which is why you need a break. Come on, get your handbag; we have a plane to catch.' Jonathon put the cases down near the front door then came back to give his mother, then the baby a peck on the cheek. 'Bye, son. Keep your grandmother in line and don't let her start you on the ballet lessons just yet.'

Ivy looked sheepish.

'You can play him Mozart instead,' he grinned, bringing a look of surprise from both his mother and his wife. 'Ready, Sophia?'

'Yes. Have you said goodbye to Maud?'

'Sure have. Don't worry about coming outside to wave us off, Mother. There's a bit of a breeze and it might wake Godfrey. See you in a little over two weeks. Open the door for me, Sophia. God, these cases are heavy.'

Once the front door was shut and the baby was out of sight, Sophia turned her thoughts to the holiday ahead of her. 'Just think. Two whole weeks on a tropical island. Are you sure I haven't forgotten anything, Jonathon?'

'Only the kitchen sink,' he laughed, 'and I'm not absolutely certain you haven't packed that either.

What on earth have you got in here?' he asked as he slung the cases into the boot.

'Only clothes.'

He waggled his eyebrows at her as he came round to open the passenger door. 'You won't be needing too many of those.'

'Neither will you,' she countered with a saucy grin.

Jonathon bent to help her put her seatbelt on, taking advantage of the moment to kiss her.

Maud broke the highly charged moment by bursting forth from the house and running down the steps. 'I'm glad I caught you before you went. Wilma just called to wish you *bon voyage* and tell you not to worry about anything at the office while you're gone. She has everything firmly under control.'

'I don't doubt it,' Jonathon muttered drily under his breath. 'By the time I get back, she'll probably have control of the whole company.'

'You're the one who offered her a partnership,' Sophia reminded him on the quiet.

'In a moment of weakness before Godfrey was born. The woman's a vampire!' He straightened to throw Maud a parting smile. 'Thanks, Maud. If you're talking to Wilma, tell her not to do anything I wouldn't do.'

'Which gives her a wide range of options,' Sophia commented drily as Jonathon drove off.

'It does not!' he countered. 'I happen to be a very conservative businessman.'

'But not so conservative in the bedroom.'

'I don't notice you complaining, wife. Not that I've had all that much opportunity to show my talents lately.'

'Which is why we're off to Bora Bora for two

weeks. Just think, Jonathon. Moonlight strolls along the white sands...skinny-dipping at midnight in the warm water...sharing a hammock under the softly swaying palms. Oh, I can't wait.'

He groaned. 'Keep up those descriptions and I won't be able to either.'

They glanced across at each other, their eyes glittering with anticipation.

'I do so love you, Mr Parnell,' Sophia said softly.

'And I love you, Mrs Parnell.'

'There's only one thing that would make our lives perfect.'

'Oh?'

'A little brother or sister for Godfrey.'

'You want another baby already?'

'Uh-huh. I know you suggested that I go on the Pill for a while, and I did get some from the doctor, and I should have started taking them last week, but I...I didn't.'

'Where are they?' he asked, frowning.

'I...um...I left them behind.'

'She left them behind,' he repeated drily.

Sophia gulped. 'You don't mind, do you?'

'Mind? I'm very disappointed!'

'You are? Oh, dear. Well, in that case I...I...'

'There I was,' he interrupted curtly, 'thinking that when I got to the airport you could open your case and throw the damned pills away. It would have made the luggage so much lighter.'

'Jonathon Parnell, you're teasing me.'

'Would I do such a thing?' He grinned.

Not once, she thought. When she first met him, he would never have done such a light-hearted thing. But he was a different man now, a different man in every way. Love had changed him. Oh, she was so happy. So very happy.

'I tell you what,' he said with a wicked smile and glittering blue eyes. 'What say when we get to the car park I open your case and you leave all your underwear behind?'

'Jonathon Parnell, I will do no such thing. You behave yourself!'

'Not on your Nelly. This is the first time I've had you all to myself for months and I'm not going to waste a minute. The underwear stays behind! You can start with those sensible cotton knickers I saw you putting on this morning. Take them off.'

'I can't do that!' she gasped. 'I…I'd be self-conscious all the time. I wouldn't be able to look at you in the airport or on the plane without knowing that you knew I was naked underneath.'

'That's the general idea.'

'Oh…'

When she blushed, Jonathon laughed. But softly, teasingly. His hand came over to gently stroke her cheek. 'I do so love you, Mrs Parnell. If the idea really embarrasses you, forget about it.'

'I…I'll think about it.'

'You do that, darling.'

She slanted him a sharp look, well aware that he was depending on her thinking about it, the devil. And in the end she would do what he wanted. She always ended up doing what he wanted!

There again…she always ended up wanting what he wanted anyway.

Her soft chuckle carried a wry acceptance of her weakness in loving this man so much.

'May I share the source of your amusement?' he asked, smiling.

She smiled back. 'I'm sure you will, you bad man. The very first chance you get.'

THE MARRIAGE CAMPAIGN

HELEN BIANCHIN

CHAPTER ONE

IT DIDN'T matter how far or how frequent the journey, returning home had a significant effect on her emotions, Francesca mused as the jet banked over the harbour and prepared its descent.

Sydney's cityscape provided a panoramic vista of sparkling blue ocean, numerous coves and inlets, tall city buildings, the distinctive bridge, the Opera House.

Brilliant sunshine held the promise of warm summer temperatures, a direct contrast to those she'd left behind in Rome the day before.

The Boeing lined up the runway and within seconds wheels thudded against the Tarmac, accompanied by the scream of engines thrown into reverse, followed by the slow cruise into an allotted bay.

Collecting baggage and clearing Customs was achieved in minimum time, and Francesca was aware of a few circumspect glances as she made her way through the arrivals lounge.

The deep aqua-coloured trouser suit adorning her tall, slender frame was elegantly cut, her make-up minimal, and she'd caught her dark auburn hair into a loose knot atop her head. The result was an attractive image, but downplayed her status as an international model.

There were no photographers or television cameras in sight as she emerged onto the pavement, nor was there the customary chauffeured limousine waiting at the kerb.

Francesca reached for her sunglasses and slid the dark-lensed frames into place.

She wanted, *needed*, a few days' grace with family and friends before stepping onto the carousel of scheduled modelling assignments, contracted photographic shoots and public appearances.

Cabs formed a swiftly moving queue at the kerb and she quickly hired one, providing the driver with a Double Bay address as he slid out into traffic exiting the international terminal.

Cars, buses, trucks—all bent on individual destinations. Warehouses, tree-lined parks, graffiti decorating—or desecrating, depending on one's opinion—numerous concrete walls. It could be any city in the world, Francesca mused.

Yet it was her city, the place where she'd been born and raised of an Italian immigrant father and an Australian mother who had never quite come to terms with the constraints of marriage.

Francesca retained a vivid recollection of voices raised in bitter recrimination, followed soon after by boarding school, with vacation time spent equally between each parent.

Happy families, she mused with a rueful grimace as she reflected on the years that had followed. Three stepfathers: two who'd bestowed genuine affection and one whose predilection for pubescent girls had become apparent during a school vacation soon after the honeymoon. Acquired step-siblings who had passed briefly in and out of her life. And with a card from her father, who had inscribed an identical greeting.

The answering machine recorded no less than five messages, and she played them through. A call from her agent; the rest were social. Seven faxes, none of which were urgent, she determined as she flicked through the pages. All, she decided, could wait until she'd had time to shower and unpack. Then she'd go through her mail.

It was good to be home. Satisfying to see familiar things and to know that she would enjoy them for several weeks.

Oriental rugs graced the marble-tiled floor, and there were soft leather sofas in the large lounge area. A formal dining room, modern kitchen, two bedrooms with *en suite* facilities, and floor-to-ceiling glass. Ivory drapes flowed on from ivory silk-covered walls, and the marble tiles were ivory too. Framed prints in muted blue, pink, aqua and lilac graced the walls, the colours accented by several plump cushions placed with strategic precision on sofas and single chairs.

Understated elegance combined with the rich tapestry of individual taste. Lived in, and not just a showcase, she assured herself silently as she took her bags through to the main bedroom.

Unpacking could wait until later, she decided as she stripped off her clothes and entered the *en suite* bathroom.

A leisurely shower did much to ease the strain of too many hours' flight time, and she riffled through her wardrobe, selecting casual cotton trousers and a matching sleeveless blouse, then thrust bare feet into low-heeled sandals.

Collecting shoulder bag and keys, she rode the lift down to the underground car park.

Sydney traffic was swift, but civilised, and far different from the hazardous volume of cacophonous vehicles that hurtled the city streets of Rome.

Italy. The birthplace of her paternal ancestors and the place where she'd met and married world-renowned racing-driver Mario Angeletti three years ago during a photo shoot in Milan, only to weep at his funeral a few months after their wedding when a spectacular crash claimed his life. Last week she'd stood beside an adjacent grave site as her widowed mother-in-law had been laid to rest.

Nothing could be achieved by focusing on the sadness, she rationalised as she drove to the nearest shopping complex.

Her immediate priorities were to access Australian currency and do some food shopping.

Minutes later she parked the car, then crossed to the bank.

There were several people queuing at the automatic teller machine, and she opted for the bank's air-conditioned interior rather than wait in the blazing heat, only to give a resigned sigh at the lengthy column of customers waiting for vacant teller locations.

For a moment she considered saving time by utilising her bank card at the foodhall, then dismissed the idea.

The man in front of her moved two paces forward, and her attention was captured by his cologne. A light, musky exclusive brand that aroused a degree of idle speculation over the man who wore it.

Impressive height, dark, well-groomed hair. Broad shoulders, the muscle structure outlined beneath a fitted polo shirt. Tapered waist, well-cut trousers. Tight butt.

Accountant? Lawyer? Probably neither, she mused. Either would have worn the requisite two-piece suit during office hours.

The queue was dissipating more quickly than she'd anticipated, and she watched as he moved to a vacant teller.

Mid-to-late thirties, Francesca judged as she caught his features in profile. The strong jaw, wide-spaced cheekbones and chiselled mouth indicated a European heritage. Italian, maybe? Or Greek?

The adjoining teller became vacant, and she moved to the window, handed over her access card and keyed in her PIN code, requested an amount in cash, then folded the notes into her wallet.

Francesca turned to leave, and collided with a hard male frame. 'I'm so sorry.' The startled apology tumbled automatically from her lips, and her eyes widened at the steadying clasp of his hand on her elbow.

Dominic's scrutiny was unhurried as it slid negligently down her slim form, then travelled back to linger on the soft curve of her mouth before his eyes lifted to capture hers.

There was something about her that teased his memory. Classical fine-boned features, clear creamy skin that was too pale, gold-flecked brown eyes. But it was the hair that fascinated him. Twisted into a knot at her nape, he wondered at its length. And imagined how it would look flowing loose down her back, its vibrant colour spread out against the bedsheets.

It was an evocative image, and one he banked down.

The breath caught in Francesca's throat at the primitive, almost electric awareness evident, and for endless seconds the room and its occupants faded into obscurity.

Crazy to feel so *absorbed* Francesca decided shakily as she forced herself to breathe normally.

She came into contact with attractive men almost every day of her life. There was nothing special about *this* particular man. Merely sexual chemistry, she rationalised, at its most magnetic.

Recognition was one thing. It was quite another to feel the tug of unbidden response.

She didn't like it, didn't want it.

And he knew. She could see it in the faint curve of that sensually moulded mouth, the slight darkening of those deep, almost black eyes. His smile deepened fractionally, and he inclined his head in silent acknowledgement as he released her arm.

Francesca kept her expression coolly aloof, and with a deliberately careless movement she slipped her wallet into the capacious shoulder bag, then turned with the intention of exiting the bank.

He was a few paces ahead of her, and it was difficult to ignore the animalistic grace of well-honed muscle and sinew. Leashed power and steel. Of body, and mind.

A man most women would find a challenge to explore, mentally as well as physically. To discover if the hinted knowledge in those dark eyes delivered the promise of sensual excitement beyond measure.

Ridiculous, she dismissed, more shaken than she was prepared to admit by the passage of wayward thought. It was merely a figment of an over-active imagination, stimulated by the effects of a long flight and the need to adjust to a different time-zone.

There was a slight tilt to her chin as she emerged onto the pavement. The sun was bright, and she lowered her sunglasses from their position atop her head, glad of the darkened lenses.

Head high, eyes front, faint smile, practised walk. Automatic reflex, she mused as she crossed the mall.

The foodhall was busy, and she took care selecting fresh fruit before adding a few groceries to the trolley. With various family members and friends to see, breakfast was likely to be the only consistent meal she'd eat in her apartment.

Family. A timely reminder that she should make the first of several calls, she determined wryly as she selected milk from the refrigerated section, added yoghurt and followed it with brie, her favourite cheese.

'No vices?' Low-pitched, male, the faintly accented drawl held a degree of mocking amusement.

Francesca was familiar with every ploy. And adept at dealing with them all. She turned slowly, and the light, dismissive words froze momentarily in her throat as she recognised the compelling dark-haired man she'd bumped into at the bank.

He possessed a fascinating mouth, white, even teeth, and a smile that would drive most women wild. Yet there was something about the eyes that condemned artifice. An assessing, almost analytical directness that was disturbing.

Had he followed her? She cast his trolley a cursory glance and noted a collection of the usual food staples. Perhaps not.

Humour was a useful weapon. The edges of her mouth tilted slightly. 'Ice cream,' she acknowledged with a trace of flippancy. 'Vanilla, with caramel and double chocolate chip.'

Dark eyes gleamed, and his deep husky laughter did strange things to her equilibrium.

'Ah, the lady has a sweet tooth.'

There was a ring on her left hand, and he wondered at his stab of disappointment. His cutting edge style of wheeling and dealing in the business arena hadn't stemmed from hesitation. He didn't hesitate now.

He reached forward and placed a light finger against the wide filigree gold band. 'Does this have any significance?'

Francesca snatched her hand from the trolley. 'Whether it does or not is none of your business.'

So she had a temper to go with that glorious dark auburn hair, Dominic mused, and wondered if her passion matched it. His interest intensified. 'Indulge me.'

She wanted to turn and walk away, but something made her stay. 'Give me one reason why I should?'

'Because I don't poach another man's possession.' The words held a lethal softness that bore no hint of apology, and his expression held a dispassionate watchfulness as she struggled to restrain her anger.

Dignity was the key, and she drew in a calming breath, then slowly raked her eyes over his tall frame from head to foot, and back again.

'Attractive packaging,' she accorded with silky detachment. She met his gaze squarely and held it. 'However, I have no interest in the contents.'

'Pity,' he drawled. 'The discovery could prove fascinating.' There was droll humour apparent, and something else she couldn't define. 'For both of us.'

'In your dreams,' she dismissed sweetly. The check-out lane was located at the far end of the aisle, and she had everything she needed.

He made no effort to stop her as she moved away, yet for one infinitesimal moment she'd had the feeling he'd seen into the depths of her soul, acknowledged her secrets, staked a claim and retreated, sure of his ability to conquer.

Insane, Francesca mentally chastised herself as she loaded carrybags into the boot and returned the trolley. Then she slid in behind the wheel of her car and switched on the ignition.

She was tired, wired. The first was the direct result of a long flight; she owed the second to a man she never wanted to meet again.

Re-entering the apartment, she stowed her purchases into the refrigerator and pantry. Rejecting coffee or tea, she filled a glass with iced water and drank half the contents before crossing to the telephone.

Fifteen minutes later she'd connected with each parent and made arrangements to see them. Next, she punched in the digits necessary to connect with Laraine, her agent.

Business. For the past three years it had been her salvation. Travelling the world, an elegant clotheshorse for the top fashion designers. She had the face, the figure, and the essential *élan.* But for how long would she remain one of the coveted few? More importantly, did she *want* to?

There were young waifs clamouring in the wings, eager for fame and fortune. Designers always had an eye for the look, and the excitement of a fresh new face.

Fashion was fickle. *Haute couture* a viperish nest of designer ego fed by prestigious clientele, the press, and the copy merchants.

Yet amongst the outrageousness, the hype and the glitter, there was pleasure in displaying the visual artistry of imaginative design. Satisfaction when it all came together to form something breathtakingly spectacular.

It made the long flights, living out of a suitcase in one hotel room or another, cramped backstage changing rooms, the *panic* that invariably abounded behind the scenes worthwhile. A cynic wouldn't fail to add that an astronomical modelling fee helped lessen the pain.

Financial security was something Francesca had enjoyed for as long as she could remember. As a child, there had been a beautiful home, live-in help, and expensive private schooling. Yet, while her mother had perpetuated the fairytale existence, her father had ensured his daughter's feet remained firmly on the ground.

There were investments, property, and an enviable blue chip share portfolio, the income from which precluded a need to supplement it in any way.

Yet the thought of becoming a social butterfly with no clear purpose to the day had never appealed.

Perhaps it was her father's inherited Italian genes that kept the adrenalin flowing and provided the incentive to put every effort into a chosen project. 'Failure' didn't form part of her father's vocabulary.

Which brought Francesca back to the present. 'A week's grace,' she insisted, and listened to her agent's smooth plea to reconsider. 'Tomorrow morning we'll confer over coffee. Your office. Shall we say ten?'

She replaced the receiver, stretched her arms high, and felt the weariness descend. She'd make something light for dinner, then she'd undress and slip beneath the sheets of her comfortable bed.

CHAPTER TWO

FRANCESCA leaned across the desk in her agent's elegantly appointed office and traced a list of proposed modelling assignments with a milk-opal-lacquered nail.

'Confirm the cancer charity luncheon, the Leukaemia Foundation dinner. I'll do Tony's photo shoot, and I'll judge the junior modelling award, attend the gala lunch on the Gold Coast.' She paused, considered three invitations and dismissed two. 'The invitation-only showing at Margo's Double Bay boutique.' She picked up her glass of iced water and took an appreciative sip. 'That's it.'

'Anique Sorensen is being persuasive and persistent,' Laraine relayed matter-of-factly.

The fact that Francesca was known to donate half her appearance fee whenever she flew home between seasons invariably resulted in numerous invitations requesting her presence at various functions, all in aid of one charity or another.

'When?'

'Monday, Marriott Hotel.'

'Tell me it's for a worthwhile cause, and I'll kill you.'

'Then I'm dead. It's for the Make-A-Wish Foundation® of Australia.'

'Damn,' Francesca accorded inelegantly, wrin-

kling her nose in silent admonition of Laraine's
widening smile.

'But you'll do it,' the agent said with outward
satisfaction.

'Yes.' Francesca stood to her feet, collected her
bag and slid the strap over one shoulder. She had
a particular sympathy for terminally ill children.
'Fax me the details.'

'What are your plans for the rest of the day?'

'A secluded beach,' she enlightened. 'A good
book, and the mobile phone.'

'Don't forget the block-out sunscreen.'

Francesca's smile held a teasing quality. 'Got it.'

An hour later she sat munching an apple beneath
a sun umbrella on a northern beach gazing over the
shoreline to the distant horizon.

There was a faint breeze wafting in from the
ocean, cooling the sun's heat. She could smell the
salt-spray, and there was the occasional cry from a
lonely seagull as it explored the damp sand at the
edge of an outgoing tide.

The solitude soothed and relaxed her, smoothing
the edges of mind and soul.

Reflections were often painful, and with a determined effort Francesca extracted her book and read
for an hour, then she retrieved a banana and a peach
from her bag and washed both down with a generous amount of bottled water.

Phone calls. The first of which was to a dear
friend with whom she'd shared boarding school
during emotionally turbulent years when each had
battled a stepmother and the effects of a dysfunc-
tional family relationship.

She punched in the number, got past Reception, then a secretary, and chuckled at Gabbi's enthusiastic greeting and a demand as to when they would get together.

'Tonight, if you and Benedict are attending Leon's exhibition.'

The flamboyant gallery owner was known for his *soirées*, invitations to which featured high on the social calendar among the city's fashionable élite.

'You are? That's great,' Francesca responded with enthusiasm. 'I'm meeting Mother for dinner first, so I could be late.'

'Have fun,' Gabbi issued lightly, and Francesca laughed outright at the unspoken nuance in those two words.

It *was* fun listening to Sophy's breathy gossip over chicken consommé, salad and fruit. Sophy's permanent diet involved minuscule portions of fat-free calorie-depleted food.

A gifted raconteur, she had a wicked way with words that was endearingly humorous, and it was little wonder her mother gathered men as some women collected jewellery. All of whom remained friends long after the relationship had ended. With the exception of Rick, her first husband and Francesca's father. He was the one who had remained impervious to Sophy's machinations.

It was after nine when the waiter brought the bill, which Francesca paid, and she saw Sophy into a cab before crossing to her car.

Twenty minutes later she searched for an elusive parking space within walking distance of Leon's fashionable Double Bay gallery, located one, and made her way towards the brightly lit main entrance.

There were people everywhere, milling, drinking, and it was difficult to distinguish the muted baroque music beneath audible snatches of conversation.

'Francesca, *darling!*'

Leon—who else? She acknowledged his effusive greeting and allowed him to clasp her shoulders as he regarded her features with thoughtful contemplation.

'You must have a drink before you circulate.'

Her eyes assumed a humorous gleam. 'That bad, huh?'

'*Non.* But a glass in the hand—' He paused to effect a Gallic shrug. 'You can pretend, *oui*, that it is something other than mineral water.' He lifted a hand in imperious summons, and a waiter appeared out of nowhere, tray in hand.

Dutifully, she extracted a tall glass. 'Anything in particular you can recommend to add to my collection?'

'A sculpture,' Leon announced at once. 'It is a little raw, you understand, but the talent—' He touched fingers to his lips and blew a kiss into the air. '*Très magnifique.* In a few years it will be worth ten, twenty times what is being asked for it now.' He smiled, and brushed gentle knuckles to her cheek. 'Go, *cherie*, and examine. Exhibit Fourteen. It may not capture you immediately, but it grows, fascinates.'

An accurate description, Francesca accorded several minutes later, unsure of the sculpture's appeal.

Yet there was something that drew her attention again and again.

Leon was an expert in the art world, she trusted his judgement, and owned, thanks to his advice, several items which had increased dramatically in value since their date of purchase. Therefore, she would browse among the other exhibits, then return and perhaps view it from a fresh angle. It was certainly different from anything she owned.

There were a few fellow guests whose features were familiar, and she smiled, greeted several by name, paused to exchange polite conversation, then moved on, only to divert from her intended path as she glimpsed the endearingly familiar features of an attractive blonde threading a path towards her.

'Francesca!'

'Gabbi.'

They embraced, and tumbled into speech. 'It's so good to see you.'

'And you. Where's Benedict?' It was unlike Gabbi's husband to be far from his wife's side.

'Eyes right, about ten feet distant.'

Francesca caught the dry tone and conducted a casual sweeping glance in the indicated direction. Benedict's tall, dark-haired frame came into view, together with that of a familiar female form. Annaliese Schubert, a model with whom she'd shared a few catwalks both home and abroad.

'Your dear stepsister is in town, and bent on creating her usual mayhem?' An attempt to seduce Benedict Nicols appeared Annaliese's prime motivation. That she had been unsuccessful both before and after Benedict's marriage didn't appear to bother her in the slightest.

'Perceptive of you,' Gabbi replied wryly. 'How was Rome?'

Francesca hesitated fractionally, unaware of the fleeting darkness that momentarily clouded her eyes. 'The catwalks were exhausting.' Her shoulders lifted slightly, then fell. 'And Mario's mother lost a long battle with cancer.'

Empathetic understanding didn't require words, and Francesca was grateful Gabbi refrained from uttering more than the customary few.

'Let's do lunch,' Gabbi suggested gently. 'Is tomorrow too soon?'

'Done.'

'Good,' Gabbi said with satisfaction. She tucked a hand through Francesca's arm. 'Shall we examine the art exhibits for any hidden talent?'

They wandered companionably, slowly circling the room, and when Gabbi paused to speak to a friend Francesca moved forward to give closer scrutiny to a canvas that displayed a visual cacophony of bold colour.

She tilted her head in an attempt to fathom some form or symmetry that might make sense.

'It's an abstract,' a slightly accented male voice revealed with a degree of musing mockery.

Francesca's stomach muscles tightened, premonition providing an advance warning even as she turned slowly towards him.

The bank, the foodhall, and now the art gallery?

Dominic had witnessed her entrance, and noted her progress around the room with interest. And a degree of satisfaction when she was greeted with such enthusiasm by the wife of one of his business associates. It made it so much easier to initiate an introduction.

She regarded him silently. The deeply etched male features, the hard-muscled frame tamed somewhat beneath superb tailoring. Also apparent were the hand-stitched shoes, Hermes tie, and gold Rolex.

The smile reached his eyes, tingeing them with humour, yet there was a predatory alertness beneath the surface that was at variance with his portrayed persona.

A man who knew who he was, and didn't require any status symbols to emphasise his wealth or masculinity.

Power emanated from every pore, leashed and under control. Yet there was a hint of the primitive, a dramatic mesh of animalistic magnetism that stirred something within her, tripping the pulse and increasing her heartbeat.

'Francesca.'

The soft American drawl caught her attention, and she turned at once, her expression alive with delight.

'Benedict!' Her smile held genuine warmth as she leaned forward to accept his salutary kiss. 'It's been a while.'

'Indeed.' Gabbi's husband offered an affectionate smile in acknowledgement before shifting his attention to the man at her side. 'You've met Dominic?'

'It appears I'm about to.'

Something flickered in Benedict's eyes, then it was masked. 'Dominic Andrea. Francesca Angeletti.'

The mention of her surname provided the key to her identity, Dominic acknowledged, as details fell into place.

He was Greek, Francesca mused, not Italian. And the two men were sufficiently comfortable with each other to indicate an easy friendship.

'Francesca.'

Her name on his lips sounded—*different*. Sexy, evocative, alluring. And she didn't want to be any one of those things with any man. Especially not *this* man.

Dominic wondered if she was aware the fine gold flecks in her eyes intensified when she was defensive…and trying hard to hide it? He felt something stir deep inside, aside from the desire to touch his mouth to her own, to explore and possess it.

'Are you sufficiently brave to offer an opinion on my exhibit?'

He couldn't be serious? 'I'd prefer to opt out on the grounds that anything I say might damage your ego.'

His husky laughter sent a shivery sensation down the length of her spine. 'Benedict and Gabbi must bring you to dinner tomorrow night.'

If Dominic Andrea thought she'd calmly tag along he was mistaken! 'Why?'

'You intrigue me.' He saw her pupils dilate, sensed the uncertainty beneath her cool façade. And was curious to discover the reason.

'No. Thank you,' she added.

'Not curious to see my artist's attic?'

'Where you live doesn't interest me.' Nor do you, she wanted to add. And knew she lied. For there was an invisible pull of the senses, a powerful dynamism impossible to ignore.

A man who sought to forge his own destiny, she perceived, not at all fooled by the smile curving that generous mouth. The eyes were too dark and discerning, *dangerous.*

She had the strangest feeling she should be afraid of the knowledge evident in those depths. An instinctive sureness that he was intent on being a major force in her life.

'Six-thirty. Gabbi will give you the address.' His lips tilted slightly as he slanted her a mocking glance. 'If you'll excuse me?'

'Extraordinary man,' Francesca commented, silently adding lethal and persistent as she watched him thread his way to the opposite side of the gallery.

'A very successful one,' Benedict informed her mildly. 'Who dabbles in art and donates a lot of his work to charity.'

'Accept Dominic's invitation,' Gabbi added persuasively. 'If you don't, I'll be outnumbered, and the conversation will be confined to business.'

Francesca rolled her eyes. 'Not really a hardship. You excel in business.'

Gabbi's eyes sparkled with impish humour. 'Take a walk on the wild side and say *yes.* You might enjoy yourself.'

All Francesca's instincts shrieked a silent denial. She liked her life as it was, and didn't need nor want any complications that might upset its even tenure.

Although it might prove a challenge to play Dominic Andrea at his own game and win.

'What do you think of that sculpture in steel?' Benedict queried, successfully diverting their attention.

Ten minutes later Francesca chose to leave, indicating to Gabbi quietly, 'I'll see you at lunch tomorrow.'

Leon was effusive as she crossed to his side and thanked him for the invitation, and as she turned towards the door she saw Dominic Andrea deep in conversation with a stunning diminutive blonde.

Almost as if he sensed her gaze, his head lifted and dark eyes pierced hers with mesmerising awareness.

There was nothing overt in his expression, just an unwavering knowledge that had an electric effect on her equilibrium. It was almost as if he was staking a claim. Issuing a silent message that he would enjoy the fight, and the victory.

Fanciful imagination, Francesca dismissed as she gained the foyer, then she descended the short flight of steps and took the well-lit path to her car.

With the ignition engaged, she eased the vehicle forward and entered the busy thoroughfare.

Dominic Andrea had no part in her life, she assured herself silently as she headed towards her Double Bay apartment.

Francesca put the finishing touches to her make-up, examined the careless knot of hair she'd swept on top of her head, then stood back, pleased with the overall image.

Halter-necked black dress, sheer black tights, perilously high stiletto-heeled black pumps. Cosmetic artistry provided a natural look, and a brilliant red gloss coloured her lips. Jewellery comprised a diamond bracelet and matching ear-studs.

Without pausing to think, she collected a slim evening purse and car keys, walked out of the apartment and took the lift down to the basement car park.

Traffic was heavy as she drove through the city, and once clear of the Harbour Bridge she by-passed the expressway and headed towards Beauty Point.

Exclusive suburbs graced the city's northern shores, offering magnificent views over the inner harbour.

Dammit. *What was she doing?* Dressed to kill, on her way to attend a dinner she had no inclination to share with a man she hadn't wanted to see again.

She could turn back and go home, ring and apologise, using any one of several plausible excuses.

So why didn't she? Instead of turning between wrought-iron gates guarding an imposing concrete-textured Caribbean-style home situated at the crest of a semi-circular driveway?

All because of Gabbi's subtle challenge issued the previous evening, and endorsed and encouraged over lunch. Now it was a little late to have second thoughts.

Francesca parked behind Benedict's sporty

Jaguar and cast a quick glance at the digital clock before she switched off the engine.

Perfect. By the time she emerged from the car and walked the few steps to the front door, she would be ten minutes late.

A silent statement that she was here on her own terms.

Subdued melodic chimes echoed as she depressed the doorbell, and seconds later the thick, panelled door swung open to reveal a middle-aged housekeeper.

'Miss Angeletti? Please come in.'

High ceilings and floor-to-ceiling glass created a sense of spaciousness and light, with folding white-painted wooden shutters. Expensive art adorned the walls, and there were several Oriental rugs adorning pale cream marble floors.

She was escorted into a large lounge where Dominic's tall frame drew her attention like a magnet.

Dark trousers and a casual blue shirt lent an elegance she knew to be deceiving, for beneath the sophisticated veneer there was strength, not only of body but of mind.

'Please accept my apologies.'

Dominic's dark eyes held hers, quiet, still. He wasn't fooled in the slightest, but his voice was smooth as silk as he moved forward to greet her. 'Accepted.' He swept an arm towards a soft-cushioned leather sofa. 'Come and sit down.'

She crossed to a single chair and sank into it with elegant economy of movement.

A further insistence on independence? 'What can I offer you to drink?'

Something with a kick in it would be nice. Instead, she offered him a singularly sweet smile. 'Chilled water, with ice.'

'Sparkling or still?'

She resisted the temptation to request a specific brand-name. 'Still. Thank you.'

There was that glance again, laser-sharp beneath dark lashes, the slight lift of one eyebrow before he crossed to the cabinet.

Benedict looked mildly amused, and Gabbi shook her head in silent remonstrance. Francesca merely smiled.

Dominic returned and placed a tall glass within her reach on the side table.

'Thank you.' So achingly polite. *Too* polite?

Within minutes the housekeeper appeared to announce the meal was served, and they made their way into a large dining room adjacent to the lounge.

The table was beautifully set with white damask, on which reposed fine china, silver cutlery and stemmed crystal glasswear.

Francesca's gaze idly skimmed the mahogany chiffonnier, the long buffet cabinet, the elegantly designed chairs, and silently applauded his taste in furniture. And in soft furnishings, for the drapes and carpet were uniform in colour, the contrast supplied by artwork and mirrors adorning the walls.

Dominic seated Francesca beside him, opposite Gabbi and Benedict.

The courses were varied, and many, and, while exquisitely presented, they were the antithesis of designer food. There was, however, an artistically displayed platter of salads decorated with avocado, mango, and a sprinkling of pine nuts.

A subtle concession to what Dominic suspected was a model's necessity to diet?

Francesca always ate wisely and well, with little need to watch her intake of food. Tonight, however, she forked dainty portions from each course.

'You have a beautiful home.' The compliment was deserved, and she cast a glance towards the original artwork gracing the walls. Not any of them bore the distinctive style of the abstract she'd sighted at Leon's gallery.

As if reading her mind, Dominic enlightened musingly, 'I keep my work in the studio.'

One eyebrow lifted, and her voice held a hint of mockery. 'Is that a subtle invitation to admire your etchings?'

His fingers brushed her wrist as he leaned forward to replenish her glass with water, and a chill shiver feathered its way over the surface of her skin in silent recognition of something deeply primitive.

The knowledge disturbed her, and her eyes were faintly wary as they met his.

'The expected cliché?' The drawled query held wry humour, and his eyes held a warmth she didn't care to define. 'At the risk of disappointing you, I paint in the studio and confine lovemaking to the bedroom.'

Something curled inside her stomach, and she lifted her glass and took a generous swallow before setting it down onto the table. 'How—prosaic.'

His husky chuckle held quizzical amusement,

and an indolent smile broadened the sensual curve of his mouth. 'Indeed? You don't think comfort is a prime consideration?'

The image of a large bed, satin sheets, and leisurely languorous foreplay sprang to mind...a damning and totally unwarranted vision she wanted no part of.

Francesca had a desire to give a stinging response, and probably would have if they'd been alone. Instead, she aimed for innocuous neutrality, and tempered it with a totally false smile that didn't fool anyone, least of all Dominic, in the slightest. 'Not always.'

'The chicken is delicious.' Dear sweet Gabbi, who sought to defuse the verbal direction of their exchange.

Francesca cast her a sweeping glance that issued a silent statement—*I'm having fun.* And saw her friend's eyes widen fractionally in answering warning.

'How was your trip to Italy, Francesca?' Benedict issued the bland query. 'Were you able to spend any time outside Rome?'

She decided to play the social conversational game. 'No,' she enlightened evenly. 'However, I'm due in Milan next month for the European spring collections.' Closely followed by Paris.

Her life was like riding a merry-go-round...big cities, bright lights, the adrenalin rush. Then, every so often, she stepped off and took time out in normality. A vacation abroad, or, more often than not, she flew home to spend time with family and friends. They were her rock, the one thing constant in her life she could rely on.

'You enjoy the international scene?'

Francesca turned slightly to the man seated at her side, glimpsed the remarkable steadiness in his gaze—and something else she was unable to interpret. 'Yes.'

'Would you care for more salad?'

A subtle reminder that she was scarcely doing the sumptuous selection of food much justice? It hardly made sense that she was deliberately projecting the image of a diet fanatic, but there was a tiny gremlin urging her to travel a mildly outrageous path.

'Thank you.' She reached for the utensils and placed a modest serving onto her plate, then proceeded to fork small portions with delicate precision.

There was a dessert to die for reposing on the chiffonnier, and she spared the exquisitely decorated torte a regretful glance. A slice of mouthwatering ambrosia she'd have to forego the pleasure of savouring in order to continue the expected accepted image.

'Did Leon manage to sell your abstract?' She sounded facetious, and felt a momentary pang for the discourtesy.

'It wasn't for sale,' Dominic relayed with seemingly careless disregard, and smiled as her eyebrows arched in silent query.

'Really?' Francesca let her gaze encompass his rugged features and lingered on the strong bone structure before meeting the musing gleam in those dark eyes. 'You don't *look* like an artist.'

His mouth quirked slightly at the edges. 'How, precisely, is your impression of an artist supposed to look?'

Harmless words, but she was suddenly conscious of an elevated nervous tension that had no known basis except a strong, instinctive feeling that she was playing a dangerous game with a man well-versed in every aspect of the hunt.

Akin to a predator prepared to watch and wait as his prey gambolled foolishly within sight, aware that the time was of his choosing, the kill a foregone conclusion.

Now you're being fanciful, she chided, suddenly angry with herself for lapsing into an idiotic mind game.

'Shall we move to the lounge for coffee?' Dominic suggested with deceptive mildness.

In a way it was a relief to shift location, and she breathed a silent sigh as the evening moved towards a close.

The impish gremlin was still in residence as she declined coffee and requested tea. 'Herbal, if you have it.' Long lashes gave an imperceptible flutter, then swept down to form a protective veil.

'Of course.' The request didn't faze him in the least. It was almost as if he'd been prepared for it, and within minutes she nursed a delicate cup filled with clear brown liquid she had no inclination to taste.

Terrible, she conceded as she studiously sipped the innocent brew. And smiled as Gabbi, Benedict and Dominic savoured dark, aromatic coffee she would have much preferred to drink.

Hoist by her own petard, Francesca acknowledged with rueful acceptance. It served her right.

'Another cup?'

Not if she could help it! 'Thank you, no. That was delicious.'

Benedict rose to his feet in one smooth movement, his eyes enigmatic as they met those of his wife. 'If you'll excuse us, Dominic?'

'It's been a lovely evening,' Gabbi said gently as she collected her purse.

Their imminent departure provided an excellent excuse for Francesca to leave. It was what Dominic expected. But she was damned if she'd give him the satisfaction.

Fool, she mentally chastised herself as he escorted Gabbi and Benedict to the front door. Pick up your evening bag and follow them.

Too late, she decided a few minutes later when he returned to the lounge.

Francesca watched as he folded his lengthy frame into a cushioned chair directly opposite.

'Your friendship with Gabbi is a long-standing one?'

'Are you going to express a need to explore my background?'

'Not particularly.'

'No request for an in-depth profile?' she queried drily.

Dominic was silent for several seemingly long seconds, wanting to tear down the barrier she'd erected but aware of the need for caution and a degree of patience. 'I'm aware of the professional one,' he drawled with assumed indolence. 'Tell me about your marriage.'

She stopped breathing, felt the pressure build, and sought to expel it slowly. She wanted to serve him a volley of angry words, throw something, *anything* that would release some of her pain. Instead, she resorted to stinging mockery.

'Gabbi failed to fill you in?'

His eyes were steady. 'Minimum details.'

'It can be encapsulated in one sentence: *champion racing car driver Mario Angeletti killed on the Monaco Grand Prix circuit within months of his marriage to international model Francesca Cardelli.*'

Three years had passed since that fateful day. Yet the vivid horror remained. It didn't matter that she hadn't personally witnessed the tearing of metal, the disintegration of car and man as fuel ignited in catastrophic explosion. Television news cameras, newspaper photographs and graphic journalistic reports ensured no detail remained unrecorded.

Family and close friends had shielded her, protecting and nurturing during the emotional fall-out. And afterwards she had stepped back onto the catwalk, aware every move, every nuance of her expression was being carefully watched for visible signs of distress.

Some had even attempted to provoke it. Yet not once had she let down her guard. Only those who knew her well saw the smile didn't quite reach her eyes, and recognised the smooth social patter as a practised façade.

'It must have been a very painful time for you.'

Francesca was unable to verbally denounce his sympathy, for there was none. Merely an empathetic statement that ignored conventional platitudes.

'Would you like a drink? Some more tea, coffee?' The smile held musing warmth. 'Something stronger, perhaps?'

Francesca stood to her feet, her expression wary as he mirrored her action. 'I really must leave.'

'Do I frighten you?' The query was voiced in a soft drawl, and succeeded in halting her steps.

No doubt about it, his target aim was deadly.

'Fear' was a multi-faceted word that encompassed many emotions. Slowly she turned towards him and met his gaze. Her chin tilted fractionally. A mental stiffening of her own resources? 'No.'

His eyes never left hers, but she felt as if he'd stripped every protective layer she'd swathed around her frozen heart and laid it bare and bleeding.

Oh, God, what was happening here? She'd known he was trouble the first time she saw him. *Walk away,* a tiny voice bade silently. *Now.*

A faint smile curved the edges of that sensual mouth, and there was a transitory gleam of humour apparent in the depth of those dark eyes. 'I'm relieved to hear it.'

'Why?' The demand seemed perfectly logical.

He looked at her carefully, weighing his words and assessing the damage they might do. And how he would deal with it. 'I want you,' he stated gently, lifting a hand to trace a gentle forefinger down the edge of her cheek.

His touch was like fire, and her pulse jumped, then raced to a quickened beat, almost as if in silent recognition of something she refused to acknowledge.

'Tangled sheets and an exchange of body fluids?' Inside, her emotions were shredding into pieces. Her eyes seared his, and her chin tilted fractionally as she took a step away from him. 'I don't *do* one-night stands.'

Courage. And passion. Banked, reserved. But there. He wanted it all. And knew she'd fight him every inch of the way.

'Neither do I.'

His words sent a shiver feathering down the length of her spine. What was it with this man? She found it annoying that just as she was about to categorise him, he shifted stance.

Dominic watched the play of emotions in her expressive eyes. No matter how much he wanted it to be different, he could wait. The temptation to pull her up against him and let her feel the effect she had on him was strong. To cover her mouth with his own, explore and vanquish.

He did neither. It would keep. Until the next time. And he'd ensure there was a next time.

Francesca felt the need to escape, and good manners instilled since childhood ensured she uttered a few polite words in thanks.

'Why, when you merely sampled a bird-like portion from each course, then picked at the salad?'

She experienced a momentary tinge of remorse

for the manner in which she'd eaten the delectable food. Did he suspect it had been deliberate? Somehow she had the instinctive feeling he saw too much, *knew* too much of the human psyche.

'My loss of appetite bore no reflection on your housekeeper's culinary ability.'

'In that case, I'll refer the compliment.'

Francesca turned and walked from the room to the front door, acutely aware of his presence at her side. She paused as he reached forward to pull back one of the large, panelled doors.

'What were you doing shopping for food in a supermarket when you employ a housekeeper?'

He could have used any one of several glib excuses, or employed a deliberately flattering remark. Instead he chose honesty. 'I wanted to see you again.'

Her stomach lurched, and an icy chill feathered her skin at the directness of his gaze.

'Goodnight.' She moved past him and stepped quickly down to her car, unlocked it and slid in behind the wheel.

The engine fired with a refined purr, and she resisted the temptation to speed down the driveway, choosing instead to ease the vehicle through the gates onto the road before quickly accelerating towards the main arterial road leading towards the Harbour Bridge.

Damn him. Francesca's fingers tightened on the steering wheel until her knuckles shone white. He was fast proving to be an intrusive force—one she didn't need in her life.

The sky was a deep indigo-blue sprinkled with

stars, and beneath them lay the city, dark velvet laced by a tracery of electric lights that had no discernible pattern. Bright neon flashed, providing vivid colour as one advertisement vied with another. A commuter train slipped by in electronic silence, its carriages illuminated and partly empty.

It was still early, yet there was already action in the city streets. Professionals worked the pavements, hustling and touting and evading the law as they mingled with the tourists and the curious.

Francesca took the expressway through the Domain, bypassed Kings Cross and headed towards the main arterial road leading to Double Bay.

Her head felt heavy, and she would have given much to be able to stop the car and walk in the clear night air. Instead she drove to her apartment building, garaged the car, then rode the lift to her designated floor.

A leisurely cool shower followed by an iced drink while she viewed television would have to suffice.

Yet nothing provided a distraction from the man who disturbed her thoughts.

Sleep didn't come easily, and even when it did, there were jagged dreams that made little sense. Except one, from which she awoke damp-skinned and damp-eyed. A vivid recall of Mario's laughing features as he stepped into his racing-car and donned his helmet prior to lining up for the last race of his life.

On the other side of the city Dominic stood looking out at the glittering lights across a darkened harbour as he reflected on the woman who had not long driven away from his home.

Sleep was elusive. At worst he could make do with six hours, five if he had to. Tonight he had the feeling he'd have to manage with less.

The fax machine shrilled in another room, and he ignored it.

What he needed was a carefully constructed strategy. A campaign that would leave nothing to chance.

Tomorrow he would make a call to Benedict Nicols in the hope that Gabbi might be persuaded to reveal details of Francesca's social calendar.

Subterfuge was permissible in the pursuit of an objective.

CHAPTER THREE

THE next few days were relaxing as Francesca caught up with friends, did some shopping, and enjoyed a rescheduled lunch with her father in an exclusive restaurant close to his office building.

The food was excellent, the ambience superb.

'How is Madeline?' Her stepmother was hardly the wicked kind, but Madeline viewed Francesca as a contestant for Rick's affections, and waged a subtle war to test her husband's priorities whenever Francesca was in town.

'Fine.' The warmth in his voice was unmistakable, and as long as Francesca continued to hear it she was prepared to forgive Madeline almost anything.

'And Katherine and John?' They were close, and Francesca regarded them as sister and brother rather than step-siblings. 'We must get together.'

'Is tonight too soon?' her father queried with a degree of wry humour. 'Katherine has, she assures me, an outfit to die for, and John seems convinced a new suit will elevate him in years to the enviable position of escorting his famed stepsister to an élite restaurant, where, God willing, some super-vigilant photographer will take a photo which will appear in tomorrow's newspaper, whereupon he'll be the most sought-after beau of the student ball.'

Francesca laughed. A glorious, warm, husky

sound. 'I take it I should wear something incredibly glamorous?'

Rick Cardelli's smile held philosophical humour. 'Obscenely so, I imagine,' he said drily.

Concern clouded her features. 'I don't want to overshadow Katherine.' Or Madeline.

His dark eyes gleamed, and the edges of his mouth curved upward. 'My dear Francesca, Katherine wants you to shine—vividly.'

'Done.' Francesca lifted her glass and touched it to the rim of her father's wine glass. '*Salute*, Papà,' she said solemnly.

'*Ecco*. Health and happiness,' he added gently.

She picked up her cutlery and speared a succulent prawn from its bed of cos lettuce decorated with slices of avocado and mango. The dressing was divine, and she savoured every mouthful.

They were halfway through the main course when Francesca became aware of a strange prickling sensation at the back of her neck.

Almost as if she was being watched.

Recognition was an aspect of her profession that she had come to terms with several years ago, and she dealt with it with practised charm.

But this was different. Mild interest in her presence didn't usually elicit this heightened sense of awareness, an acute alertness, as if something deep inside was forcing her attention.

She turned slowly, allowing her gaze to idly skim the room. And came to a sudden halt as she caught sight of Dominic Andrea sharing a table with two men a few metres from her own.

At that moment he glanced up, and her eyes collided with his dark, piercing gaze. He offered a slow, musing smile, which merely earned him a brief nod before she returned her attention to the contents on her plate.

Her appetite diminished so as to be almost non-existent, and she declined dessert, choosing to settle for coffee.

'Francesca?'

She looked up at the sound of her name and realised she hadn't taken in a word her father had said. 'I'm sorry, what did you say?'

'Is there a reason for your distraction?' Rick queried, and she wrinkled her nose in wry humour.

'An unwanted one.'

Her father chuckled. 'Now that I have your attention...Madeline would like you to join us at home for dinner. Does Wednesday suit?'

'I'll look forward to it.'

The waiter cleared their table and brought coffee.

Francesca was conscious of every movement she made, aware as she had never been before of one man's veiled scrutiny.

No one would have guessed to what degree Dominic's presence bothered her, or how much she longed to escape.

'A refill?'

'No, thanks.' She cast her father a warm smile. 'This has been lovely.' She watched as he summoned the waiter to bring the bill.

'Rick. How are you?'

Even if the faint aroma of exclusive male cologne hadn't warned her, the slow curl in the pit of her stomach did.

Dominic Andrea. Dark eyes, inscrutable expression behind the warm smile.

'Francesca.' The intimate inflexion he gave her name made the hairs at her nape rise in protest. Something that irritated the hell out of her and lent a very polite edge to her voice as she acknowledged his presence.

Dominic leaned down and brushed his lips against her temple. The contact was brief, his touch light. But something ignited and flared through her veins, potent, alive—*electric*.

She wanted to kill him. In fact, she definitely would kill him the next time she saw him. *If* she saw him again. How *dare* he imply an intimacy that didn't exist? Would never exist.

'You know each other?' Rick queried, interested in the expressive play of emotions that chased fleetingly across his daughter's features.

'We dined together earlier in the week,' Dominic enlightened smoothly.

Damning. Francesca cursed, all too aware of his intended implication.

'Really?' Rick absorbed the information and wondered whether anything was to be made of it. 'You'll join us for coffee?'

'I'm with two colleagues. Another time, perhaps?' His eyes shifted to Francesca, who met his steady gaze with equanimity. 'If you'll excuse me?'

He reminded her of a sleeping tiger. All leashed power beneath the guise of relaxed ease.

Francesca watched as he turned and threaded his way back to his table.

'I didn't realise you were on such close terms with Dominic Andrea. I have one of his paintings.'

She couldn't imagine her father coveting anything resembling the colourful abstract resting in Leon's gallery. A mental run-through of the artwork gracing Rick and Madeline's walls brought a mental blank.

'The vase of roses in the dining room,' Rick enlightened. 'Madeline assures me it is perfect for the room.'

Francesca had to agree. She'd silently admired it numerous times. Such painstaking brushwork, a delicate blending of colours. Velvet curling petals, the perfection of leaf foliage, the drops of fresh dew. Displayed in a glazed ceramic bowl against a shadowy background. The work of a man, she conceded, who possessed infinite patience and skill. Did those same qualities extend to pleasuring a woman? Somehow she imagined that they did.

Sensation feathered the surface of her skin, and she consciously banked down the acute ache deep within. She experienced guilt, and mentally attempted to justify it.

'Shall we leave?' Rick suggested as he settled the bill. Together they threaded their way towards the exit and parted with an affectionate kiss as they reached the pavement.

Shopping, a visit to the hairdresser and the beautician took care of the afternoon, then she drove home and dressed for the evening ahead.

Obscenely glamorous. Well, the gown was certainly that! Indigo lace over raw silk, form-fitting. A lace bolero, high-heeled pumps and evening purse. Her favourite perfume added a finishing touch.

Familial affection was in evidence during dinner, and Francesca relaxed in the warmth of it. There were gifts to distribute that she'd collected in Rome, and the photographer appeared at their table right on cue.

If Madeline knew it was a set-up, she didn't let on. It was enough that she and her children would appear on the social pages, their names in print.

Sunday brought abnormally high summer temperatures, and Francesca was glad she'd made arrangements to join her mother for a day cruising the harbour on a friend's boat. The breeze made for pleasant conditions, and for the first time in ages she slept the night through, rising later than usual the next morning at the start of what promised to be a hectic week.

Francesca drummed her fingers against the steering wheel in an increasingly agitated tattoo as it took two and sometimes three light changes to clear each computer-controlled intersection.

Traffic into the city was heavier than usual, and a silent curse formed on her lips as green changed to amber, then red.

In less than five minutes she was due to check in backstage in readiness to appear on the catwalk for a charity fashion parade.

The first of many she'd agreed to do during her stay on Australian shores.

Damn. Another red light. Was everything conspiring against her?

Ten minutes later she swept into the main entrance of the hotel, handed her keys to the valet, took the parking stub, then hurriedly made her way into the foyer.

The Grand Ballroom was situated on the first level, and she tossed up whether to take the stairs or the lift.

The stairs won, and minutes later she threaded her way through milling guests to the main doors. Inside uniformed waiters were conducting a last-minute check of the tables, and harried committee members conferred, consulted and made small changes to existing seating arrangements.

'Francesca. *Darling!*' Six feet tall, Anique Sorensen, society doyenne and leading fundraiser, embraced her stature by clothing it as expensively and outrageously as possible. This year the focus appeared to be jewellery. Masses of gold chains round her neck and adorning each wrist. On anyone else it would have looked garish, even tacky. But Anique managed to make it appear a fashion statement. 'I'm so grateful you can be here today. You look fabulous. Just fabulous.' She paused to draw breath and clasped Francesca close in a bear-hug, then did the air-kiss thing before releasing her hold. 'How *are* you?'

Francesca said what she knew Anique expected to hear...in one syllable. 'Fine. And you?'

'Ask me after the show.' The smile was in place, but there was an edge to it. 'I'm waiting on two models.'

A fashion showing might *look* smooth and display professional co-ordination out front, but organised chaos ruled behind the scenes.

'Traffic's heavy,' Francesca offered, shifting her garment bag from one shoulder to the other. 'Who?'

'Annaliese and Cassandra.'

Cassandra was a doll, laid-back, easy to get along with and professional. Annaliese, on the other hand, was a sultry cat who played diva to the hilt both on and off the catwalk.

'They'll be here,' Francesca assured her, and caught Anique's wry smile.

'I know, darling. But *when*?' Her sharp gaze circled the room. 'The guests are due to be seated any minute, in ten the compère will announce the charity's chairwoman's introductory speech, and five after that we need to roll.'

'It'll all come together.'

'It always does,' Anique agreed. 'I'd kill for a cigarette and a double gin.' She gave a long-suffering sigh. 'I swear, next year I'm not going to be on *any* committee.'

'You will. They need you.' It was true. 'No one can pull in the people the way you do.'

The eyes softened, their expression sincere. 'You're a sweet girl, Francesca.'

The usual bedlam reigned backstage, with racks of clothes and accessories and fellow models in various stages of undress fixing their make-up. Designers' assistants, co-ordinators, were each running numerous preliminary checks in the countdown to showtime.

Always there were last-minute changes, alterations that had to be noted on everyone's list. Mostly, they got it right.

Francesca checked the clothes and accessories she was to wear, and their sequence, then she shed her outer clothes and got to work on her make-up.

'Fran, sweetie.' Cassandra, tall, willowy and a natural blonde squeezed in to grab some mirror space. 'I need someone to tell me I'm sane.'

'You're sane,' Francesca said obligingly. 'That bad, huh?'

Cassandra delved into her make-up bag and seconds later her fingers flew with lightning speed, a touch of blusher here, eyeshadow there, and an experienced twist with the mascara wand. 'My daughter has tonsillitis, I broke a nail on the car door latch, snagged a run in my tights, and got caught in traffic.' She outlined her mouth and applied brilliant red gloss. 'Annaliese has yet to put in an appearance out front, and Anique...' She paused, and rolled her eyes in a wonderfully expressive gesture.

'Is about to go into orbit?' Francesca completed drily.

'You got it in one.'

The compère's introduction could be heard in the background. 'Five minutes,' one of the co-ordinators warned, whirling as a figure dressed entirely in scarlet flew into the room. 'Annaliese. You're impossibly late.'

The leggy, dark-haired model gave a careless shrug, tried to look apologetic and failed. 'Blame the cab-driver.'

'We'll run you last in the first segment,' the co-ordinator improvised. 'Just *hurry*, will you?' She altered her list, and moved quickly to ensure the alteration was duplicated.

Francesca stepped into casual shorts, secured them, added a top, and slid her feet into heeled slingback white sandals. Then she picked up the wraparound skirt and hitched it over one shoulder.

The chairwoman's speech finished, the compère completed his spiel, and the music began.

'OK, girls,' the co-ordinator announced. 'This is it. Cassandra, you first. Then Francesca.'

Upbeat music, flashing lights, *showtime*.

It was a familiar scene, different catwalk, another city. Francesca waited for her cue, smile in place, then she emerged on stage. Each movement was perfectly co-ordinated as she walked to the centre, paused, and turned before taking the catwalk. Choreographed action that displayed the clothes to their best advantage.

Resortwear, swimwear, city and career wear, collections, formal evening wear, bridal.

Designers fussed, assistants frowned, and the co-ordinators soothed and cajoled and kept everything moving smoothly.

Francesca effected one quick change after another, exchanging shoes, accessories. The bridalwear segment was the designers' *coup de grâce*, and each gown was modelled solo to give specific impact. Slow music and a slow pace down the length of the catwalk and back.

Then all the models appeared on stage together, the guests gave a noisy ovation, the compère wound down and the designers slipped out to stand beside the model wearing their creation. Then it was all over.

Waiters began appearing, bearing trays laden with plates of food, and drink waiters hovered unobtrusively as they took and delivered orders.

Francesca emerged backstage and began discarding the heavy satin beaded gown. Her own clothes felt comfortable by comparison, and she crossed to the mirror to tone down her make-up.

On the agenda was something light to eat, then she'd drive back to the apartment, change and swim a few leisurely lengths of the pool.

'Will you be at Margo's tomorrow?'

She glanced up at the sound of Cassandra's voice. 'Yes. You too?'

'Uh-huh.'

'I don't do it for free,' Annaliese declared in bored tones as she joined them.

'Really?' Cassandra queried sweetly, unable to let the unintentional *double entendre* escape unmentioned. 'As a matter of interest, how much do you charge?'

Francesca saw Annaliese's eyes narrow, glimpsed the anger tighten that full mouth. 'Jealous, *sweetie*?'

'Why, *no*, honey. I don't relish the attached strings.'

'Pity you didn't consider *strings* when you opted to travel the hard road as a single mother.'

Oh, my, Francesca accorded wryly. Much more of this and there would be a cat-fight.

'Annaliese, why don't you hush your mouth before I do it for you?' Cassandra queried silkily.

'One hopes that's an idle threat, darling. If not, let me warn that I wouldn't hesitate to lay assault charges.'

'Bitch,' Cassandra muttered as soon as Annaliese vacated the changing room. 'She likes to rattle my chain.'

'It's her favoured pastime,' Francesca enlightened as she collected her garment bag and slung it over one shoulder. 'I'm out of here.' Her lips curved into a generous smile. 'See you tomorrow.'

As she emerged from backstage Anique snagged her arm and heaped ebullient praise for a job well done.

Ever polite, Francesca paused to exchange a greeting with various women, some of whom she knew and others she did not. Consequently it seemed an age before she was able to escape into the main lobby and summon the valet to collect her car.

'A message for you, ma'am.'

Who? she queried silently as she took the envelope from the valet's hand. 'Thanks.' She switched on her mobile phone and checked her voicemail, then she lifted the envelope flap and extracted a business card.

Dominic Andrea's business card, with a message *Call me* penned on the back above a series of digits. Francesca didn't know whether to be annoyed or amused, and slipped the card into her bag as she stepped through the automatic sliding doors to wait for her car.

Within seconds it swept into the curved forecourt. The valet jumped out and held open the door as she slid in behind the wheel.

It took longer than usual to reach her apartment, and once inside she tossed down her bag, slipped off her shoes, then padded barefoot into the kitchen for a cool drink.

Ten minutes later she took the lift down to the ground floor and made her way towards the indoor pool.

The soft, clear water relaxed her, easing the kinks from tired muscles as she stroked several laps, then she turned onto her back and allowed her body to drift with the movement of the water for a while before reversing her position.

Employing a slow breaststroke, she made her way to the side and levered herself up onto the tiled edge. Water streamed off her body as she stood to her feet, and she caught up her towel and dealt with the excess moisture.

It was almost five when she re-entered the apartment, and with automatic movements she crossed into the bedroom, entered the *en suite* bathroom and turned on the shower.

Ten minutes later she pulled on a towelling robe and began blowdrying her hair, then she moved into the kitchen to prepare something light to eat.

An omelette, she decided. Eaten in the lounge while watching television.

The phone rang twice during the evening. Her mother suggesting lunch, and Gabbi issuing an invitation to the theatre.

CHAPTER FOUR

MARGO'S boutique was one of several in the exclusive Double Bay boulevard catering to the city's rich and famous.

An astute woman with a love of fashion, Margo had opened the boutique soon after her husband's death in a bid to channel her energies into something constructive. Adhering to instinct, she stocked expensive designer originals that were classically elegant. Her window display held one mannequin, whose apparel was changed every day. A selection of bags were offered to complement designer shoes.

Margo's quarterly invitation-only fashion showings were offered to a valued clientele, with the request that they each bring a guest. Champagne and orange juice flowed, catered refreshments were served with coffee and tea. Margo offered a ten per cent reduction in price on everything in the shop and donated a further ten per cent of the day's take to her favoured charity.

A fondness for using fledgling unknown models had boosted the careers of several, a few of whom had gone on to achieve international recognition.

Francesca had been one of them. Hence, if a visit home coincided with one of Margo's showings, Francesca donated her services *sans* fee, out of respect and affection for a woman who gave far more to charity than was generally known, and who insisted such philanthrophic gestures were never reported in the press.

Parking wasn't a problem, and Francesca crossed the square at a brisk pace, dodging small puddles accumulated from an early-morning rainfall. An elegantly clad vendeuse stood at the door, welcoming guests and checking their invitations. Outside there was hired uniformed security.

Collectively, the jewellery adorning fingers, wrists, necks and earlobes would amount to a small fortune.

Francesca counted two Rolls-Royces and a Bentley lining the kerb, and three chauffeurs engaged in transferring their employers from car to pavement.

The boutique's air-conditioned interior provided a welcome contrast to the high humidity that threatened, according to the day's forecast, to climb into the nineties.

'Francesca.' Margo's greeting held warmth and genuine enthusiasm. 'It's so good to see you. Cassandra arrived a minute ago, and the three novices are already quaking out back.'

A smile tugged the edges of her mouth. 'Quaking?'

Margo's eyes held a musing sparkle. 'Almost literally. And desperately in need of professional wisdom to help put them at ease.'

Francesca thought back nine years to the time she had stood consumed by nerves in one of Margo's changing rooms for the first time and doubted *any* words would make a difference.

'I'll do my best.'

'I'm counting on it.'

Francesca moved through the vestibule to the changing rooms, greeted Cassandra, the co-ordinator assigned to accessorise each outfit and detail their order of appearance, and smiled at the three girls whose expressions bore witness to a sense of awe and trepidation.

They were so *young*. Humour was the only way to go, and her eyes assumed a mischievous sparkle. 'You've forgotten everything Margo said, are convinced your limbs will freeze the instant you go out there, and, failing that, you'll trip and fall flat on your face.' Her mouth curved with impish wit. 'Right? None of which is going to happen. Trust me.'

Margo was an exemplary organiser, and with plenty of staff on hand the fashion showing began without a hitch. Champagne flowed, and the guests were receptive. Seating was arranged three deep in two opposing semi-circles.

Francesca was first out, and she paused, executed a slow turn, then completed a round of the inner circle.

It was as she turned back to the audience that she saw him. Dominic Andrea, attired in a formal business suit, blue shirt, navy tie. Looking, she noted wryly, very comfortable with his surroundings, and not at all daunted at being only one of three men present in a room filled with women.

What the hell was he doing here?

Francesca's smile encompassed everyone and her eyes focused on no one in particular. Head held high, shoulders squared, she went through a familiar routine.

Yet she was acutely aware of the darkly attractive man whose attention she sensed rather than saw, and she had to actively steel herself against the faint shivering sensation that spiralled the length of her spine.

'What gives?'

Francesca cast Cassandra a harried glance as she slid down the zip fastening and stepped out of a tailored skirt. 'Be specific.' She unbuttoned the blouse and discarded it, then reached for an elegant trouser suit.

'There's a man seated third row, centre,' Cassandra declared as she donned tailored trousers and slid the zip in place, 'who seems to be showing an intense interest in your every move.'

As the morning progressed Francesca became increasingly aware of Dominic's presence. And his attention.

Why did she feel so *exposed* beneath his encompassing scrutiny? She hadn't felt this… 'Nervous' wasn't strictly accurate. She'd walked down too many catwalks, appeared at too many fashion showings to allow nerves to undermine professionalism.

Aware. That about summed it up. Attuned to one person to such an infinite degree that you were able to *sense* every glance without seeing it. The tingle that feathered down her spine, the slight heaviness of her breasts as each nipple tightened, and the slow, soft curling sensation deep within.

All this as a result of a few chance encounters

with the man, a few shared hours in company of mutual friends over dinner, and the brush of his lips against her temple? It was crazy.

Even more absurd was the feeling that she'd entered a one-way street from which there was no return.

Wayward thoughts, she dismissed. Her life was pleasant, she had command of it, and memories of Mario filled her heart. What more did she need?

Shared passion. A warm body to hold onto in the long night hours.

Where had that come from?

Fleeting pain darkened her eyes as guilt, remorse, *anger* tore at something deep inside, and for one split second she wanted to run and hide.

Yet she did neither. Professionalism ensured she tilted her head a fraction higher, curved her lips to make her smile a little brighter, and she walked, turned, paused with the ease of long practice.

Intimate, classy, *successful*, Francesca dubbed the event as it came to a close. Everyone bought. Garments, shoes, bags. Each was folded reverently in tissue paper and deposited into one of Margo's stylish carrybags.

Francesca pulled on an elegant Armani trouser suit, slid her feet into high-heeled pumps, then caught up her capacious carry-all and slid the wide strap over one shoulder.

She entered the salon, saw the number of guests milling in groups, and took a steadying breath as she glimpsed Dominic deep in conversation with an attractive woman on the other side of the room.

Why was he still here?

Almost as if he sensed her glance, he raised his head and cast her a penetrating look, then returned his attention to the woman beside him.

Shattering, Francesca perceived. The effect he had on her senses. She'd been supremely conscious of his scrutiny each time she'd circled the salon, and had managed to successfully ignore him.

'Francesca.'

He had the tread of a cat. Francesca turned slowly to face him. 'Dominic,' she acknowledged with due solemnity.

His smile was warm, and his eyes held amusement as he took hold of her hand and lifted it to his lips.

The touch was fleeting, yet she felt as if she'd been branded by fire. Heat flared through her veins, travelling a damning path. If he'd wanted to disconcert her, he'd succeeded.

Potent sexuality at its most lethal, she thought shakily. Wielded by an infinitely dangerous man who, unless she was mistaken, would play the game by his own rules.

He sensed the slight quiver of nervous awareness, felt the startled tightening of her fingers, and allowed her to pull free of him. For now.

During the past hour he'd watched her display a variety of clothes, admired her body's graceful movement, the tilt of her head, the warm generous smile.

Outwardly cool, she schooled her features into a polite mask, and knew that she hadn't fooled him in the slightest.

'If you'll excuse me?' She wanted, needed to get away.

'No.'

The refusal startled her. 'I beg your pardon?'

'No,' he repeated quietly.

Francesca pitched her voice sufficiently low so that no one else could hear. 'Just what the hell do you think you're doing?'

His gaze was steady. 'At this precise moment?'

She lifted one hand and let it fall to her side in angry resignation. 'OK, let's go with "this precise moment".'

A fleeting smile lightened his features, and she caught a glimpse of gleaming white teeth. 'Inviting you to lunch.'

Now it was her turn. 'No.'

His eyes gleamed with dark humour. 'I could add persuasion and kiss you in front of Margo's guests.'

Her voice lowered to a furious whisper. 'Do that, and I'll *hit* you.'

'It might be worth it to see you try.' He didn't give her time to think as he captured her face and lowered his head down to hers.

It wasn't a gentle touching of mouths, or a sensual tasting. Nor was it particularly brief.

This was claim-staking. Possession. Erotic, evocative, and intensely sexual.

Shock reverberated through her body, and she instinctively lifted her hands in an attempt to effect leverage against his chest.

He eased the pressure a little, and she tore her mouth away from his.

'You—'

He stilled the flow of angry words by placing a finger against her lips. 'Not here, unless you want to cause a scene.'

Her eyes sparked with fury, and her mouth shook as she sought to gain some measure of control. She became aware of her surroundings, the salon's occupants, and she wanted to verbally damn him as he took hold of her arm and led her outside.

'You arrogant, egotistical *fiend*,' Francesca accused the second they were alone.

'You didn't respond to my message, and with your telephone and mobile number ex-directory, your address unlisted, you left me no alternative.' He didn't add that he possessed sufficient influence to infiltrate the tight security screen she'd erected around her public and private persona.

'You inveigled an invitation to Margo's showing on that basis?' Anger was very much to the fore, sharpening the gold flecks in her eyes, accentuating the tilt of her head, stiffening her stance. She wanted to rage at him with a torrent of words that would singe the hair on his head.

He shrugged his shoulders. 'It was an interesting experience.'

'That's all you have to say?'

'It gave me the opportunity to watch you at work.'

Being one of few men in a room filled with avid women fashion-followers couldn't have held much appeal. 'I hope you suffered!'

Dark eyes gleamed, and his lips parted to form a quizzical smile. 'Oh, I did, believe me.'

Her chin lifted, and her eyes sparked furious fire.

'What is it with you? Do I present a challenge or something?'

Mockery was very much in evidence. 'Or something.'

It was a loaded statement, one that she refused to examine. 'Let me make it quite clear.' She drew in a deep breath. 'You're wasting your time.'

'That's a matter of opinion.'

Francesca closed her eyes, then opened them again. 'You know my father. Gabbi and Benedict Nicols are mutual friends.'

'What we share has nothing to do with your father, Gabbi or Benedict. Or anyone else for that matter.'

Emotion clouded her features, fleeting and pain-filled. 'We don't share *anything*.'

'Not yet,' Dominic said quietly. 'But we will.' He cupped her cheek in one hand and brushed his thumb along the length of her jaw. And didn't miss the movement in her throat as she compulsively swallowed.

Francesca glimpsed the deceptive indolence apparent in those deep eyes, the silent assurance of a man who knew what he wanted and would allow nothing to stand in his way. The knowledge tripped her pulse and made her heart beat faster. She had to put some distance between them.

'Please let me go.'

It was the 'please' that did it. He trailed his hand down her cheek, outlined her lips with the pad of one forefinger, then he dropped his hand down to his side as he offered a quizzical smile.

'I guess we don't get to eat together?'

'I have to be in the city in half an hour.' And lunch was going to be a salad sandwich and bottled water she'd pick up and eat along the way.

'Another modelling assignment?'

'A photographic shoot.' She took one step back, another to the side. 'I really must go.'

Francesca turned and crossed the road. She could feel a distinct prickle of awareness between her shoulderblades, and she was conscious of every step she took along the pavement.

It was only when she was safely behind the wheel of her car that the tension began to ease, and by the time she reached the city Dominic was firmly expelled from her mind.

The fashion shoot was exhausting, with the designer insisting the photographer do numerous takes from every conceivable angle. Accessories were changed countless times, her make-up touched and retouched, her hairstyle switched from loose and unruly to casually upswept, then confined in a sleek French pleat.

'Anything planned tonight, darling? I'd like to move outdoors, capture you on a lonely beach against the backdrop of a fading sunset.'

It was after six, and she was battling the onset of a headache. More than anything she wanted to step into her own clothes, climb into her car and drive back to her apartment. And sink into a spa and sip a long, cool drink, she added silently.

As a photographer, Tony was a perfectionist. And she was sufficiently professional to want to work *with* rather than against him.

'Are you going to allow me time to eat?' she queried with resignation.

'Of course, sweetie.' His smile was quick, and his eyes held a humorous gleam. 'I'm not an absolute monster.'

'Although you'll want me here early in the morning for dawn shots,' Francesca accorded with cynicism.

'How well you know me.' There was a certain wryness evident. 'But I'm the best.'

Knowledge, not vanity. He won awards every year for his photographic skill, and harboured a genuine love for the camera. Able to combine subject and background to maximum effect on celluloid, and an exceptional strategist, he loathed temperament, lauded professionalism and went to any length to achieve the look he wanted.

Together, they worked as a team, stowing clothes and equipment before adjourning to a nearby café for a meal eaten alfresco at a verandah table offering splendid views over a leafy green park.

Afterwards they headed north in a small convoy of vehicles to a designated cove where a makeshift tent was erected in which Francesca could change.

The cool breeze from the ocean whispered across her skin and lifted a few loose tendrils of hair as she moved at Tony's bidding, providing one pose after another as he clicked off rolls of film.

'Just a few more, Francesca. I want to do some black and white shots.'

Dusk began to dim the peripheral fringes, providing shadows that grew and lengthened, shading colour and merging lines.

'OK, that's it,' called Tony.

The equipment was dismantled, the clothes restored into individual garment bags and packed into the van. Lights along the boardwalk provided illumination, in direct contrast to the expanse of indigo sea.

Tony stowed his camera in the car, then turned towards her. 'Care to join me in a drink? There's a trendy little bar two blocks away.'

'Will you be offended if I say no?' Francesca countered.

'A date, darling?'

She smiled as they left the sand and stepped onto the bricked walk. 'With my bed. Solo,' she added as she anticipated his response. 'I imagine you'd prefer me bright-eyed and vivacious tomorrow?'

'As a photographer, yes,' he grinned. 'As a man, I'd derive pleasure from seeing you languorous and sated after a long night of loving.'

An arrow of pain lanced her body's core, and it cost a lot to inject a degree of humour into her voice and keep it light. 'You don't give up.'

'Maybe one of these days you'll say yes.'

He was a nice man. Personable, intelligent, and easy to talk to. She'd worked with him frequently in the past, and wanted to continue to work with him in the future.

'To a drink?'

His laughter brought a smile to her lips. 'Know all the angles, darling?'

'Almost every one,' she assured.

'So,' he concluded slowly, 'no shared nightcap, not even coffee?'

'I'm taking a raincheck, remember?' She leaned forward and placed a fleeting kiss to his cheek. '*Ciao*, Tony. I'll see you in the morning.'

CHAPTER FIVE

ELECTRONIC chimes brought Francesca into a state of wakefulness, and she uttered a faint groan as she rolled over to hit the 'stop' button.

Damn Tony and his photographic inspiration. Yet, even as she silently cursed him, she was sufficiently professional to recognise his vision. And doubtless she would applaud it when she sighted the finished prints.

A shower swept away any vestiges of the night's cobwebs, and a glass of fresh orange juice did much to revitalise her energy. It was too early for breakfast, so she merely extracted a banana from the bowl of fruit in the kitchen.

Attired in stylish loose-fitting cotton trousers and matching top, basic make-up complete, she slid her feet into low-heeled sandals, collected her bag, then took the lift down to the underground car park.

Within minutes she reached the main arterial road. Traffic at this early hour was minimal, and there was almost an eerie solitude in traversing darkened streets whose only illumination came from regulated electric lamps.

There was a tendency to be introspective and allow one's thoughts free passage.

Dominic Andrea. An intriguing man, with diverse interests and recognised as a skilled entrepreneur. There could be little doubt that that skill ex-

tended to the bedroom…or wherever else he chose
to indulge in sex.

She drew the line at defining it as lovemaking.
'Love' was a definitive word that had little to do
with a mutual slaking of the senses as two people
took pleasure in each other's body without trust or
commitment.

The thought of Dominic Andrea in the role of
lover aroused feelings she found difficult to dispel.
To tread such a path would be madness.

Dear heaven, what was the matter with her?

Francesca reached forward and switched on the
car radio, grateful for the busy sound of rock music
and the artificial brightness of an early morning DJ.
It helped redirect her focus.

Which, she rationalised, was a dawn fashion
shoot that needed to be set up in early-morning
darkness with everything in readiness for the first
sign of light on the horizon.

Three cars and a van hugged the kerb when she
slid to a halt behind Tony's distinctive BMW.
Lights were already set up on the beach, the tent
was in position, and as she drew close she could
hear the sound of muted voices.

'Morning, everyone.'

Tony gave her a weary smile as she entered the
tent. 'Good girl, you're on time.' He cast his watch
a quick glance. 'Ten minutes, OK? Same gown,
hairstyle. Less make-up.'

The sky was just beginning to lighten as
Francesca assumed position within a metre of the
receding tide. Wet sand gleamed like well-oiled
gunmetal, melding with a smooth liquid sea.

Before their eyes grey shadows melted beneath the emergence of soft colour, like the transforming brush from an artist's palette. And the air bore a freshness untouched by the sun's warmth.

'Let's get this show on the road. We won't have long,' Tony warned as he lifted his camera. 'Francesca?'

'Ready when you are.'

The camera clicked, shutter moving forward as he called for her to move this way, then that.

'Head up a little higher. That's it. Hold it. Now turn towards me and smile. Mona Lisa, darling.' Shot after shot was taken. 'OK, now we want happy. Not quite laughing. Got it.'

The shutter whirred at a fast pace. 'Movement, sweetie,' he directed. 'Let's see that skirt swirl, shall we? More. Again. And again.' He was moving rapidly, his hands and body co-ordinating perfectly as he talked. 'Damn. The light's coming up fast.'

Five minutes later he capped the lens. 'That should do it. Thanks, everyone.'

It was shaping up to be a hectic day, Francesca perceived a trifle ruefully as she shed the gown, then pulled on her trousers and top. At lunch she was booked to tread another catwalk, and this evening she was due to dine at her father's home. With deft movements she twisted her hair into a knot atop her head, then slid her feet into sandals.

'Care to share coffee before we each get on with the day?' Tony queried as she emerged from the tent.

'Love to,' Francesca accepted, grateful for their

easy friendship as they trod a path across the sand
to the parked cars.

They each stowed their bags, locked the boot,
then crossed the road to the beachside café.

'I'll order,' Tony indicated as they slid into an
empty booth. 'Short black?'

'Please,' she responded gratefully, and sipped the
dark aromatic brew from the cup placed in front of
her shortly afterwards.

'You're covering today's charity luncheon at the
Hilton?'

''fraid so, darling.' He drained his cup and sig-
nalled for the waitress to refill it.

'All those dowagers dressed to kill, fawning over
you in a bid to have their photo appear in the society pages, huh?' Francesca teased, and caught his
faint grimace.

'They send me gifts. Champagne, expensive trin-
kets. One matron even went so far as to offer an
unforgettable all-expenses-paid weekend on
Hayman Island.'

'Tell me you declined.'

He offered a wry smile. 'I don't accept bribes,
as tempting as some appear.'

It was almost eight when Francesca slid behind
the wheel of her car and drove to the gym. An
exercise routine was so much a part of her daily
regime that she scarcely gave it a thought.

There was little time to spare when she returned
to her apartment in order to shower, dress, and drive
into the city.

The fundraising luncheon in aid of the Australian
Cancer Society was a major event. The venue was

prestigious, and the guest list read like an excerpt from the city's register of the city's rich and famous.

'Sell-out' was whispered from one to the other as the speeches progressed and lunch was served. Then the compère announced the start of the fashion parade and the music began.

The main lights dimmed and strategically aimed arc lights lit the catwalk. Showtime.

Afterwards, Francesca tidied her hair, retouched her make-up, then collected her bag. With luck she'd be able to slip out and make an exit without too much delay.

She was halfway across the room when she heard a familiar voice call her name.

'Francesca.'

Her stepmother, with Katherine at her side, seated at a nearby table. 'You'll join us for a coffee, won't you?'

Madeline was adept at making a query sound like a command, and there was little Francesca could do other than slip into the indicated seat.

Katherine offered a conspiratorial wink, well aware that her mother's main purpose in issuing the invitation was to bolster her own social prestige. Smart girl, Katherine.

It was thirty minutes before Francesca could orchestrate her escape, and a further half an hour before she joined the flow of traffic leaving the city. Consequently it was almost five when she re-entered her apartment.

After a day exchanging one elegant outfit for another, she would have preferred to slip on a robe,

eat a light chicken salad, watch television, then settle for an early night.

Instead, she selected a stunning black silk trouser
suit, added a touch of gold jewellery, applied minimum make-up, highlighted her eyes, and left her
hair loose to cascade onto her shoulders.

Lights blazed in welcome as Francesca traversed
the long, curved driveway leading to Rick and
Madeline's elegant double-storeyed Tudor-style
home situated high in suburban Vaucluse.

The interior reflected Madeline's exquisite taste,
and Francesca greeted Katherine and John with affection, brushed cheeks with her stepmother and accepted Rick's warm bear-hug.

'Have a seat, Francesca,' Madeline bade. 'Rick
will get you a drink.'

Diplomacy and an adeptness born of many years'
experience in recognising Madeline's *modus oper-
andi* ensured that Francesca kept within the un-
written boundaries. Once you knew the game, it
was relatively easy to play.

'Orange juice? A wine spritzer?'

'A spritzer would be great,' she accepted
warmly.

The sound of the door chimes provided an inter-
ruption, and Madeline turned towards Rick. 'That
will be Dominic. Let him in, darling.' She turned
to Francesca. 'You don't mind the inclusion of another guest?'

There was nothing she could do except smile. 'Of
course not.'

Rick knew better than to matchmake. Madeline,
however, had no such qualms, and was adept at

assembling people together in order to create an interesting evening.

Dominic Andrea's motives for accepting the invitation were open to conjecture.

'He's really a hunk, isn't he?' Katherine enthused with teenage fervour, and Francesca was saved from making comment as her father ushered Dominic into the lounge.

In her line of business she came into contact with many visually attractive men, but few possessed this man's aura of power. It went beyond the physical, and meshed with a dangerous sexuality that threatened a woman's equilibrium. A potent combination, she conceded as she took in his expensive suit, silk tie, hand-stitched shoes, before allowing her gaze to settle on those broad, chiselled features.

Generous mouth, cleaved from a sensual mould. Eyes so dark, yet as expressive as he chose them to be. At this precise moment there was a tinge of humour beneath the projected warmth.

'Madeline.' He moved forward with fluid grace, took hold of his hostess's hand, then turned towards her stepdaughter.

'Francesca.'

'Dominic,' she acknowledged coolly. She felt on edge already, and he'd only just entered the room. What on earth would she be like at the end of the evening?

Unsettled, if he had anything to do with it.

'A drink, Dominic?' Rick was a considerate host who kept a well-stocked liquor cabinet designed to cater to the whim of any guest.

'Thanks. A soda.'

Madeline smiled. 'The need for a clear head?'

'Perhaps Dominic has an ulcer,' Francesca offered sweetly. 'I imagine an artistic temperament and the pressure of business play havoc with the stress levels.'

'Not an inclination to minimise alcohol to one glass of wine with the evening meal?'

She tilted her head and viewed him in silence for several long seconds. 'How.' She paused deliberately. 'Boring.'

His mouth curved slightly. 'You prefer a man whose mind and actions are clouded with alcohol?'

Oh, my. Was she the only one present who picked up on that *double entendre*?

Francesca silently willed the evening to pass quickly so that she could make her escape at the soonest possible moment without causing Madeline or her father offence.

She caught Dominic's faintly raised eyebrow, and realised that he'd accurately assessed her thoughts.

'I had no idea you were joining us tonight.' As a conversational gambit, it lacked inspiration.

His eyes held hidden warmth and a degree of cynical humour. 'Madeline issued an invitation to look at the positioning of two of my paintings in her home.'

Her head tilted fractionally. 'Do you make it a practice to approve where your paintings hang in all your buyers' homes?'

'Rarely,' he conceded.

'Rick and Madeline should feel duly honoured.'

His soft laughter was unexpected, the humour

tilting the curve of his mouth and fanning tiny lines from each corner of his eyes. Eyes that were remarkably steady, even watchful as he caught each fleeting expression on her finely boned features.

'Perhaps.' Dominic lifted a hand and tucked a stray tendril of hair behind her ear in a gesture deliberately designed to startle. 'Although let there be no doubt that the main reason I'm here tonight is *you*.'

He glimpsed the faint widening of her eyes, the momentary shock, before she successfully masked her expression.

'Dinner is served, ma'am.' The cook's intrusion was a timely one, and Francesca expelled a relieved sigh as Madeline led the way.

Seating was arranged with Madeline and Rick facing each other at the head of the table, Katherine and John on one side, with Dominic and Francesca seated together.

Vichyssoise was followed by barbecued prawns on a bed of rice, with steamed fish, hollandaise sauce and salad as a main course. Crème caramel and fresh fruit sufficed as dessert.

A pleasant meal in what would have been relaxing company—if it hadn't been for Dominic's presence. Francesca was acutely aware of his every action, the smell of clean tailoring mingling with the subtle tones of his exclusive cologne.

He used his cutlery with precise, decisive movements, his enjoyment of the food evident, and he skilfully drew Katherine and John into the conversation, transforming John into an amusing raconteur while Katherine bloomed beneath his attention.

Madeline was at her best. Fame or fortune in a guest was a bonus. To have two dine at her table who could lay claim to both was a considerable *coup*. Rick, sensing his wife's satisfaction, became more expansive as the evening progressed.

'Shall we adjourn to the lounge for coffee?' Madeline queried, signalling just that intention by standing to her feet.

Everyone followed her directive, but Francesca was unprepared when Dominic moved behind her and drew out her chair.

She hadn't expected the courtesy, didn't want it, and had to consciously refrain from pulling her arm away as his fingers lightly clasped her elbow.

'Katherine, John,' Madeline invited graciously. 'If you choose, you can retire upstairs and view television.'

An exemplary mother, and a very shrewd one. Political correctness and good manners were something Madeline insisted upon. It said much that neither of her children grasped the excuse to leave.

Fifteen minutes max, Francesca decided, then she would express her thanks and depart. She sank gracefully into a lounge chair and accepted coffee.

It had been a long day, and tomorrow, after seeing her mother, she'd agreed to join a panel of judges assembled to select three junior models from twenty young hopefuls parading their stuff on the catwalk.

Friday, Saturday and Sunday were free, and she'd designated them as *hers*. For pampering, a professional haircut, a massage. Sheer indulgence.

Unbidden, her eyes met those of Dominic, and

she glimpsed the degree of sensual warmth evident in those dark depths. He presented a disturbing factor, and she was in no doubt of the steel-willed determination beneath the surface.

Francesca finished her coffee, declined a refill, and rose to her feet. 'If you'll excuse me, I really must leave.' Her warm smile encompassed Rick, Madeline, Katherine and John. 'It's been a lovely evening.'

'Likewise,' Dominic accorded with ease as he unwound his length from the chair. 'It's been very enjoyable.'

Why was he timing his departure to coincide with her own? Why shouldn't he? a silent voice demanded as she crossed the lounge at Rick's side, brushed a quick kiss to his cheek at the front door, then stepped quickly down the steps.

'Running away?' Dominic's voice held slight amusement as he matched his pace to her own.

She withdrew a keyring from her evening purse in readiness, and walked past a black Lexus to where her own car was parked. She selected a key and inserted it into the door.

His arm brushed hers as he reached forward and undid the latch, then drew open the door.

'How was your day?'

She slipped past him and slid into the driver's seat. 'You can't really want to know.'

He placed an arm on the roof and leaned in towards her. 'Yes. Humour me, Francesca.'

She slid the safety belt across and clipped it into position. She should have felt in control, yet somehow the advantage appeared to be his.

'A three-thirty a.m. start for a dawn photographic shoot, a fashion parade at the Hilton, dinner with family.'

'And guest.'

'Unexpected guest,' she amended.

'Whom you would have preferred not to be present.'

She tilted her head in order to meet his gaze. 'Perhaps you'll enlighten me as to how you came by the invitation.'

'I occasionally do business with your father.' His shoulders shifted in a slight shrugging gesture. 'Madeline appears to appreciate my paintings. It wasn't difficult to make a phone call.'

No, she supposed. Not difficult at all for a skilful manipulator to pose a few pertinent questions within a conversation in order to gain his objective.

She looked at him carefully, and his sloping smile had the strangest effect, causing sensation to unfurl deep inside and creep insidiously through her body.

'What should I expect next?' She kept her voice deliberately cool. 'The "Your place or mine?" spiel?'

Dominic regarded her steadily. 'Interpreted as, "Let's get between the sheets and I'll show you what you're missing"? I don't play that particular game.'

'With any woman?'

'With you,' he declared with soft emphasis. He reached forward and caught hold of her chin between thumb and forefinger. 'Now, shall we begin again? Tomorrow—'

'There isn't going to be a tomorrow.' Her voice sounded thick and vaguely husky.

'Yes,' he said quietly. 'There is. The day after, or the one after that. Next week. Whenever.'

Francesca looked at him long and hard, saw the calm awareness in his eyes, and felt *exposed* in a way she'd never experienced before. Fear, apprehension—both were prevalent. And a strange sense of recognition. Almost as if something deep inside her had sought and found the matching half of a whole.

She didn't want to deal with it, with *him*, and what he represented. She wanted time to think, to evaluate. Saying yes to this man, on any level, would lead her towards a path she was hesitant to tread.

'This is one situation where your persistence won't pay off,' she assured him.

'You don't think so?'

'I know so.'

'Then prove me wrong and share lunch with me. Nominate a day.' A challenge. Would she accept or refuse?

Fine, she accorded a trifle grimly. If that was what it took to convince him she wasn't interested, she'd agree. Besides, lunch sounded *safe*. Broad daylight, with the excuse of work as a legitimate escape route.

Francesca gave him a long, level look. 'Friday,' she capitulated. 'Name the restaurant, and I'll meet you there.'

'Claude's, Oxford Street, Woollahra. One,' he said without missing a beat.

A fashionably chic French eating place where advance bookings were a must. 'Fine.' She slid the key into the ignition and fired the engine, watching as he stood back and closed the door.

Seconds later she cleared the gates and entered the wide, tree-lined suburban street, following it down until it joined with New South Head Road.

Electric streetlights shared a pattern uniformity, vying with colourful flashing neon signs illuminating the city's centre. Ferries traversed the dark waters of Port Jackson, and a large cruise ship was ablaze with light and life as a tugboat led it slowly towards the inner harbour.

Magical, Francesca reflected silently, and felt a strange pull towards another harbour in another city on the opposite side of the world. Another car, a Ferrari Testarossa, driven by Mario through the steep winding hills above Rome. And how she'd delighted at the sight spread out before her, laughed with the joy of life, then gasped at the speed with which Mario had driven home in order to make love with her.

Mad, halcyon days that couldn't last. Even then she'd been afraid the candle that burned so brightly within him was destined for a short life.

It was almost eleven when she garaged her car and took the lift up to her apartment. With care she shed her clothes, removed her make-up, then she donned a slither of silk and slid in between cool percale sheets.

CHAPTER SIX

AN ELEGANT woman, Sophy adored being *seen*. Consequently her choice of venue was one of the city's currently trendiest meeting places in town.

'*Drinks*, darling,' Sophy had specified the get-together, and Francesca slid into a reserved chair and ordered coffee.

Her mother would be late. After all these years it was accepted Sophy had no sense of time. Excuses, many and varied, were floated out with an airy wave of the hand, and her family and friends inevitably forgave her the lapse.

Thirty minutes wasn't too bad, Francesca conceded wryly as she glimpsed her mother making an entrance. There had been occasions when she'd waited for up to an hour.

Titian hair styled in a shoulder-length bob, exquisite features, and slim curves a woman half her age would die for. Add an exclusive designer outfit, and Sophy presented a visual image that drew appreciative admiration.

'Sorry, sweetheart.' Sophy effected a careless shrug as she slid into the seat opposite. 'Armand…' Her mouth tilted wickedly. 'You know how it is. The French—everything is *l'amour*.'

'I thought you were through with Frenchmen,' Francesca said equably.

'Ah, but they are so *gallant*.' Sophy cast her

daughter an impish smile. 'Besides, darling, he is fantastic in bed.'

'How nice.'

'Yes,' her mother agreed, and her eyes gleamed with humour. 'It's a lovely bonus.'

Francesca wondered with philosophical resignation if Armand was even more unsuitable than his illustrious predecessor, who had squired her mother for a record ten months before Sophy discarded him.

'Now, sweetheart. Tell me what you think of your father. The last time I saw him I thought he was looking quite…' Sophy paused, then added delicately, 'Mature. A few more lines. I recommended my cosmetic surgeon, but you can imagine your father's response.'

Indeed. Voluble, to say the least.

'Madeline makes so many demands, and of course there's the children.'

An emotional minefield Francesca had no intention of entering. 'Would you like coffee?'

'Please.' Her eyes sharpened fractionally. 'You look—different.' Speculative interest was evident. 'Yes. Definitely.' Her mouth curved. 'It's a man, isn't it?'

A man. It seemed such a tame description for someone of Dominic Andrea's calibre.

'Now why would you think that?' Francesca countered evenly, and her mother smiled.

'Am I right?'

'Not really.'

'Ah,' Sophy declared with ambiguous satisfaction, and changed the subject. 'You have yet to mention Mario's mother. So sad. There was a nurse, of course?'

'Yes, round the clock.' Francesca didn't add that she'd shared each shift and snatched sleep as and when she could.

Frequenting the trendiest café ensured there were interruptions, as first one, then another of Sophy's friends stopped by. Introductions rarely identified Francesca as Sophy's *daughter*. Age was something her mother guarded jealously and refused to acknowledge to anyone—for how did a woman who *looked* thirty admit to a twenty-five-year-old progeny.

Armand duly arrived to collect his *amour*, and Francesca wondered how her mother could not see that the man was too attentive, too smooth, and too intent on feeding not only Sophy's ego but his own.

However, Francesca had long given up worrying about her mother's succession of paramours. Sophy was aware of all the angles.

The day after…next week…whenever. Dominic's words echoed inside Francesca's head as she considered calling him to say she'd changed her mind about meeting him.

Except she had the feeling all that would do was postpone the inevitable.

Perhaps it would be better to get it over and done with. They'd talk, eat, and discover whatever he thought they had in common didn't exist. And pigs might fly, she denounced disparagingly.

What existed between them was primeval chemistry, pure and simple. The question was, what was she going to do about it? More pertinently, what was she going to allow Dominic to do about it?

Oh, for heaven's sake. What are you afraid of? she silently berated herself.

Good question, Francesca noted wryly as she entered Claude's and was greeted by the *maître d'*.

'Ah, yes. Mr Andrea is already here.' His smile charmed, as it was meant to do. 'Please. Follow me.'

It was crazy to feel nervous. *Act*, a tiny voice prompted. You're good at it.

Dominic watched as she threaded her way through the room. He observed the number of heads turn in her direction, witnessed the speculation and admiration, and felt a certain empathy for their appreciation of Francesca's beauty.

Experience had taught him that the packaging didn't always reflect what existed in the heart, the mind, the soul, and that physical lust was an unsatisfactory entity without love. Consequently, he refused to settle for anything less.

As she drew close he sensed the imperceptible degree of nervousness beneath the sophisticated veneer, and discovered it pleased him.

He rose to his feet as she reached his table. 'Francesca.'

Her response was polite, and he smiled, aware of the defence mechanism firmly in place...and wondered how long it would take to demolish it.

The *maître d'* held out a chair and she sank into it. 'Madame would prefer a few minutes before she orders a drink?'

'I'll have an orange juice.'

'I shall inform the drink steward,' he said gravely, and with a snap of his fingers a formally clad waiter appeared out of nowhere, took her order, then disappeared.

The lighting was low, the tables small. And Dominic seemed much too close.

Francesca looked at him carefully, and his features seemed more finely chiselled, the bone structure more pronounced in the dim illumination. Dark hair, dark eyes, dark suit. It accentuated his breadth of shoulder and emphasised a physical fitness most men would aspire to.

A complex man, she decided instinctively, who was capable of savagery and great tenderness. It was evident in his painting, for he possessed hands that could slash bold colour on a canvas yet brush strokes on another with such sensitivity the contrast was vast—too vast to imagine the artists were one and the same.

And as a man, a lover? Was he wild and untamed? Sensitive and loving? Were his emotions always under control? *Did she want them to be?*

Oh, God, where had that come from?

With a sense of desperation she picked up the menu and began to peruse it.

'If I say you look beautiful, will you hold it against me?'

His voice held mild amusement, and she lowered the menu, cast him a level look, then offered him a singularly sweet smile.

'Probably.'

A soft chuckle escaped from his throat. 'Should

we aim for polite conversation, or opt for companionable silence?'

'You could tell me what you did yesterday, then I'll tell you what I did,' she said with marked solemnity. 'That should take care of ten minutes or so.'

'Yesterday? I caught an early-morning flight to Melbourne, attended a meeting, lunched with a business associate, flew back mid-afternoon, and played squash.'

'You were meant to stretch that out a bit, not condense it into thirty seconds.'

He reached for his wine glass, lifted it, sipped from the contents, then replaced it onto the table. 'And you?'

'Sat on a panel judging junior models, caught up with my mother.'

'And thought of any number of reasons why you should cancel lunch today?'

It was a stab in the dark, but an accurate one. She opted to go with honesty. 'Yes.'

One eyebrow slanted. 'Do I pose such a threat?'

'You unnerve me.' The words slipped out without thought.

'That's a plus,' Dominic drawled.

She decided to set a few boundaries. 'We're sharing lunch. Nothing more.'

'For now,' he qualified. 'Shall we order? I can recommend the escargots.'

It was an acquired taste, but one she favoured.

The waiter appeared, noted their selection, and disappeared.

Francesca lifted her glass and took a long sip of

iced water, then set the glass carefully on the table. Her eyes met his, their expression wary, faintly wry.

'Do you have anything planned for the weekend?' Dominic queried, and she rested the fork onto her plate then took time to dab her mouth with the napkin before answering.

'A quiet few days—no family, no social engagements.'

'Time out?'

Her fingers strayed to toy with the stem of her drinking glass. 'Yes.'

'There's a function in one of the major city hotels tomorrow evening for which I have tickets. Gabbi and Benedict suggest we join their table.'

Gabbi was a dear friend, whose company she enjoyed. Dominic was something else entirely. The thought that he had no willing partner he could call upon was ludicrous.

'I lend my support to a few charities, but rarely attend their social functions.'

Was her expression so easily readable? She wouldn't have thought so, yet this man possessed an uncanny ability to read her mind.

'Then why are you attending this particular one?'

He leaned back in his chair and regarded her with studied ease. 'Because it provides me with an opportunity to ask you out.'

'And no doubt you meant to sweeten the invitation by joining up with two of my best friends?'

The waiter cleared their plates, and inclined his head as they declined dessert and settled for coffee.

'A simple yes or no will do,' Dominic mocked, and she gave him a brilliant smile.

He always seemed to be one step ahead of her, and for once she felt inclined to reverse the process by doing the unexpected. 'Yes.'

He didn't display so much as a flicker of surprise, nor did he indicate satisfaction at her answer. 'Let me have your address and I'll collect you.'

She wanted to protest, acknowledged the foolishness of taking independence too far, then gave it, watching idly as he penned the apartment number and street on the back of a card.

It was after two when they emerged from the restaurant.

'Where are you parked?'

Francesca felt the touch of his hand on her arm and wanted to pull away, yet stay. A true contradiction in terms, she acknowledged wryly as she fought the deep, curling sensation that slowly unfurled and began spreading through her body.

'About fifty metres to the left.'

It was mid-afternoon and there were several people within close proximity. So why did she feel *threatened*? Fanciful thinking, she dismissed, and resisted the inclination to dismiss *him*, here, now, and walk quickly to her car.

Minutes later she paused at the kerb and withdrew her car keys.

He seemed to loom large, his height and breadth intimidating, and the breath caught in her throat as his head lowered down to hers.

A kiss, brief, in farewell. She would accept the

firm brush of his lips, then step back and smile, slip into her car and drive away.

Francesca wasn't prepared for the warm softness of a mouth that seemed far too attuned to her own, its wants and needs.

Unbidden, her hands crept up to tangle together at his nape as he pulled her close, and a soft protest rose and died in her throat as he deepened the kiss to something so intimate, her whole body flamed with an answering fire.

An invasion of the senses, exploring, savouring. He conquered in a manner that made her forget who she was, and where.

When he lifted his head she felt lost, almost adrift, for the few seconds it took for her to regain a sense of reality.

Her eyes were wide and luminous, and she felt a sense of shock. And shame.

'Tomorrow,' Dominic reminded her gently. 'Six-thirty.' His smile was warm. 'Drive carefully.'

He wasn't even breathing quickly, whereas she felt as if she'd just been tossed high by an errant wave and carried breathless and choking into shore.

She didn't say a word. Couldn't, she rationalised as she stepped from the kerb and crossed round the car to unlock her door.

With every semblance of calm, she started the engine, reversed the necessary metre to allow her clear passage into the flow of traffic, then moved the car out onto the road.

It wasn't until she was several kilometres distant that she began to breathe normally, and later that night, as she lay sleepless in bed, she could still feel the possession of his mouth on her own, the imprint of his body against hers, and the intoxication of her senses.

Francesca woke early, and after a leisurely breakfast she showered and dressed, then drove to a Double Bay clinic for her scheduled massage, facial and manicure.

Lunch was followed by a leisurely browse through several boutiques. One outfit really impressed her, together with shoes and matching bag. Her experienced eye put them all together and transposed them onto her stepsister's slender frame, and she smiled with pleasure as she anticipated Katherine's reaction when she received the gift.

There was time for a coffee with Margo, and it was after four when she slid into the car and headed home. The sun was strong, and she automatically reached for her sunglasses, only to discover they weren't atop her head. They weren't in her bag, either, and she cursed beneath her breath at the thought of having misplaced them.

Sensitivity to strong sunlight occasionally triggered a migraine, particularly if she was under stress, and it was a situation she took precautions to avoid.

By the time she reached her apartment block the familiar ache had begun behind her right eye. If she was lucky, ordinary painkillers would arrest it, otherwise prescription pills and several hours' rest were the only source of relief.

Francesca gave it half an hour, then she rummaged in her bag for Dominic's card and reached for the phone.

He answered his mobile on the third ring. 'Andrea.'

The sound of his voice increased the splintering pain in her head. It hurt to talk, and she kept it as brief as possible.

'I'm in the vicinity of Double Bay. I'll be there within minutes.'

'No, don't—' It was too late, he'd already cut the call.

She didn't want him here. She didn't want anyone here. Even thinking hurt, so she didn't even try to qualify anything, she simply retrieved the packet of prescription pills and took the required dosage.

When the in-house phone buzzed she answered it, then pressed the release button as Dominic identified himself.

Francesca was waiting at the door when he came out of the lift, and he took one look at her pale face, the dark bruised eyes, then gently pushed her inside the lounge and closed the door.

'That bad, hmm?' He brushed his lips to her temple. 'You've taken medication? OK, let's get you into bed.'

She struggled between comfort and propriety. 'The couch.' Her protest was less than a whisper, for it would be heaven to rest her head against his chest and close her eyes.

Ignoring her, he put an arm beneath her knees, lifted her into his arms, and took a calculated guess as to which room was hers.

The bedroom was much as he had imagined it

would be. Feminine, but not overly so. There were no frills, no clutter on flat surfaces, and the colour scheme was pale peach and green.

Without a word he closed the drapes, folded back the bedcovers, then, ignoring her protest, he carefully removed her outer clothes and gently deposited her onto the bed.

'Comfortable?'

The medication was allowing her to sink into numbing, almost pain-free oblivion. 'Yes.'

Dominic drew the sheet up to her shoulders then sank into a nearby *chaise*, his expression enigmatic as he watched her breathing deepen.

Unless he was mistaken, she'd sleep through until the early-morning hours. He'd stay for a while, then he'd leave.

She looked peaceful. Her features in repose bore a classic beauty, the facial bone structure in perfect symmetry, alabaster skin as soft and smooth as silk. And a generous mouth that could tilt with laughter and curve with sensual promise.

Yet there was a vulnerability evident he knew she would just hate anyone—him especially—to witness. An inner fragility that tugged at something deep inside him and made him feel immensely protective.

Dammit, he wanted the right to be part of her life. To earn her respect, her trust. And her love. The *forever* kind. Commitment. *Marriage.*

After one union that had ended tragically, it wasn't going to be an easy task to persuade her to marry again. Nor would she readily believe it was *love* he felt for her, not merely physical lust.

The temptation to cancel out of tonight and be here when she woke was strong. However, she'd resent such vigilance rather than thank him for it.

He left quietly, secured the door, then took the lift down to the lobby and drove home.

It was dark when Francesca stirred, and she opened her eyes long enough to determine she was in bed, then she closed them again, drifting easily back to sleep.

The sun was filtering through the drapes, lightening the room when she woke again, and she groaned as she glanced at the bedside clock.

Food. And something to drink. She tossed the sheet aside, slid to her feet, then padded into the kitchen.

A glass of fresh orange juice did much to begin the revitalising process, and she switched on the coffeemaker, slid bread into the toaster, and nibbled a banana while she waited. Cereal, a hardboiled egg, toast and an apple ought to do it, she mused as the coffee began to filter. Toast popped up, and when the coffee was ready she sank onto a high stool and took the first appreciative sip of caffeine. Bliss. Absolute bliss.

When she'd finished eating she'd take a leisurely shower, then dress and decide what to do with the day.

Meanwhile, she reflected on Dominic's ministrations, and his presence in her bedroom before the medication had taken its full effect. How long had he stayed? And *why*? She wasn't sure if she wanted to know the answer.

The phone rang twice while she was in the shower, and when she checked the answering machine the first call was from Dominic, the second from Gabbi.

She dialled Gabbi's number first, and apologised for her absence the previous night.

Gabbi's voice was full of concern. 'Are you sure you're OK?'

'Fully recovered and ready to face the day,' she reassured her. 'How were things last night?'

There was a momentary pause. 'It was a sell-out. Dinner was fine, and everyone declared the fashion parade to be a huge success.'

'You're hedging, Gabbi. I take it Annaliese played up?'

'You could say that.'

'Much as it goes against the grain, I think you're going to have to get down and dirty with that young lady.'

'Ah, now there's a thought. Any suggestions?'

'Yell? Throw something?'

'All out war, Francesca?' There was amusement evident. 'Think of the repercussions.'

Francesca wrinkled her nose. 'Benedict wouldn't give a damn.'

'Annaliese and her mother are a formidable pair,' Gabbi responded soberly.

Indeed. Francesca considered herself fortunate her own step-siblings were of the loving kind. And Madeline, although fiercely territorial, wasn't sufficiently vindictive to deliberately drive a wedge between Rick and his daughter.

'I suggest you sharpen your claws,' Francesca

indicated with a touch of wry humour, and heard Gabbi's laugh echo down the line.

'Filed and ready.'

They ended the call on a light note, and Francesca was about to punch in the digits to connect with Dominic's mobile when the phone rang.

'Francesca.' Her pulse quickened and went into overdrive at the sound of Dominic's voice. 'You slept well?'

'Yes. Thank you,' she added politely.

'For what, precisely?'

His indolent query raised goosebumps where goosebumps had no right to be. Why was she thanking him? For caring enough to be there for her? Ensuring she was comfortably settled and waiting until the medication took effect? 'Just—thank you.'

She could almost see his features relaxing with a degree of humour, and that sensuously moulded mouth curve into a smile.

'Want to join me on a picnic?'

The question startled her, and she hesitated, torn by an image of finger food eaten alfresco.

'If I refuse, will you seclude yourself in the studio and paint?'

He gave a husky laugh. 'Something like that.'

There was a pull of the senses she found difficult to ignore, and she aimed for a light response. 'How about a compromise?'

'Shoot.'

'I'll come watch you paint, *then* we go on a picnic.'

'You just want to see my etchings.'

She couldn't help the smile that curved the edges of her mouth. 'You've seen *me* at work.'

'Much more glamorous than a pile of blank canvas, numerous quantities of oil paint and mineral turps, I can assure you.'

'We have a deal?'

'Deal,' he responded easily.

'Give me five minutes and I'll be on my way.'

She retrieved a spare pair of sunglasses from the bedroom and slipped them into her bag. Should she contribute some food? Her refrigerator wasn't exactly a receptacle of gourmet treats. Fruit and frozen bread did not a feast make. OK, so she'd stop off somewhere *en route* and collect a few things.

Which was precisely what she did, arriving at Dominic's front door with no less than two carrybags held in each hand.

'I invited you to join me on a picnic, not provide one,' he remonstrated as he divested her of her purchases.

'I got carried away. Besides, I owe you a meal.'

'You don't owe me anything.'

She followed him through to the kitchen. 'Humour me. I have an independent streak.'

A friendly room with modern appliances, she decided as he unpacked the bags and stored a coldpack in the refrigerator.

She cast him an all-encompassing look, appraising the sleeveless shirt, the cut-off jeans, the trainers on his feet.

One eyebrow slanted. 'What did you expect? An enveloping artist's cape?' His eyes gleamed as he reached out a hand and touched one cheek,

glimpsed the faint uncertainty evident and sought
to alleviate it. 'Shall we go?'

She didn't resist as he led her to the glassed
walkway, connecting the large studio above a multi-
car garage to the house.

It was, she conceded, an artist's dream, with sec-
tions of floor-to-ceiling glass and sliding floor-to-
ceiling cupboard doors closing storage areas. Even
the roof held panels of glass to capture every angle
of sunlight.

There were the tools of trade in evidence—pots
and tubes of oil paint, three easels, canvas,
frames—all tidily stored on racks.

Yet she saw splotches of paint on the bare
wooden floor, denoting it as a functional room
where work was achieved.

'Do you need to paint in silence? Or doesn't
noise bother you?'

'Depends on the mood, and the creative muse,'
Dominic answered, watching her closely. This was
his sanctum, a room which revealed more of himself than he liked. Consequently he allowed very
few people access.

'Tell me where you'd prefer me to sit or stand
while you paint.'

'You don't want to explore?'

'I imagine if there's something you want to show
me, you will,' Francesca said evenly.

'Take a seat, while I create a colourful abstract
to be auctioned off for charity next week.'

She watched him turn a blank canvas into a visual work of art. First the block of colour, covered
by bold strokes and strong slashes. It looked so

easy, his movements sure as one hour passed, then another, and she sat there enthralled by his artistic ability to transfer image to canvas. It didn't seem to matter that she possessed little comprehension of the portrayed abstract or its symmetry. The creative process itself was inspiring.

His involvement was total, and interest, rather than curiosity, impelled a strong desire to see some of his completed works. She would have given much to examine the tiered rack where several canvases were stored. Maybe next time.

At last he stood back satisfied. 'That's enough for today.' He deftly deposited brushes, cleaned paint from his hands, then crossed to a nearby sink and washed.

'Let's get out of here.'

He left her in the kitchen. 'I'll go shower and change while you pack food into the cooler.'

He reappeared ten minutes later, dressed in casual trousers and a short-sleeved polo shirt.

They drove north to a delightful inlet that was relatively isolated.

'Hungry?' Dominic queried as he spread a rug on a grassy bank overlooking a curved half moon of sand and sea.

It was almost mid-afternoon. 'Famished.'

Francesca began unpacking the cooler while he unfurled a large beach umbrella and staked it firmly into the ground to provide essential shade.

She set out plates, fresh bread rolls, sliced ham, chicken and salads, brie, fruit.

'A soda?'

'Please,' she accepted gratefully, uncapping the bottle and taking a long swallow of iced liquid.

Dominic split the bread rolls in half and began filling them, then handed her one. 'OK?'

She took a bite, then grinned. 'Excellent.' She felt relaxed, despite the intimacy of their solitude. Carefree, she realized. Something she hadn't experienced in a long time.

Deep down she knew she should be wary, on guard against the mood between them taking a subtle shift. As it inevitably would. But not today. Today she needed some light-hearted fun, and the opportunity to get to know Dominic Andrea, the man beneath the projected persona.

'Tell me about yourself.'

He finished one bread roll and filled another. The look he directed her was piercing, steady. 'What do you want to know?'

'Where you were born, family.'

'The personal profile?' he mocked gently. 'Athens. My parents emigrated to Australia when I was seven. I have two younger sisters, one lives in America, the other in Santorini. My mother returned there five years ago when my father died from a heart attack.'

'Do you see them often?'

His smile held amusement. 'Every year.'

Somehow she'd pictured him as self-sufficient and a loner. 'I guess you have nieces, nephews?'

'Two of each, aged from three months to six years.'

It wasn't difficult to imagine him hoisting a squealing child astride his shoulders, or playing ball. Why hadn't he married and begun a family of his own?

'How about you?'

It was a fair question, and one she sought to answer with equal brevity. 'Sydney-born and educated. Two step-siblings on my father's side. Several from my mother's numerous marriages.'

She wasn't willing to provide him with any more facts than he already knew. 'Let's walk along the beach.'

She rose to her feet in one graceful movement and glanced at her watch, saw that it was four. 'What time do you want to leave?'

'There's no particular hurry to get back.' He stacked the remains of their picnic in the cooler, then stored it in the boot together with the umbrella and rug.

Together they traversed the grassy slope down onto the sand and walked to the water's edge. There was a slight breeze that teased the length of her hair and gently billowed the soft material of her blouse.

The inlet was small, with a rocky outcrop bordering each point as it curved into the sea. Dominic reached for her hand, and she didn't tug it away, nor did she protest when he indicated they walk the width of the inlet.

They exchanged anecdotes, enjoyed shared laughter, and Francesca was aware of a growing friendship that was quite separate from the sexual attraction simmering between them.

The awareness was always there, sometimes just hovering beneath the surface. And on other occasions, when she became conscious of every breath she took, every beat of her heart. Part of her wanted to relax and let her emotions go any which way, and be damned to the consequences. Then logic kicked in and persuaded her to take the cautious path.

It was almost five when they returned to the car, and Dominic deactivated the alarm then unlocked the passenger door.

Francesca reached for the latch, then caught her breath as he placed an arm either side of her, caging her in an inescapable trap.

She glimpsed the darkness in his eyes in the one brief second it took for his head to descend, then his mouth was on hers, seeking what she was too afraid to give.

His lips were warm, evocative, and his tongue slid between her teeth before she had the chance to think.

He was patient, when all he wanted to do was possess. Gentle, not willing to frighten. And coaxing, persuasive, waiting for her response.

Francesca felt the betrayal of her body, the rapid pulse-beat, the slight quiver that began deep inside and invaded her limbs. The ache of awareness throbbed, radiating until she felt *alive* with sensation, and she kissed him back, luxuriating in the brush of his tongue against her own in a light mating dance that soon began to imitate the sexual act itself.

She wanted him closer, much closer, and her arms lifted to encircle his neck as she leant against him.

His arousal was a potent force, and a silent gasp

died in her throat as his hand slid down to cup her bottom, pressing her even closer.

Then he began to move, slowly, creating a barely perceptible friction that was so evocative it became almost unbearable to have the barrier of clothes between them.

A hand moved to her breast, outlined its shape, then slipped inside her blouse, beneath the lacy bra to tease the sensitised peak.

Her faint moan was all he needed, and his lips hardened as he took total possession of her mouth.

No one had kissed her with quite this degree of passion. Desire was there, raging almost out of control. His, hers. There was no sense of time or place, just total and complete absorption in each other.

It was a child's voice, pitched high and piercing, that succeeded in bringing a rapid return to sanity.

Dominic's breathing was no less heavy than her own as he buried his forehead in her hair. Her skin was warm and moist, as was his as she withdrew her arms and tried to gain leverage against the powerful body pressing far too close to her own.

'Dominic—' The protest left her lips and he lifted his head.

'I know.' With effort he straightened and unlatched the front passenger door, waited until she slid into the seat, then closed it before crossing to the driver's side.

Seconds later the engine fired and the car reversed in a semi-circle, then purred towards the gravelled apron bordering the bitumen road.

Francesca reached for her sunglasses and slid them into place, grateful for the tinted lenses. Dear heaven, they'd behaved like unrestrained teenagers! Hard after that came the thought of what might have happened had they not been interrupted.

Dominic could feel her withdrawal, and sought to prevent it. With a skilled movement he pulled onto the side of the road and brought the car to a halt.

Her face was pale, her eyes far too large as she turned towards him. 'Why are you stopping?'

He leaned an arm on the steering wheel and shifted in the seat. 'Don't close up and go silent on me.'

'What do you want me to say? Shame about the timing?' Her eyes were clear, and there was a faint tilt to her chin. 'Or perhaps I should attempt to comment about the weather, the scenery, in a banal attempt at conversation.'

'I wanted you. You wanted me. If there's any blame, it falls on both of us. Equally. That's as basic as it gets,' he said hardily.

'We were like two animals in heat. In a public area, in full sight of anyone who happened by.'

'Fully clothed,' he reminded her. 'And in control.'

Her mouth opened, then closed again. That had been *control*? What the hell was he like without it? 'Let's forget it, shall we?'

'Nice try, Francesca.' His voice was satin-smooth with a hint of dry humour as he fired the engine and eased the car back onto the road.

She wanted to hit him, and would have if the car had been stationary. He should consider himself fortunate that it took thirty minutes to reach his

home at Beauty Point. By then her temper had
cooled down somewhat.

As soon as the car drew to a halt she slid from
the seat, closed the door, and prepared to cross to
where her own car was parked.

He took his fill of her set features, the straight
back, and her defensive stance. 'Running away
won't achieve a thing.'

Her eyes sparked with a mixture of residual temper and pride. 'Maybe not. But right now I'm going
home.'

'I intend to see you again.'

He was right, she discovered shakily. Running
away wouldn't achieve anything. But she needed
space, and time to *think*.

She took the few steps necessary to her car,
paused, then turned back to face him. 'I have a
modelling assignment scheduled for Tuesday, and
a reasonable night's sleep is a prerequisite to looking good.'

He followed her to the car, and stood within
touching distance. The breath caught in her throat
as he took hold of her shoulders and lowered his
head down to hers.

She wanted to cry out a verbal negation, but it
was too late as his mouth closed over hers in a kiss
that tore at the very foundation of her being.

As he meant it to do.

The knowledge frightened her on a sensual level,
and made her aware of a primitive alchemy that was
shattering in its intensity.

'Tuesday night. Be here, Francesca,' Dominic
commanded silkily.

She was incapable of uttering so much as a word, and her fingers shook as she unlocked her car. The engine fired seconds later and she cleared the gates, aware her breathing vied in raggedness with her fast-pulsing heartbeat.

CHAPTER SEVEN

THE Leukaemia Foundation luncheon was well patronised, the venue excellent, and the fashion parade succeeded without a visible hitch.

Behind the scenes it was a different story. Annaliese arrived late and in a dangerous mood, taking pleasure in denigrating a designer, which reduced him in a very short space of time to a quivering wreck. Nothing assigned from Wardrobe pleased her, and she insisted on making changes, which caused frayed tempers, hand-wringing, and mutterings among the ranks of fellow models, not to mention everyone else involved backstage. It wasn't the worst session Francesca had participated in, but it came close.

Choosing what to wear for the evening took considerable thought, and Francesca cursed as she riffled through the contents of her wardrobe. Relaxed and casual? Or should she aim for sophistication?

The tension knotted inside her stomach as she considered crossing to the phone and cancelling out.

Her fingers momentarily stilled as Dominic's image came vividly to mind. A curse fell from her lips and her eyes clouded with pensive introspection. *What was she doing?*

Why did she have the feeling that he would appear at *her* door within an hour of her failing to appear at *his*?

After much deliberation, she selected an elegant three-piece silk trouser suit in deep emerald-green. Jewellery was minimal, and she stepped into matching stiletto-heeled pumps.

It was a glorious evening. Clear sky, blue ocean, creating a perfect background for various harbour craft taking the benefit of a slight breeze drifting over the sea.

The worst of the traffic making a daily exodus from the city was over, and Francesca experienced no delays at computer-controlled intersections.

Consequently, it was six thirty when she turned into Dominic's drive, and within minutes she cleared the gates and drew to a halt close to the main door.

She hadn't suffered such a wealth of nervous tension since her early modelling days.

Dammit, get a grip, she counselled herself silently as she pressed the doorchimes. Seconds later the door opened, and she summoned a warm smile. 'Hello.'

Dominic's eyes narrowed slightly at the huskiness evident, the faint shadows clouding her expression.

Attired in dark tailored trousers and a cream cotton shirt unbuttoned at the neck, he looked relaxed and at ease.

It would be wonderful to move into those arms and lift her face for his kiss. For a wild moment she almost considered doing just that.

'Bad day?'

Francesca offered a faintly wry smile. 'I guess you could say that.'

'Want to tell me about it?'

'What part do you want to hear?'

'Let me guess. One of the models went ballistic, a designer threw a tantrum, and whoever was in charge of Wardrobe threatened to quit.' One eyebrow slanted in humour. 'Close?'

'Close enough.'

He took hold of her arm and led her into the lounge. 'Mineral water or wine?'

'It's sacrilege, but can I have half of each?'

She felt too restless to sit, and she crossed the room to examine a small painting that had caught her attention on a previous occasion.

It was beautiful in every detail, soft blues, pinks and lilacs, a garden scene. She glimpsed the signature in the lower right corner, and almost forgot to breathe. There was little doubt as to its originality.

'You admire Monet?'

Dominic had moved silently to stand behind her, and she felt his nearness, sensed the warmth of his body.

She turned slowly to face him. 'Who doesn't?'

He handed her a tall frosted glass, and Francesca gestured a silent toast. 'Salute.'

Dinner was a casual meal of barbecued prawns with a variety of salads, eaten informally on the terrace.

'Heavenly,' Francesca accorded as she selected slices of cantaloupe and plump red strawberries from a fruit platter. There was also ice cream. Vanilla, with caramel and double chocolate chip.

She caught his teasing look, and laughed. 'You remembered.'

His eyes gleamed with latent humour. 'Will you eat it? That's the thing.'

She wrinkled her nose at him and selected a spoon. 'Just watch me!'

The view out over the harbour was magnificent as the sun began to fade towards the horizon and the shadow of dusk cast a stealthy haze. Streetlights sprang into life, regulated pin-pricks of white light spreading out over suburbia as far as the eye could see. In the distance was the heat and the beat of the city, flashing neon, bright lights, action.

Yet here it was peaceful, almost secluded, with high walls and cleverly planted shrubbery providing privacy from neighbouring properties.

'Would you like to go indoors?'

Francesca wiped her fingers on a serviette, then let her head rest back against the chair. 'I don't think I want to move.' She sighed at the thought of checking in to the airport at six the next morning.

A fashion parade at the Gold Coast Sheraton Mirage, followed by a photographic shoot, then cocktails with a public relations executive and his colleagues.

Soon she had to fly to Europe for the designer collections. After which she intended secluding herself for a week of rest and relaxation. No phones, no contact whatsoever with the outside world. Where the resort staff were bound to secrecy and the guests paid a fortune for the privilege of total anonymity.

A few weeks ago she'd been sure of her future and its direction. Now she was beginning to query what she really wanted.

'Coffee?'

Francesca turned her head slightly to look at him. 'Please.'

Dominic stood to his feet and moved indoors, and she followed, suddenly restless for something constructive to do.

In the kitchen she watched as he filled the coffeemaker, added ground beans, opened cupboards, withdrew sugar, then set out cups and saucers on the servery counter.

His hands were sure, their movements economical, and her eyes travelled, encompassing the muscular forearms exposed by the turned-back cuffs, the breadth of shoulder, the expanse of chest covered in cream chambray, up to that defined jaw, sensuous mouth, sculpted cheekbones. Those eyes, so dark, so steady as they met hers.

The breath locked in her throat at what she saw there.

Desire. Raw and primitive.

Her pulse quickened to a thudding beat that was audible to her own ears. Visible, she felt sure, as her whole body began to reverberate with answering need.

'Come here.' The command was gently spoken, and she placed her fingers onto his outstretched palm and allowed herself to be pulled into his arms.

His mouth was firm as it settled over her own,

shaping, exploring the soft contours, then nibbling at the lower fullness.

She felt his breath, warm and vaguely musky as he teased his tongue against her teeth, and she stifled a faint gasp as he began to invade the moist crevices, tasting, laving each ridge, each slight indentation, before creating a tantalising foray that deepened into total possession.

One hand slid down her spine and cupped her bottom, lifting her close up against him so that she could be in no doubt of his arousal.

She fitted as if she was meant to be there. *His*. All he had to do was convince her of that.

He could feel her acceptance of *now*, but he sensed her indecision and knew that afterwards she would feel she'd betrayed her dead husband's memory.

Francesca's hands clutched his forearms, then slipped up to his shoulders as his mouth left hers and trailed down to savour the fast-beating pulse at the base of her throat.

Her neck arched, allowing him free access, and she groaned out loud as his lips travelled down to the valley between her breasts and lingered there, caressing the soft fullness with his tongue as he edged the material down to reveal one burgeoning peak.

Dominic breathed in deeply as he tasted the wild honey that was her skin, and wanted more. Much more. He contented himself with the fact that a journey was made up of many steps. If he was to succeed, he'd have to exert patience and take one step at a time.

She wanted to feel his skin, and her fingers moved to the buttons of his shirt, freeing each one, then, not content, she pulled it free of his waistband.

Dear God, he felt good. Tight-muscled midriff, taut chest, and a generous mat of dark hair that just begged to have her fingers curl into its length.

His mouth closed over the roseate peak and he suckled shamelessly, nibbled, then caught the nipple between his teeth and took her to the edge between pleasure and pain.

Her hand slid down over the fold of his zip-fastening, trailing the rigid length before seeking the tab and slowly releasing the nylon teeth.

Fingers feathered over silk briefs to explore what lay beneath, and she felt a momentary sense of panic at the size and thickness of him.

She needed gentle persuasion, reassurance, and above all he had to show her that this was more than just sex.

'Dominic—'

His mouth took possession of her own, cutting off her protest as he utilised every ounce of skill he possessed in showing her part of his heart.

She was vaguely aware of being swept into his arms and carried up a flight of stairs to a bedroom.

His, she decided dimly as he switched on a bedside lamp on a pedestal next to a large king-size bed. Slowly he let her slide down to her feet.

Oh, God—what was she doing? 'I don't think—' She halted as he took her face between his hands and lowered his mouth to hers.

'Don't think,' Dominic bade against her lips. 'Just feel.'

I'm not sure I can give what you want. How would he react if she said those words aloud?

His teeth nipped the tip of her tongue. 'Yes.' His tongue soothed hers and his hands gentled the agitated movements of her own. 'You can.'

He wanted her so badly, *needed* the advantage of joining his body with hers so that he could show her how much he cared. How *right* this was—for both of them.

He kissed her deeply, gently coaxing in a manner that made every bone in her body turn to jelly. Dominic uttered the two words he hoped would make the difference. 'Trust me.'

Dared she? She didn't have any choice as her body proved to be its own traitorous mistress by leaning in to his kiss, giving him access to her mouth so he could plunder at will.

Her clothes, his, were quickly, easily dispensed with, and she stood almost breathless at his male beauty.

Warm, sun-kissed skin sheathed strong muscle and sinew, defining superb musculature with a sculptor's precision. Tight flanks curved down from a narrow waist, his stomach taut with an arrow of dark hair that led down to the juncture at his thighs, thickening in growth as it couched his manhood.

He stood watching her appraisal, at ease with his nudity, and her eyes skimmed the potent thickness of his arousal, skittered to his chest, and came to rest at his chin.

'Look at me.'

I just have. She lifted her face fractionally and met his intense gaze.

He reached for her, closing his hands over her arms as he slid them up to capture her shoulders.

'Open your eyes, Francesca,' Dominic bade her as his breath feathered her cheek. 'I want you to see me. Only me.'

He pulled her forward and lowered his head down towards the soft hollow at the edge of her neck.

His mouth worked an evocative magic as he savoured each and every pleasure pulse until she quivered in his arms.

Heat shimmered through every vein as she went up in flames, and he hadn't even begun.

Beautiful, he thought reverently. The faint edge of shyness appealed, even as it appalled him. She didn't possess that fierce fervour of a woman well-versed in experiencing an explosive climax. Or of one who was fully aware of the pleasure her own body could give, not only to her partner but to herself.

Slow, he determined. Slow and easy. They had the night.

Francesca groaned softly as his fingers trailed low over her stomach, then tangled in the hair curling at the apex of her thighs.

His mouth suckled at one breast, tormenting its peak into a turgid arousal, and just as she thought his touch unbearable he crossed to render a similar assault on its twin.

Fire arrowed from the centre of her being, the flame licking through her body until she felt every nerve, every cell overheating as his skilled fingers probed the moist folds, and she cried out as he stroked the small nubbin, caressing until her whole body shuddered and she sank against him.

A strangled gasp left her lips as he sank down onto his knees and traced the same path with his tongue, tasting the indentation of her navel before savouring the line of her hipbone.

Teasing, tantalising, until he reached the soft hair guarding entrance to her womanhood.

'Dominic—no—' The cry was one of stark disbelief, but he ignored the tug of her hands as she took hold of his head.

But it was too late, much too late as she began to experience the most intimate kiss of all. And as his tongue wrought havoc she went up in flames, unaware of the soft, guttural cries that emerged from her throat, the purring pleasure as he took her higher, or the subdued scream as he held her there before tipping her over the edge.

Dear God, she was sweet. An intoxicating mix of honey and musk. He suckled her moisture, savouring it like a fine wine, and held her firm when she would have fallen.

It was too much, Francesca thought dimly as she sought to retain a hold on her emotional sanity. Way too much. She wanted to beg him to stop, yet the words wouldn't formulate, let alone escape from her throat.

His lips began a slow path over her stomach, then travelled up to her breasts to caress each peak in turn, settled briefly on the rapidly beating pulse at the base of her throat, then took possession of her mouth.

She could taste herself, then only him as he encouraged her tongue to participate in a duelling dance with his own.

It was like nothing she'd ever experienced before. Total capitulation, complete possession, and she was hardly aware of the soft mattress beneath her back until he paused to extract a small foil package from the nearest pedestal drawer.

Quick, deft movements, then his hands moulded her slight frame, caressed, then gentled as he prepared her to accept his length.

She was slick with need, aching as she'd never ached for a man, and she gasped when her flesh stung slightly as he gained entrance. She could feel the expansion of muscles and tissue, the gradual acceptance as he buried himself to the hilt inside her.

Then he began to move, slowly, almost withdrawing before carefully plunging in again, angling his shaft slightly until he felt her muscles seize and grip him. Then, when she was ready, he gradually quickened his movements until she lifted her hips to take him even deeper.

Francesca had thought it couldn't get any better, but she was wrong. His oral onslaught had heightened her senses and stimulated desire to fever-pitch. Now he took her to a higher plane, where mind, body and soul reached perfect accord and transcended anything she'd ever experienced on a sensual level.

So much for control. She had none. Nor did she want any, she decided dazedly as the spiral of sensation reached its zenith.

Perhaps she cried out as he shuddered in the

throes of his own climax, for his mouth settled over hers, soothing, gentling, as he held her close.

For a while she didn't move. Couldn't. She felt warm, and wondrously lethargic. Later she'd feel the pull of unused muscles. But for now she was content just to lie here, and savour the tumultuous aftermath of passion.

She lifted a hand and let her fingers drift down the column of his back, lingering at the indentations of his spine as she explored each vertebra until she reached the strong splay of pelvic bone.

His buttocks flexed, and she felt him swell slightly inside her.

'Uncomfortable?' His voice sounded deep and faintly husky as he grazed the hollow at her neck.

'No.' She liked the closeness, the feel of his large body, the heat and the smell of it. 'Do you want to...?' She paused, suddenly hesitant, and she felt his mouth move to form a smile.

'Disengage? Not particularly.' He shifted his weight so that he rested the bulk of it on his elbows.

He could tell from her expression, the slightly dazed look in her eyes, the soft pink tingeing her cheeks and the glow of her skin that she felt good. Lord, she excited him as few women had in the past. He wanted to take her again, to feel the tightness as she sheathed him and experience the way she moved beneath him.

Yet perhaps not so soon. There was time to tease a little, to play.

Francesca felt him shift slightly as his hands curled beneath her shoulders, then he rolled onto his back, carrying her with him.

He lifted his hands and threaded his fingers through her hair, dislodging most of the pins which held its length in what had once been an elegant French twist.

'Hmm, that's better.' His smile was slightly crooked, his eyes deep and warm as he regarded the tumble of hair falling loose about her shoulders.

He traced the outline of her mouth with his fore-finger, then probed the ridge of her lower teeth.

She bit him, not hard, but sufficiently firmly to see his pupils dilate. Then she suckled the tip of his finger, swirling it with her tongue, just once, before releasing it.

So, the ball wasn't entirely in his court after all, he mused.

There was a certain degree of power in sitting astride a man. Francesca felt in control and wholly sexual, exulting in the flare of passion evident as she used her knees to exert a little leverage, then began rocking, ever so gently, watching as his eyes darkened.

There was a faint line of sweat beading his upper lip, and she leaned forward and carefully removed it with her tongue.

He let his hand slip to her breast, caressing its peak as he cupped the fullness of its twin. Beautiful and firm, the slopes were as smooth as satin to his touch.

With care he urged one engorged peak into his mouth, laving its nipple into button-hardness, and heard her almost inaudible groan as sensation pooled deep within. He could feel her response in the faint tensing of internal muscles, and his own reaction in the burgeoning of his shaft.

For what seemed hours, he had commanded her body, her senses. Now she wanted to tip the scales a little in her favour.

And she did, tentatively at first, then as her confidence grew she took complete control, riding him as hard as she dared until he grasped hold of her hips and surged into her, again and again, lifting her as he arched his body higher and higher, so that his shoulders and his feet were the only parts of him anchored to the bed.

Afterwards he cradled her close, caging her to him as he smoothed his lips across her sweat-drenched brow, his hands soothing her shuddering body until she lay limp and spent.

She must have slept, for she remembered stirring a few times and being gently rocked in strong arms before slipping back into that blissful state that was neither true sleep nor part wakefulness.

'I must go,' she murmured, not once, but twice, only to succumb to the drift of his fingers, the persuasive touch of his mouth.

'Dominic,' she groaned in the early pre-dawn hours. 'I have an early flight to catch.'

He rolled out of bed and scooped her into his arms, then carried her, protesting, into the *en suite* shower.

He bathed her, then swathed her slim form in a voluminous towel. 'Why not come back to bed?' He kissed her nose, then gently savoured that soft mouth. 'To sleep. I promise.' He brushed her lips with his own. 'I'll set the alarm and cook you breakfast.'

It was tempting, oh, so tempting. 'I really have to go home.'

He dried her carefully, offered her a selection of toiletries, then watched as she quickly donned her clothes.

What did she say to him? *Thanks, it was great*?

Dominic saved her the trouble by placing a finger over her lips. 'Take care.'

There was a sense of unreality driving through almost empty streets. There were no stars, no moon. Just an eerie pre-dawn light lifting the greyness of night.

Precisely what time was it? The illuminated clock on the dashboard revealed it was almost four. Two hours from now she needed to front up at the airport check-in counter.

Hardly enough time to snatch little more than even an hour's sleep, she decided without a trace of weariness as she garaged the car and rode the lift up to her apartment. After the night's activity, she should have been almost dead on her feet. Yet she felt strangely exhilarated, *alive* as she hadn't been in the past three years.

Inside, she brewed a cup of strong coffee and drank it black with sugar, then she checked her bags, added a few last-minute items, and made herself breakfast. Fresh juice, fruit, muesli, toast. And more strong coffee.

Awake. And waiting wasn't such a good idea, for it provided time for thought.

Last night she'd slept with a man. A hollow

laugh rose and died in her throat. Hell, *sleep* hadn't even been a consideration!

A complexity of emotions raced through her brain, clouding her perspective.

This relationship— Oh, who was she *kidding*? She groaned out loud. *What* relationship?

And what came next? Did she get to spend a night at his place, he at *hers*, escape for the occasional weekend together?

Good sex without emotional involvement. Responsible. A slightly hysterical bubble of laughter rose and died in her throat at the thought of blood tests, prophylactic protection.

Then she sobered as she became prone to introspection, and she succumbed to the inevitable feelings of guilt at having betrayed everything she held dear about Mario. The shared love, the laughter, her hopes and dreams, her fear for him. The stark replay of that fateful crash.

But tears were for the weak, and she'd shed them long ago.

With determined resolve she reset the answering machine, tidied the apartment, and at five-thirty she collected her bags, locked the door and rode the lift down to Reception, where a cab stood waiting to transport her to the airport.

CHAPTER EIGHT

THE one-hour flight to the Gold Coast was un-eventful, and a friendly hostess escorted Francesca into the terminal and introduced her to a waiting chauffeur, who collected her bag and saw her seated into the rear of a luxury limousine.

There were some advantages in having acquired a degree of fame and recognition, Francesca acknowledged silently as she extracted sunglasses and slid them on.

The fact there were also many disadvantages couldn't be discounted, but this morning she was grateful for Laraine's organisational skills as the limousine headed towards Surfers Paradise.

Long, sandy beaches, gently rolling surf, deep blue ocean, and at this early morning hour a soft azure sky. The many highrise apartment buildings appeared like concrete sentinels in the distance, and as they drew close she could sense the pulse of a thriving industry dedicated to the tourist dollar.

The Sheraton Mirage was a luxury low-rise hotel, with wonderful views and access to a uniquely de-signed shopping complex and marina.

Unpacking was achieved in minutes, and Francesca looked longingly at the large bed, then checked her watch. She had a few hours before she needed to present herself behind the scenes in the grand ballroom downstairs. Time she could kill by browsing the shopping complex, or, what was more sensible, catching up on some lost sleep.

No contest. The bed won. And she quickly slid out of her shoes, discarded her clothes, slipped on a wrap, set the alarm, then lay down.

Not such a good idea, she decided a short while later as she dwelt on the hours she'd spent in another bed.

The only precautions taken had been Dominic's use of prophylactic protection.

Dear heaven, it had been good. Better than good. She tried to come up with a superlative, and failed. Her body still ached from his invasion, and her skin burned as she vividly recalled every detail.

He had taken his time, seducing, making everything a feast of the senses.

To become involved with a man like Dominic Andrea was dangerous, for it would be all too easy to become addicted to his brand of lovemaking, to *him*.

She'd given her heart once, and had it broken. She never wanted to feel that bereft again.

Francesca must have dozed, for she woke to the sound of the alarm and was surprised that she'd managed to sleep at all. A shower would refresh her, then she'd tend to her make-up, her hair, dress, and present herself downstairs.

There was a bowl of fresh fruit in her room, and she selected a banana, peeled and bit into it *en route* to the bathroom.

The Gold Coast Mirage was built right on the beach, with an expanse of marble floor, a stunning indoor waterfall, and a massive pool with an island bar.

The ballroom was situated on the ground floor, and one glance was all it took to determine the social glitterati had turned out in force.

The luncheon was a tremendous success, with capacity seating. Backstage chaos was minimal. There were few mishaps, and none that gained public notice.

At last she was able to escape, albeit briefly, to nibble on some finger food before the scheduled photographic shoot was due to proceed.

The photographer was over-friendly—and, worse, a toucher. Whatever image the assistant instructed Francesca to present he wanted to change—personally.

After two hours of posing in various parts of the hotel and around the pool, Francesca was almost at screaming point. He was too much in her face, and she wanted to tell him so. Almost did, on one occasion, and only barely held her tongue.

At last the final shot was taken, and she could escape to her suite for a brief respite before it was time to change and show up for the cocktail party.

Classic black, long straight skirt split to mid-thigh, a black sequinned singlet top, black tights, high-heeled stiletto pumps, hair piled up on top of her head with a few loose tendrils falling beside each ear, a wide gold necklace and matching bracelet. Retouched make-up.

Francesca snatched up a slim black evening purse, slipped the long gold chain over one shoulder, collected her key, and made her way to the lounge bar.

One hour, tops, then she'd retire gracefully and return to her suite, where she'd order a room service meal, then shower and fall into bed.

Several more guests began to wander into the lounge, and there were introductions, polite small talk, as well as a few informal speeches while canapés were served.

The photographer gravitated to her side and made such a nuisance of himself that when he tried to get too close she aimed her stiletto heel and brought it down on his instep.

His face whitened, then flared blood red. 'Bitch.'

Without a word she turned away from him, located the hostess, then the organiser, and exited the lounge bar.

She reached her suite, and once inside put the safety chain in position. Then she leaned wearily against the door.

Damn. She hadn't needed aggravation at the end of a long and difficult day. Following a sexually active, sleepless night.

An audible groan escaped from her lips, and she levered herself away from the door and crossed the room to the bar fridge, where she selected cold bottled water, removed the cap, and poured the contents into a glass.

Francesca kicked off her shoes, removed her earstuds, then carrying the glass into the bathroom, she began cleansing her face of make-up.

A sharp double knock on the outer door came as a surprise. She had yet to order room service, and it was way too early for the maid to turn down the bed.

She wiped her hands on the towel and crossed the room. 'Who is it?'

'Dominic.'

Dominic?

Francesca opened the door a few inches. 'What are you doing here?' The words slipped out before she could prevent them, and she saw one eyebrow lift.

'This is not the most ideal way to have a conversation,' he drawled, and she immediately freed the chain.

Attired in tailored dark trousers and an indigo cotton shirt unbuttoned at the neck, he exuded raw masculinity.

'I guess you just happened to be in the neighbourhood and decided to drop in.' As an attempt at flippancy, it failed miserably.

She didn't look as if she had weathered the day any better than he had. Fragile, definitely—and, if he wasn't mistaken, feeling acutely vulnerable.

He lowered his head and kissed her with gentle thoroughness, then pulled her into his arms and kissed her again.

When his mouth lifted fractionally from her own, she ventured, 'I should ask what you're doing here.'

He traced light kisses along her lower lip, then caught it between his teeth and bit gently. 'Should you?' His lips moved to one ear and trailed a path down her neck to one sensitive hollow, savoured it, and began exploring her throat. 'I didn't want to spend the night without you.'

Well, that certainly spelled it out. And momentarily rendered her speechless.

His soft laughter was almost her undoing. 'Did you manage to get any sleep at all?'

Francesca rolled her eyes expressively. 'I look that bad, huh?'

He lifted a hand and trailed fingers along the edge of her jaw. 'Slightly fragile.' He lowered his head and brushed his lips against her own.

'I think you can safely say that's an understatement.'

She felt rather than saw his faint smile. 'Then I think I should feed you.'

The sensual heat of his body was matched by the increasing desire in her own. If they remained in the suite they probably wouldn't get to eat at all.

'Let's walk across the road and choose one of the several restaurants overlooking the Broadwater,' she determined, and saw his lips curve with amusement.

'Safety among a crowd?'

She offered a witching grin. 'Yes.' She moved a few paces, slid her feet into heeled pumps, collected an evening bag, and tucked her hand in his.

They chose Saks, and within minutes they were seated at a window table. Soon the sky would darken and night would fall, but until it did they had a clear view of boats lining the marina and people strolling along the wooden boardwalk.

Francesca ordered a starter, a main course, and a delicious dessert.

It was an excellent meal, eaten leisurely, and afterwards they took their time over coffee. Then

Dominic settled the bill and they took the overhead footbridge to the hotel.

No sooner had they entered the main lobby than a male voice announced, 'Well, well, look who's here.'

The photographer. Slightly inebriated, and, if Francesca wasn't mistaken, out for vengeance.

He positioned his camera and reeled off some film. 'Our famed ice maiden, and escort.' His smile was vaguely feral as he subjected Dominic to a raking appraisal before focusing his gaze on her. 'No wonder you skipped the party, darling.'

With camera in hand, he held a powerful weapon. Francesca pinned a smile in place and kept walking.

'Both staying here together?'

He followed them towards the guest wing, and ventured past the 'Private—Guests Only' glass sign.

Dominic paused, then turned so that Francesca was shielded behind him. 'One step further and I'll alert the management and have charges filed against you for harassment.'

'I'm only doing my job.'

'Then I suggest you go do it some place else.'

When they reached her suite Dominic held out his hand for her key. 'Is there any need to initiate damage control?'

Francesca preceded him into the room. 'A phone call to my agent.' She tossed her evening purse down onto the nightstand and lifted the handset. 'Help yourself to a drink.'

Five minutes later she replaced the receiver and turned to find Dominic watching her.

'You've encountered this sort of problem before?'

The stalker, the pervert, the fanatic. The nightmare no one wanted.

Only her father knew about the letters she'd received for months after Mario's death. Words cut from newspapers, magazines, pasted onto blank paper and sent through the post. Compiled by a sick but shrewd mind. It had taken six months for the police to pin him down, and in that time she'd learnt to defend herself. The down and dirty kind of fighting that wasn't taught in any dojo.

Dominic caught the fleeting shadows, calculated the reason, and decided not to pursue it. There would come a time when she trusted him enough to share, and he could wait.

Francesca met his dark, discerning gaze with equanimity. 'The photographer wasn't a problem, merely a nuisance.' She crossed to a single chair and sank into it.

Last night she'd shared every intimacy imaginable with this man. Now she didn't know how to proceed. Or even if she should. A hollow laugh rose and died in her throat.

She wasn't aware of him moving. Yet his hands rested on her shoulders, soothing, gently massaging the cricks, the stiffness out of tense muscles.

It felt like heaven. 'Don't stop,' she begged, and, closing her eyes, she gave herself up to the magic of his touch.

Minutes later she groaned in protest when he

lifted her into his arms and deposited her on the bed. With deft movements he dispensed with her shoes, then her skirt. Next came her top.

'Dominic—'

He drew the bedcovers back, then pressed her forward to lie on her stomach. 'Just relax and enjoy.'

Francesca thought every muscle in her body would melt, and after the initial few seconds she simply pillowed her head on her arms.

It was impossible to fight against the tiredness as she reached a state of total relaxation and drifted to sleep.

She didn't feel the mattress depress slightly as Dominic carefully eased himself to his feet. Nor was she aware that he pulled the covers over her, or that he divested himself of his clothes, crossed round to the other side of the bed and slid between the sheets.

Francesca stirred, sensed the comfort of warm flesh and muscle, and in the depth of her subconscious mind she didn't question it. Merely shifted slightly to seek closer contact. And sighed with satisfaction as fingers lightly drifted the length of her spine.

It was a dream. A hazy, lazy vision she didn't want to lose. The faint musky male scent mingling with a subtle remnant of cologne merely added another dimension.

Lips grazed her cheek, then slipped to nuzzle the hollow at the edge of her neck. Mmm, that felt good. So good, she almost purred as the lips trailed to her breast, savoured, then suckled gently before sliding slowly to the curve of her waist where they traced a path to her navel, settled, succoured, and continued down over the soft concave of her belly.

Francesca moved restlessly with anticipatory pleasure, then groaned her disappointment when they began a caressing pattern close to her hip.

Fingers teased the short curls guarding her feminine core, then slid inward to stroke the sensitive clitoris.

This was one hell of an erotic dream, she mused as sensation built to a slow ache and began spiralling through her body. So acute that it seemed much too real to belong in anyone's subconscious mind.

The sweep of a hair-roughened leg against her own provided the catalyst that broke the dream and plunged her into reality.

There was a faint click, then the room flooded with light.

Francesca's lips parted, then closed, and her eyes felt incredibly large as she stared into masculine features mere inches from her own.

A dark shadow covered his jaw, a night's growth of beard that lent a raw sexuality to broad bone structure. His eyes were warm, dark, and incredibly sensual.

'Good morning,' Dominic said gently as he trailed a forefinger down the slope of her nose, then slipped down to trace the soft fullness of her mouth.

What followed was a sensual tasting—a prelude to slow and languorous loving when heightened senses flared to fever pitch, only to subside in a long sensuous aftermath.

'What time is it?'

Dominic angled his wrist in order to read the luminous dial on his watch. 'Ten past seven. Want me to order room service?'

She was hungry, and said so. At the sudden gleam in those dark eyes she quickly qualified, 'For food.'

His smile melted her bones, and he leaned forward to brush her lips with his own, then slid from the bed and stood to his feet. Unashamedly naked, his superbly muscled frame was sleek and potently male.

Far too potent, Francesca reflected as she watched him walk through to the *en suite* bathroom. Wide shoulders, a well-defined waist, tight buttocks, and long, muscular legs.

He moved with the natural ease of a physically fit man who was comfortable with his body. Assured, confident, and animalistically graceful, combining strength and power that was beautiful on an intensely male level.

As soon as the door closed behind him she pushed aside the bedclothes and reached for her robe.

Ten minutes later they walked through to the beach. White sandy foreshore and startlingly blue sea stretched as far as the eye could see to the south as the shoreline hugged the land mass.

At this hour of the morning the air held a clean freshness, warmed by the sun but without the intensity of heat that would follow as the day progressed.

'Is this going to be a brisk aerobic walk or do we stroll?' Dominic enquired as they cleared the perimeter of crunchy dry sand and gained the level, tightly packed variety fringing an outgoing tide.

Francesca cast him a considering look, taking in the casual shorts, the shirt slung carelessly across his shoulders and knotted at his chest, the peaked cap and the joggers. 'Aerobic,' she determined, and set the pace.

He shortened his stride to hers, and she shot him a winning smile.

'An attempt to expend any excess energy?'

'Mine or yours?'

His laughter was low and husky. 'Both, I imagine.' The dark, gleaming glance he threw her held more than humour, and she fought against the surge of heat flooding her veins.

He was getting too close. Much too close for her peace of mind. Invading her space, her time, and infiltrating her emotions. With a controlled determination set to destroy each and every one of her carefully erected defences.

She had a strong, instinctive feeling that with Dominic Andrea it would be all or nothing. And she wasn't anywhere near ready to examine *all*.

The beach was far from isolated. People walked, jogged, some casually, others with an intensity that spelled adherence to a fitness regime.

They reached Narrowneck, so named for the narrow strip of land separating river and ocean at that particular point, and followed the Esplanade into the heart of Surfers Paradise.

Tall, high-rise apartment buildings were positioned one after the other, and there were numerous

outdoor cafés and ice cream parlours geared to at-
tract the tourists.

'Want to stop for coffee?'

Francesca spared him a sweeping glance. 'And
croissants?' she added, feeling ravenously hungry.

He smiled as he caught her hand in his and led
her onto the boardwalk.

'A pre-breakfast snack?'

She wrinkled her nose at him and laughed. The
day seemed suddenly brighter, and it had nothing
to do with the sunshine.

They headed for the nearest café, took an outdoor
table, and Dominic ordered from the waitress.

A large table umbrella protected them from the
sun's encroaching heat, and Francesca sipped the
ruinously strong brew as she idly viewed the ocean
and the few people enjoying an early-morning
swim.

He watched as she split open a croissant and
spread each half with jam. She looked refreshed,
alert. Yet he sensed the slight defensive edge beneath her smile. If he wasn't careful, she'd attempt
to put him at arm's length.

'Want to do the return trip by sand or pavement?'
Dominic queried when they had finished.

'Sand,' she said, without hesitation, and he directed her a lazy grin.

'Not afraid I might toss you into the ocean?'

'Chance would be a fine thing.'

They walked at a measured pace, and reached the
hotel complex in good time. Francesca skirted the
large outdoor pool, sank down on her haunches to

remove her joggers, stripped down to a bikini, then slid into the cool water.

Heaven. For a few minutes she simply let her body cool, then she followed Dominic with a few leisurely laps before levering herself onto the ledge.

A towel was placed in her hand by a diligent hotel employee, and she blotted the excess moisture from her skin, aware Dominic was mirroring her actions. She stopped to collect her outer clothes, wrapped a towel round her slender curves sarong-wise, then walked ahead of Dominic to her suite.

'You take the shower first. I'll pack.'

'We'll share.'

A droll reply rose to her lips, then died. It was OK to be sassy in a public place, but here in the confines of a private suite it was a different matter. 'There's breakfast, and a plane to catch,' she managed lightly. 'With not much time to spare.'

'Five minutes of sex in the shower isn't my idea of satisfaction.' He caught her close, sliding his hands up to cup her face as he lowered his head. 'And taking a later plane isn't an option.' His mouth hovered over hers. 'So this will have to do.'

Warm, and devastatingly sensual, his mouth plundered at will, taking, giving, until she sank in against him, wanting more, much more.

When he finally broke the kiss, she was incapable of moving, and he looked down at her slightly swollen lips, the glazed, almost dazed expression in those incredibly brown eyes, and smiled.

'The shower,' he insisted gently, urging her towards the bathroom.

I've slept with him, had sex with him. What's the

big deal about sharing a shower? It isn't as if this is the first time you've shared a shower with a man.

With Mario, it had been fun and laughter.

But this was different. Way, way different.

There would be nothing humorous about sharing a shower with this man. Evocative heat pulsed through her body at the mere thought of standing a breath apart from his naked, virile frame.

She watched as he pushed down the knit boxer shorts, together with the thin black silk briefs beneath them.

Without a word she undid her bikini bra strap and discarded the scrap of Lycra, then stepped out of the matching briefs.

Water cascaded onto the tiled floor and she reached for the soap, studiously avoiding eye contact—*hell*, body contact—with Dominic.

Impossible, of course. His movements were vigorous, his use of the soap generous, and he made no attempt at modesty. Nor did his state of arousal appear to faze him.

Francesca liked to think she was adept at dealing with any situation, but this one left her fraught with nerves.

As soon as Dominic exited the shower cubicle Francesca reached for the shampoo, lathered and rinsed, then closed the water dial.

With a towel fastened round her slim form, she used the portable blowdrier on her hair, then quickly applied basic make-up and moved into the bedroom to scoop up fresh underwear and a change of clothes.

Ten minutes later she was ready, dressed in

cream tailored trousers and matching top. A long silk scarf in brilliant shades of peacock-green and blue added a dash of colour.

'We'll leave our bags with the concierge while we have breakfast.' Dominic slid the zip fastener closed on his, waiting while she added a few last minute items to hers, then caught one in each hand.

The lagoon restaurant was almost empty, consequently service was swift. Fresh orange juice, coffee, followed by cereal, fruit, toast, scrambled eggs and mushrooms.

A limousine was waiting for them, their bags stowed in the boot, as they emerged from the foyer.

Flashbulbs, one after the other in quick sequence, took them unawares.

Francesca caught sight of yesterday's fashion shoot photographer, and swore softly beneath cover of an artificial smile.

'"*Francesca Angeletti and prominent Sydney entrepreneur Dominic Andrea check out of Gold Coast Sheraton Mirage Resort together. Society's hottest new couple?*" Good caption, don't you think?'

So he'd done his homework. She'd suspected he might make it a mission, simply to get back at her. She didn't bother commenting, merely stepped into the rear of the limousine ahead of Dominic, glad of tinted windows and the driver's skill as he cleared the resort's entrance in record time.

With no luggage to check in, they moved directly through to the departure lounge and boarded the Boeing jet immediately prior to take-off.

'I'll pick you up at seven,' Dominic indicated as

he dropped her off outside her apartment building. At her blank look, he prompted, 'We're joining Gabbi and Benedict at the theatre, remember?'

The car slid away from the kerb before Francesca had time to say a word. Minutes later she rode the lift up to her apartment, checked her answering machine for messages, collected three faxes and sorted through her mail.

Then she walked through to her bedroom and unpacked her bag, her expression pensive as she reflected on just how she was going to deal with Dominic.

She had the strangest feeling that the ball wasn't in her court at all, and that when it came to keeping score he was way ahead of her.

The thought stayed with her throughout the afternoon, bothered her as she showered and dressed for the evening ahead, and endorsed her decision to take control of the situation.

CHAPTER NINE

FRANCESCA swept her hair into a smooth knot above her head and secured it with pins, then she completed her make-up and crossed to the walk-in wardrobe where she removed a gown in deep ruby red velvet. Its style and cut gave credit to a little known designer who, in Francesca's opinion, would soon earn kudos in the international arena. There were matching heeled pumps and an evening purse, and she added a diamond pendant and attached diamond studs to each ear.

The intercom buzzed right on time, and she reached for the receiver. 'Dominic? I'm on my way down.'

He was waiting for her in the foyer, and the sight of him took her breath away. Attired in a black evening suit, with pin-pleated white cotton shirt, he looked every inch the sophisticated social dilettante.

Yet only a fool would fail to discern the leashed power beneath the surface. Or miss the faint ruthless edge that set him apart from most men.

A valuable ally, she acknowledged silently as she slid into the front passenger seat of the gleaming Lexus. And a feared enemy.

Gabbi's husband Benedict possessed similar qualities, she reflected as Dominic eased the car off the bricked apron and onto the road. Both were hardened by the vicariousness of a cut-throat busi-

ness world and the men and women who inhabited
it.

Traffic into the city flowed relatively smoothly,
and Gabbi and Benedict joined them at a prear-
ranged meeting place within minutes of their arrival.

'You look fantastic,' Francesca accorded softly
as she brushed her cheek to Gabbi's.

'Same goes,' Gabbi responded with a quiet
chuckle.

'Shall we mix and mingle, drink in hand?'
Benedict queried. 'Or would you prefer to go directly into the auditorium?'

'Dominic—*darling*. How *are* you?'

Francesca heard the breathy feminine voice and
turned, interested to see who would project such an
intimate greeting.

Petite and blonde, it was the same woman
Dominic had been deep in conversation with at
Leon's gallery a few weeks ago.

Francesca, unprepared for the arrow of jealousy,
watched as the blonde clung a few seconds too long
as Dominic brushed his lips to her cheek. The beautifully lacquered pink nails lingered as they trailed
down his jacket, and the smile, although brilliant,
didn't quite mask the edge of sadness in her eyes.

'Simone,' Dominic said gently. 'You know
Gabbi and Benedict. Have you met Francesca?'

'No. Although I've often admired you on the catwalk and in the glossies.'

The lights flickered, signalling patrons to enter
the auditorium and take their seats.

'Perhaps we could have a drink together some time?' Simone ventured wistfully as they parted.

Francesca noted that although Dominic's smile held warmth, he didn't commit himself to an answer, and she wondered at the sudden spurt of anger that rose to the surface and made her want to demand what Simone meant to him.

Their seats were excellent, and, although Francesca had seen a stunning cast production in London some time ago, the Australian version was excellent, and as always the music, the theme, tugged at her emotions.

When the curtain came down on the first act it was Gabbi who suggested they move into the lobby for a drink.

There was an underlying hum of excitement evident among the mingling patrons, several of whom were society matrons determined to be seen by the few photographers commissioned to cover the night.

Francesca, well-used to the careless and frequent use of the 'darling' greetings, thought if she heard just one more in the next five minutes, she'd scream.

'Damn.'

Francesca heard the softly voiced curse and looked at Gabbi, raised one eyebrow, then lowered it in full comprehension as she saw Annaliese making her way towards them through the crowded lobby.

'Want to escape to the powder room?'

'And spoil her fun?'

'You mean we get to stay and watch?'

'Oh, yes,' Gabbi said firmly, slipping her hand into Benedict's large one.

Francesca watched as Gabbi's husband cast his wife a gleaming glance and lifted her hand to his lips.

'Benedict. Wonderful to see you,' Annaliese purred as she reached them. She turned towards Dominic and cast him a smile that would have melted most men into an ignominious puddle. 'Dominic. So kind of you to take pity on Francesca.'

Grrr. Kittens played. Cats fought. 'All alone, Annaliese?' Francesca queried smoothly.

'Of course not, darling.' The smile was saccharine sweet. 'How was the Gold Coast? I believe you became embroiled with a certain photographer at the Mirage? Word has it your reaction was...' She paused for maximum effect. 'Physical.'

Francesca sharpened metaphorical claws and aimed for the kill. 'Not nearly as physical as you were in Rome, or Paris. And then there was that much publicised débâcle in Milan, if I recall?' She arched one eyebrow and offered a slight smile that was totally lacking in humour. '*Touché*, Annaliese?'

'I think we've each run the media's gauntlet at one time or another,' Benedict indicated smoothly.

It was perhaps as well the next act was due to commence. Patrons were beginning to drift back into the auditorium, and anything she might have said was lost as the music started and the lights began to dim.

The finale gained enthusiastic and well-deserved

audience applause, and at its close they rose to their feet and joined patrons exiting the auditorium.

'Let's go somewhere for supper,' Benedict suggested as they gained the car park. 'Dominic, Francesca? You'll join us, won't you?'

'Where?' Gabbi queried, and Francesca caught Benedict's faint smile as he responded.

'Double Bay.' The smile broadened. 'I doubt Annaliese will consider following us there.'

Or Simone, Francesca added silently, and admonished herself for being uncharitable.

It was almost midnight when Dominic brought the car to a halt in an allocated bay outside her apartment building.

Francesca reached for the door latch. 'Thanks for a pleasant evening.'

'We slept together last night, and made love the night before—not to mention this morning.' He caught hold of her chin and tilted it towards him. 'Tonight you want to dismiss me?'

A tiny shiver feathered through her body. 'I'm not sure I like where this is leading.'

'Define "this".'

She was afraid—of him, herself. 'You. Me.' Her eyes met his bravely. 'Soon I fly to Europe.' She felt his thumb trace her lower lip, and sensed its slight tremble at his touch. 'I won't be back in Australia for several months.'

'So...no strings?' Dominic queried in a dangerously silky voice. 'Just enjoy each other, responsibly. Alternate nights in your apartment or mine, as and when the mood takes us? Then we kiss each other goodbye and say, Hey, that was great, let's do it again some time?' He was icily angry, so much so that he wanted to shake her, *hard*. 'Is that all it meant to you?'

She could end it now, she decided dully. Say the careless words that would ensure she walked away and never saw him again.

It was what she should do—if she wanted to retain her emotional sanity.

Acute pain pierced her body and punctured her soul at the thought of never experiencing the touch of his hands, his lips grazing over her skin, or the feel of his powerful body possessing her own.

'No.'

For a few mindless seconds he didn't say anything. He was content to brush gentle fingers across one satin-smooth cheek then thread them in her hair.

'Simone threw you off balance?'

Was she that transparent? 'It's obvious she cares deeply for you.'

'We were engaged briefly in our early twenties when I was a struggling artist hell-bent on resisting my father's efforts to join him in business. Simone disliked the idea of travelling around Europe for two years on a pittance.' He shrugged. 'We argued, I walked, and Simone married someone else.'

Francesca looked at him carefully in the dim light. 'So now you're simply good friends.'

Maybe there was something in her voice, the intonation she gave, for he smiled. 'Simone is aware it can never be anything else.'

Was that supposed to be reassurance? The thought of him arousing another woman to a state of mindless abandon, his strong body urging her towards ecstasy, caused pain of a kind that made her feel ill.

'It's late.' She released the latch and opened the door. He slid out from behind the wheel and crossed round to clasp her arm. 'Dominic—'

A finger touched her lips. 'Tell me you want to be alone, and I'll go.'

She almost said yes. Then she thought how darned *good* it felt to be held in his arms, to go to sleep knowing he would be there whenever she woke through the night.

It was a tantalising vision. Part of her wanted to accept what they had together without questioning where it might lead or how it would end. Simply live for the *now*, without pondering what the future might bring.

She wanted the sweet sorcery of his touch, the sensual magic no other man had been able to evoke.

'You get to make breakfast,' Francesca capitulated lightly.

He extended a hand for her keys, and once through security they rode the lift together in silence.

Why did she feel so nervous, for heaven's sake? And alive, so gloriously wonderfully *alive*.

Such a complex mix of emotions, she acknowledged on entering the apartment.

Out of habit she slipped off her shoes, then crossed the lounge to the kitchen. 'Coffee?'

He shrugged off his jacket, folded it over a chair and followed her. 'Please. Black, one sugar.'

She took down two cups and set them on saucers.

She shouldn't feel awkward, but she did. Maybe because it was her apartment, her territory, and not the neutrality of a hotel suite.

Theatre seemed a safe topic, and they discussed other shows they'd each enjoyed, and a few dramatic productions.

Dominic replaced his empty cup, removed her own, and held out his hand. 'Turn off the lights and come admire the view with me.'

He looped his arm over her shoulders as they reached the wide expanse of floor-to-ceiling glass. A touch on the remote control module and the drapes slid back to reveal a panoramic vista. Pinpricks of electric light formed a magical pattern that extended as far as the eye could see.

Francesca made no protest when he turned her towards him, and her arms lifted, encircling his neck as his head lowered down to hers.

Mesmeric, gentle, he made kissing a sensual feast, building up a slow heat until she burned with need. Then he swept her into his arms and carried her through to the bedroom.

Her fingers were feverish as she sought to free the buttons on his shirt, and she dragged the material free from his trousers, then reached for his belt. She didn't want any barrier restricting access to his naked flesh. Or her own. And seconds later the velvet gown slid to the floor, followed by a gossamer-fine lace teddy.

They tumbled down onto the bed, and she voiced a faint protest as Dominic reached out and snapped on the bedside lamp.

'I want to see you,' he growled. 'I want you to see me.'

Francesca was past caring whether there was light or the comfort of darkness. His fingers brushed a path up her inner thigh and traced a fiery pattern before sinking into the moist tunnel in a simulation of the act itself.

Her body arched beneath him, seeking the solace he offered, then she cried out when blind need drove her over the edge.

Dominic slid into her with one powerful movement, matching each thrust to a timeless rhythm as she urged him harder and faster until they reached the pinnacle, poised there for seemingly long seconds before soaring towards a shattering climax that left them both labouring for breath.

Francesca lay limp and totally enervated, her skin moist with sweat. In her mind she'd cried out, soft, guttural sounds that had built in frequency and pitch until she was no longer conscious of where or who she was.

Dear heaven, she hadn't realised, hadn't known it was possible to lose oneself so totally in the sexual act.

To know your emotional sanity, your very existence was dependent on another caused fear of a kind she wasn't sure she wanted to deal with.

'Open your eyes,' Dominic commanded softly.

Francesca felt the drift of his fingers as they brushed her cheek, and wasn't sure she wanted to obey. For then she would have to face him, visually, physically, and acknowledge what they'd shared together.

'Tell me how you feel.'

She couldn't find the words even to begin to describe the magic euphoric state of her body and mind. Where did she start? What did she say? That her skin was a mass of acutely sensitised nerve-endings so highly attuned to *him* that it reacted to his touch as if it had received an electrical charge? Radiating heat through veins and nerve fibres to the centre of her sensual being until her entire body *sang* like a piano tuning fork?

Or perhaps she could attempt to explain the incredible meshing of mind with body? How on some deep mental level there was recognition of a kind that was like some incredible discovery, almost as if they'd known each other in another era, a former age.

The thought it could even be a possibility tore at everything she knew. It made her question *love*, and what it meant. Worse, she was forced to accept that love could assume many guises and with Mario she had experienced only one of them. And that wasn't something she wanted to examine right now.

If Dominic wanted an insight into her mind at this precise point, she would allow him to see anger. The confusion, the self-doubt. The glimmering of an enlightening revelation was hers alone.

Francesca's eyelashes fluttered upwards. 'You want assurance on how you scored?'

Something dark moved in his eyes, creating a shadow that made her feel suddenly afraid.

He had watched every fleeting expression, divined each one of them, and felt a growing frustration at being almost completely powerless to exorcise them. There was only one path to travel, that of total honesty, even if it was accorded confrontational.

'This isn't about "Was it as good for you as it was for me?" You were with me every step of the way, and we both went up in flames.'

The heat began to diminish, chilled by her own hand. A part of her bled for that loss, while another urged her towards re-establishing emotional self-preservation.

'You're a skilled lover.' Dear heaven. An understatement if ever there was one.

He was silent for a few heartstopping seconds, then he spoke in a chillingly soft voice that sent icy shivers down her spine. 'Is that all you thought it was?' His breath feathered against her cheek. *'Technique?'*

It was impossible to read his expression, and she didn't offer a word as he caught her face between both hands and tipped it so she was forced to meet his gaze.

'Francesca?' His eyes raked her features, glimpsing the defensiveness apparent in her eyes, and he swore softly beneath his breath.

'What *is* this?' Her eyes were dark and furious. 'Twenty questions?' She wanted to vent some of her anger, verbally, physically. 'What do you want to hear, Dominic? That you're the first man I've had sex with in three years?' She was like a runaway train, unable to stop. 'That having had sex with you, I'm going to allow you to be part of my life?'

He fastened his mouth on hers, effectively halting

the flow of words in a plundering possession that ravaged each and every layer guarding her soul.

It went on for what seemed an age, and when at last he lifted his head she had to struggle to regain her breath.

'I'm not giving you a choice.' His voice was deep, smoky, and filled with intent.

With an anguished cry Francesca launched herself at him, hands bunched into fists as she sought to inflict damage wherever she could connect. 'The *hell* you're not.'

She heard him grunt as she landed a blow to his ribs, and experienced a short-lived surge of satisfaction before he caught hold of one wrist, then the other and forced them behind her back.

He soon rendered her legs ineffectual by trapping them between his own, and she struggled against him, unable to gain any purchase except with her mouth, which she used without thought or aim, sinking her teeth into a hard muscled shoulder.

His retaliation was swift as he shifted slightly and took hard succour from her breast before leaving his mark on its sensitive curve.

Francesca renewed her struggle and gained nothing except a knowledge of his strength.

'Enough. You'll hurt yourself.'

She was breathing hard, her eyes molten with self-rage as she was forced to concede defeat. While he didn't look as if he was doing more than restraining a recalcitrant child.

'I hate you.' It was said almost matter-of-factly, without venom, and a muscle tensed along his jaw.

'No, you don't.'

The anger was beginning to fade a little, yet it was still there, waiting to flare given the smallest opportunity.

'Damn you.' Her eyes hurt with angry tears she refused to let fall. 'For three years I've been able to convince myself I'm doing fine.' Her vision misted. 'And I was. Until you swept into my life.' And tore it apart.

Dominic lifted a hand and traced the fullness of her lower lip with his thumb. 'I don't drive fast cars or take any unnecessary risks.'

Francesca froze with pain, then reaction set in and she reared back from him, scrambling to the edge of the bed.

'That was uncalled for, and unfair.'

'It's the truth.'

'I'd like you to leave.' Cool clear words, as cool as the ice beginning to form round her heart. She stood to her feet and snatched up a robe, then pulled it on and tied the belt.

He didn't move, and her eyes were stormy with anger as she turned to face him. 'Get dressed, and get out of here.'

Had anyone told her how beautiful she was when she was mad? With her hair tumbling onto her shoulders in disarray, her skin flushed and her eyes sparking anger, she resembled a tigress.

He slid to his feet, collected briefs and trousers and pulled them on, then stood facing her across the width of the bed.

'I'm alive,' Dominic said quietly. 'Remember that before I walk out of here.' His eyes held hers, equally as dark as her own. 'And we both lose something we could have had for the rest of our lives.'

She watched as he reached for his shirt and shrugged into it. Then he retrieved his shoes and socks and put them on.

'That's emotional blackmail.'

He paused in tying his shoelaces and cast her a long, steady look. 'It's a statement of fact.'

'A manipulative one,' Francesca corrected heatedly.

'You think I don't know how difficult it is for you to let go of the past?' There was something primitive in his expression, a ruthlessness that was harnessed, yet exigent beneath the surface. 'Or how afraid you are to let any man too close in case you get hurt?'

Her eyes were still stormy. 'It's called self-preservation. Emotional survival.'

'You think so? Destruction might be more apt.' He paused, collected his jacket and hooked it over one shoulder, aware as he said the words that he was taking the biggest gamble of his life. 'Be happy enclosed in your glass house, Francesca.'

The image was vivid, almost frightening. Inaccessible, destined always to be alone, leading an empty, shallow existence devoid of emotion. An observer, never a player. Was that what she wanted?

'Every time I take one step forward, you force me to take another,' she cried in anguish. She lifted one hand and let it fall helplessly to her side. 'I don't even know the direction, let alone the destination.'

Dominic skirted the bed and moved to stand within touching distance. 'I want it all. My ring on your finger. *Marriage.* And the right to share the rest of your life.'

Francesca felt the blood drain from her face. 'You can't mean that.'

'Can't I?' The demand was dangerously soft, and she shivered at its silent force. 'No other woman has taken control of my emotions the way you do. I doubt anyone else could.'

She was hesitant in her need to choose the right words. 'That's not a good enough reason.'

Something flared in his eyes, a flame that was quickly masked. 'What about love?'

The breath locked in her throat. *Love?* The everlasting kind? 'I had that once. It nearly killed me when I lost it.'

Dominic tossed his jacket onto a chair, and she was powerless to evade his fingers as he caught hold of her chin and tilted it so she had no recourse but to look at him.

'Life doesn't come with a guarantee, Francesca.' His hands slid to cup her face, his eyes dark with latent emotion. 'You make the most of what you have for as long as it's there.'

His mouth settled on her with a wild, sweet eroticism, seeking, soothing, seducing in a manner that sent the blood coursing through her veins, heating her body almost to fever-pitch.

Francesca lost all trace of time or place as she became caught up in the magic of his touch, the feel of his body as his arms shifted to bind her more closely against him.

She kissed him back, hungrily wanting as much as he could give, meeting and matching him every step of the way.

He broke free slowly, easing the pressure, the intensity, as he trailed his mouth gently over the swollen contours of her own, then he placed light, open-mouthed kisses along the edge of her jaw, traversed the column at her neck, then settled in the hollow beneath her throat.

'Will you tell me about Mario?' Dominic queried gently. 'I think I deserve to know.'

She moved back a pace, putting minimal distance between them.

Oh, God. Where did she start? Much of their lifestyle had been portrayed by media hype, some of it fact, mostly fiction. Dominic could access that any way he chose. No, it was the private story, the personal details he wanted.

'We met at a party in Rome,' she began slowly. 'We were both celebrating a personal victory. He'd won on the race circuit and I'd signed a modelling contract with a famed Italian designer.' She struggled to keep it light. 'Mario was...outgoing, gregarious.' How did you explain one man to another? Simple things, like the way he drew people, women especially, like a magnet?

'We had a whirlwind romance, and married three weeks later.' She hugged her arms tightly over her midriff in a protective gesture, and stared sightlessly ahead. 'He lived and breathed the race circuit. There was the constant adrenalin rush of the practice sessions, improving lap times, always needing to go faster, be better than anyone else. Each time he went out on the track I mentally prepared myself for the fact he mightn't come back in one piece.'

Dominic pulled her close and she wound her arms around his waist as she absorbed his strength.

They stood together like that for an age, then she felt his fingers drift up and down her spine in a soothing gesture, and there was the touch of his lips on her hair, at her temple.

'I love you.'

His hands captured her face, and she almost died at the expression in his eyes before his head descended and his mouth closed over her own.

A slight tremor shook her slim form, at what he sought to give and what she was almost afraid to take. Then she let herself go with the magic of his touch, matching his passion with such a wealth of feeling she had no recollection of anything other than the moment and the need for total fulfilment.

Their loving held a primitive quality, wild and so incredibly intense that it surpassed anything they had previously shared together. It was a long time before their breathing slowed and they lay sated, completely enervated by the depth of their emotions.

They must have slept, for Francesca stirred at the drift of fingers tracing a lazy pattern across the soft curve of her hip. Then she murmured a faint protest as the hand slipped lower and began an intimate exploration that warmed her blood and turned her body into a molten mass of malleable sensuality.

This time there was none of the heat and hunger of the night before, only a slow, leisurely loving that displayed exquisite care.

Francesca's eyes met his and held them, witnessed the strength, the purpose, and she knew she didn't want to lose him. Whatever it was they shared, she wanted the opportunity to explore it.

He saw the subtle change, felt the tension in her body begin to ebb, and sought to provide the reassurance she needed.

His mouth was gentle yet possessive as he loosened his hold and traced the indentations of her spine.

Heaven was the mutual giving and taking of pleasure, discovering, wanting to test his restraint as he tested hers until nothing else mattered but the moment. Each time they came together it seemed as if she gifted him a little bit of herself.

They slept a little, then made love whenever one or the other stirred into a dreamy state of half-sleep, part-wakefulness.

Something which happened often, Francesca acknowledged as she felt the soft passage of Dominic's lips across one cheek.

'I have an exhibition in Cairns on Saturday,' Dominic imparted close to her ear. 'Cancel any plans you have and come with me for the weekend. We'll fly up tomorrow and have a day in Port Douglas.'

From the soft dawn light filtering through the drapes, 'tomorrow' had already arrived.

She gave in to the temptation to tease him a little. 'I'll give it some consideration.'

'Minx,' he accorded huskily. 'Do you have to think about it?'

'The exhibition sounds fun. It means I get to

view some of your work. Not to mention being able to observe you in the role of artist.' She was on a roll. 'And the far north holds special childhood memories for me.'

'Is that a yes or a no?'

She smiled in the semi-darkness. 'What time do you want to leave?'

'Eight. I need to collect my bag from the house.'

She'd call her parents to let them know she'd be out of town.

His lips traced a path to the corner of her mouth. 'Hungry?'

'For you, or food?' she teased, and felt his smile.

'Both.'

She ached in places she hadn't thought it was possible to ache. 'I guess that means I don't get to snatch an hour's sleep before we need to shower, change and have breakfast?'

'Do you *want* to sleep?'

'You're offering something better?'

He didn't answer, merely showed her. It took quite a while. And afterwards he tested the speed limit, and they were last to board the flight north.

CHAPTER TEN

IT WAS hot and sultry in Cairns, with high humidity, dull skies and the threat of an imminent tropical Wet Season.

Soaring outdoor temperatures hit them like a wall of heat as they left the comfort of the air-conditioned terminal and walked the short distance to their hire car.

Francesca stripped off her cotton jacket and tossed it onto the rear seat, and Dominic loosened the top few buttons of his shirt.

The air was different up here, the pace of life less frenetic than the southern cities, and the foliage covering the ranges bordering the coastline was a lush dark green.

Port Douglas lay approximately seventy kilo-metres further north, with wide sweeping beaches bounding the eastern fringes and an inner harbour to the west of a narrow promontory.

Sugar cane country, Francesca mused as they passed acres of freshly farrowed paddocks. Mechanical planting and cutting now. Only firing the cane remained the same as it had in years gone by. Small rail tracks crossed the road at intervals, connecting one farm to another, so that cut cane could be loaded and transported to the mill.

She remembered holidaying in this region as a child, visiting Italian grandparents who'd owned vast cane holdings and a farmhouse that was filled with exotic cooking smells, much love and laughter. Now her grandparents lay buried side by side, and the land had been divided and sold off in part to developers.

There were several resorts bordering each side of the four-kilometre stretch leading into Port Douglas, and Dominic took the long, curved driveway that led to the exclusive Sheraton Mirage.

Their suite was luxurious, with sweeping views of the ocean. 'I need to make a couple of calls,' Dominic relayed as he stowed their bags. 'Then we can swim, explore, drive up onto the Tableland. Or,' he suggested, closing the space between them, 'stay here and order in as the mood takes us.'

Francesca moved into his arms and lifted her face for his kiss, loving the feel of his mouth on hers, the gentle possession that rapidly led to hunger of a kind neither of them wanted to deny.

He was a caring lover, pacing his needs to her own, then, when he'd driven her to the point of wildness, he tipped her over the edge and held her as she fell.

There was no sense of time or place in the long afterplay. The drift of fingers, the exploration by lips and the slow sensual tasting that teased and lingered, incited, until only total fulfilment would suffice.

It was dark when they rose from the bed, showered and dressed.

Dominic regarded her quizzically as she applied minimum make-up and stepped into heeled sandals.

'Does this mean you'd prefer to eat dinner in the dining room?'

Francesca's eyes held a devilish gleam, and her smile was almost wicked. 'I need food as an energy boost to last me through the night.' She touched her lips with the tips of her fingers and blew him a kiss. 'Besides, it would be nice to enjoy the ambience, don't you think?' The corners of her mouth lifted with delicious humour. 'A light white wine, seafood. The local barramundi is superb, and when we've had coffee we can stroll through the grounds.'

Dominic pulled on trousers, added a polo shirt, and slid his feet into loafers. 'Just remember this was your idea.'

A soft bubble of laughter emerged from her throat. 'Think of the anticipation element.'

He bestowed upon her a brief, hard kiss, then caught hold of her hand. 'I'll bear that in mind.'

The dining room was well patronised, the food excellent and the wine superb. They lingered over coffee, then elected to traverse the extensive pool perimeter before retreating to the covered walkways linking the resort's various guest villas together.

Dominic's arm curved round her shoulders, pulling her close, and she smiled in the semi-darkness. It felt good. Better than good. It felt *right*.

Their air-conditioned suite was blessedly cool after the heat of the night, and it was she who moved into his arms, pulling him close for a long, hungry kiss.

Clothes soon became an impossible barrier, and

they took pleasure in the process of discarding them before tumbling down onto the bed.

This time there was no feeling of guilt, no sense of shame. It was Dominic's features she saw, the passion she experienced solely for him.

In the morning they woke late, enjoyed a leisurely breakfast, then checked out of the resort and took the inland highway through Julatten and Mount Molloy to Mareeba, before heading east via the Kuranda range to Cairns.

A late lunch, a check of the gallery, then they returned to their hotel for dinner. Invited guests were scheduled to arrive at the gallery at eight, and a limousine was to be despatched to the hotel to transport them the two blocks distant.

Francesca had selected black Armani evening trousers and matching jacket, high-heeled pumps and discreet gold jewellery. Her make-up was understated, with emphasis on her eyes.

'Sensational,' Dominic commended with a slow sweeping appraisal that made her heart beat faster. He fixed his black bow tie, adjusted cufflinks, then shrugged into his suit jacket. The look was that of a high-powered business executive, sophisticated, at ease and in total control.

Dominic reached into his pocket and withdrew a slim jeweller's case. Inside was an exquisite gold chain, and she watched as he extracted it and fastened it around her neck.

His eyes met hers and held them as he lifted her left hand and pressed the intricate gold band to his lips.

The gesture shocked her, and a sensation akin to

pain settled deep in her heart. She could only look at him in silence, incapable of uttering so much as a word, and she made no protest as he caught hold of her hand and led her from the suite.

The gallery was in a converted old Queenslander-style home, with wide covered verandahs bordering each of the four external walls. Double French doors led onto the verandah from every room, and the effect was one of rambling spaciousness.

Dominic was greeted effusively, Francesca recognised, and accorded equal reverence.

There was little opportunity to wander at will and admire the exhibited paintings before the first of the guests began to arrive.

'You're a hit,' Francesca murmured later as the gallery filled and the erudite examined and essayed an opinion as they conferred with apparent knowledge on style and form. A 'Sold' sticker appeared on one painting after another.

'Me, or my art?' Dominic teased, and saw her eyes gleam with hidden laughter.

'Both,' she said succinctly. 'Think you can hold things together for a while?' There was no doubt he could. 'I intend to appraise the exhibits.'

'Why is it that your opinion makes me nervous?'

She cast him a musing smile, then saw that he meant it. 'Afraid I might get a glimpse of your soul, Dominic?'

'Perhaps.'

How did one judge the complexities of a man who was capable of such artistic expression? Was any part of it an extension of the man himself, or merely a practised style?

'He's very talented, don't you think?'

Francesca turned at the sound of a male voice, and smiled at the elderly silver-haired gentleman. 'Yes. Yes, he is.'

He indicated the abstract. 'What do you see in this?'

'It intrigues me,' she said honestly. 'I look for hidden meanings, and find none.'

'Precisely. But one cannot easily give up the search for a key which could unlock the puzzle, hmm?'

'You're right,' she conceded slowly, and he lifted an imperious hand.

'I shall buy it. As an investment it will increase threefold in value over the next few years. It will also provide my guests with a conversation piece.' He lowered his hand as an assistant hurried forward. 'Now, my dear, what takes your eye?'

He accompanied her from one room to another, his interest keen, his charm and wit entertaining. It was more than an hour before Francesca rejoined Dominic, and she met his faintly raised eyebrow with a smile.

'I've been conversing with a very interesting gentleman.'

'Samuel Maxwell, art critic and collector,' Dominic acknowledged.

'He thinks you're very talented.'

His eyes gleamed with mocking humour. 'I'm honoured.'

'He bought an abstract.'

'And flattered,' he said steadily. 'Maxwell is selective.'

'There you go,' she said lightly. 'Another fan.'

'And you, Francesca. Are you a fan?'

'Of the art, or the man?'

She was saved from answering when his attention was caught by a dowager of generous proportion who flirted outrageously. Francesca cast him a faintly wicked smile, and moved to the far side of the room.

It was a further hour before they could slip away. The evening was, according to the ecstatically fulsome gallery owner, a tremendous success.

A limousine returned them to their hotel, and they took the lift to their floor.

'Tired?' Dominic queried as they entered their suite.

'A little.' She slipped off her shoes and loosened her jacket.

He lifted a hand and lightly traced the gold chain to where it nestled in the valley between her breasts. 'You have beautiful skin.'

Her eyes lightened with humour. 'Are you seducing me?'

'Am I succeeding?'

Every time. She had only to look at him and her body went into sensual overdrive. All evening she'd been supremely conscious of him, part of the scene yet apart from it. And knew that he was equally as aware of her as she was of him. It had been evident in every glance, the touch of his hand whenever she drifted into his orbit, the warmth of his smile.

He made her feel so incredibly alive. A warm, sensual woman in tune with her own sexuality and aware of its power.

It was an awakening, a knowledge that heightened the senses and brought another dimension to the physical expression of shared sex. The body and mind in perfect accord with that of another. Mutual pleasuring gifted freely without self-thought.

Francesca lifted her arms and pulled his head down to hers, loving the feel of his lips as they grazed across her cheekbone, traversed her jaw, then settled with unerring accuracy on her mouth.

They had the night. Tomorrow they'd board a flight south and resume the hectic tenure of their individual lives. But for now it was enough to savour the loving.

Francesca awoke slowly to the light trail of fingers creating a pattern over the concave of her stomach, and she felt the rekindling of desire as lips settled fleetingly on one shoulder and trailed a path to her breast.

She could feel the faint rasp of his night's beard as it grazed lightly over her skin, and she gave a soft, exultant laugh as he caught her close and rolled onto his back.

There was a feeling of power in taking control, and he allowed her free rein as she tantalised and teased, then it was he who set the pace and she who clung to him in a ride that tossed her high, so high she had no recollection of anything except acute sensual pleasure, and the knowledge he shared it with her.

Long afterwards she lay cradled against his chest, his arms caging her close as he smoothed her tumbled hair and stroked fingers over her silken skin.

It was late when she woke, and they showered

together, ordered in breakfast, then dressed and checked out in time to connect with the Sydney flight.

Several hours later they disembarked, exited the airport terminal, and entered into the stream of traffic heading towards the city.

'I have to be in Melbourne tomorrow,' Dominic informed her as he negotiated a busy intersection, and Francesca felt a sense of loss.

'When will you be back?'

'Wednesday at the earliest. Probably Thursday.'

She'd miss him. 'I have a photographic session Wednesday, another scheduled for Thursday.'

They were traversing the Harbour Bridge before she realised he hadn't taken the Double Bay turn-off.

'Dominic—'

'Stay with me tonight.'

She didn't need to think, didn't *want* to think. She'd have enough time to do that while he was away.

It was after eight the next morning when Dominic deposited Francesca outside her apartment building on his way to the airport.

She rang Rick, then Sophy, caught up with Gabbi, and had a long conversation with her agent. An international fax from her mother-in-law's Italian solicitor needed an immediate response, which entailed a search through copies of legal correspondence.

Lunch comprised a salad sandwich followed by fruit, and she cooked pasta for dinner.

Dominic called her at nine, and the sound of his voice produced an unbearable longing. 'Missing me already?'

You don't know how much. 'A little.'

'It'll keep, Francesca.'

She hadn't fooled him in the slightest. 'Sleep well,' she lightly mocked, and she heard his soft chuckle.

'Promises?'

'Maybe.'

It was late when she slipped into bed, and she lay awake for an age, damning her inability to fall asleep. After an hour she switched on the television and changed channels for a while. Her head felt heavy with tiredness, and she lifted the weight of hair from her nape in an effort to ease the kinks.

Her fingers touched on the gold chain at her neck, and she absently traced its length as she thought of the man who had put it there, and why.

What she'd had with Mario had been special. No one could take it away. But would he have wanted her to live the rest of her life alone? To deny herself happiness and love—a different kind of love perhaps—and children, with another man? Somehow she didn't think so.

Without questioning her actions she drew off Mario's wedding ring and attached it to the chain, feeling the weight nestle in the valley between her breasts.

There were roses waiting for her in Reception when she entered her apartment building late the following afternoon, and she rang Dominic on his cellphone, only to discover he was in a meeting and unable to talk freely.

'I can say anything, and you'll be hampered in your response?' Francesca teased.

'I can always reschedule.'

She laughed. 'For something terribly decadent, with fresh strawberries and expensive champagne?'

'Is that a definite?'

'Would you prefer yoghurt or whipped cream?'

'Count me in.'

'I'm offering seconds.'

'That, too.'

'What would your associates think if they knew you were indulging in mild phone sex?'

His voice deepened. 'I'll look forward to settling with you in a day or two.'

She gave an irrepressible chuckle. 'I'll hold that thought.'

It was no easier to summon sleep than it had been the night before, and Francesca lay awake in the darkness caught up in a web of reflective thought.

Love. Was *this* what it was? An inability to *think*, to function without him? To want, *need* with such intensity it became difficult to focus on anything else?

Wednesday's fashion shoot went way over time, and an unexpected summer shower saw Tony transfer the shoot indoors, to his studio, before moving on as scheduled to a major city department store.

It was almost closing time when the final shot was taken. Staff were packing up, and only a few last-minute shoppers remained.

In the changing room Francesca stepped into cotton trousers, fastened the zip, then pulled a skinny-rib top over her head.

The store's background piped music clicked off as she stepped into heeled sandals and gathered up her bag.

'Who the hell are you, and what are you doing here?'

'Waiting for Francesca,' a deep male voice drawled in response.

Dominic.

She smoothed nervous fingers over the length of her hair, then emerged from the changing room to see Tony regarding Dominic with hard-eyed suspicion.

He turned towards Francesca as she moved forward. 'You know this man?'

Her eyes met Dominic's, and what she saw there made her catch her breath. Then she smiled. 'Yes.' She didn't hesitate, just walked straight into his arms and raised her face for his kiss.

Dominic was very thorough, and it was several minutes before he lifted his head. 'The lady is with me,' he said with deadly softness, for the benefit of anyone who might have held the slightest doubt. Then he looked down at her. 'Isn't that so?'

He was asking much more than that, and she gave him his answer. 'Yes.'

Later, much later, they lay entwined in the shadowy dark hours of night, sated and deliciously drowsy after a long loving.

'You are going to marry me?'

Francesca lifted a hand and gently traced a finger over the length of his jaw. 'Am I?'

Dominic let his teeth nip at a delicate swell of flesh, felt her shudder, and sought to soothe the tiny bruise with a gentle open-mouthed kiss.

'That was meant to be a statement, not a question.'

'Ah.' She smiled in the darkness. 'Being masterful, are we?'

'Soon.' The insistent undertone made her want to tease him a little.

'Next year?' The query earned her an evocative kiss that made her forget everything.

'Next week.'

'That could be difficult.'

She felt rather than heard his soft laughter as he trailed his mouth down the edge of her neck. 'Nothing is difficult.'

No, it wasn't, if you had the money to pay a horde of people to organise everything.

'Like to hear what I have in mind?'

She let her fingers traverse the indentations of his back, then conducted a slow sweep to one hip. 'Why is it I get the feeling you've already set a plan in motion?'

'A ceremony in the gardens at my home, a celebrant, family and immediate friends.'

It sounded remarkably simple. And romantic. Francesca could almost see it. A red carpet rolled out on the spacious lawn, glorious stands of trailing roses framing the gazebo. She even had a dress she'd never worn that would be perfect.

She sensed the faint tightening of muscles beneath her straying fingers, felt the increased beat of his heart and was unable to continue teasing him. 'OK.'

'OK? That's it?'

'Yes,' she said gently. 'There's just one consideration.'

'Tell me.'

'I'm due in Milan, remember? Then Paris.'

'My darling Francesca,' Dominic declared with deceptive indolence, 'I'll not only be sharing your flight—' he placed his lips against a particularly vulnerable part of her anatomy and felt her indrawn breath '—I'll be standing at the rear of every function room wherever you appear on the catwalk.' He suckled gently and felt her fingers rake through his hair. 'And occupying your bed every night.'

'Mmm,' she murmured with satisfaction. 'I was hoping for that.'

His laugh was low and smoky. 'Should I be brave and ask which has priority?'

As if he needed to ask! Her lips curved to form a winsome smile. 'It's nice to share travel with a companion.'

'Really?'

'Uh-huh. And of course it will be reassuring to know you're in the audience.' The smile widened. 'Although you should be warned that designers are temperamental creatures who won't tolerate distractions.'

'Guess I don't get to go backstage.'

'Not if you value your life.'

'They're likely to get physical?' He was deliberately baiting her, and she responded in kind.

'No, but I might.' Too many women in various stages of undress wasn't something she felt inclined to share with him.

'You've left out something.'

'I have?' She gave a tiny yelp as he rolled onto his back and carried her with him. A slow, sweet smile lightened her features and she lifted her arms high in a graceful cat-like stretch. 'Oh, yes. You get to share my hotel suite each night.'

'Witch,' Dominic accorded lazily.

It was a while before Francesca could summon sufficient energy to talk.

'A rooftop apartment in Paris, and a delayed honeymoon would be a nice way to bring my career to a close.'

Something jerked at his insides, and he carefully controlled it. 'You're thinking of giving up modelling?'

She hadn't needed to give it much thought. 'Professionally.'

There was silence for a few seemingly long seconds. 'Don't you want to ask me why?' Francesca queried gently.

This was one time he found it difficult to co-ordinate the right words. 'Tell me.'

'I want to have your child. Children,' she corrected. 'That is, if you—'

Dominic didn't allow her to finish as he brought her head down to his, and his mouth was an evocative instrument as he kissed her with such passionate intensity it melted her bones.

When at last he lifted his head, she could only press her cheek into the curve of his neck, and a slight tremor shook her slender frame as he cupped her face and shifted it so that he could see her expression in the slim stream of moonlight arcing across the room.

'You'll make a beautiful mother,' he said gently.

She felt the prick of tears, and consciously banked them down, but not before he'd glimpsed the faint diamond-glitter drops on the edge of her lashes.

His mouth possessed hers with a soft, evocative hunger that was so incredibly tender she could almost feel her whole body sigh in silent acceptance of a joy so tumultuous it transcended any rationale.

CHAPTER ELEVEN

THE limousine carrying Francesca, Gabbi and Katherine swept smoothly across the Harbour Bridge, then headed towards Beauty Point.

It was a glorious summer afternoon, the sky a clear azure with only a nebulous drift of cloud to mar its perfection.

Francesca lifted a hand and absently fingered the single strand of pearls at her neck. It held a pendant, a pearl teardrop surrounded by diamonds. There were earstuds to match. Dominic's gift to his prospective bride.

Her gift to him was simplistic, but meaningful. A secret smile curved her lips, and her eyes softened as she imagined his reaction.

Her fingers sought the slim gold chain, and failed to find it. A slight frown creased her forehead. It must be directly beneath the pearls. She remembered taking it off before she showered...and had a mental image of lifting the pearls from their flat jeweller's box.

She'd left the chain on the bedside pedestal.

'We have to go back.' The words slipped out before she was even aware she'd voiced them.

'But we're almost there,' Gabbi protested. And at the same time Katherine expressed in consternation, 'Francesca, we'll be late.'

Somehow she didn't think Dominic would mind. Although first she needed to instruct the driver, then she had to make a call from the car phone. When both were achieved, she sank back against the cushioned seat.

'Are you going to tell us what this is all about?' Gabbi asked curiously.

'I left Dominic's gift at my apartment.'

'You could have given it to him later,' Gabbi rationalised.

'Yes,' Francesca agreed, 'I could. Except it wouldn't be the same.'

Thirty minutes later the limousine drew to a halt at the apex of Dominic's driveway, and Francesca slid out from the rear seat to stand still as Gabbi and Katherine ran a last-minute check on the exquisitely pale champagne gold sheath dress with its cream antique lace overlay Francesca had chosen to wear for her wedding.

Gabbi grinned and gave her approval. 'Let's get this show on the road.'

Rick was waiting inside the house, and he came forward the instant they entered the lobby.

'Francesca.' He caught hold of her shoulders and held her at arm's length. 'Everything OK?'

'Very much OK,' she assured gently as she leaned forward and brushed his cheek with her own. She made an attempt to lighten the situation. 'That is, if Dominic is still waiting out there for me.'

'With considerably more patience than most men would be able to summon in similar circumstances,' Rick accorded drily.

'Then let's not keep him waiting any longer, shall we?' Francesca suggested lightly.

The gardens were beautiful, the flowers and shrubs clipped to perfection, and the lawn a carpet of green.

There were a few guests seated behind members of her immediate family, but she hardly saw them. Her focus was centred on the white-painted gazebo and the tall, dark-suited figure who stood watching her progress as she walked the length of red carpet with Rick at her side.

Francesca looked into Dominic's eyes and saw everything she needed to know laid bare. Her own eyes misted, and there was a slight quiver to her lips as she summoned a slow, sweet smile.

A few more steps and she'd be able to place her hand in his, feel its warm strength and accept what he offered for the rest of her life. There was no lingering doubt or apprehension, only love.

Dominic gathered her in close and kissed her with such passion it was all she could do to keep a hold on her sanity.

It could have lasted seconds or minutes, she had no recollection of the passage of time.

Minutes, she decided, as she heard the sound of faint amusement from those assembled behind her.

'Mr Andrea, it's usual to kiss the bride *after* the ceremony.'

'Believe me, I intend to do it then, too,' Dominic drawled with musing indolence.

The celebrant chuckled, then cleared his throat. 'Shall we begin?'

'Could you wait just a moment?' Francesca requested. 'There's something I need to do first.'

She turned towards Dominic, caught his faintly raised eyebrow, and smiled as she lifted both hands to her neck. Seconds later she placed the long thin gold chain holding Mario's wedding ring in the palm of his hand.

Would he realise the significance of her action? *Know* that by gifting him Mario's ring she was willingly giving Dominic her heart? All of it.

Francesca wasn't aware she was holding her breath until his mouth curved into a warm smile, his eyes liquid with comprehension, and she released it shakily, only to catch it again as he lifted her left hand to his lips and kissed the bare finger awaiting the placement of *his* wedding band.

'Thank you,' he said gently.

'I thought it would mean more to you than anything else I could gift you,' she responded softly, adding with a faintly wicked smile, 'At this moment.'

His eyes flared, then became incredibly dark.

Francesca turned a radiant face towards the celebrant. 'We're ready.'

It was a simple ceremony, and afterwards Dominic kissed his wife with such incredible gentleness the men among the guests shifted uncomfortably and the women were seen to blink rather rapidly.

The food was superb, with catering staff serving at tables set out on the wide terrace with its pano-

ramic view of the harbour. The cake was cut and
photographs were taken.

Francesca barely remembered tasting a morsel,
and she merely sipped from a flute of champagne.

She was supremely conscious of Dominic seated
at her side, the touch of his hand, the way his body
brushed against her own. His eyes, those dark, almost black depths, liquid with emotion whenever
she caught his gaze, tugged at an answering need
deep inside her.

A musing smile curved her lips as he leaned his
head close to her own.

'I guess it wouldn't do to leave early.'

She turned her head slightly and brushed her lips
against his. 'I don't think so.'

'Damn,' he cursed lightly.

Her lashes curled upwards, revealing a wicked
gleam in those stunning liquid brown eyes. 'Another hour won't kill you.'

His mouth curved in answering humour. 'It
might.' His lips feathered close to her ear. 'I have
this pressing need to...' In a voice as soft as the
finest silk he proceeded to explain what he meant
to do the instant they were alone.

Her body began to melt, curving into his like
warm wax. 'I think we should mingle,' she said
unsteadily. 'Otherwise we're in danger of shocking
the guests.'

His mouth drifted over hers, savoured briefly,
then he caught hold of her hand.

Together they circled the tables, lingering, laughing, until it was time to change, collect their bags

and slip into the limousine that would transport them to a city centre hotel.

'This is…' Francesca paused in the centre of a sumptuous penthouse suite. 'Overwhelming.'

Dominic closed the door, then walked to where she stood. '*You* overwhelm me.' He lifted a hand and brushed his fingers against her cheek. He didn't care that they were slightly unsteady as he glimpsed the emotion evident in her wonderfully luminous eyes. For him. Only him.

'I love you,' he said gently. 'Today. All the to-morrows.' He traced the curve of her mouth with his thumb, felt its soft fullness, and wanted the sweetness inside. 'I can promise never to willingly hurt you. You have my heart, my soul.'

She ached so much, so deeply, that her eyes hurt with the strength of her emotions. 'I didn't think love could happen twice.' She had to blink to keep the prickle of threatening tears at bay.

He smiled and drew her close, his breath catching as her arms lifted to his shoulders then crept to encircle his neck.

Her lips touched his, opening like the petals of a rose as he took possession, deepening the kiss until she lost recognition of everything except the man.

He filled her senses and made her *want* as he offered the promise of heaven on earth. More. He delivered. And then some.

But then, so did she. Willingly, wantonly. Gifting him more than her body. Everything.

Tonight there was none of the urgency, little of a driven need. Just a long, slow loving that took them to the heights several times and beyond. They slept a little, then woke to exult in each other again until the sunlight chased away the shadows of night.

Francesca lifted a hand, pushed back her tangled hair, then she met his eyes and smiled. 'I love you.'

Her pulse-beat had returned to normal after a passion so incredibly tumultuous every nerve-end still hummed with acute sensation.

'Do you know how much it means to me to have you say that?' Dominic queried huskily.

His hand began to drift as his fingers traced a lazy pattern across her stomach, explored her navel, then moved to tease the whorls of hair at the apex between her thighs.

The scent of her drove him crazy. Her skin was so delicate, so fragile, he almost felt afraid to touch her. Yet she shared his hunger, and exulted in his possession, until he forgot who he was in the need to gift her not only his body but his mind. It was frightening to give up so much power, to lay oneself so open and bare. Yet he doubted she would ever use the advantage against him.

His head lowered to her breast and he began grazing a tender nipple with the edge of his teeth.

The tug of renewed desire arrowed through her body, and she trailed her fingers across his back, exploring the muscular ridges, aware of the strength and the power, and wondered for the nth time how she had existed, believed she'd lived, before meeting this man who was now her husband.

Almost as if he read her mind his head lifted and he settled his mouth over hers, soothing, gentling, marking her as his own as surely as if he'd branded her flesh with fire.

The strident peal of the telephone sounded loud in the silence of the room, and Dominic shifted, then reached for the receiver.

'Our wake-up call?' Francesca hazarded as Dominic replaced the handset.

'We have fifteen minutes to shower and dress before room service deliver our breakfast.'

She looked at him with mock solemnity. 'It was your idea to book an early-morning flight to Athens.'

His eyes held a wicked gleam. 'Ah, but I had the foresight to organise a stop-over *en route*.'

A smile tugged the edge of her mouth. 'How thoughtful.' The temptation to tease him a little was irresistible. 'Shall we hit the shower separately or together?'

'You really want me to answer that?'

She slid out from the bed and walked unselfconsciously towards the adjoining bathroom. When she reached the door she turned and shot him a tantalising smile. 'Can't stand the heat, huh?'

She'd barely made it to the shower cubicle when firm hands fastened around her waist, lifting, turning her until she was positioned astride his hips.

A laugh bubbled up in her throat, then died as he bestowed upon her a brief, hard kiss before lowering his mouth to settle at the acutely sensitive pulse at the base of her throat.

She shuddered as sensation spiralled through her body, and she arched up against him, groaning out loud as his teeth closed over one swollen nipple, teasing, suckling, until she was almost driven to the brink of sanity.

Francesca cried out when he shifted his head and rendered a similar salutation to the twin peak.

His eyes were impossibly dark when they finally met hers, and she felt herself drowning in those dark depths, seriously adrift as his mouth lowered to possess hers in a kiss that echoed the deep, pulsing thrust of his powerful body.

She rose with him, wrapping her arms round his neck as she held on and gloried in their shared passion.

And afterwards she buried her lips in the hollow of his neck, too enervated to move as her racing heart slowed and steadied to its normal beat.

His hand travelled slowly up and down her spine, soothing as he pressed his lips to her hair.

It was heaven to rest against him like this, to feel that what they shared meshed the physical and spiritual in a rare coupling that few were fortunate to attain.

She felt him burgeon inside her, sensed the increased urgency, and rode with him one more time, slowly, gently, as if they had all the time in the world.

A hard double knock on the outer door brought them both back to the reality of the day, and a faint curse escaped Dominic's lips as he carefully lifted her down onto her feet.

'Breakfast.' He reached for a towelling robe and tugged it on, then he leaned forward and pressed a gentle kiss to her faintly swollen mouth. 'Stay there. I'll be back in a minute.'

She could imagine him crossing the suite, opening the door, signalling for the waiter to deposit the tray.

The thought of cereal and fruit, scrambled eggs and toast gave her an appetite, and she reached for the dial, set it to warm and released the lever.

Seconds later the glass door slid open and Dominic stepped into the stall, removing the soap from her fingers as he lathered every inch of her skin. Then he held out the soap. 'Your turn.'

'Oh, no,' Francesca denied, laughing softly. 'You're on your own.' She reached up and pulled down his head for one brief, soft kiss. 'Too many challenges and we'll not only miss breakfast, we'll miss the plane.' She shot him a dazzling smile. 'Besides, I'm *food* hungry.'

He let her go, with a devilish smile that hinted her escape was only temporary.

As the giant jet taxied down the runway Dominic reached for her hand and lifted it to his lips.

'No regrets?'

Francesca looked at those strong features, the raw emotion evident in his eyes. She lifted shaky fingers to his cheek, then trailed them to the edge of his mouth, and stifled a gasp as he drew the tips in between his teeth. 'Not one.'

He reached for her, uncaring of the fellow passengers sharing the first-class cabin, or the hostess who was waiting to serve them.

His mouth on hers was incredibly gentle, and when he lifted his head he glimpsed the faint shimmer of tears.

'We have a lifetime.'

Her bones liquefied at the warmth evident in those dark eyes. 'Yes,' she affirmed simply.

Carpe diem. Seize the day. And she would, with both hands, and rejoice in every one of them.

Modern Romance™
...seduction and
passion guaranteed

Tender Romance™
...love affairs that
last a lifetime

Medical Romance™
...medical drama on
the pulse

Historical Romance™
...rich, vivid and
passionate

Sensual Romance™
...sassy, sexy and seductive

27 new titles every month.

*With all kinds of Romance for
every kind of mood...*

MILLS & BOON®

Makes any time special™

MAT4RS

Sensual Romance™
4 brand new titles each month
...sassy, sexy and seductive.
Available on subscription every month from the Reader Service™
GEN/21/RS2

Tender Romance™
6 brand new titles each month
...love affairs
that last a lifetime
Available on subscription every month
from the Reader Service™
GEN/02/RS2

Medical Romance™
6 brand new titles each month
...medical drama
on the pulse.
Available on subscription every month
from the Reader Service™
GEN/03/RS2

Historical Romance™

4 brand new titles each month

...rich, vivid
and passionate

Available on subscription every month
from the Reader Service™

GEN/04/RS2